Love's Golden Dream

Bobbie Shafer

Publishers Note:

This is a work of fiction. All names, characters, places, and events are the work of the author's imagination. Any resemblance to real persons, places, or events is coincidental.

Original Cover Art: Justin James

Copyright Bobbie Shafer ©2014
All rights reserved
2nd Edition
ISBN 13: 978-0615954233
ISBN-10: 0615954235

DWB PUBLISHING
www.dancingwithbearpublishing.com

Love's Golden Dream   Bobbie Shafer

For my husband, Gordon, for his undying support.
And for my children: Connie, Kim, Kelly, and Cary for
their hard work, help, and advice.

Love's Golden Dream   Bobbie Shafer

~ One ~

San Francisco
Thursday, August 20, 1857

Aimee McKay's throat was so dry she could not swallow. She pinched her lips together to quell their trembling. This voyage would not solve all her problems but it was her only chance for freedom, if she wanted to survive.

Gripping the rail until her knuckles turned white, she leaned over the edge, her eyes sweeping over the faces of people on the wharf. She moved back, out of sight from the throng of locals on the dock, and slumped wearily against the bulkhead of the S.S. Sonora, taking deep breaths to slow her pounding heart.

In her haste to be at sea, her fellow passengers appeared to move in slow motion, as they ambled up the gangplank from the Vallejo Street Wharf in San Francisco.

All around her, newlyweds celebrated with glasses of champagne while rough-clothed miners, flamboyant entertainers, and a variety of men, women, and children leaned over the rail, blowing kisses, and waving wildly to the well-wishers on the dock. These passengers were preparing to depart on the first leg of a voyage that would take them to Havana, where passengers and cargo would transfer to the S.S. Central America. From Havana, the ship would proceed to its final destination in New York City.

Clusters of friends and family members strolled along the deck, toasting one another, and chatting happily. The festive atmosphere spread to the crowd on the dock below. The locals, browsing in the shops along the pier, were caught up in the excitement of the moment and waved to those about to depart.

Toe-tapping music filled the air with the local band's lively rendition of the popular tune, *Old Susanna*, and brightly colored streamers streaked through the air as the travelers hurled the paper strips overboard. The children raced back and forth along the deck, blowing on noisemakers, whooping and hollering, while slinging handfuls of confetti into the air.

As Aimee watched the merriment on board, thoughts of the past year, the horror she went through, and all the dreams she lost, spun through her mind. She shook her head to clear the unpleasant memories away, and then glanced up to see a handsome young man with sun-bleached hair gazing at her. When he caught her eye, he nodded, smiled, and touched his finger to his forehead.

Warmth spread throughout Aimee's body. She looked away and began fidgeting with her purse. Digging for a handkerchief, she fought the urge to glance up and see if the young man still watched her.

A woman walked up beside her and said, "Isn't this exciting?"

Startled by the woman's words, Aimee's head jerked up.

"Y-es, yes it is." Aimee pulled her stiff, black hat lower to make sure the scar along her hairline was covered. Aimee silently prayed the woman would go away.

Although she wore the green dress her father gave her for her last birthday, the only decent outfit Marcus hadn't sold, she worked hard to play down anything that would make her stand out in the crowd. A veil covered the upper part of her face, while a pair of half-moon spectacles she purchased from a street vendor, balanced on her nose. Plain gloves covered her hands and she wore sensible, high button shoes.

Aimee hoped that on a ship with almost five hundred passengers and crewmembers, she could travel unnoticed. Her face burned with the painful memories that no self-respecting, young woman would ever wish to look back upon.

"My name is Adeline Easton, and that's my husband, Ansel over there. He's the tall, dark, and handsome one wearing the white Panama hat. He bought that hat just for this trip. Doesn't he look dashing? The couple over there is Virginia Birch and her new husband. They were married yesterday, and the handsome young man standing beside Virginia is her brother, Lucas Chase. He was best man at their wedding.

"Weddings are so exciting, aren't they? Ansel and I were married just this morning, so this is our wedding trip and we're on our honeymoon. We're going to New York to live. Is that your destination, Mrs.?" She paused, her eyes dropping to the ring on Aimee's finger—the plain gold band Aimee bought in a pawn shop that very morning helped hide curiosities of a woman traveling alone.

Aimee took a deep breath, her mind racing to recall the story she concocted for herself in case someone forced her into conversation. Again, she tugged the veil down over her scar, lifted her chin and smiled.

"McKay, Mrs. John McKay. Yes, I'm heading to New York to visit family."

The woman smiled and turned slowly, looking right and left, then turned back to Aimee, her lips pursed with a puzzled look.

"Isn't your husband with you?"

"No, uh, he—he was called to a very important meeting at the very last moment. He's planning on joining me as soon as he can get away."

"Oh, mercy me. I would be terrified to travel alone. You are so brave," Adeline said, as she fanned her hands in front of her face. "I'm just so helpless. My family would never permit me to travel alone."

"This was, uh, an emergency. There is an illness—a family illness. I just hope there are no delays and I'm able to arrive in time." The lies were painful and tears filled Aimee's eyes.

Misreading her tears, Adeline gasped. "Oh, my dear, I didn't mean to imply... How thoughtless of me. I hope the illness is not serious. I do not know what I would do if anything like that happened to me right now.

"I didn't realize you were in such a desperate state. Please, if there is anything..." the blast of the departure horn drowned out the rest of her words. She patted Aimee's arm as a shout from her husband caught her attention.

Ansel waved his Panama hat, motioning for his wife to join him. A void of loneliness swept over Aimee as she watched Adeline Eason rush to her husband's side. For a while the gangplank filled with departing visitors and family members. A second warning blew and as soon as the gangplank emptied, the dockhands swung the walkway back to the dock, and fastened the gate along the deck securely in place.

The horn blew for the third time and the rumbling sound of the anchor raising announced imminent departure.

"Mister Dorcus, take us out," came a voice from above.

Aimee looked over her shoulder and saw the window to the bridge open and the captain looking toward the dock.

"Bring in the anchor," the man beside the captain shouted, and two burly men began to crank a huge handle.

The grating, rhythmic rattle vibrated the deck as the anchor chain wound up through an opening on the front of the ship onto a spool in the belly of the ship beneath the deck.

"Release the lines," the helmsman called down, and the men on the dock wrestled the immense loops of rope from the dock anchors, dropping them in the water.

"Secure all lines," the second-in-command ordered, and the crew hauled the rope from the water, coiled it around a circular rack, and tied it down.

The crowds on Vallejo Street Wharf yelled their goodbyes, wildly waving handkerchiefs and parasols as parting gestures. Visitors and well-wishers pushed and shoved to get a last look at their family and friends as the whistle screamed one final time.

Aimee moved toward the rail. Most of the passengers returned the waves and blew kisses but not Aimee McKay. She had no friends and she prayed no one she had ever met realized she was aboard. She only wanted to watch California fade away.

As the ship inched away from the dock, she reached the rail. Her spirits rose as the space between the ship and dock widened but the joy quickly became a shiver of fear when a familiar voice sounded from the dock.

"Aimee Amelia McKay, where in blazes do you think you are going?" The slurred words made her cringe. "Get down here this instant, you stupid cow."

The sound caused her stomach to lurch wildly. Her body went numb as her gaze found the source of the threat. Staring in horror at the last person on earth she ever wanted to see again, Aimee felt faint.

Fate had been cruel when it allowed the man on the dock to stumble upon her departure. Dressed in the latest fashion, Marcus Alexander weaved arrogantly along the wooden walkway, waving a half-empty bottom of whiskey, scowling up at her. His other hand gripped the arm of a heavily jeweled, tightly girdled woman. Here was the man who destroyed her life.

He shaded his eyes, which she knew from experience were so blood-shot they would appear to glow red, as he squinted up at her.

"Didn't I tell you to stay home, you sorry wench? How did you get out? Where did you get the money to buy a ticket?" His bellowing drew the crowds' attention and the mob searched for the object of his rants.

"Did you pick somebody's pocket or were you hiding some of your poor, old dead mama's cheap jewelry from me? Where are you heading, little Aimee, back to Papa? He doesn't want you, not anymore, and your brother? Even dear, sweet Edward doesn't want a stained sister. Nobody wants you now. Nobody! I made sure of that."

Marcus' booming laugh grated against her very soul. He stumbled, clutched his companion to steady himself, and laughed manically. Releasing his companion for an instant, he placed his hand across his mouth and blew her a kiss.

"I'll find you, little Aimee McKay. Make no mistake about that. Keep looking over your shoulder, you sly little heifer, every minute of every day. I'll search this world over until the day I die. I'll find you and my face will be the last thing you'll ever see.

"You can't get away from me. You're mine. You'll always belong to me. Do you hear me, little Aimee? Dead or alive. Sooner or later, I'll find you."

Marcus then whispered something to his escort and they burst into laughter. He continued to bawl obscenities, but as the distance between them widened, his words were lost in the rumble of the departing vessel.

With Aimee's heart pounding in her chest, and her eyes watering with unshed tears, the ship eased farther and farther from the dock. Marcus Alexander became smaller and Aimee prayed it would be her last glimpse of him.

Aimee glanced around to see if anyone had witnessed the incident, and rubbed her aching forehead with trembling fingers. She saw an older man wearing a dark suit, facing into the wind, reading a small book. If he had heard the conversation, he pretended not to notice. He kept his face buried in his book, never looking up.

Aimee knew she couldn't return home. She would rather her family think her dead than to subject her father and brother to a lifetime of gossip, embarrassment, and shame. They had warned her that Marcus was evil but she had turned a deaf ear. She shuddered to think what gossip they must have already had to endure.

Aimee made her way to one of the deck chairs where a crewmember offered her a cool drink. Sipping lemon water with shaved ice, a smile played in the corners of her mouth. Life felt as if it had more meaning as the miles between her and Marcus increased.

The little old man she noticed earlier at the rail sat to her right still reading his weathered little book. Two men sauntered down the deck and sat down in two chairs to her left. A waiter came hurrying from the dining room and placed a bottle, two glasses, and a bucket of ice on the small table between them. The little old man waved his hand at the waiter but the waiter ignored him, pretending not to notice.

Even though the heavier of the two men who sat near her tried to keep his voice low, Aimee heard every word.

"Horace, old boy, have you noticed how low this ship is riding in the water?" he asked his companion, his jowls quivering with excitement.

"As a matter of fact, I did, but I just assumed it was the new engine I heard one of the crewmen mention," his friend answered.

"Well," the heavy man rasped.

Aimee leaned back and pretended to close her eyes, instead she peered at him through thick lashes, and watched him looking up and down the deck.

"It is not the engine, my friend. It's gold! Yellow, thick, delicious, mouth-watering gold!" The man continued.

"Cornelius, what are you talking about?"

"Edward Hart, an old chum of mine, and I were at a party last night and he confided to me that I would be traveling with over thirty thousand pounds of pure gold, one-third of all the gold mined during the California gold rush.

"There are cartons and cartons of gold coins and countless boxes of ingots and hundreds of crates of golden bricks, not to mention bags of gold dust. The banks of the eastern states eagerly await their arrival, my friend. They've issued immense loans and promises of credit against the delivery of this very shipment. Horace, my boy, we are truly traveling in style."

"This is incredible, Cornelius. Did he mention how much this shipment is worth?

"Oh, yes."

Aimee heard a chair scrape the deck and lifted her lashes enough to see the heavy man move closer to Horace.

"It's worth over one point six million dollars."

Horace downed his glass of bourbon in one gulp and poured himself another.

"That's not all," Cornelius continued. "He said that most of the passengers are carrying thousands of dollars of gold in belts, bags, purses, and pouches. They felt it was safe aboard a ship captained by an officer of the United States Navy".

"Navy?" Horace asked, his brow shooting to his hairline.

"Oh, yes indeed. This is also a United States mail ship. There is over thirty thousand pieces of mail aboard. The security of this voyage is all but guaranteed".

"I had no idea," Horace said.

"Neither does anyone else." Cornelius guffawed as the two rose to continue the conversation elsewhere.

Aimee looked around at the well-dressed passengers, and could see there were many on board the S.S. Sonora who did not worry about money. She rose and began walking along the deck, her mind racing.

After purchasing her ticket and a few pieces of clothing for a disguise, Aimee calculated she had just enough money for one scant meal a day for a month, and if need be, she would only eat every other day. Determined to survive, she vowed never to repeat the disastrous mistake she made in her one and only foolish attempt at love.

A year with Marcus had destroyed her dreams, had scarred her face and her soul for life, and she felt the heavy weight of age in her mind. Though she was still frightened, she was more determined than ever to be her own person.

Someone touched her arm. "I hope you'll join us at the Captain's table for dinner, Mrs. McKay. Mister Billy Birch, a well-known San Francisco entertainer and his wife, Virginia, will be there. He may perform and it will be a lovely diversion for us all, I'm sure. We'd be delighted to have you attend also," Adeline Easton said, and walked with Aimee around the deck.

"I'm afraid not, Mrs. Easton. I'm not accustomed to sailing and I'm not feeling at all well. I think I'll rest this evening," Aimee said. "I simply can't get my ailing... uh, mother off my mind." Her stomach churned and she truly did feel ill.

"If we can do anything, please don't hesitate to call on us." Adeline patted Aimee's shoulder and moved away.

~ * ~

One evening, when most of the passengers were in the dining room enjoying a lavish dinner, Aimee slipped away to the deck for a breath of air.

Two couples sat on deck, and then the old man Aimee had noticed the day of their departure shuffled to a group of chairs and sat down. Dressed in a black wool suit, his stiff collar rode high under his chin. Although his hair was short in the back, the man had two long gray curls dangling down each side of his face. He removed his wide-brimmed, black hat and took a seat. Smiling, the little man looked at those around him. The two couples sniffed, gathered up their belongings and departed in a huff, glaring at him as they passed. With a sigh, his shoulder sagged and his head drooped.

Despite her efforts to remain unnoticed, Aimee felt a kinship with this man for some strange reason. She noticed that not only the passengers, but the crew also seemed to go out of their way to ignore this man. Their prejudice of his lifestyle was unacceptable to her.

"Excuse me," she said softly. There was no response. "Sir, excuse me. Sir, are you all right?"

The old man looked around. "I'm sorry," he murmured. "Are you addressing me?"

17

"Yes," Aimee said, smiling. "Are you all right? Perhaps you'd like a cup of tea?"

She sat next to him, and reached into her pocket and pulled out a handkerchief that she waved to attract the waiter's attention. He came to her side immediately.

"We'd like... I'd like a pot of tea and two cups, please," Aimee said.

The waiter glanced toward the old man.

"Is there a problem?" She narrowed her eyes, her glare daring the waiter to refuse her.

"No, of course not, ma'am," the waiter said. "Will that be all?"

"No, two slices of cake would be nice." Money was tight but this was a special moment.

"Yes, ma'am, right away, ma'am," he said in a practiced clip and hurried away.

"How do you do, sir? My name is Aimee McKay. I'm pleased to meet you. You do drink tea, don't you"?

The old man shook his head and pulled himself up straight. "Please forgive my rudeness and my poor English. I am Abram Ginsberg. I am most happy to meet with you." His heavy accent sounded pleasant to Aimee's ears and his smile warmed her.

"I would love a cup of tea but please allow me the luxury of presenting you with this snack."

"But I invited you," Aimee protested.

"Yes but you give kindness and I give tea, yes? Please?"

"Of course," Aimee relented.

The waiter returned with the tea and two small flat cakes. When he left, Aimee poured the tea and handed a cup, along with a piece of cake, to Abram.

He smiled, lifted the cup in mock salute, and took a sip.

Aimee sipped hers and smiled. "It's really good."

"The cook must not have known it was for me," Abram said, sarcasm lacing his words.

18

"The world is full of fools, bigots, and unsavory characters. Their judgments must not rule our lives."

"Such dark philosophical thinking from someone so young."

"Youth does not always mean naïve. Are you headed to New York on business?"

"Yes and no," Abram said. His face flickered with a hint of pain. "My father invested in gold mining ventures some time ago and I am returning home with the profits. I recently received news that a fever brought from the old country by a relative has taken my entire family from me. There is no... no one left." He paused and inhaled a shaky breath.

"Oh, Mister Ginsberg, I am so very sorry for your loss. I know what it feels like to be alone, though I cannot imagine losing everyone you love. Please accept my deepest sympathy."

"Of course, my dear but now there's no one left, what good is this gold? Why was I saved?" His shoulders jerked with a silent sob.

"Mister Ginsberg, I am sure you have much knowledge, experience, and so much life to share with others. You still have a great deal to give. Search your heart, ask for guidance, and you'll discover why you were spared."

"My dear Mrs. McKay. Your words move me. They have eased an old man's pain. An angel must have put you on this ship."

"He wasn't exactly an angel but I did mean every word I said."

"I know you did, dear child, and I have much to think about." He laid a coin on the bill on the table. "That should take care of that. Now, if you'll excuse me, I think I'll follow your suggestion and read my book again." He smiled. "I have much to ponder."

~ * ~

Aimee succeeded in keeping to herself most of the time, although she and Mister Ginsberg met now and then to chat. Despite her hopes of remaining unnoticed, Aimee occasionally did run into a few passengers while on deck to enjoy the fresh air.

Aimee stood by the rail, watching the men on dock secure the ships ropes, when a gentle touch brought her out of her reverie.

"Excuse me, ma'am. My name is Lucas Chase and I believe this is yours."

Whirling around, she saw the smiling young man holding out a pale green, silk scarf she had draped around her neck before leaving her room.

"I didn't even realize it had blown off. Thank you, sir."

"Don't mention it. Glad I was around to retrieve it, Miss...?"

"Mrs. John McKay," she replied.

He joined her at the rail watching as the boat was secured.

"I hope you're enjoying the voyage, Mrs. McKay."

Before Aimee could answer, a woman hurried around the bulkhead wildly waving a handkerchief.

"I believe someone is trying to get your attention," Aimee said when she saw Virginia Birch heading toward them.

Lucas turned and rolled his eyes upward. "Yes, I promised I would hang on to my sister's travel bag. She's terrified her expensive face powder and perfume will get lost. You'll have to excuse me. Perhaps we can talk again?"

"Perhaps," Aimee said, frowning. She was surprised at the irritation she felt at Virginia's interruption.

~ * ~

The passengers disembarked and all their belongings, along with the mail and the secret gold shipment, were loaded onto the Panama City Railroad for the three and a half hour ride to the Aspinwall Dock.

Aimee strolled along the vendor's exhibits that lined the outer edge of the docks. Noticing Mister Ginsberg buying fresh fruit, she purchased bananas, oranges, lemons, and a few limes.

Stuffing her purchases, along with two loaves of bread, into her bag, she jumped at the soft, sweet voice of her new friend.

"Mrs. Aimee, I insist you sit with us on the train ride to the ship. I am greatly concerned with your traveling alone. My husband speaks a little Spanish and has traveled extensively. We don't want you getting lost, do we?" Adeline Easton said.

Since no feasible excuses popped into her mind and Abram had disappeared, Aimee nodded. The train whistle blew and the passengers boarded. Aimee prayed time would pass swiftly. Adeline introduced Aimee to her husband, and to Mr. and Mrs. Birch. When Lucas joined them, Virginia touched Aimee's arm and tugged on her brother's sleeve.

"Mrs. McKay, I believe you've met my brother, Lucas Chase. Lucas, Mrs. McKay is on her way to New York to visit her ailing mother. Her husband is to join her later."

Lucas smiled and nodded to Aimee, who shyly returned his smile.

"Luke here has been playing the grubby old, gold prospector for the past year or so, Mrs. McKay, and he's done quite well, if I might brag. He found... What did you call it, Luke, a mother's lore?"

Lucas laughed and Aimee couldn't help but smile as she noticed his sky-blue eyes, the soft, curly, light brown hair, and bronze tint to his skin, obviously from working the gold fields.

"Lode, sister dear, mother *lode*. Just luck, that's all. We were chipping in the right cave at the right time."

"I'm sure it was more than luck, Mister Chase. Congratulations on your strike," Aimee muttered, turning her face toward the window.

The train jerked once, then again before slowly beginning to move down the tracks. The wo-men began to chat about the woes of finding good servants, the latest clothing styles, and where they could find the finest quality accessories. Their husbands discussed rumors of discontent in the north, the advantages of researched investments, and the economic conditions of the country.

After a while, Ansel Easton leaned toward Aimee. "Mrs. McKay, I don't recall my wife mentioning what sort of business your husband is in."

The dreaded question caused Aimee's heart to pound, her pulse to race, and the palms of her hands became clammy.

"A dealer, he... he, ah, deals... that is, he deals in money, mostly gold... gold exchange. Yes, he deals in gold exchange." Being a gambler, winning and losing was sort of a gold exchange business, she thought. "He and his father have always been involved in the money world that is, moving money from here to there. You know? Hand to hand."

Marcus had once told her that he had learned everything he knew about gambling from his father.

"Oh, he's a banker?" Ansel asked.

"No. That is, not exactly." Aimee closed her eyes and prayed for the right words. She opened her fan and fluttered as perspiration began to form in her hairline.

"I'm afraid I'm not very knowledgeable when it comes to the business world. He has explained it all to me but you know how women are, in one ear and out the other. All I know is that the money and gold is transferred from here to there, now and then, from one hand to another," she repeated and fanned herself again. "You must think me very foolish."

"My dear Mrs. McKay," Ansel paused and chuckled, while glancing at his wife. "Lovely ladies like you have no need to understand the complicated financial world. That is our job. Wives are trained to care for the men who care for the money and that's not at all foolish." He laughed again as he reached over and patted his wife's hand.

The other men nodded their agreement and muttered the same sentiment, but Aimee noticed that Lucas had not agreed, however, and had instead, he looked quickly out the window.

"Excuse me, please," Aimee murmured.

She stood and made her way to the end of the car, where she stepped onto the small railed porch. Her entire body felt feverish. The fresh air cooled her damp face, as her heart began to slow.

Smoothing her forest green skirt and jacket, Aimee remembered the day her father had first seen her wearing the lovely outfit. He kissed her cheek and brushed his hand over her dark hair, his words etched into her memory.

"You look beautiful, Aimee. Your dress matches your eyes. Those beautiful green eyes cannot tell a lie. Remember that, my dear. Your eyes always give you away."

At the sound of the door opening behind her, Aimee pulled herself together.

"Mrs. McKay, please forgive me if I'm out of line," said Virginia Birch. "But I have a feeling things are not quite right here. I don't think the others have noticed, as most of them are wrapped up in their own little worlds right now, and everything is all about them. Is there anything you want to talk about?"

Aimee felt faint. Until now, she thought she might get away with her deception but Virginia Birch was smart. She swallowed hard. Had Virginia discovered her lies?

~ Two ~
Winds of Change

"I could see the strain on your face when your husband was mentioned. Don't worry dear, every marriage runs across bumps in the road, and there are little clouds that block the sunshine in everyone's blue sky. I'm sure it isn't anything serious. If you ever want to talk about, well, about anything, I'd be happy to listen. Sometimes just talking unburdens the soul, if you know what I mean."

A wave of relief swept over Aimee. "Oh, no, it's not that. I've never traveled alone. I never even ventured out of our little county. I was always so sheltered, so protected. I was Papa's little girl until... well, now here I am."

"No explanations are necessary, my dear. I'm afraid I don't agree with my husband's philosophy that women's existence is caring for the men in their lives. If all the fathers allowed their daughters to have the same education they gave their sons, and allowed us to learn a little independence, then traveling alone would not be so stressful. Let's return to our seats so you can relax and think about getting home soon. You're in good hands with us."

Conversation was light for the next few hours and soon they arrived at the Havana Dock to board the S.S. Central America, which gave Aimee freedom from the need for further lying.

Her cabin was small and plain. Although there were two narrow beds, she was the only one assigned to the room. There was one small chest and a metal desk with a chair in the corner bolted to the floor. The hundred and fifty dollar steerage ticket took most of her money, and it was all she could afford, yet she would have paid twice that amount to escape San Francisco.

The S.S. Central America remained docked overnight until they departed early the next morning. Aimee had sewn a hidden pocket into her petticoats, and one into her cloak where she stuffed a few meager coins that remained wrapped with handkerchiefs. Rumors circulated about purse-snatchers and pickpockets on the city streets and docks. Aimee wasn't taking any chances of losing her last penny.

Tuesday morning, warmed by a bright sun, Aimee stood alone watching the water churn behind the ship. The sky was clear blue, with a few white puffy clouds here and there. A gentle breeze danced across the deck and the weather couldn't have more perfect. Watching Havana slip away in the distance lifted Aimee's spirits.

The crew worked twenty-four hour shifts and most of the passengers quickly settled down to card games, checkers, chess, or backgammon. Some read or chatted on deck, while others strolled around the deck getting sun and exercise.

Abram approached and invited Aimee to sit on deck with him for a while. Lucas Chase caught her attention and when their eyes met, he tipped his hat and smiled. She thought his blue eyes warm and sincere; his smile intoxicating. She stiffened and looked away. Although his look caused her cheeks to heat, she stood firm. Not again. Not ever again.

When Commander William Lewis Herndon was not in the wheelhouse, he walked the decks, greeting the guests, stopping to engage in conversation now and then.

The first night passed quietly, and Aimee fell into a deep sleep. For the first time in many months, she enjoyed a night-mare-free night.

The next morning a fresh breeze kicked up and the sea filled with tiny, foamy whitecaps.

"Having a pleasant voyage, Madam?" A deep and gentle voice asked.

Looking up, Aimee saw Commander Herndon smiling at her. She relaxed knowing the captain of a ship this size had no interest in the personal life of his passengers. He was simply being polite and courteous. Besides, as a United States Navy Commander, his concern was the safety of his passengers, crew, and cargo.

"Yes, thank you. The crew is most helpful and courteous." A sudden gust of wind tugged at her hat and caused her to sway.

The captain looked at the flags snapping overhead. "Wind's picking up a bit but not to worry, this ship is large enough to with-stand a gale or two, and our equipment is first class. With our ex-perienced crew, I assure you, everyone is definitely in good hands," he said, steadying himself as the ship rolled gently.

With a tip of his hat, Commander Herndon continued his walk along the deck, nodding and greeting other travelers.

Within a few hours, the gusts turned into a steady breeze that grew into a strong wind. Many of the women and some of the men went inside to the main room, where they continued their games and reading. As the wind grew into a gale, the other pas-sengers abandoned the decks for the main room or the dining room.

Even Abram Ginsberg had to beg Aimee's indulgence as he staggered to his room, clutching his abdomen, his face a light shade of green. Still, no one seemed concerned, even though sev-eral other passengers became seasick. Games were abandoned, crowds on the deck dwindled, and most of the passengers huddled in their cabins as the ship swayed and lurched in the rough seas.

Only Aimee and a few others braved the deck. Her months locked in Marcus's shanty resulted in a slight case of claustrophobia, and the hours in her tiny cabin wore on her nerves. Amy stood and struggled to stay on her feet as the ship heaved from side to side.

"Not to worry," the first mate shouted above the wind. "This iron lady can handle an irate storm or two. She has all the latest equipment, and I assure you, this crew has seen their share of rough seas, my friends. It'll blow itself out in no time." He smiled, tipped his hat, and moved on.

The other crewmembers smiled and nodded but Aimee noticed that although the crew seemed confident enough, their smiles did not quite reach their eyes.

Even though the sea churned all night and the ship bucked and rolled, Aimee kept faith in the words of the captain and crew.

Thursday morning, the storm built to its full fury and Aimee heard the crew rushing around, securing the cargo as water cascaded across the railings onto the decks, and the ship tossed over one mountainous wave after another.

As Aimee dressed, she bounced from side to side, and then struggled to make her way to the deck. Climbing the narrow staircase proved almost impossible when the ship bucked wildly, thrusting her backward causing her hand to slip from the wet banister. Grabbing for the railing, she came up with air, and prepared herself for a painful fall. Suddenly, a strong hand grasped her arm, steadying her and preventing the backward stumble.

"Careful, ma'am," a deep voice shouted over the roar of the storm. Lucas Chase held her firmly and wrapped his other arm around her waist as the ship lurched from side to side. "I've taken my share of falls down mine shafts and hills, and this staircase doesn't look too safe right now. You best get back to your cabin. This storm should be over soon."

"I must have fresh air. I'm suffocating in my cabin," she wheezed, gasping for breath. "I'll be fine once I reach the deck."

The ship rolled again and threw Aimee against Mr. Chase's chest. He gripped her tightly, as her hat slipped from her head, and her hand flew to cover her scar.

"Good grief, you've been hurt."

"No, uh, well, y-yes. It happened a little while back. It's nothing."

"Still, I'm sorry. It must have been quite painful. I need to get you back to your cabin."

"No," she said loudly. "I can't breathe down there."

Lucas raised a brow and shook his head. He steadied her and continued to assist Aimee up the wet, slick steps. The scene on deck was shocking. Sails had shredded and debris covered the floor. Deck hands desperately tried to anchor down wind-blown chairs, tables, and other loose objects.

"Sorry, ma'am, you'll have to go below. We have a squall on our hands and we cannot guarantee your safety. Please, ma'am," shouted a young deckhand. His words ripped away by the wind and rain that pelted his face. "It'll be over soon, ma'am. They usually don't last too long."

Aimee turned and with Lucas steadying her, she went back to her cabin. She glanced back to see Lucas hurrying up the steps to help the young deckhand tie down equipment.

Jamming her belongings into the carpetbag, Aimee checked to make sure her coins were secure in her hidden pockets.

Even though the young crewmember tried to reassure her, she read the fear and concern on his face and the faces of the other men as they scrambled around. By what she could see of the ocean, they should all be concerned. The few times she glanced out the porthole in her room, it was under- water. Somehow she knew this was not an ordinary squall. They could sink. Fear rose like bile in her throat. This was not the way she wanted her sad, little life to end - poor, disgraced, and alone.

~ * ~

28

Within a few hours, the S.S. Central America found herself trapped in a full-blown hurricane that continued all day and into the night. Hours passed and the passengers began to panic. Saturday morning Aimee struggled from a fitful sleep to ominous silence. The engines had stopped and there was no sound of the paddlewheel turning.

She left her room and started upstairs, where the other passengers gathered in the upper hallway. She paused on the steps, as a man's high-pitched voice announced that the men in the engine room were unable to stoke coal into the boiler due to flooding in the engine room.

Another terrified man stuttered, "I h-heard the fi-fi-fire went out and the engine di-died. So did the paddle-paddlewheel."

Aimee recognized the third voice as Virginia Birch. "I just heard that Captain Herndon ordered our flag to be hoisted upside-down. You know what that means don't you? We're in distress. Heaven help us. I think we're sinking!"

Shortly before noon, Aimee heard the crew knocking on doors asking the men to join the bucket brigade to bail water from the ship. The Captain announced there was danger of taking on too much water and capsizing. The crew needed every able-bodies man on deck.

The eye of the storm passed but the seas remained violent. Although the S.S. Central America was still afloat, the ship had sustained mortal damage. The massive sails hung in strips from the masts; cargo had been tossed around and pummeled the sides of the ship causing cracks and holes, allowing water to pour in.

Aimee hurried up the steps to help bail but her assistance was politely refused. They worked feverishly and Aimee saw several of the men pull out their shirts, unbuckle their hidden treasure, and throw gold-filled money belts to the deck.

When her eyes widened and her mouth dropped open, one man explained. "My desire for gold will not be the death of me," he said. "If I fell overboard, the weight would surely drag me to the bottom of the sea. If I've discovered anything on this voyage, it's that riches aren't everything."

He kicked the belt out of his way and when others saw what he had done, they, too discarded their belts and pouches, then continued passing buckets. The men fought the wind and rain as they concentrated on bailing the rising water.

Aimee returned to the dining room and huddled with other woman against the walls. The secured tables remained but all the chairs had been stored elsewhere. Tired and frightened, she sat in the corner and clutched her worn carpet bag; her only possession.

"Miss Aimee? Can I get you anything?"

Aimee opened her eyes and smiled at the worried face of Abram Ginsberg, as he stiffly sat down beside her.

"No, Mister Ginsberg, but thank you. I'm just contemplating the nothingness that I've accomplished in my short life."

"I feel as if you and I have been friends for a very long time. Your friendship was so unexpected and appreciated, that I treasure it as one of the finest gifts I've ever received."

"Please, Mister Ginsberg..."

"I think, considering the circumstances, we could dismiss the formality, don't you, Aimee?" He said with a wide grin.

"Yes, Abram, I do."

"As you know, I take great stock in repaying my debts."

"Yes, I do know," she smiled, remembering his insistence on paying for the tea the first day they met.

"Once again I find myself in debt to you and I am thrilled that I can repay your kindness, friendship, and lovely company. You were right when you told me we all had a purpose. I see now what mine is."

Aimee frowned at his words and was shocked to see him unfasten the lower button on his shirt.

He turned his back to the other passengers and unbuckled a strap hidden beneath, and then pulled a wide, bulky, leather money belt from his waist. He buttoned his shirt and straightened

30

his vest, then reached down and slipped the belt from his lap to hers.

"Here, my dear. Put this belt on under your cape and hide it beneath your blouse. It's very, very heavy and it's going to be difficult for you to move around but you must. There's a great deal of gold in that belt and even more in this bag. I want you to have it. I'm sure you will make me proud."

Making sure no one was watching, Abram opened her bag and transferred her meager belongings into his leather bag and shoved it toward her. "This is your future. You will use it wisely, I know."

"No. No, I can't. I won't. It's yours and you must see that it is used wisely." Her voice cracked, as tears gathered.

Abram place his finger over her lips and shushed her with a whisper.

"My sweet, gentle Aimee. Don't you think I know of your tragedy, your pain, and your fear? I saw that brute at the dock, heard his threats, and felt your pain as you grasped on to a thread of hope when the ship pulled away.

"Yet, with all your worries, you found room in your heart and mind to comfort a stranger. You brushed away the clouds of despair and sorrow that surrounded me. You went out of your way to befriend me. You did not hesitate to show me that there was more to life than wallowing in tears, anguish, and the bigotry that hounded me. You were the blessing I so desperately needed and I want to give that back."

He shook his head as Aimee started to speak.

"I'm embarrassed to say, especially now, that I don't know how to swim and I have a feeling that most of us will be in the water soon. No, do not talk about life preservers and jackets. I am old and weary. Bone weary. I recognize the fact that it is my time but I have one last chance to give, and to share just as my book said.

"I searched my heart and made my decision. This gold can make dreams come true and how blessed I feel to be able to give you a chance to fulfill your dreams. Will you allow me this? Aimee, I need you to let make my last act on earth be this good deed."

Aimee watched the tears trickle down his leathery cheeks and felt her tears match his. All she could do was nod, and that nod brought a beaming smile to his weathered face.

~ * ~

A few minutes after noon one of the crew spotted a ship on the horizon, heading their way. Captain Herndon ordered the lifeboats lowered. The first two swamped as soon as they touched the raging sea but the last three made it safely into the water. As ordered by the Captain, the crew lowered all the women and children into the remaining boats by ropes tied around their waists. The men deposited the passengers in the lifeboats one by one with their one small bag while the Marine waited in the distance to pull them safely on board.

As Aimee and her carpetbag were lowered, she smiled wryly as she heard one sailor remark, "She looks like such a tiny thing, you wouldn't think she'd be so heavy."

He panted as he struggled to lower her and Abram's carpetbag into the waiting boat for the trip to the distant brig.

Due to the churning waves and high winds, it took each lifeboat two hours to reach the rescue ship and two hours back to S.S. Central America. High waves pushed the waiting frigate further from the sinking Central America. The Marine was only able to rescue one hundred and eight souls, which amounted to all the women and children on board.

At eight o'clock that night Aimee, wrapped in a seaman's rough, wool, blanket stood at the rail of the Marine, her carpetbag securely trapped between her feet.

Aimee and the other women watched, and saw the faint flare of a rocket fired from aboard the floundering ship; the final acknowledgement of doom. Three tremendous waves slammed into the S. S. Central America causing the mighty ship to shake and quiver.

With the shattering of the mast, and cracking of splintering wood, the helpless vessel began to break apart. She gave a desperate shudder as one end rose up high above the waves and the bow slowly began to slip into the sea. Captain Herndon stood bravely on the paddle-box, while over two hundred remaining passengers and crewmembers leaped into the ominous, choppy seas.

All of the treasured cargo of gold coins, bullion, dust, and ingots sank to the bottom of the sea. Some of the women screamed, and hid their faces, as others fell to their knees and began to weep for their loved ones, friends, and fellow passengers left behind.

The scene unfolding before Aimee's eyes paralyzed her; she had never known such loss. Her long hair came unfastened and wet strands blew across her face, her tears mingling with salt water.

She bowed her head, closed her eyes, and sobbed, "Goodbye, Abram Ginsberg, my dear, dear friend. You'll always be in my heart." As she brushed her hair back and opened her eyes, the ship was gone.

The wind swept the Marine too far away for further rescue efforts, and Captain Hiram Burt, from Boston turned his vessel toward Charleston, South Carolina to deliver his passengers and the survivors of the S.S. Central America to the safety of land and away from the horrific scene of the tragedy.

Aimee watched as the purser of the Marine walked sympathetically between the shivering women and children, taking down their names and addresses for notification of their families. The crew had provided them with some of their trousers and shirts to get them out of their wet clothes and wrapped them in blankets for warmth.

This was the answer to her unuttered prayers. Aimee now had the opportunity to hide the belt filled with gold that Abram had presented to her. Looking at the other survivors, she realized she would never have recognized any of them walking down the street dressed as they now were. This was her chance to erase the past and start anew. Her problem had been how to start a new life and, as she watched the purser walk among her fellow passengers, she saw the solution before her eyes.

Within a few hours, the Marine docked and word of the disaster spread like wild fire. The wharf quickly filled with doctors, nurses, city fathers, and a variety of morbid curiosity-seekers who came to the dock to survey the survivors of the tragedy at sea.

As soon as Aimee stepped off the gangplank, she discarded the blanket and clutching the heavy carpetbag, wormed her way through the gathering crowd. When she was sure no one noticed, she slipped down a dark alley. Away from the limelight, she fingered the heavy, bulging belt through the damp, salty, clothes and once she was satisfied the gold was safe, she headed for the nearest second-hand store, half-dragging Abram's bag with her.

Entering the dark emporium, she clutched one of the two silken handkerchiefs she had tied around the strap of her chemise. She was afraid that spending any of the gold coins from Abram's belt might look suspicious, considering the way she looked. She pulled her hair back in a knot as she walked through the door.

Aimee selected a pair of worn, patched trousers, a pullover undershirt, and a thick, warm, work shirt and laid them on the counter. She added to her purchases a pair of heavy socks, thick soled second-hand boots, and a full-length, well-worn drover's coat that covered her entire frame.

On her way to pay for her clothes, she snatched up a woolen, dark brown, flat baker's boy cap. She paused and picked up a pair of worn scissors sticking out from a bucket of junk. Aimee reached the narrow counter where the vendor waited, pulled out her handkerchief and began to unknot it. She counted out the money carefully, stuffed the clothes into her bag, and set out to find an out of the way place where she could change.

For two bits, she rented a cramped little room in a shabby hotel where she entered and sat heavily down on the worn, sagging bed. Aimee had not realized how exhausted she was. The gold-laden belt rubbed her hips raw and dragging the heavy car-petbag sapped her strength. Her body ached from head to toe from the weight of Abram's gift, although she did not consider it a burden. Her discomfort was nothing compared to the fate of the men aboard the lost ship.

Unbuckling the money belt and dropping it on the bed, Aimee stood for several minutes in her bloomers and chemise, al-lowing her skin to breathe and her muscles to relax. After peeling off the damp chemise and drying her skin, she slipped on the newly bought undershirt, then refastened the money belt over the undershirt and pulled on the work shirt. Pulling on both pairs of pants, she hoped to plump up her small stature.

With a sigh of regret, she pinched her lips tightly together and reached for the scissors. Taking a deep, shaky breath she grabbed a handful of hair, closed her eyes and began to cut the waist-length tresses. Tears streamed down her face as strand af-ter strand of long, dark hair fell to the floor.

When the last fistful of hair wisped to the floor, what was left was a scraggly-chopped, three-inch shaggy head of hair strug-gling to curl. Grabbing up the cap, she wiped the tears from her face, and jammed the hat down firmly, pulling the bill low on her face. She wrestled into the long coat and eyed herself critically in the dirty mirror.

The disguise startled her, and though not perfect, it would do for now. The reflection no longer showed a bedraggled, young woman but a poorly dressed young man, down on his luck and dressed for travel. Flipping up the collar of her shirt and coat, she rubbed some of the dirt from the windowsill across her jaw and chin, and then eyed the change. The scar now showed but per-haps that would help with her disguise.

Leaving the seedy hotel by the rear door and dragging her carpetbag and the blanket filled with her old clothes and hair, she walked into the edge of the woods, buried the seaman clothes un-der leaves and limbs and scattered her hair in a wide circle, shov-ing some under logs and fallen tree limbs. Satisfied that no one would discover the discarded items any time soon, Aimee went directly to the livery stable where, after some haggling she left with a tired, old horse, a dry, cracked saddle and a small, scarred mule with a pack harness. She now had less than two dollars left.

Aimee rode down the street and made a wide circle back to the woods where she transferred the green traveling outfit from her father into one of the packs and secured them to the rack on the mule. Taking some of the gold bars from the leather bag Abram gave her, and placed them into the saddlebags and evenly distributed the heavy load on the mule. The horse could not carry much more and she wasn't sure how long she might be traveling.

Trotting to the edge of town, she stopped and looked back at a strange world, an old life, and swore to fill all her tomorrows with atonements for her mistakes, and then urged the old horse forward.

A young and immature young girl had let love blindside her and lead her to ruin but now her eyes were wide open and love did not stand a chance.

~ Three ~
Masquerade

Aimee rode the horse, leading the mule behind her as she headed northeast from Charleston. She stopped in the small but growing settlement of Dawson City, and slipped feedbags over the animals' heads, and then went into a small trading post. She purchased several slices of bacon, a loaf of homemade bread, and a small sack of oats. Feeling nervous that someone would question her, Aimee kept a cautious eye out but customers who weren't engrossed in card games were deep in conversation, and the bored clerk wrapped her purchases without a word.

The question of what to do with the gold plagued her. How would she ever explain such an amount?

Riding until it was nearly dark, she would like to have made better time and gotten farther from Charleston but her poor old horse just couldn't trot for very long at a time. Whenever she stopped to let the animals rest and stretch her tense muscles, the horse nuzzled her as if grateful for the break.

Aimee left the road and guided her horse about a hundred feet into a sheltered private spot. Clearing a small area, she bordered with stones and started a small fire, before setting up her shelter and preparing her bed. Slipping the tack from the horse, she then unloaded the mule. With a grunt and clenched teeth, she dragged the bundle into the underbrush and located a large stick that she carried back to the campsite.

Hobbling both animals and slipping the oat-filled feed sacks over their heads, she fried several slices of bacon and cut off a thick chunk of bread. While the bacon was frying, Aimee's stomach growl-ed and churned. It was hard forcing herself to chew the bacon slowly when she really wanted to devour it, and the bread, in one mouthful. At first her stomach cramped but after a few swallows of water and bites of bread, the cramping quieted. She continued chewing slowly and couldn't remember a meal tasting so good.

Aimee sat on the edge of her blanket, leaned back, and thought she'd rest her eyes for just a second before pulling off her boots and coat.

A bright light struck her face, causing instant panic. Yanking the stick from under the saddle, she shielded her face, blinked her eyes, and looked around. Sleep had overcome her from the moment her head hit the blanket until the sun woke her. The horse and mule grazed nearby and a light breeze blew through the trees. As she struggled to her feet, her leg cramped, causing her to stumble and fall against a tree. The weight of the belt seemed to have doubled. A slight moan escaped her lips as she rubbed her upper thighs and calves. Not having ridden for so long, it was going to take a while to work out the soreness. Her shoulders and hips were stiff and aching but Aimee wouldn't give in. Abram had warned her that carrying his gift wasn't going to be easy but it was worth any pain she might have.

On the second day, she gave her faithful steed his name. He was, as usual, nuzzling her as she walked around and stretched her body. When she turned and patted his neck, road dust filled the air. Aimee sneezed and the horse blew loudly through his nose.

"You need a bath, you dusty old thing." She paused, smiled and patted him again, though softer this time. "Dusty, that's what I'll call you, old fellow, Dusty. Don't worry, I'll give you and... Well, you and your friend here will both get a good bath at the end of our journey, wherever that may be. Stick with me, dear friends and you won't be sorry."

By mid-afternoon, a thick forest appeared along the road. She could see bountiful game, streams abundant with fish, and the farther she traveled, the safer she felt. She knew the distance to Dawson City wasn't that far, and on a younger, healthier horse she would have made twice the distance in half the time, or better. Still, Dusty and the donkey were doing their best and she appreciated each mile they carried her, even though she felt she could have made better time on foot.

A weather beaten sign on the side of the road announced they were approaching Sycamore Grove.

"You know, Dusty, I like the sound of Sycamore Grove. Maybe it's a good omen. Let's check it out and see." Aimee patted the horse's neck and urged him forward.

Sycamore Grove was a small community but a couple of new buildings told Aimee it was a growing town.

Stopping in front of the general store, Aimee slid stiffly off Dusty's back and looped the reins over the hitching post. The general store sat in the center of the block with a bank on one side and a hotel on the other.

For the last mile or so, Aimee rehearsed the story she would use to explain the gold. It was dangerous to travel with so much gold in her possession, so with a deep breath, Aimee straightened her posture, and headed into the bank.

Slipping in quietly, she looked around and headed toward the counter.

"I'd like to speak to the man in charge," Aimee said, lowering her voice to almost a growl.

"What is your business, sir?" The teller asked.

"A deposit."

"Just a moment," the teller said, and disappeared into a back room.

In a few moments, a large man in a dark suit came striding into the room. He had graying hair, sparkling brown eyes, and a wide, sincere smile. His friendly demeanor told Aimee this wasn't going to be as hard as she first thought. However, at the sight of the oddly dressed young boy, the banker's smile wavered before regaining his composure.

"My name is Ernest Gaines, President of Sycamore Grove Banking and Savings. Come right in, young man. "Lacey, get us some coffee right away. Make yourself at home, Mister... I'm sorry. I didn't get your name.

"Kaymey, Mack Kaymey. I'm from California," Aimee said gruffly.

"Mister Kaymey, welcome to Sycamore Grove. What can I do for you? Mister Lacey said you wanted to make a deposit."

"Thank you, Mister Gaines. Yes, I am considering setting up an account here. Let's just say that the gold fields in California were very good to my father and me. He is no longer with us and I find myself alone and searching for a place to call home. I like the looks of this town and am interested in settling down here."

"Excellent. Sycamore Grove is a growing little town, Mister Kaymey, and I think you have made a wise choice in choosing us for your new home. Now, just how much gold are we talking about here, sir, if you don't mind my asking?"

"I-I'm not exactly sure," Aimee said. My father was in charge of the gold. Do you have an assay office nearby where I can have it weighed and counted?"

"You have come to the right place, Mister Kaymey. Mister Lacey, my assistant is a certified assay officer and can evaluate your gold."

"Mister Gaines, I can see that you are a businessman and a professional. I must insist that you keep any transactions between us in the strictest of confidence. Do I make myself perfectly clear?"

"Yes, you do, Mister Kaymey. And I give you my word that Mister Lacey and I never discuss the business of our clients outside this institution."

"Very well. I will bring in the gold and I give you *my* word that if anything we discuss slips out, I will pull my money out faster than you can blink an eye. I prefer to bring it in the back door. You do have a back door, don't you?"

"Yes, indeed. I will meet you there whenever you say."

"I will bring my pack mule around now. Please have someone there to help me."

Aimee didn't want to travel anymore with the gold on the back of the mule and she was not sure how long she could stand up to the weight of the belt around her waist. The mule was exhausted and she was tired, hungry, and needed rest. However, she wasn't ready to put her entire fortune in one place.

Leading the horse and donkey to the rear of the bank, Aimee carefully transferred most of the gold to the saddlebags and made sure her money belt remained secure beneath her shirt. With a trembling hand, she knocked on the door and Ernest Gaines opened it. Then he and Mister Lacey toted the gold inside.

After placing the gold in the safe, Mister Hiram Lacey began to pour the gold dust from the pouches onto the delicate weight. "I'll save the bars and coins to weigh and count later," he explained, his eyes never leaving the scale.

Aimee and Ernest sipped coffee in the corner and watched the assayer verify the weights, figure the dollar amounts, and record it in a ledger.

It took the better part of the afternoon to weigh, calculate, and record the weight and values of the dust, nuggets, bars, and coins. When he finished, Mister Lacey brought the ledger to Mister Gaines, placing it on the table. He remained by the table, his eyes trained on this employer as he watched Ernest examine the numbers.

Aimee watched the banker's eyes widen before passing it to her for veri- fication. She looked at the final total in the ledger and realized that Abram had under- estimated the amount he had given her. Then, she thought, perhaps had hadn't. Perhaps he didn't want to overwhelm her with the knowledge that she was carrying over sixty-eight thousand dollars on her person, and that did not include the gold in the money belt.

"Mister Kaymey, as you may or may not know small banks like ours rarely keep gold in our safe. I'll make arrangements to have this transferred to a larger bank and you will have a line of credit to draw upon."

"Mister Gaines, how often do you send large amounts of gold to Charleston?" Aimee asked softly.

"We've never had this large of a deposit..."

"That's the point I'm trying to make, Mister Gaines. I am afraid sending this much gold overland by stage might breach my privacy. Isn't there any other way you can handle this?"

"We could sell off this gold to several banks in the state without arousing any attention. It might take a few months. Would that be satisfactory?"

"Yes, actually, that would be best. I'm in the market for a piece of land, preferably with a house. I can do any improvements on it slowly. Is there anything available?"

"Certainly. In fact, I think I have just the thing for you. However, it is a ways out of town. There are a couple of available houses near town, but they only have small yards. Anything with large acreage will be further out. We will handle your account and this transaction most discreetly, assuring your anonymity."

"Actually, I prefer a country place, as long as it's close enough to drive in for supplies once in a while." Aimee stood, stretched and rubbed the small of her back. "I've been on the road for a while. I need a hot bath and a good night's sleep. Could we look at the property tomorrow morning, and may I have a copy of the assay?"

"Absolutely. That will be perfect. We'll get your gold into the vault and set up your account. I assure you that you have nothing to worry about. As soon as you finish breakfast, come by and we'll be on our way to see the property. How much money do you think you'll need to get by for now?"

Aimee's heart pounded and breathing was difficult. Her papa had taken care of all the expenses when she lived at home and Marcus never allowed her to have any cash. However, in the past few weeks, she learned the value of the dollar.

Straightening up, Aimee swallowed hard and said, "I'll take a couple of hundred dollars. That should do for now."

~ * ~

When Aimee walked into the general store, the owner identified himself as Mathew Barker. Aimee bought a fresh set of men's clothing, several pairs of socks, and a decent pair of boots.

Walking the horse and mule slowly over to the livery stable, she had them watered and fed. Assured the animals were well taken care of, she rented a room at the hotel and took a hot bath. After she was clean and dressed in the new clothes, Aimee went down to the dining room and had the biggest steak dinner on the menu.

Aimee couldn't take another bite, and her eyes felt as if lead weights were attached to them. She took the stairs one faltering step after another, then slid into the first bed she had slept on since leaving home.

The next morning, after coffee and toast, she left the hotel and headed toward the bank.

"Good morning, Mister Kaymey. Ready to take a ride?" Ernest Gaines asked.

"I just need to saddle my horse," Aimee replied.

"Nonsense, I have my buggy harnessed and ready to travel. Martha, my wife, fixed a lovely picnic since we might not be back in time for the midday meal."

"I'm ready," Aimee said in her low, boyish voice.

The August heat had lessened somewhat and a cool breeze danced across her cheeks. Still a little shy, Aimee turned up her collar and pulled down on her hat. The banker drove at a slow pace, pointing out lush meadows and plentiful game. The trip took almost an hour before Mister Gaines turned off on a small, unused road that climbed upward to tree-covered hills.

Conversation was not a problem as Ernest Gaines talked constantly. First, he talked about the town, the various businesses, who owned what, their families, his family, and the future of Sycamore Grove. Very little of his chatter was absorbed by Aimee, who was lost in the beauty of the hills, meadows, forests, and endless sky.

"You ought to see these hills in the fall, Mister Kaymey. They look like jewels on a crown with gold, orange, red, and bright yellow leaves. My grandfather came here in the fall and said that was the main reason he settled here. The Indians called the tallest hill Eagle's Roost. There are some giant pines and cedars up there with eagle's nests in the tallest ones. Lots of folks just call this place Eagle Creek."

"How much land are we talking about?" Aimee asked.

"It begins where we turned off back at the main road and a little over nine hundred acres runs back past the creek that comes from a natural spring to prominent markers on each side. The spring runs down from those hills back there through the property and some is underground. The well by the house contains that very same underground natural spring water and has never been known to run dry."

"Who owns this property and how much are they asking for it?" Her heart sped up as she tried to hide her appreciation of the land.

"Ralph Duncan, the late mayor of Sycamore Grove owned this property. He heard a rumor of a cotton mill going in here and thought the mill workers might want to buy some property. As it turned out, the mill went in over at Dawson City and so did the workers. Mayor Duncan passed away a year or so ago and none of his kin were interested in paying taxes on property since none live around here. It's been for sale for nearly a year now."

"The price?" Aimee repeated.

"It started out at a dollar and twenty-five cents an acre, but it's negotiable."

Aimee had never made a business decision in her entire life, but she was not afraid.

"I'll give you fifty cents an acre here and now," Aimee said.

"I don't know. I was thinking more along the line of a seventy-five or eighty-five cents an acre."

"What you're thinking and what I'm offering is the difference between being for sale and being sold. Take it or leave it. I've got plenty of time to look around," Aimee said in a voice she hoped sounded intimidating.

"Now, now, let's not be hasty. I think we can work something out. You haven't seen the house yet. It does need some work. It wasn't more than just a two room cottage for old Ralph."

"Is that it?" asked Aimee as they drove up to a drooping gate between two leaning posts.

"Yes, that's it. Quite homey, don't you think?" The buggy circled around the weed-infested driveway up to the vine-covered cabin.

"Still looks in good condition." Aimee observed.

"I'm sure it is. Duncan built it in hopes that people would want to build one like it. He had grand dreams of opening a lumber mill using the trees from the property. I'm afraid the dream died as soon as the announcement that Dawson City was getting the mill.

"It is sound enough but you may need new glass for the windows, new shelves, and we'll have to make sure the stove still works."

Aimee climbed down from the buggy and walked to the front door. Pulling the vines away, she reached for the knob.

"Here, Mister Kaymey, let me. I've got the key."

Ernest pushed the large key into the tarnished lock and gave it a firm twist. There was a click and when he turned the knob, the door swung open with a whine and screech.

Aimee stepped inside, squinting into the darkness. She walked to the window and jerked a dusty curtain across a wooden rod. Ernest pulled the other curtains aside until light struggled in from three grimy windows.

Peace, calmness, a kind of comfortable feeling like home swept over Aimee. This was it. This is home. Controlling the urge inside of her to whoop and holler, she lowered her head and smiled into her collar.

"It really does need some work," she heard Gaines repeat. "I think he intended to make it a two story cottage from the way the roof looks. The window glass is good though, so you won't need new glass and the stove looks like it works fine. Mister Barker at the general store can order building supplies from Dawson City. The lumber mill there can cut your order in no time. Have you any idea what size house you want, that is, if you are still interested?"

"I'd like to see the barn and check out the well, if you have time," Aimee said, peering out the back window.

"Of course you would. And I have all the time in the world."

The well-built barn only needed a few boards replaced and there were only a few warped planks that pulled loose. The well water was cold and clear. A small corral off the barn needed some rails reattached and there were signs of a new fence started, then abandoned.

"Mister Gaines, I would like to close the deal on the property today, just as soon as we get back into town. This is where I intend to spend the rest of my life. As soon as the paperwork is finished, and I want it finished today, I plan to move in and get settled as soon as possible. That is, if you accept my offer." Aimee frowned and held her breath as she waited for his response.

"I'll be honest with you, Mister Kaymey. There won't be any problems at all. I've been trying to sell this piece of land for over a year now and I'm happy to wrap up the sale today. I have limited power of attorney to sell this property at my discretion. If you're sure you want it, we can sign the papers today and you will be the owner by nightfall. Are there any other family members that will be joining you later, sir?"

"No. No one is joining me. I have no family."

"I'm sorry, Mister Kaymey. I didn't know."

Aimee smiled at the banker and took another deep breath. "Life is not always fair, but we must take responsibility for our own lives, mustn't we, Mister Gaines?"

"Yes, we do. You're absolutely right. I think you're going to be happy here. The land is good and rich, and I don't doubt for a minute that you'll have this place turned around and paying for itself in no time. Are you ready to head back or do you have time for a bite of Martha's crispy fried chicken? And, please, call me Ernest."

~ Four ~
Eagle Creek

With the table cloth spread Aimee made a split-second de-cision she prayed she wouldn't later regret. She had that same feeling about Ernest as she did when she befriended Abram.

"Ernest, I'm going to put my trust and faith in you. I have no one else. I need a friend and you've been honest with me. I need someone to help invest some of my money and help me with my finances. I thought about it and realized I'm not qualified to do this alone. I want to start my new life legally.

"While we eat your wife's delicious smelling fried chicken, I need to tell you a story and you must promise that what I'm about to tell you remains between you and me. If, after I confide in you, you decide you cannot be a party to this, I'll just move on because I won't be able to stay otherwise. There will be no hard feelings and I'll understand completely."

"Mister Kaymey, I have a good feeling about you. I think you and I are about to start a life-long friendship and lucrative re-lationship. I'll tie the horses in the shade where they can graze. You get the dishes from the basket. I think Maggie put in a bottle of wine. I'll tell you a little secret. I've got the deed and bill of sale right here in my briefcase."

Aimee set the table. She dusted off the chairs and pushed them up to the table when Ernest entered with his briefcase.

After filling the plates and pouring the wine, Aimee cleared her throat and removed her hat.

"Mister Gaines..."

"Call me Ernest, please," the banker insisted.

"Ernest, there's something you must know. In order to make this sale legal, you must hear me out.

"My name is not Mack Kaymey and I'm not a man. My name is Aimee Amelia McKay. I cannot sign those papers legally with a false name and as a woman, I'm not sure I can even buy property. I need your advice." Aimee stared at her plate, afraid to look Ernest Gaines in the eye.

Mister Gaines took a sip of wine and said softly, "I'm listening."

"I have failed as a woman." She paused and fingered her scar. "I made foolish decisions that could have killed me when I turned my back on my family. They tried to warn me but I didn't listen. The good Lord gave me a second chance when I reached the end of my rope. Ironically, I ended up in another life-threatening situation. I'm sure you are aware of the sinking of the S. S. Central America?"

Ernest frowned and nodded as Aimee continued. "I was aboard that magnificent ship when we sailed into the hurricane and I survived the devastating horror. The crew and most of the men died.

"Aboard that ship was a kind and gentle old man named Abram Ginsberg, whose heart and spirit was broken due to the loss of his family. We became friends and shortly before the captain ordered the woman and children to be in the lifeboats, this sweet, lovely friend gave me his money belt and a suitcase filled with gold.

"I don't understand why I am still alive when so many good, hard-working men are not. I cannot – no, I *will not* make foolish mistakes again. I have the chance to start over but I can't do it alone. I also have the chance to make the gift from Abram stretch across the years. I think he'd like that. Will you help me?" She looked into his eyes, as tears flowed down her cheeks.

Ernest Gaines reached over and patted Aimee's hand.

"My dear Miss McKay, you are too hard on yourself. We all make mistakes. I don't know what particulars led you to Sycamore Grove to settle but the Lord knew what He was doing when He led you here. My mother was a survivor, too. She kept a smile on her face when my father abandoned her.

"The family and neighbors whispered about her, and through it all, she made sure we all had good educations, married well, and set up in life. We might have starved to death as far as my father cared. My mother sold what jewels she had and what furniture we could do without. She also took in boarders.

"I was very young when I began to learn the sacrifices and the depths of the hearts of women. Mother has gone now but a day doesn't pass that I don't think about the pain of her loneliness. Raising us and never showing how lonely she really was, or how she suffered at the hands of my father never prevented her from being a good and kind woman and a dedicated mother.

"I'm not only a banker, Miss McKay, I'm also the only Sycamore Grove lawyer and a Justice of the Peace. We'll draw up change of name papers, and by the end of the day, you will be Mack Kaymey and owner of Eagle Creek Farm. You said you have the gift for a second chance, and I feel I have a second chance, too. I have a chance to make my mother proud. She would certainly approve of me helping you."

He stuck his hand toward Aimee and as she grabbed it, a sob stuck in her throat.

After they finished the fine meal Mrs. Gaines had made and cleaned up the dishes, they headed back to Mister Gaines' office.

When they entered town, Ernest turned to Aimee. "Well, Mister Kaymey..."

"It's Aimee, Ernest."

"Not for long." He grinned. "Soon it will be Mister Mack Kaymey. But what I was going to say, Aimee, is that I should confess something to you, too."

"Confess? It's really n-not necessary," Aimee blustered.

"Oh, I think it is. You see, obviously no one else noticed but I began to have my suspicions about your identity. If you don't mind, I'll be happy to give you a few pointers if you're sure that you want to remain Mack Kaymey."

"H-how... w-hat? I don't understand."

"For starters, you need to work on your walk, the way you sit, the way you stand, and the way you eat, just to mention a few. You need to hide your delicate hands and perhaps some darker face powder to distract from your flawless skin."

Aimee's face turned beet red. "I thought I'd done a pretty good job," she said sheepishly.

"I imagine since you've changed your appearance, I'm probably the only person to talk to you for more than just one or two words, right?"

"Yes, I've only bought clothes in Charleston and here. I rented a room and ordered supper last night. Do you think anyone else has noticed?"

"Absolutely not. It probably never occurred to anyone around here that someone would try to become someone else. You're safe but it wouldn't hurt to remember the little things I mentioned."

"I really appreciate your help, Ernest. This is what I must do and I couldn't do it without you."

At the bank, Ernest wrote out a change of name certificate and finalized the sale of Eagle Creek. After completing their business, Ernest accompanied Aimee to the hotel to collect her things and have coffee in the dining room.

"Don't hold your little finger out when you pick up your cup," Ernest warned in a whisper. "Just grab the cup and take a long drink. Our parents attempted to teach all their children manners but young boys just don't worry about etiquette.

"Now, if you cross your legs, cross them at the knee, not the ankle unless your legs are stretched out in front of you. When you walk, take long strides and swing your arms. Keep your voice low and say as little as possible. Most men are not big talkers unless they are at a men's club or a poker game, but you do not have to worry about that.

"When you stand, keep your feet apart, hands in your pockets, and keep your head down. That smooth skin on your face is a dead giveaway, plus Miss Aimee, your eyes are too pretty for a man. You need to wear tinted glasses.

"Get yourself a wagon to load up on provisions so you don't have to come into town too often. When you get ready to improve your cabin, we'll get together and I'll pass your instructions on to a builder. There's no hurry. We can get the cottage snug for winter and worry about building next spring. Any questions?"

"Not that I can think of."

"Give me an hour or so. Remember what I said, and go on over to the livery stable and see about buying a wagon."

"I need a couple of good horses. The one I have is old and worn out but I want to keep him and the donkey. They saved my skin and I'll give them both a good home."

"I think Ephraim Walker at the stables has a pretty good selection of horses and he's a fair man. You do not have to worry about Matthew cheating you at the general store. They are both good, honest people. In fact, most of the citizens here are good folks, but you'll find some bad apples in nearly every barrel."

"Ernest, I'll try to remember what you've told me. I don't doubt that I may give a few people reason to gossip, but I assure you that I intend to live my life in a solitary manner. I'll get the wagon and see about the horses, and then meet you at the general store in about an hour." Aimee stood, wiped her mouth roughly, grinned and walked out taking long, heavy strides.

An hour later Aimee drove to the general store in a sturdy used wagon pull by a young, fresh team of horses with Dusty and the mule tied to the back. As Aimee entered the store, she saw Ernest with another man and he motioned for her to join them.

"Matthew," Ernest said. "I want you to meet Mack Kaymey. Mack just bought Ralph Duncan's old place. He'll be living out there in the old cottage until next spring when the weather gets warmer and he has a chance to add on or build a bigger house. I expect Mister Kaymey will need you to order a few supplies when the time comes."

Matthew Barker stuck out his hand with a wide welcoming smile and pumped Aimee's hand. "Welcome to Sycamore Grove, Mister Kaymey. Will Mrs. Kaymey be joining you later?"

"Mister Kaymey is a bachelor, Matthew. He... he's recovering from a long illness and is looking for a peaceful, quiet place to regain his strength." Ernest gave Aimee a quick smile.

"Yes, the doctor recommends a long rest and this looks like a good place." Aimee said, deepening her voice.

"Indeed it is," Matthew agreed. "We'll be happy to deliver your supplies on a regular basis. All you need to do is send a list and we'll take care of the rest. Do you have someone to take care of you out there?"

"Delivering won't be necessary and I can take care of myself, but I appreciate the offer."

"Whatever you say, Mister Kaymey. If you'll excuse me, I'll get this order filled and have my son, Nathaniel, and my clerk, Wayne, load up your wagon. It's nice to meet you, sir. I expect I'll see you later. Nice to see you, Ernest." Matthew hurried away to fill Aimee's order.

"Would you like me to ride out with you, Mack?" Ernest grinned.

"No, thank you. I've taken up enough of your time. I need to settle in on my own. I don't know how to thank you."

"It's been my pleasure. I'll ride out in a few days and see how things are going." He shook Aimee's hand and looked deep into her eyes. "Everything's going to be fine, you'll see."

Ernest waved as he left the store and Aimee set about picking up a few personal things. She chose thread, needles, and several yards of off-white muslin, and placed the items on the counter. When she spotted a heavy iron for pressing clothes, she added it to the growing pile.

She picked out two pair of work pants, a couple of shirts, and a heavy jacket, then selected an inexpensive pocket watch from beneath the glass counter that Matthew carefully set out for her. She bought dishes, pots and pans, and when she finished, the clerk boxed them up. As soon as everything was loaded, she quickly paid Matthew in cash, although he tried to insist on opening a charge account in Mack's name.

Climbing onto the wagon and taking a deep breath, Aimee started home. *Home.* What a wonderful word.

Aimee had not realized how far Eagle Creek was from Sycamore Grove and the unfamiliar land muddled the amount of time to get there. Even so, she was pleased that it was far enough out she didn't have to have to deal with passersby or nosy townsfolk. Spotting the turnoff road, she pulled on the reins and the horses turned down the private lane toward the cottage with Dusty and the mule trotting along behind.

The well-trained horses were easy to handle. They followed the road with little or no prompting. As they plodded along the path, Aimee's gaze wandered over her new property. The more she saw, the happier she became.

Overhead a pair of eagles soared lazily, catching the drafts coming off the hills. A rustle along the side of the road caught her attention, and the white tails of two deer were visible as they darted deeper into the woods. Squirrels scampered along the upper branches of nearby trees, chattering noisily, and a flock of quail fluttered from a clump of weeds close by. The whistling and warbling of vibrant birds filled the air, and the meadows came to life with the colorful flight of dozens of butterflies darting from blossom to blossom. Aimee felt as if she had moved to a fairyland.

The horses slowed as Aimee day- dreamed and she realized they had stopped at the curve of the driveway that circled to the front of the house. With a flick of the reins, the horses continued to the front door. Aimee climbed down, looped the reins through the ring of an iron weight, and dropped it near the lead horse.

With a quick turn of the key, the front door opened. Aimee locked the door behind her, unbuckled the worrisome money belt, and pulled it free from her chafed waist. After shoving it under the moss filled mattress, she opened the front door and began to carry in the supplies. She unloaded box after box until the wagon was empty.

Plopping down on the last two boxes by the front door, Aimee stretched her stiff back and rested a few moments before leading the horses to the barn, where she unhitched the team and turned them loose in the large corral behind the barn, along with Dusty and the donkey. Walking toward the house, Aimee caught a furtive movement in the bushes. She peered into the woods, but saw nothing. *Just a bird*, she thought.

Inside the house, she took off her hat, gloves, and jacket, and then began to put away her supplies. The anticipation of a future filled her with the joy. Pulling out the supplies, Aimee was delighted to see that Ernest had been well aware of a woman's needs, as well as the needs of living alone so far from town.

On the shelf above the wood-burning stove, she placed coffee, tea, and sugar, and placed a kettle of water on the stove and lit a fire. Living with Marcus, Aimee had to learn to do for herself; something she had never had to do before she left her privileged life at home. In California, however, she learned to build a fire, cook on a wood stove, and wash the laundry in a large pot over an open fire in the yard. Living with Marcus had been an education in more ways than one

While the water heated, Aimee continued to unpack the boxes. In a wrapped package, she found two sets of new bed linens, towels and washcloths. In another box, there was a loaf of fresh baked bread, a variety of dried beans, a sack of potatoes, two sacks of flour, baking powder, and salt.

The second box contained a slab of dried beef, ground pepper, canned peaches, milk, a couple of jars of homemade jams, and a jar of honey. The last box held a basket of eggs, a crock of butter, slab of bacon, smoked ham, and at the very bottom, she discovered a pistol and several boxes of ammunition. There were also a bag of cabbage sprouts, onion shoots, and some unknown greens with a note from Matthew Barker.

"Mister Kaymey, I am enclosing, at no charge, these starters for a fall crop of cabbage, onions, and turnip greens. There is still plenty of time to get these in the ground so you will have a small winter crop of fresh vegetables. Good Luck, Matthew Barker."

A shadow at the window made Aimee pause but she pretended not to notice. Walking to the table, she picked up the pistol, loaded it, and went to the front door. Snatching the door open, she stepped outside with the gun in front of her.

"I know you're there. Come out before I start shooting," she growled.

Slowly a small, dark-skinned boy emerged from around the corner. His wide eyes filled with tears, and his lips trembled as he reluctantly shuffled forward. The boy wore a clean, if ragged blue shirt and a pair of well-patched overalls that were at least one size too large for him. The chopped-off pant legs didn't reach his ankles and his thin, bare, ankles stuck out of a pair of hand-me-down boots with no laces.

"P-please, don't s-shoot. I weren't gonna take n-nothing, honest. I wuz j-jest lookin'," he said, his eyes glued to the gun.

Aimee lowered the pistol and stared at the small, trembling boy.

"What's your name, son?" she asked. "And what are you doing here?"

"It's Isaac, suh, Isaac Washington, and I wuz jest a'lookin', honest. I wuz just a'lookin'." A large tear trickled down, making a damp track on his dusty face.

Aimee looked at him, trying to decide how to handle this frightened boy like a man would, instead of how a tenderhearted woman might.

"Are you hungry, Isaac?" she asked, turning toward the house. "I got some bread, butter, honey and jam inside. You want some? Come on," she said softly.

Isaac reached up and swiped at the tear with the back of his dusty arm, smearing the wet trickle across his cheek. "You ain't g-gonna s-shoot me?"

"Not today, Isaac, not today." She grinned and hesitated at the door until he nervously entered.

"I just got here and the place is kinda dirty," Aimee said. "Just grab one of the rags over there and wipe off that chair against the wall. I'll fix us something to eat. Would you rather Would you rather have honey or jam?" she asked the boy.

"Whutever you wants." Isaac dropped his gaze to the floor and wiggled his foot.

"Fine, let's have jam. When I was a young girl…, uh, lad, we used to have bread and jam for tea. It's a little early for tea, but we can pretend, can't we?"

"Yas suh, I reckon, but I-I thought you drank tea," he said, his eyebrows wrinkling together.

Aimee giggled and the boy looked at her hard. She coughed and cleared her throat. Grinning, she put the bread on a plate, picked up the butter, jam, and honey, and set them on the table.

"Well, I can see your confusion. You do drink tea, that's right, but an afternoon snack for some people is also called teatime. They usually drink tea with the snack, and I guess that's where it got its name. This is a special occasion. You are my first guest."

"Yas suh," Isaac replied, his brow still knitted.

"You live around here, Isaac?" Aimee asked.

"Yas suh, I live back in the woods a bit," he mumbled, as he bit into his buttered bread smeared with peach jam.

"Do your parents live there, too? How big is your family?"

Isaac eyes widened and his hand twitched.

"Thanks for the bread and jam, but I gotta go."

"Go? Go where, Isaac?"

"I gotta gits home, it's purdy far. Ma'll git worried."

"You want a job, Isaac? I could use a strong boy like you to help me get this place cleaned up. I've got some sprouts for a small fall garden that needs put in soon. Do you think your folks will let you work here a while? I can pay you."

"Dunno, I'll ask, but I doesn't think so. I gots to go," he repeated as he inched toward the door.

"Come back in the morning if it's okay. You can bring your father if you want to. I'd like to meet him. It's good to know your neighbors."

"We ain't rightly neighbors an' we don't bother nobody. We jest mind our own business."

"We ain't rightly neighbors an' we don't bother nobody. We jest mind our own business."

"Still, bring him if he'll come. I have a job for him, too, if he's interested," Aimee added.

"Yas suh," Isaac mumbled, then turned and shot out the door.

By the time Aimee reached the door, there was no sign of Isaac. The boy had disappeared into the forest like a sprite.

After sweeping and dusting the entire cabin, Aimee tackled the weeds and vines around the front door. She stretched her aching back and decided to inspect the condition of the few small outbuildings.

The chicken coop needed a few repairs, and the barn needed new boards and hinges, but the buildings seemed fairly sound.

Making a mental list of tools she would need, Aimee added a milk cow and a few laying hens to the list. As the sun began to set, Aimee realized how exhausted she was.

Sitting on a stump near the door, she pulled off her boots and damp socks, then wiggled her toes in the one clump of cool grass near the house. A smile spread across her face. It felt so good, so right, and she knew that since she had arrived at Sycamore Grove, she had probably smiled more than she had the entire past year.

The evening breeze refreshed her, in spite of the dust that clung to her sweaty skin, and Aimee felt free and clean. Dirt certainly wasn't the worse thing in the world, especially if you were happy, and Aimee was finally happy. There was a future for her on the horizon, even if it was as someone else.

~ Five ~
Unexpected Help

The sun rose in the eastern sky, spilling rose colored hues and golden rays across Aimee's pillow. She stretched and listened to the chirping of the birds and was filled with peace. After her bath last night, she had put on clean bloomers and chemise before sniggling into bed beneath the new sheet. About to turn over and snuggle back down, the sound of a barking dog jolted her upright.

Leaping out of bed, she yanked on a clean pair of work pants, slipped into a new shirt, pulled on her socks, and jammed her feet into her boots. While cramming her shirttail into the waist of her pants, she heard Isaac's singsong voice.

"Go git it, girl. Bring it here."

Aimee ran a brush through her short, curly brown hair and yanked on the cap she bought in Charleston.

Before she opened the front door, she put a couple of pieces of wood in the stove, stirred up the coals until the flames caught, and sat the coffee pot on top.

Leaning against the doorframe, Aimee watched Isaac toss a stick down the road. He clapped his hands together, while making little clucking sounds until the young, shaggy pooch raced after it, wagging her tail so hard her entire body wiggled.

The boy jumped when Aimee called out. "I didn't think you were coming back. Does your Pa know you're here? I don't want to make any enemies my first day."

"He ain't nobody's enemy." Isaac stood tall and his eyes flashed. "My Pa's a good man. He don't bother nobody. None of us do. I jest didn't want to worry him, and we could sure use the money." He approached Aimee, dragging his feet with each step while looking down at his bare toes.

"Isaac, I don't want to get on your pa's bad side and I certainly don't want you getting into trouble. If you simply talk to him and get his permission to work here, I'll feel a lot better. In fact, from what I could tell yesterday when I was walking around, I could probably use several pairs of hands. If he isn't too busy working his place, perhaps he could work for me a couple of days a week?"

"I don't think Pa'll come out of them hills. He don't trust people much," Isaac said.

"I'll tell you what. You come inside and have breakfast with me, and we'll get a small patch of ground cleared for the garden, clean out some weeds near the house, and then we'll go talk to your Pa. Maybe I can convince him."

Isaac grinned but shook his head. "Mister Kaymey, I done had my breakfast. Ma gets us all up a'fore dawn, makes us dress, and we's fed a'fore the sun comes up. She sez she don't want nobody underfoot while she's a'workin'.

"I'm supposed to be training Dolly to fetch. Pa wants to make her a coon dawg, but she don't act much like a coon dawg to me. George Cooley, from the camp, found 'er one day. She was skin and bones and I guess she sorta belongs to everybody since we all feed her a bit."

"Well, don't give up. She'll come around. After all, she's young. Maybe she'll work all her playfulness out and when she gets a little older, she'll train better. Since you've had breakfast, I don't suppose you want a biscuit with honey, do you?"

"I reckon I have room fer a biscuit or two," Isaac said with a grin.

Aimee went inside, poured herself a cup of coffee and mixed up a batch of biscuits. Slipping them in the oven, she remembered the first time she made biscuits after she and Marcus were together. They were so hard Marcus couldn't even break them when he threw them against a tree. However, the long days alone in the shanty in California gave Aimee plenty of time to improve her cooking.

Soon the flakey biscuits were golden brown and she and Isaac smeared on butter and smothered them in honey. After they ate, the pair walked outside and began pulling weeds from around the house and stripping the clinging honeysuckle vines from the eaves and windowsills.

"You need to git yerself some hoes and a scythe," Isaac said with a sigh, wiping the sweat form his forehead.

"A scythe? What's a scythe?" Aimee huffed and puffed as she struggled to uproot a large clump of grass near the door.

"You doesn't know what a scythe is?" Isaac shook his head, rolling his eyes. "Whut kinda farmer is you, Mister Kaymey?"

"Sometimes when folks have to start over that means doing something they've never done before; like your puppy there. That's why I need you and your father's help, Isaac. I don't want to fail - I can't fail. This is my new life and I have to succeed. This is my second chance. Do you understand?" Aimee's lips trembled.

"Yas suh, I does understands about second chances. I kin hep you. First of all, a scythe is a long, sharp, curved blade that attaches to a wooden handle. You needs it for grass, weeds, hay, cornstalk, or whatever you needs to cut. I reckon the store in town has one or could get you one and you really does need it, sir."

Aimee and Isaac accomplished a lot, but without a hoe or scythe, the clearing would take days, weeks even, and by then, it would need re-weeding. Aimee began to realize she would need more help than she imagined.

"Isaac, let's wash up, cool off, and head for your place. I need to talk to your Pa and Ma today."

Isaac backed up, frowning. "I don't reckon we should, Mister Kaymey. They doesn't like strangers. I ain't sure you'd be welcome. They's good people but they doesn't trust most folks. You jest don't understand."

Aimee saw how uncomfortable Isaac was as he fidgeted and frowned, and then suddenly realization struck her. She shook her head like Isaac had. How stupid could she be? She had seen numerous slaves since she'd been in South Carolina, and Isaac told her that his entire family, plus others, lived deep in the woods. They scraped a living from the earth and were terrified of strangers.

Why hadn't it dawned on her before? Isaac and his family were escaped slaves. They lived terrified that bounty hunters would find them and return them to the plantation. They would probably be beaten or killed for escaping. She slapped her hand over her forehead in exasperation and promised herself she would open her eyes, as well as her mind in the future. Taking a deep breath, she forced herself to smile.

"Isaac, I find myself in need of a great deal of help. Sometimes people can help one another without realizing they can. Your father and you can really help me out and perhaps, just perhaps, I can help him too. I know you said your family doesn't like strangers, and I can understand that.

"However, as close as we live, we can't afford to be strangers to one another. We're neighbors now, whether you understand that or not. Now, I am going to meet your family, so you might as well get used to that idea. Come on, let's get ready."

Isaac's shoulders sagged. "Yas suh, iffen you say so."

After they cleaned up and had a long drink of clear, cold spring water they started into the woods toward the hills. Aimee was surprised to find they had walked a little over half an hour before Isaac stopped, turned to her, and placed his finger over his lips.

"Sh-h-h-h. Let me tells 'em we's a'comin'. They doesn't like to be surprised."

From what Ernest told her about her property, the Washington family and their friends must be living on the wooded side of the nine hundred acres. She had no problem with that as there was plenty of land, yet, this might be to her advantage.

Isaac cupped his hands around his mouth and began to howl like a wolf. He listened and then repeated the cry. A few seconds passed and the sound of a whip-poor-will cut through the air.

"That's my Pa. He heard me. Come on but you better holds your arms out with your hands open so's he kin see you ain't got no gun or nothin'. Walks slow, an' don't make no sudden moves."

Words were not very frightening but the way Isaac acted, Aimee wondered if she might be the one to have something to be frightened about.

Walking slowly behind Isaac, Aimee kept her arms outstretched, and the pair entered a large clearing.

There were five or six small, makeshift shacks and a lean-to built around the edge of the clearing. Each building had a small limb-covered porch and the occupants hung ragged cloths to cover the windows. A large fire burned to the right of the clearing and Aimee could see a steaming pot of water filled with clothes, hanging over the fire.

Someone had stretched a thin rope between trees to hold wet clothes and the lines were heavy with newly washed shirts and well-worn pants. Smaller items were hung over bushes and small trees. The clearing appeared deserted. In fact, if it hadn't been for the well-tended fire, Aimee wouldn't have suspected anyone lived there at all.

"Mister Washington?" Aimee called out in a husky voice. "My name is Mack Kaymey. I just bought the old Duncan place down toward the road. I need some help getting the place fixed up and I hope that perhaps we can work something out.

"I mean you no harm. As I told your son, I need some experienced workers. Won't you please just come out and talk to me? I am unarmed and all I want to do is talk."

Several minutes passed and the snap of a dry twig broke the silence. Turning her head slowly, she saw a tall man with cocoa colored skin slowly amble from behind the first house. He held a homemade hoe and looked suspiciously at Aimee through his heavily hooded eyes. The door of the shack slowly opened and a handsome woman stepped out. She held a broom with both hands and the grim look on her face told Aimee Isaac had been right to warn her.

"Wha'cha want?" The man said gruffly, adjusting the hoe.

"How about a cup of coffee and some conversation?" Aimee said gently, still holding the same position.

"I gots some tea water a'heatin'. Come in. Albert mind your manners. Ain't no use being rude now, is there? He's here and there ain't nothing we can do about it. You can see what he has to say," said the woman, although she continued to grip the broom tightly.

Aimee could now see wide-eyed faces peering from the windows of the other shanties.

She pulled her cap off as she walked to the tiny porch, and the woman held the door open for her.

"My name is Rose and that there's my man, Albert. The boy that brung you is... well, I guess you knows he's our Isaac."

"Yes, ma'am," Aimee replied. "I met Isaac yesterday. He did not want to bring me here but I insisted. He's a good boy and didn't mean to disobey you."

A slight smile flitted across the woman's face. "He is a good boy."

Albert leaned the hoe against the side of the house and followed them inside, motioning for Isaac to remain outside.

A full size mattress rested on a frame of saplings and there was a pile of thinly stuffed quilts folded in the corner. A crude table with three small benches around was the only other furniture, and a rough-made fireplace stood in the corner. Aimee shivered as she tried to imagine how anyone could raise a family in this place.

Rose poured tea in three bent metal cups. When she reached for a loaf of bread, Aimee noticed Albert frown and Rose quickly jerked her hand back and sat down.

Aimee sipped the hot, bitter liquid. She forced herself to swallow the strange concoction.

"W-hat can we d-do for you, Mister, uh..."

"Mack Kaymey, Mrs. Washington. I think we can help each other, so I'd like to get right to the point. I am in the process of starting a new life for myself. You don't have to be concerned, I'm not a criminal, nor am I an escaped lunatic.

"I would like to hire Mister Washington and anyone else here that is willing to work, to help get my place in order. In return, I will provide you with a fair salary and in five years' time I will provide a deed in your name for ten acres of your own."

Albert Washington blinked as Rose jerked her head toward him. He gave a little shake of his head but Rose narrowed her eyes and pinched her lips tightly together.

"Mister Kaymey," Albert finally spoke. "I don't thinks you understands our position. We been here almost three years and we's use to doing for ourselfs. We ain't a'wantin' to mingle with folks from the outside world. You said you wuzn't runnin' from the law. Well, if certain folks come up on us, I don't know if we'd live long 'nuff to be sent back. You see... " he paused and Aimee saw a tear trickle down Rose's cheek.

"I am so sorry," Aimee said, and reached over to pat Rose's hand.

When Albert stiffened, she quickly jerked her hand back.

"Please forgive me," she said. "I do understand your situation and I think that if you give me the chance I can make things right for you. I have a friend who can draw up some papers and to anyone concerned, it will look as if everyone here belongs to me. When it's safe, you will receive your papers of freedom. I do not now, nor have I ever believed that one man should belong to another.

"Slavery is a cruel and despicable practice, and I swear to you that all of you will soon be free men and women in charge of your own lives. I desperately need your help and I know I can help you. Will you at least think about it?"

Rose and Albert looked stunned. "Why would you do this for us? You jest now met us. You don't even know us." Rose said in a shocked whisper.

Aimee looked into Rose's eyes and then at Albert.

"You're my neighbors. We're going to grow old together living side by side. You never know when you're going to need a friend, and I don't think you can ever have too many friends. What do you say? Do we have a deal?"

Albert looked at Rose for a long time. When she nodded, Aimee breathed a sigh of relief.

Albert spoke softly. "Yas suh, Mister Kaymey, it's a deal. When does you want me to start?"

"I'm going to have to buy some equipment. Isaac says we need a hoe and a scythe. I didn't even know what a scythe was. If you'll come by as soon as you can and make a list of the things we're going to need, I'll pick them up in town. The barn and fences need work and so does the springhouse, which was never finished.

"An extra corral needs built for a cow I plan to buy, and eventually, we need to fence off some pasture for the horses. I don't have a clue as to what all I need, or how much wire or post is required. That's where you come in. I may build a new house in the future and your cabins need some work."

Albert hung his head and murmured, "You doesn't have to do that, sir. We's fine."

"Nonsense. You work for me now and I want my employees comfortable in their living quarters. Do you think any of the others would be interested in a job?"

"George Cooley, Dewey Jackson and their family is plannin' on headin' west next spring, if'n things gets worse. Rose's ma and my brother, Rufe is a'stayin'. Maybell Cooper and her husband likes it here. I reckon they could all use some money for the winter and others fer their trip, iffin they's decides to go."

"I can use all the help they're willing to give."

"Sir?" Rose said shyly. How much does you think you be a'payin' for the job?"

"Rose," Albert snapped sharply.

"That's a fair question. I'm thinking fifty cents a day and bonuses when certain jobs are finished on or ahead of time. Does that sound fair?"

Rose gasped at the amount and Albert nodded excitedly.

"That sounds mighty fair, sir. We'll work hard and make you proud," he said.

"I'm already proud, Mister Washington. Proud of having such fine neighbors as you all."

"Would you like more tea, Mister Kaymey?" Rose asked.

Aimee shuddered slightly and shook her head. "No thank you, Mrs. Washington. I really need to get home. Do you think Isaac could take me part of the way back? I'll probably get lost if he doesn't, and that would be embarrassing."

"Please, sir, we is jest Rose 'n Albert. Isaac will be pleased to see you home."

"Excellent, I can't tell you how pleased I am with our arrangement. I was beginning to think I would never be able to make the improvements I need."

Aimee rose and put on her hat. She noticed Rose watching her carefully. She might be able to fool most men since they were not as critical as women but Rose could possibly expose her. Aimee hoped if there was any doubt, Rose would come to her first. She'd just have to keep her fingers crossed.

~ * ~

By the time she and Isaac reached the field behind Aimee's house, the sun had set low in the sky.

"I don't remember crossing this meadow," Aimee said, looking around.

Isaac grinned. "No, suh, I led you the long ways to our place but I tooks a shortcut back. I wants to show you this field. It runs right up to the corral. You might wanna think 'bout fencin' this spot in for horses."

Aimee grinned. "Were you listening at the door, Isaac?"

"Yas suh, but I didn't means no harm."

"No harm done, son. You are absolutely right. This will make a wonderful grazing pasture and all I'd have to do is open the corral to put them out. Be sure and mention this to your father."

"Yas suh, I will. Sees you tomorrow."

"You bet," replied Aimee as she turned and started toward the house.

The air here was clean and crisp, the soil rich, and the grass deep green and thick. In her mind, Aimee saw a small herd of beef cattle grazing lazily in the meadow and perhaps other cultivated fields filled with crops for summer and fall. She also imagined a small herd of young horses racing across the pasture. The army was always in the market for horses. It certainly was something to consider.

Aimee was excited about all the possibilities that stretched out before her, and all because of the faith Abram had in her.

Thinking of Abram caused a hitch in her breath, so she inhaled deeply and offered a silent prayer of thanks for him.

Even though she felt fortunate to have met Ernest but she couldn't count on many people feeling like he did toward women. And if she had to, she would keep up her masquerade until the day she died. It was matter of survival. She had lived through Marcus and a hurricane and she would certainly live through this.

~ Six ~
A New Life Begins

Once again Aimee woke up to the sounds of Isaac and the dog. When she walked into the main room, she inhaled the aroma of fresh coffee. She poured herself a cup and added some canned milk, sugar, and closed her eyes as she passed the cup under her nose.

The sound of hammering brought her to her feet. Out the window, she could see Isaac and Albert already at work repairing the barn.

Opening the door, Aimee stepped outside. "Good morning," she called. "How about some coffee? Did you make it, Isaac?"

Isaac turned around with a wide, beaming smile. He said something to his father, who shook his head, answered quickly, and kept hammering.

"Pa reckons since we jest started, so's we better keep a'workin'."

"Albert?" Aimee called out. "I know you and Rose have rules that your family live by at your place. Well, I have rules too, and one of them is when I tell you to take a break, then you take a break. All right?"

Albert frowned, hung the hammer on a board by the claw, and started toward Aimee. Isaac trotted along behind him.

Aimee hurriedly poured two more cups of coffee and set the can of milk and sugar on the table, along with bread and jam.

"How about some bread and jam?" she asked.

"Naw suh, we's fine," Albert replied.

He picked up his cup while Isaac poured milk and added sugar to his coffee. Aimee saw his face soften and his lips formed a smile as he drank the first swallow.

"Good." Albert smiled broadly. "This is really good."

"I'm glad you like it. Everybody should start the day with a good cup of coffee. At least, that's my opinion," Aimee said. "I'm

curious, what kind of tea did Miss Rose serve yesterday?"

Albert frowned. "That stuff is some kind of root tea that Dewey Jackson's momma fixes. It's all we gots, so it has to do."

"No, it's not all you have now. Did you make up that list of supplies we need?"

"Well," he lowered his head and Isaac looked unhappy.

"We cain't writes it down, 'cause we cain't write," Albert answered, dropping his eyes to the ground.

70

Aimee could have kicked herself. Once again, she had made a hurtful blunder.

"We really don't need a list. It's probably best that we go to town ourselves. We might see other things we need," Aimee said. "I'll just take Isaac with me and I'll bet he can remember, can't you, son?"

Isaac nodded vigorously.

"I can't say as I approves of that. You truly reckon it's safe?" Albert stiffened and pinched his lips together.

"Albert, you said it's been three years since you came here. Besides, I'm sure Isaac probably doesn't look a thing like he did three years ago. I need to talk to my lawyer friend about getting those papers I told you about. You don't need to worry."

Albert sighed heavily. "I don't reckon I'll ever not worry 'bout my family."

Aimee poured him another cup of coffee. "I aim to see that you don't have to worry quite so much in the future."

"I still doesn't understands why yous doin' this."

"A man named Abram Ginsberg did something similar for me. I didn't feel I deserved it either but I have to pass that blessing on. Besides, we both win this way. You get your freedom and I make friends."

Suddenly a voice cut through the morning air.
"Hello in the house. Is anyone home? Hello?"

Albert leaped up, knocking his chair across the room. Fear and terror contorted his face, and grabbed his father's arm,

clinging tightly.

Aimee stood and held out her hand. "Calm down. Go into the bedroom and stay there. Don't come out, whatever you do. Stay there until I come for you. Do you hear me, Albert? Do you?"

Albert nodded numbly.

Aimee jammed on her baker's boy cap, folded her collar up around her neck and walked quickly outside. She froze at the sight. There, sitting on a beautiful roan stallion, was Lucas Chase.

She couldn't believe he was the very same handsome, blue-eyed, young man she met on the voyage.

Having left Charleston so quickly, she never learned the fate of those who leaped into the water as the ship sank, and sadly assumed that most drowned. She had no idea that other ships responded to the news of the disaster and rescued fifty men who clung to floating debris.

"Good morning. I'm Lucas Chase and I've lost my way. I wonder if you can direct me to Sycamore Grove." He removed his hat and wiped his forehead with the back of his sleeve.

Pulling her cap down to her eyes, Aimee lowered her chin into the collar of her shirt and coughed. "Go back to the main road and take a right. It's about six miles straight ahead. You can't miss it."

"I thank you, sir. I'm not familiar with this part of the country. Do you mind if I water my horse and get a cup for my-self?"

Aimee shook her head and pointed toward the corral. "There's a cup hanging on the post," she said hoarsely.

"Again, much obliged. You don't know of any property around here for sale, do you?" Lucas asked as he dismounted and started toward the corral.

"Naw, I surely don't," she growled.

"How long have you lived here?" Lucas asked, narrowing his eyes, as he stared at Aimee.

"You git your water and be on yer way," Aimee snapped. "I don't mean to be rude but I got work to do and I ain't got time to jaw."

"Sure, thanks anyway," Lucas said.

With her heart pounding wildly in her chest, she whirled around and took long strides to the house. Inside, she rushed to the window, and watched Lucas water his horse, drink from the pump, and remount.

Sweat stood out on her upper lip, as her breath came in short gasps, she felt faint, and a slight ache began above her right eye. She watched Lucas heel the horse into a trot until he was out of sight, and then she collapsed into the nearest chair.

Aimee heard the bedroom door creak open, followed by Isaac's footsteps.

"Mister Kaymey, sir, is you all right? Pa, come quick. I think Mister Kaymey done fainted."

"No," Aimee said weakly. "No, I'm all right. It's okay, Albert, you can come out now. It was just a stranger passing through."

"Then why is you so pale and trembly?" Isaac asked, worry evident in his voice.

"I was in bad health a while back and need some rest. Sometimes when I get overly excited, my body reminds me that I should slow down. It's okay. I'll be fine if I just sit here a spell and catch my breath."

"You want I should hook up the team if we's goin' to town?" Isaac asked.

"Not right now. Let's have some more coffee and then we'll talk about what all has to be done around here. I-I think I'll go into town tomorrow."

Aimee had a bad feeling that she hadn't seen the last of Lucas Chase, and she wasn't sure what to do about it.

"Yas suh," Isaac said, still looking at Aimee with a frown.

The rest of the day went quickly. Albert collected reusable nails from the loosened boards in the barn, hammered them straight, and reattached boards that were still in good condition. He explained they didn't need to buy fence posts as he and Dewey, who would be there tomorrow, would scour the woods and cut young saplings for posts.

They would also walk off the area for the new corral and pasture and decide the amount of wire needed for fencing. Some of the barn wood was rotten and more lumber was required. Aimee insisted they stop work at five so they could get home in plenty of time to do their chores. She stood at the back fence and waved, watching father and son walk through the meadow on their way home.

Aimee couldn't believe all the repairs Albert and Isaac made that first day. Albert salvaged most of the barn and worked steadily until he ran out of nails. He and Isaac readjusted most of the split rail fence around the corral and stepped off the addition Aimee wanted to add for the cow.

The place was already looking better, and if only Lucas hadn't stopped by, it would have been a perfect day, especially if she could just stop thinking about him. Pictures of him flashed in her mind, his twinkling blue eyes, the wild, light golden-brown curls, his endearing smile, and the glances he had given her during the trip. She blinked hard and shook her head.

I must be going mad, Aimee thought and squeezed her eyes tightly shut.

No longer could she afford thoughts like that. She had made her choice and now she must pay the price. Only cruel fate could send a man like Lucas into her life. Was it a test? She failed life's test once and she would not fail again.

Her fingers went to the scar Marcus had given her. Even though her growing hair covered it fairly well, she never forgot it was there, and it served as a reminder that she should always be cautious and strong. She had to be someone who never gives in and never weakens. She smiled as she hid the scar under a curl. It was very good to have something to keep her focused.

~ * ~

The next morning, Aimee was up, dressed, and finishing her third cup of coffee by the time Isaac and Albert tapped on the door. She put on her cap and invited them in, surprised to see Rose standing beside Albert, smiling and holding a wrapped object.

"Morning, Mister Kaymey. Momma had bread in the outdoor oven when we wuz ready to leave and made sure that I brung you a fresh loaf."

74

Aimee stood back and motioned for them to enter. Rose came inside but Albert remained in the yard. He gestured to someone out of sight and when Aimee stepped onto the porch, she saw a short, stocky man come from around the corner.

"This here is Dewey Jackson. George Cooley'll be along directly. They's gonna start cuttin' fence posts. Maybell's husband, John, is a'comin' with George, 'n him and me is gonna pull all that there grass from around the house."

Aimee nodded numbly and returned the kitchen. Rose filled Aimee's cup and her own, as Aimee sat down.

"You look surprised," Rose said smiling.

"I am. I expected Albert but I wasn't sure about the others."

"Well, we's jest plain tired of makin' ends meet. Our young'uns is hungry and we eats the same thing day after day. Everybody talks about making life better but it jest don't happen. With the thought of a little money 'n better food, things seem a little brighter, a little better. You weren't foolin' us 'bout them papers wuz you?"

Aimee reached over and quickly patted Rose's thin arm. "I'm going into town in just a little while and get things started. No, Rose, I was not fooling. My life, your life, and the lives of everybody up there in the hills are changing for the better. Now, tell me the names of everyone who needs papers."

Aimee used the paper the clerk wrapped her muslin in to make the list, and wrote with a piece of charcoal from the stove. The first thing on the list was a tablet, pen and ink. After getting the names she needed, she added nails, hoes, a scythe, several rolls of wire, and a large question mark. She folded the paper, put on her coat with her good hat, and nodded to Rose, as she walked outside.

~ * ~

Trying to remember all the tips Ernest had given her on how to act manly, Aimee repeated them over in her mind all the way into town. The wagon pulled up in front of the general store, and when they climbed down, Aimee put her hand on Isaac's shoulder and directed him to the bank.

Ernest Gaines was saying goodbye to a customer when Aimee and Isaac entered. He welcomed her with a wide smile and raised his brow when he glanced at Isaac. Without a word, however, he escorted them into his office.

"Well, now, what do we have here?" His booming voice intimidated Isaac and he cringed behind Aimee.

"Ernest, I seem to have run across a small problem. I have discovered that I've lost my bill of sale for some slaves I bought earlier and were just delivered."

Ernest's mouth dropped open and his eyes bugged out comically. "I beg your pardon," he gasped. "What did you say?"

Taking a deep breath, she pulled out the list. She smiled at Ernest's stunned demeanor and slowly repeated what she had said, pronouncing each word distinctly.

"In my travels, I have mislaid a bill of sale that I was given when I purchased some slaves on my way here. I hoped that, as my lawyer, you might be able to draw up a bill of sale. I wouldn't want some unscrupulous scoundrel to come along and try to claim they belong to him. They belong to me and I want that fact on paper. Do you understand?" She stared hard at Ernest, hoping to convey her meaning.

"I'll need to contact the seller and verify the sale. Perhaps they have copies of the transaction."

"Ernest, that won't be possible. It was an unadvertised sale from the back of a wagon. A plantation had gone bankrupt and the owner lost everything. I understand he burned his place to the ground to keep the bank from getting their hands on it.

"He had his overseer take his slaves and dispose of them the fastest way possible in order for him to get some quick cash. I didn't insist on getting his name as I thought the bill of sale would suffice. Now that I've lost it, I am depending on you to make things right for everyone. Do you understand?" She repeated slowly, with one brow raised.

76

Ernest nodded slowly. He was indeed, beginning to understand. "I see. Well, since you are unable to remember the name of the seller and you have lost your papers, I suppose I could draw up a contract that would satisfy the curious. Now, mind you, if someone challenges you on its legality in court, you might possibly lose. However, I don't see that happening. Most people accept contracts at face value."

Aimee smiled and stuck out her hand. "I have the list of names here, Ernest. How long do you think this will take?"

"Maybe a couple of hours, luckily, Old Judge Harkness is in town for a day or so, and I know he owns several slaves down in Savannah. He'll be happy to sign the verification for me. We're old poker players from way back and he owes me a few favors."

"I can't tell you how much I appreciate this, Ernest. I don't think I could get my place in working order without them. Isaac and I need to pick up some equipment at the store. We'll get some lunch at the restaurant and maybe look at the livery stable. We'll check back with you in a couple of hours."

Ernest frowned, cleared his throat, and looked hard at Aimee. "I don't think it's a good idea for you and the boy to eat at the restaurant. I'm not crazy about their food and I don't think you'd be happy with the service."

Aimee immediately stiffened when she understood Ernest's message. Of course, no one would serve Isaac in a public restaurant. What was she thinking?

"You're right, of course. The last time I ate there, the beef tasted like shoe leather. Maybe Isaac and I will wait until we get home. We'll get our supplies and come back. Thank you, Ernest. You are a good friend."

Ernest took Aimee's hands in both of his. He held them for a long time, looking into her eyes.

"I admire you, Mack Kaymey. You remind me so much of someone I once knew. My wife, too, is a lot like you. I wish you two could have met under different circumstances. I know you would have been great friends."

Aimee smiled and touched his arm. "Thank you, I'm sure we would have been."

"Oh," she gasped. "I almost forgot. A man came by the house yesterday. He said he was lost and looking for some property. You haven't seen him, have you?"

Ernest looked puzzled for a moment, and then his face brightened. "Yes, now that you mention it, Matthew did send a young man down to see me about some property. Seemed like a nice fellow.

"Unfortunately, the only thing around here is an old dairy farm with a couple hundred acres about five miles on the other side of town. Somehow, he didn't look the dairy farmer type. There are a couple of houses just a mile or so from the edge of town for sale, also. He said he'd been working the gold fields in California and was ready to settle down.

"Ai- uh... Mack, are you all right? Is anything wrong? Do you know that fellow?"

Aimee took a deep breath. "As a matter of fact, we might have met once. I thought, that is, I heard he drowned."

"Oh my," Ernest said, paling. "This is an incredible coincidence. You don't think it's anything more than that do you?"

Aimee smiled. "No, Ernest, there is no reason to think otherwise. It's just unfortunate that we both decided to settle here. Perhaps he won't find anything he likes and will move on."

"I'm sure that's the case. As I said, he doesn't look like running a dairy would be his cup of tea. If I hear anything, I'll let you know immediately."

Nodding as she turned to Isaac, who looked very confused, Aimee said, "Come on, son, we've got supplies to buy."

Aimee stopped at the teller's cage and picked up another hundred dollars and the pair headed for the general store. She still had quite a bit of money left over from her initial withdrawal but wasn't sure what all would be needed, and she wanted to be able to pay Albert and the others weekly.

Matthew Barker came out from behind the counter and met Aimee before she had taken five steps into the store.

"Mister Kaymey, what a surprise. I wasn't expecting to see you for quite a while." He turned and scowled at Isaac, who hung back, looking at a stack of hoes and shovels against the front wall.

"What are you doing, boy?" He snarled. "Where's your Ma?" You don't have any business in here. Git, go on, now... git."

Isaac froze, his eyes filled with fear and he began to stumble backward.

Aimee turned and grabbed Matthew by the sleeve, jerking him around. Although she was several inches shorter than Barker, she took Isaac by the shoulder with her other hand, guided him behind her, and took a deep breath. Men stood up for what belongs to them and Aimee couldn't do any less.

She stepped up to Matthew and pulled herself up as tall as she could. "Mister Barker, I don't think you meant to be rude or discourteous to me and my hired boy here, but I don't appreciate your attitude. He belongs to me and is here to carry my purchases. Do you have a problem with that?"

Matthew Barker's face reddened as he glanc-ed around. Several customers turned away quickly, pretending not to have heard anything.

He hurriedly recovered, straightened himself, and adjusted the sleeve Aimee just released.

"I can assure you there was no disrespect intended, Mister Kaymey. I didn't realize the boy was with you. We have to be careful of shoplifters. They'll steal you blind if you're not careful. Let me offer my apologies and assure you that it will never happen again. Isaac cowered behind Aimee but nodded when he saw Aimee look down.

"It won't happen again," Matthew repeated, sincerely.

"I hope not. I have several families under my supervision and they will be dropping in from time to time to purchase necessary tools, supplies, and equipment for me. They will each have a signed note, and a shopping list from me for the goods I'll need, and I'd appreciate it if you give them the same courtesy and assistance that you give me. After all, they are following my orders and I am paying good money for my purchases, isn't that so?"

"They will certainly be treated as valued customers, Mister Kaymey. I assure you." Trying to shift the subject, the storeowner smiled and said, "Now what brings you to town?"

Aimee handed Matthew the top half of her list and turned to Isaac. "Son, you go with Mister Barker here and make sure that he understands exactly what we need. I want the finest quality you have, Mister Barker. They have to last."

"I'll see to it that you get the best, sir," Matthew said, and motioned for Isaac to follow him.

Aimee approached the counter and while Isaac picked out the tools, fencing, chicken wire, and other supplies, she decided to surprise Rose and the other women. Matthew's wife, Edna, hurried over to wait on her and smiled kindly at Aimee.

"Mrs. Barker, I have a number of workers at my place now and I need about..."

She paused and tried to remember how many families were in the hills. A finger popped up for Rose's family, George and Dewey, a woman named Maybell, and a couple of others Albert said were leaving next spring. That was at least six.

"I need six separate boxes of supplies. I want coffee, tea, flour, cornmeal, baking powder, beans, bacon, canned milk, peaches, tomatoes, and whatever else sounds good. Plus, they'll need about fifteen plates, cups and spoons, knives, and forks.

"Throw a couple dozen blankets and about six yards each of ten different patterns of dress material along with needles, thread, and scissors. You'll need their shoe sizes so they'll have to come in later for those. Add ten pounds of sugar, twenty pounds of potatoes, and a dozen bunches of onions and six separate pounds of butter and six-dozen eggs. Oh, and a dozen pair of heavy-duty work gloves. Do you have all that in stock?"

Edna Barker bent over the counter, with a pencil and paper, trying to keep up. She blinked rapidly as she wrote.

"I-I have nearly everything but the eggs. My son, Nathan, can run down the street to Mrs. Miller's house and get all the eggs she has. She'll be thrilled to get rid of them. Her chickens have been laying more eggs than we've been able to sell, so I'm sure she will have six dozen."

"I'll take all she has. That's fine, just fine," Aimee said as she rubbed her chin. "When you have the boxes filled, load them in the wagon, please. Thank you Mrs. Barker, for your help.

"As soon as Isaac and your husband has gathered up all the tools I need, just total up everything and I'll pay you for them. By the way, I wonder if you could fix us both a little snack we could eat before heading back?"

Edna beamed at the chance to please her rich customer. She was all but dancing. "It just so happens I have a fresh baked ham in the kitchen. I could fix you each a big sandwich with a baked sweet potato, and big glass of lemonade."

"That sounds delicious, ma'am," Aimee said in her disguised voice. "I surely appreciate your kindness."

"Not at all, not at all. We appreciate your business, Mister Kaymey, and we aim to please our customers, you know." She giggled and headed through the back door to the private living quarters.

Isaac joined her at the counter and Aimee noticed that Matthew busied himself with writing down all the tools and totaling up the ticket.

"Matthew, I need a good hunting rifle and plenty of ammunition added to that list. I need to get my smokehouse full by winter. Your wife's fixing us a couple of sandwiches and some lemonade. We'll be down at the pond. If you'll holler at us when they're ready... " she didn't finish before Edna popped through the door.

"Didn't take too long, did it, Mister Kaymey? I have your sandwiches wrapped here with the buttered potatoes and here is your lemonade. Do you need help taking it outside?"

"No thank you, Mrs. Barker. Isaac here will take the sandwiches and I'll take the drinks. We'll bring the glasses back soon as we're finished."

"No need to return them, Mister Kaymey. You just keep those glasses. We have plenty more," she said quickly, glancing at her husband.

"Much obliged, ma'am," Aimee said.

As she and Isaac walked out, Isaac said sadly, "She jest didn't want the one I's gonna drink out of, did she?"

"Who cares, Isaac? We don't, so don't you worry. We know what's right and that's all that matters. Besides, you can take the glasses home to your mother. I'm sure she'd love to have them."

As they ate their lunch on a bench by the pond, several townspeople passed and gave them curious looks.

When they got back to the store, Aimee paid her bill. "Matthew, could you do one more thing for me?"

"Of course, Mister Kaymey. How can I help you?"

"I need a milk cow, laying hens, a rooster, and a couple of steers."

"Yes, sir," he replied while making a note. "Shall I have them delivered?"

"No, that won't be necessary. I'll return in a few days for them."

~ Seven ~
An Unwanted Neighbor

Ernest seemed to be in a happy mood when Aimee and Isaac returned to the bank. He left his office door open and when the pair walked inside, he motioned for them to come into his office.

"My, you're in a good mood. Did you just inherit a million dollars?" Aimee asked good-naturedly.

"Almost," he said with a grin. "Martha dropped by after a trip to Doc Tucker's and just told me I'm going to be a father in six months. Also, I just opened another large account that should really impress the insurance company.

"Moreover, the judge never doubted my story concerning your lost bill of sale for one second. I filled out the, you know, second bill of sale and he signed it along with your name change without even looking at them. You are now the proud legal owner of..." he glanced at the papers. "Fifteen slaves, sixteen, counting this young man. I've also invested a little of your money in a man who is redesigning the plow. His name is John Deere and he's making new plows from steel imported from England, and there's a new invention called the Atlantic Telegraph.

"Times are changing and I feel these investments will eventually give us a nice return."

He handed Aimee the papers and folded them neatly. She looked at him through narrowed eyes and asked in a whisper, "Who was this depositor who is going to help you impress the insurance company?"

The question wiped the smile off Ernest's face. "There was nothing I could do, Ai... uh, Mack. The man insisted on opening an account. I couldn't tell him we were full. After all, this is a bank. What did you want me to do?"

Heaving a deep sigh, Aimee smiled sadly. "Of course not, Ernest, you had to do your job. You have a responsibility to this town and everyone in it. Growth of Sycamore Grove is important but I wish Lucas Chase had found another town to help grow."

Aimee left the bank after again congratulating Ernest on becoming a father and reassuring him that she understood his position concerning Lucas Chase.

Lucas hadn't bought the dairy, Ernest had been right about that, instead, he had taken a room at Mrs. Lander's boarding house. After turning down the dairy, and two other houses near town, he told Ernest he would keep looking.

If Isaac was surprised at all about the number of boxes in the back of the wagon, he didn't show it. Aimee surmised that he had learned if it didn't affect him, then he should ignore it. His daddy probably taught him a long time ago to mind his own business.

As they rode back to Eagle Creek, Aimee wondered how Albert and the rest had manage to get anything up into the hills, and how they would get the supplies she bought up to their place. The trail that Isaac used was certainly not wide enough for a wagon, and the shortcut through the field didn't look like an easy way either. She had a feeling that there was another way up there, and Albert had decided to keep it a secret.

She did notice Isaac sneaking a peak at all the things in the back now and then. She wondered what the conversation would be like when they discovered the supplies were for them.

"Mister Kaymey?" Isaac finally said. "Them papers that man gave you in town. Does them papers mean we don't have to hide anymore?" He asked with wide eyes.

"Yes sir, Isaac, that's exactly what they mean. Now, you have to understand something from the very start. I want this perfectly clear, and I want you to make sure your Pa and his friends understand. Those papers say that you, your family, and all their friends are slaves who belong to me, but that's not true.

"The papers are just to protect all of you from people who might come along and say you belong to them. Now, when the time is right, I'll have papers drawn up to say that you are all free and that you don't belong to anyone. Do you understand? They are just to protect you."

Isaac's little face broke into a beaming smile that warmed Aimee's heart. "Yas suh, I understands and I'll sees to it that Pa and the others understands. You won't be sorry, Mister Kaymey, we'll work hard for you."

"Isaac, I didn't do this so you would work hard for me. I did it because it was the right thing to do. Like I told your pa, we're neighbors now and neighbors do what they can to help one another."

Isaac grinned all the way to the house, then jumped down from the wagon and ran to Albert before Aimee had a chance to pull the team to a complete stop.

Dewey and another man Aimee wasn't familiar with came toward the wagon.

"Mister Kaymey, this here is George Cooley. Whacha wants us to do with them boxes?" Dewey asked.

"Hello, Dewey. Glad to meet you, George. The boxes of food and supplies stay in the wagon. The tools, chicken and fencing wire, nails, hammers, hoes, shovels, fencing, and that scythe go wherever Albert tells you to put them.

"There's also a brown package there on that box in the corner with gloves in it. Each of you get yourself a pair and take the rest back to the other men who live with you. I'm sure they could use them when cutting wood or doing other work."

She could see the look of disbelief on their faces. There was also a glimpse of suspicion, and she realized they weren't used to anyone doing anything for them for free.

Albert and Isaac spoke quietly and intensely and when Albert finally smiled, Aimee relaxed. She was afraid he would misunderstand the purpose of the papers of ownership.

"Albert, could you come over here for a minute?" Aimee called.

Throwing the armload of weeds into a large pile, he went to the wagon and glanced at the boxes.

When he reached over the side, Aimee laid her hand on his and said, "Albert, tell me the truth. Is there another way to reach your campsite besides the trail through the woods, or the shortcut through the meadow?"

Albert sighed and nodded. "Yas suh, there is. There's an old loggin' trail jest past the road that comes up here. We done put brush and dead saplings 'cross it so it isn't seen, but it's there all right."

"Good because you're going to have to use it to get these supplies to your womenfolk. Now, I'm not sure I have everything you need. Tell Rose to check carefully and let me know if I've forgotten anything.

"Oh, and by the way, I plan to get several rifles for you all to use for hunting. You can't keep trapping small animals to eat. Wouldn't you like turkey, venison, or a wild hog once in a while? I don't think I could live on possum, raccoon, and fish for very long."

Albert, Dewey, and George stood stock still, staring at Mack Kaymey as if he had just grown an extra head.

"Y-you mean y-you're gonna gets us real guns with r-real bullets?" Dewey asked, and his mouth went slack.

Aimee pretended she hadn't heard the disbelief in his voice. "Yes, I have one here for Albert but later on I'll get more. I don't want to raise suspicion. People wouldn't feel too safe if they knew my slaves had guns, now, would they?"

Isaac had explained to George and Dewey the fake papers Aimee had drawn up. They may have been nervous about Mack Kaymey having papers stating they were his slaves, but with him providing guns, they now knew Isaac was telling the truth.

"I may have to buy a couple of rifles here, and have my friend buy some for me out of town. It's even possible that I'll have to drive to Charleston for the rest but don't worry, we'll have them soon.

"Albert, why don't you get the tools stored and call it a day? I know it's still early but you all need to get these supplies home. You don't want that fresh butter to melt all over everything. When you bring the wagon back, it's still a good idea to hide the entrance to that logging road. I don't want anyone else to use it."

"Yas suh, I'll do jest that. Suh," he said softly. "This here is mighty fine of ya, yas suh, mighty fine."

"You all earned it, Albert. Every one of you. I'll see you tomorrow, if you're not too busy at home. Keep the wagon overnight. If you come tomorrow, you can bring it back then, if not, then whenever you can."

"You'll see us tomorrow," Albert said firmly. "Yas suh, we'll be here."

Aimee watched as the men put the tools in the barn, and Dewey and George held their new gloves, stroking them as if they were made of gold. Sadness came over her as she thought of all the hardships they had been through. The list went on and on.

There was the lack of food, no medical care, freezing nights, no way to provide clothes for their children, nor a proper house to protect them from the winter weather, nor any way to show their women how much they cared.

The helplessness the men must feel not being able to provide a safe haven for their family, and the pain the women must have endured caring for sick children, trying to prepare what food they could find to keep them alive had to be stressful. Not to mention the struggle to survive and stay out of sight from bounty hunters.

She wanted to be a part of their new beginning just as they were a part of hers, and she would make sure they never had to suffer again. Aimee's greatest dream was to have a good life for them and for herself. And all thanks to Abram. She hoped he knew.

After the men and Isaac had left, Aimee pulled off her cap at last. She could not understand why a man would want to wear a cap or hat all day. As a young girl, she hated putting on a bonnet when she went out. She had always been a tomboy at heart and playing the part of a man wasn't so bad. Still, she did miss her long hair and picking out a frilly new dress now and then. Being a girl wasn't so bad now that she thought about it. It had just depended on her mood. Now, however, moods didn't matter. She didn't have a choice.

Going into the barn, she led Dusty and Puck, the name she had given her mule, out into the corral. She pumped water into the trough and watched the mule scamper around the fence line. She laughed aloud when Puck lay down in the dirt and began to roll from side to side. Dusty just shook his head and watched Puck as if he were a naughty child.

Aimee went inside, stirred up the fire, and put on the teakettle. A sweet cup of tea would hit the spot. She went out to the unfinished springhouse, took two eggs from the spring cooler, and sliced off a couple of strips of bacon. Soon the bacon sizzled while the teakettle whistled. She pulled the kettle off the edge of the hot spot, slid the bacon over, and dropped two eggs in beside them. She wondered if Rose was preparing the same thing for their supper. It had probably been a long time since any of them had fresh chicken eggs.

Aimee sopped up the last of the yolk and popped it into her mouth when she heard the sound of hooves on the packed dirt outside. Thinking it was Albert returning the wagon she ran her hand through her hair and walked lazily to the front door.

Sitting straight in the saddle, in the middle of the yard was the only person for miles who could destroy her dreams. She turned, grabbed her cowboy hat off the hook and pulled it low over her forehead, and stepped outside.

"Good evening, sir. Remember me? I stopped by here the other day and asked directions. Chase, Lucas Chase. I didn't get your name?" He paused politely, awaiting an answer.

Aimee drew herself up as tall as she could, turned her collar up, coughed and growled, "Mack Kaymey's my name. You lost again?"

Lucas laughed a deep, warm laugh. When he smiled, the

corners of his eyes crinkled and a deep dimple creased his right cheek.

"No sir, not this time. I just came from down the road a piece, three or four miles, I think. I found a nice piece of property, and if I'm not mistaken the boundary butts right up against yours. A nice wide creek comes down through the hills, forms a small pond, and then empties out from a spillway further down. Owner's name is Henry Owens. He thought this place was empty. He didn't know anyone lived here."

"Haven't been here long, so I don't know the man," Aimee said in a clipped tone.

"He lives on the other side of the land I'm looking at. I think his father owned the land between his and yours. He died last year, and I guess Owens doesn't care anything about it. There's about five hundred acres of good soil, trees, and clear, cold, spring water."

Aimee coughed, as she shifted from one foot to the other. Her hands deep in her pockets, she tried to act disinterested. It must have worked.

"Well, I won't take up any more of your time. Just wanted to stop by and say howdy." Lucas stared hard at Aimee and moved his horse a little closer to her.

"Howdy." Aimee tugged her hat as she turned and stepped back. Inside the house, she peeked out the window and saw Lucas pause. He looked carefully around the place, smiled to himself, and kicked his horse into a gallop, disappearing down the road.

~ * ~

The day had been much the same as the one before. The men worked hard but now Aimee wanted to be a part of getting her new home into good condition. She pulled weeds, washed the outsides of the windows, and watered the onions, cabbage, and greens she and Isaac planted, and then cleaned the yard around the house.

After raking out the barn, she carried the manure to a pile to be used as fertilizer. Aimee examined the completed work on the barn, looked around and smiled, quite pleased with the progress. The time passed quickly and soon she noticed the sun sinking low on the horizon.

Aimee filled a bucket of water and poured some into the coffee pot, and set some to boil. After dark, she locked the door securely, pulled off her clothes, washed and trimmed her hair, and bathed. Feeling refreshed, she pulled on a clean shirt and fell onto the bed.

Her exhaustion came not from the trips into town and the strain of breaking the law with Ernest's help, but also from the fact that all the planning of finding a house in a small town, deep in the woods, far from Charleston had not been enough. Aimee couldn't believe that Lucas Chase - from *California* - a man she thought had died on the tragic voyage, could ruin everything. Not to mention he would soon be living a few miles down the road.

It wasn't possible to pull up stakes and move. She had bound herself to the Washington's life, their family and friends. This land was good, she had the house, the horses, the tools needed for work, and she was a known citizen of Sycamore Grove. If she disappeared now, there would be talk.
Laying a damp cloth across her throbbing head, she eventually drifted off into a dream-filled sleep of crashing waves, sparkling blue eyes, and voices warning her to be careful.

~ * ~

Rising before dawn, Aimee dressed, ate, fed the animals, and then headed back to the house where Albert, Dewey, George, and Isaac had arrived in the wagon. Rose sat on the seat beside Albert but Aimee was not surprised. She knew if she received the boxes of supplies as Rose had, she, too would have gone to personally thank the benefactor.

George jumped from the wagon and helped Rose down. Albert drove the wagon into the barn where the others climbed down and put the horses away. Rose brushed the dust off her skirt and sleeves and checked to see if her braids were still smooth and neat. She pulled herself up and started toward the house. Aimee smiled and pushed the door open for Rose to enter.

"Coffee's still hot. Can I get you a cup?" Aimee asked, keeping her voice low.

Rose nodded and Aimee could see she was struggling to keep her composure. There were tears filling Rose's eyes and her lips trembled. She had probably tried to prepare a speech of thanks the entire trip but now they were face to face, Aimee thought Rose must be too nervous, and Aimee wasn't about to embarrass her.

"Now, Rose," Aimee said, in her low, gruff voice. "Before you start fussin' about those supplies, let me tell you something. I… "

"Stop," Rose interrupted sharply. "I needs to talk. I've been repeatin' my speech since we left the house. First of all, you ain't what you seems to be. Don't deny it, I kin tell. I have the gift of seeing beyond things. My granny had it and I gots it now."

Aimee stiffened. She reached over, grabbed the coffee pot, and took an extra cup from the shelf. Rose watched silently as Aimee refilled her cup, then poured another one and pushed it toward it toward Rose.

"I don't know what you're talking about." Aimee shakily placed the pot back on the stove and picked up her cup.

"Yes'um, you do," Rose said simply, and Aim-ee caught the *yes'um* clearly.

"How did you know?" Grabbing the back of the chair, she sat with a jolt.

"I'm a watcher," Rose said. "Since I wuz a little girl hanging on my ma's skirt, I watches people. At first I jest watches the massuh and his lady, and all them fancy people that came to Deerborn Estate. I watches the servants, the field hands, the overseers, and most of all, I watches all the slaves from dawn to dark. I seen the young 'uns grow up 'n git sold away and I seen older folk get older and sadder.

"I noticed one big thing 'bout young and old. Men and women are as different as night and day, as cold and heat, as yes

91

is to no. Well, they is some people that wishes they wuz sumpin' they's not, but wishes as they might, they is what they is and you, Miss... you is what you is."

"Does everybody know?" Aimee asked in disbelief.

"Not from me they doesn't. That's for you to tell, not me. I figures you gots a mighty good reason to hide what the good Lord done gave you, and it ain't up to me to say why.

"But then there's the second thing. I know you did what you did out of the goodness of your heart. Most men wouldn't of thought of that. I saw the women of the camp cry last night... crying for joy. A joy they felt for the first time since we've been here. I thinks everybody there had hot biscuits and fresh eggs last night. The looks on our folks' faces this mornin' wuz looks of folks that had a full belly for the first time in years." Tears freely streamed down Rose's face and Aimee began to cry, too.

There was a knock on the door and Isaac called, "Mister Kaymey, Pa wants to know iffen you wants us to start on the new corral first or work on the chicken pen. We brung Abraham to help and they's ready."

"Isaac, you tells your Pa we'll be out in a minute," Rose called hoarsely. She began to wipe her damp eyes with her apron.

Less than a minute later, the door burst open, and Albert stood in the opening clutching a large stick, his eyes flaming in anger.

"Albert, has you gone mad... " Rose began, as Isaac peeked around his father's legs.

"Did he hurt you, Ma? I heerd you a'cryin'," Isaac said tearfully.

Despite the emotions of the past few minutes, Aimee burst out laughing and Rose joined her. Albert's angry look melted into a confused twist and Isaac hid.

"Albert, come in and close the door, please. Isaac, your mother is just fine and we have grown up talk right now. Please wait outside and I'll call you later," Aimee said softly.

Albert walked stiffly inside and closed the door firmly. He

still held onto the piece of wood, that Rose took from him and replaced with her cup of coffee.

"You ain't gonna be needin' this, Al. There's no danger. Sit down and behave. I reckon Mister Kaymey has something to tells you."

Aimee nodded and sat while Rose poured Albert a cup of coffee. He stared at Aimee suspiciously until Rose leaned over and gave him a hug.

"Albert... Mister Washington, I ran away from my past life just as you and your family did. I was a young, foolish girl who was blinded by what I thought was love. I turned my back on my family, and after withdrawing the money my mother left me, I ran away in the middle of the night with a man who later stole my money and gave me this scar." She paused, pulled back her hair and exposed the jagged scar on her upper temple.

"I escaped, bought a ticket to New York City but he saw me on the ship and swore he would find me. The ship sailed into a hurricane and was lost at sea, but I was rescued and hid my identity. To make a long story short, I am not a man. I am a woman and your wife figured it out.

"That's the main reason she came today and we were overcome with emotion and like most women, we started crying. That's when Isaac came to the door and heard Rose."

Albert looked stunned. His grip went slack and would have spilled his coffee from the way the cup tilted, if Rose hadn't taken it from his hand. He star-ed hard at Aimee, then slowly, his stare softened and his eyes widened.

"A woman... and you knowed this, Rose?" he asked incredulously.

"Not at first. I never looked too hard at him, I mean her. Not directly in the face at first. But once I starts studying her, likes I does everbody, I commenced to wonder, then I starts a'thinkin' and memberin', and when you came home with all that food, I just knew whut my gift done told me was true," she said with a smile.

"Who else knows?" Albert asked.

"Besides Rose, only Ernest Gaines, over at the bank. He is my banker and lawyer, and he drew up the papers I needed to say you were my slaves. I had to tell him so I could get my name changed properly in order for the bill of sale on this property to be legal. It's difficult for women to own property, and a woman alone is a prime target for every scam artist and thief in the country. I wanted Aimee McKay, which is my real name, to disappear. You understand, don't you, Albert?"

Albert chuckled harshly. "You's askin' me if I knows why someone would hide don't make much sense, Miss... What was that name again?"

"Mack," Rose snapped. "Mister Mack Kaymey. That's who's sittin' in front of us and we ain't gonna change things now or never. As far as Isaac is concerned, I doesn't think we should tell him. Hear me out," she said as Aimee frowned and opened her mouth.

"Isaac is a good boy and as trustworthy as they come, but mishaps kin happen and words kin slip out when you ain't even knowin'. It would destroy him if he knew he wuz the reason Mister Kaymey's secret was revealed. So to protect Mister Kaymey and Isaac, I sez we jest don't say nothin' now. When he's older, we can think about it."

Albert listened carefully and nodded. "You's right, Rose, as usual. He don't needs no extra burdens of life now while he's young. When he gits older, well, we'll see then, like you said. Agreed?" He looked at Aimee, who nodded, her face contorted with the pain of the lie.

Albert emptied his cup and stood. "Well, we gots work ahead for the whole day. Rose, you gonna stay and visit or is you goin' back home? I hates to see you walks so far in your condition."

Aimee looked back and forth between Albert and Rose, and when she saw Albert's proud look and Rose's shy smile, she knew.

"A baby? Rose, are you going to have a baby?" She squealed

and hugged Rose, who giggled and hugged her back.

"Now, you two has to stop that," Albert said gruffly. "How would it looks if I lets my master to go around a huggin' on my woman?"

Aimee laughed and stepped back but continued to hold Rose's hand. "He's right you know."

Rose nodded. "I nearly forgot. Isaac told me that in all his 'splorin', they's a man who lives 'bout twenty or thirty minutes from here that has a yard full of chickens. If you plans on gittin' some, maybe he's got some you kin buy."

Aimee nodded slowly. "There's one more thing I didn't think about until you mentioned the man with the chickens. Albert, do you remember that day you and Isaac hid in the bedroom when that man stopped by asking for directions?"

Albert nodded and frowned when he saw the strain on Aimee's face.

"That man was on the same ship as I when we got caught up in the hurricane. I thought he drowned but when he showed up in my front yard, I thought I would faint. After he left, I thought that was the end of it. But it wasn't. He stopped in again after you left yesterday. It seems he is trying to buy the property next to mine... Henry Owens' place? He must be the man who has the chickens. We need to stay clear of the man from the ship. He could ruin everything for me. And for all of us.

"I'm making you manager of this farm, Albert. You'll handle everything from now on, including what we'll plant where, and you'll talk to any strangers who come here. Matthew Barker, who runs the general store in town, thinks I've come here to recuperate from a long illness. We'll keep that story going. That will be a good excuse for me staying out of sight."

Albert nodded. "Yassum. Sorry, yas *suh*, I's be proud to take charge. I wuz in charge of the whole back thousand acres at Deerborn. 'Course, we only planted cotton but we got the job done and done right. In fact, I think we, uh, you, need to plant plenty of hay."

"I like the sound of 'we'." Aimee smiled, rose and put the cups in the enameled dish tub on the counter.

"Rose, next spring I intend to build me a new house right here. I may use this," she gestured around her, "as part of the house, or I may just tear it down and start from scratch. I haven't decided but when it's all finished, I'm going to need a house-keeper.

"I don't mean a maid, I mean a housekeeper, someone to run things, to hire maids and buy household supplies and see that someone cares for the yard and gardens and such. We'll also hire someone to care for your child or maybe children," she paus-ed and smiled when she saw Albert's grin. "They'll be right here with you during the hours you are here, that is, in the new house, if you decide you'd like the job.

"And Albert, I want you to think about staying on as farm manager permanently. This has been a day of unusual surprises and many things to think about, so I'll end this for now. I want you to take Rose home in the wagon and make sure she gets some rest. Then come on back and do whatever you had planned to do today. I'm going to ride over and see about some chickens."

~ Eight ~
Lock, Stock and Barrel

Aimee trotted slowly along on the horse until she saw a sign nailed to a tree that read, *Keep Out - No Trespassing - Henry Owens - Owner.*

She pulled to a stop, cleared her throat and called out in a deep voice, "Hello, Henry Owens. I need to talk to you." Urging Dusty up the trail, she stopped now and then to call out.

"Hello, Henry Owens."

After about thirty yards or so, she got an answer. "Take to the left. I'm over here by the fence."

Taking a deer path for a few yards, a man and young boy struggled to prop up a sagging fence.

"Little Henry, git this man a drink of cold water," the man said, and the boy took off toward a wagon.

"Whut kin I do fer ya?" the man asked, his wide smile exposed several missing teeth.

"Those signs at the road worried me a bit," Aimee replied, gesturing over her shoulder.

"Oh, them. My pa put them thangs up years ago. He warn't a very social feller, my pa, Henry Senior. I'm junior and this boy o' mine is Little Henry Three. I need to take 'em down. Little Henry, remin' me to take them there signs down by the road, ya hear?"

"Yes sir, Pa." The boy grinned as he handed Aimee a bent-up tin cup filled with water.

Aimee dismounted and drank the cool water in a single tilt. "My name is Mack Kaymey. I bought the old Duncan place down the road and I heard you might have some chickens for sale, Mister Owens."

"Mack, call me Henry. We don't go by no fancy city ways out here. I ain't never sold my chickens but that don't mean I won't. There's a mighty lot of them critters runnin' 'round and the more I got, the more feed I gotta buy. How many you lookin' fer?" He ask pulled off his crumpled hat and scratched his head.

"I was thinking of two or three dozen, Henry but I'd settle for one or two if you don't have enough. I'd also like to have a rooster if you have one to spare."

"Oh," he mused, as he stared into the trees. "I figure I can spare two or three dozen and," he paused, smiling slyly, "I do have a rooster. He's a mean 'un though, but I'd throw him in fer free if you take him." He chuckled. "You brung any cages or pens?"

Aimee shook her head, "No, I don't have anything like that."

"No matter. I got some old 'uns you kin use but I'd like 'em back. Never know whut you need to cage up."

"I appreciate that, sir. Do you think I could pick them up tomorrow? I'll bring the wagon."

"Tomorrow'll do fine, jest fine. Jest follow the road straight up and you'll run right into the yard. Kin you make it 'bout nine? I'll have 'em ready by then."

"Nine it is, then. Thank you, Henry. I'll see you tomorrow. Thanks for the water, son," she said to Little Henry Three. Then she turned Dusty around and headed back.

By the time she got to the house, Albert had returned. George and Dewey were working on the split rail fence while Isaac hoed the walkway. The improvements on the place brought a smile to Aimee's face.

"Albert, how long would it take to fix up that pen for three dozen chickens?" She hollered, and slid off Dusty. The horse shook himself, snorted his approval at being home and headed for the barn without being led. "I think Dusty is about ready for retirement." Aimee chuckled.

"You's right to exercise him now and then," Albert remarked, and grabbed the reins when the horse trotted by. "Them muscles'll jest turn to jelly if'n ya don't ride him some."

"About that chicken pen?" Aimee reminded him, peering

toward the barn.

"I kin do it," the new man piped up. "Howdy, Mister Kay-mey. I'm Abraham Cooper, and I kin fix that pen from the side of the barn there and tack that old wire down good. I'll build some nesting boxes on the outside wall of the barn. We kin close them boxes up in the chicken house later a'fore it gits cold."

Albert looked toward the barn and nodded. "That's good, Abraham. Is that all right, Mister Kaymey?"

Aimee grinned. "It's your call, Albert. After all, you're the farm manager now." Pulling her hat off, she pounded it against her leg, knocking off the dust. "I'm going in to rest a while. Can I get you some coffee?"

Albert smiled widely. "No sir, our women folks done fixed us lunch and this here water's jest fine. We gots work to do, so you gits some rest now. You's lookin' kinda pale."

Aimee grinned and walked inside. She pulled off her hat, gloves, and coat, and then sat at the table to tug off her boots. Flexing her tired feet, she wiggled her toes, and stretched happily. Rest sounded like a good idea, although she wasn't tired physically, she was emotionally drained. It was truly exhausting to pretend to be someone you're not.

The teapot began to whistle when she hung her hat on the rack. She hated wearing a hat so much. She would have to talk to Rose and get some pointers on how she could play the role of Mack Kaymey and be more at ease.

There was suddenly a shout and Aimee looked out the window, then let out an exasperated sigh. There was Lucas Chase, dismounting in the front yard. Albert walked up to him and the two stood talking.

She saw Albert shake his head, nod toward the house, and then look over at the barn. Lucas smiled and pointed westward. Albert nodded again and shoved his hands in his pockets. Isaac ran to them, said something to Albert, and Albert nodded. Isaac ran back to the barn, leading the team to hitch up to the wagon.

Aimee resisted the urge to join them. Lucas talked for a

few more minutes, laughed several times. After glancing toward the house again, he nodded, stepped back and stuck out his hand toward Albert, who looked suspicious and a little fearful. Lucas remained with his hand outstretched until Albert pulled his hand from his pocket and shook. It was a firm and hearty shake from Lucas who turned, mounted his handsome roan, and nodded to Albert before riding away.

Waiting until Lucas had time to reach the road, Aimee cracked the door a few inches and called to Albert.

Looking around casually, Albert strolled to the house and slipped in through the half-opened door. He quickly removed his hat, holding it in his hands.

"Albert, what did he want now? Did he say anything about me?"

"I don't reckon you need to be worryin' now. He's jest one of them friendly-like fellers who wants git to know his neighbors."

"Neighbors?" Aimee gasped. "Does that mean he really bought the land next to ours?"

"I's 'fraid so," Albert said slowly. "They's agreed on a price today. You must have jest missed him when you went to see 'bout them chickens. He's gonna start clearin' the land and wanted us to know that we might be hearin' men choppin' or sawin', but I don't think that's the case.

"His land is a fer piece away to be hearin' that noise. I think he jest wanted us to know he would be livin' down the road. I truly 'spect him to be droppin' by quite a lot. I hates to say it but he's kinda like you in that he is one o' them neighborly fellers."

"What am I going to do? I'm confident I can fool people I don't know and have never met, but to face someone I know? I don't know if I can pull this off."

"Don't you worry. We'll keep our eyes open. I was jest thinkin' that we needs to put up a gate down by the road with a big bell attached. At least we kin hear 'em when they's enter."

"That's a wonderful idea, Albert. How soon can you get it

done?"

"I's git someone started on it first thing in the mornin'. We wants it to look nice so it may take a while to do it right. One of the men at the camp does iron work. With this here place being called Eagle Creek, what do you reckon 'bout puttin' two big eagles over the entrance?"

"That sounds perfect. I do want it to look special. You go ahead and build it and use the wagon to go into town and buy any supplies you need. I'll write a letter for you to take in to Mister Barker at the store and he'll charge everything. Now, don't skimp on what you need, I can afford it."

"You sure it'll be safe fer me and George to go to town?" He asked warily.

"I've told Mister Barker my workers would be in now and then. Take Isaac with you. He knows where everything is and Mister Barker knows him. While you're there, ask Mister Barker about the milk cow. And Albert, thank you. I don't know what I would do without you."

Albert shifted uncomfortably and grinned. "We's neighbors and friends and ain't that whut you said friends and neighbors was fer?"

It was strange hearing her words echoing back at her. "You're right, Albert. That's what friends are for."

Albert shoved his hat back on and opened the door. "If you starts gittin' cabin fever, you kin always rides up to the camp and visit with my Rose. I know she'd love to see you, 'n when we gits that gate up, you kin stay outside as long as you wants to."

He went back outside and started to work while George, Abram, and Isaac drove the wagon into the woods to chop down saplings for fence posts.

~ * ~

Taking out the pale muslin she bought, Aimee began to cut out a pattern for a nightgown. She had slept in a shirt since the rescue, but now she was going to do something for herself. Aimee McKay was going to get a new nightgown and be comfortable for

101

the first time in quite a while.

She measured, fitted, cut, and started basting the pieces together until she realized that she could hardly see. A tap on the door caused her to throw a blanket over the sewing.

Albert stood there, with hat in hand, as usual. "We's finished fer the day, sir," he said loudly. "We'll be gittin' on home. The rest will be here tomorrow on time, but I may be's a little late. I need to talk to Willie 'bout designing us a pair of eagles for that gate."

As he walked away, he turned and smiled. "See ya in the mornin', boss."

Aimee smiled and watched him join the others as they started the walk home. She opened the door a little wider and called out, "Albert, why don't you all double up and take the team and Dusty to ride home? It will save you a lot of time."

Albert and the others talked quickly among themselves and he waved at her. "Thank ya, sir. We'll do that. Thank ya."

After closing all the curtains, Aimee lit the lamps on the shelf, table, and side board near the bed. After getting ready for bed, she uncovered her sewing. Humming a tune from her childhood, she continued basting the gown together, the smiled as she held up the gown. First of all, she shortened the sleeves and gave it a scooped neckline.

All of the gowns she had ever worn had buttoned at the neck. Adding an extra yard in the skirt kept it from wrapping around her if she had a restless night. She wondered if other women would like that style. Their husbands probably wouldn't allow it. However, she sighed, that wasn't a problem for her.

Continuing her sewing, Aimee wondered if there would ever come a time when all women would have the same freedom of choice that men did. Most men were so foolish to believe that women weren't as smart or clever as they were. Wouldn't they feel foolish if those she'd met knew she had deceived them so completely? Still, if women are ever given the freedom to make their own decisions, they must have their own money, or, at least the opportunity to have a job that would pay them enough to be independent.

It was not to her credit that she was independent. She humbly accepted the fact that without Abram and Ernest, she would not have gotten as far as she had. A day didn't pass that Aimee didn't say a silent prayer for her friend, Abram and all those men lost at sea.

After sewing for a couple of hours, Aimee folded up the gown, put away the scraps, and climbed into bed.

There was one problem Aimee hadn't allowed herself to face since she moved into the house - the traveling bag. The little carpetbag that started the voyage with a few clothes and stock-ings was now filled with gold coins, small sacks of sparkling gold dust, and several very large nuggets.

She knew if she had thousands of dollars in the bank, she had a great deal more than that hidden under her bed in that precious bag. She wasn't going to put it in the bank, she had already made up her mind on that. Life could change overnight. She knew it wasn't rational to feel that way but she did. Something told her to hang on to Abrams bag and she would.

Tired, though not sleepy, Aimee wished she had picked up a book or two at the store. She made a mental note to buy read-ing material next time she went in, which would be sometime next month, if everything went according to plan.

Listening to the night sounds of the birds and insects, she finally drifted off to dreamless sleep.

~ * ~

Waking to the soft sound of footsteps in her kitchen, she jumped out of bed, peeped around the divider curtain, and saw Rose preparing coffee.

"How did you get in?" she said, pulling on her shirt and trousers, and threading the belt through the loops.

"That's something I wants to talks to you about," Rose said frowning. "After we escaped the transport wagon, we hid in the woods and traveled at night. Sometimes we would come 'cross an

103

abandoned cabin and I reckon that we got into some of them jest to get out of the rain or cold. I guess you could say we gots to be smart with locks and fasteners.

"That there board placed in the brace is easily lifted up by a piece of metal or thin piece of wood and don't think for a second that there's folks that don't know how. I come in for two reasons. One was to show you how easily you could be robbed, and the other is because Albert told me 'bout that man you used to know. Albert's gonna put a new lock on that door today so you'll be safe."

"Rose," Aimee cried, "you can't spend your days watching out for me. You have responsibilities at home with this new baby coming. I'm sure Albert looks forward to a hot cooked meal when he gets home and..." she stopped when Rose held up her hand and turned away.

"Miss Aimee," Rose smiled. "My mama lives with us and she takes it on herself to do most of the cookin'. She's gittin' on in age but nobody can fault her cookin'. With Isaac being almost eight and want-in' to either wander around the woods or trail along with Albert, I really don't have many chores.

"I makes the beds, helps with the wash once a week, and straightens up the house, which don't take long, and then I jest sew or whatever the season allows. Right now, I'm here and I's decided to takes you up on housekeeper.

"Now, since I never did no proper housekeepin' work, I thought I better start learnin' now. You can teach me and I can works for free. And I'll keeps that Chase feller away from you."

Aimee listened to Rose. It was so comforting to have someone around to worry about her. Since she left her home, she felt alone and friendless but since she had been in South Carolina, she'd found allies around every bend.

"Rose, I'll allow you to do this on two conditions. When we're alone, you call me Aimee. Not Miss Aimee, not Miss McKay, not Mister Kaymey, just plain Aimee. The other is that your salary will be fifty cents a day just like the men. No one works for free.

Deal?"

Rose looked shocked and slowly shook her head. "I don't think I can do this Miss… Mister Kaymey. You have to understand that my brain jest ain't trained to call a white woman by her given name. From the time I's born, I's taught, no, trained to never, ever get friendly with my betters."

Aimee walked over, poured herself a cup of coffee, added cream and sugar, and sat down. "Rose, I too, was trained in an entirely different world than I find myself now. Tell me honestly. Don't lie to me, Rose. Do you truly, deep in your heart, think that all white people are better than you? Think hard, Rose. I'm asking you to be honest with me and you know you can be."

Rose turned quickly, and began to wipe the counter, and poured water in the wash pan.

"Rose, I'm not letting you off the hook. I'm waiting for an answer."

Rose turned toward Aimee, her mouth a tight, fine line and her eyes flashed. "No, Aimee," she said tersely. "I do not think that all white folk is better. Most jest thinks they is."

Aimee laughed and jumped up. "Oh, Rose, I knew you wouldn't fail me. I could see it on your face. You're a strong, independent woman who sees things the way they really are. You told me you're a watcher. As a watcher, you saw how things were and you also saw how things ought to be.

"Albert treats you with love and respect. He knows how smart you are and depends on you to keep the family together. One day, maybe not in our lifetime, or even in your children's lifetime but one day, people will be treated as they deserve, that is, if they wake up and demand it."

Rose relaxed and returned Aimee's grin. "You gots my dander up there fer a minute. Nobody but you coulda done that. It felt good. I hope you're right about that someday. I hope my daughter lives in that world and she gets to see her dreams fulfilled, or at least she can be the kind of woman who is a part of that there change."

"We can pray and hope, Rose. We can pray and hope."

"Oh, I'm s'pose to tell you that Abraham's uncle, Mose, is going to make them eagles that Albert wants to put over the gate. He's making him a special fire for the metalwork. He was a horse-shoer at Deerborn Plantation and is mighty good at workin' with iron if he has the right stuff. Albert says Mose and Abraham are excited that they's finally gonna git a chance to do whut they wuz trained for."

"You tell Abraham that if his uncle Mose is interested, I'd like to have him shoe all our horses. I plan to get several more in the next few weeks and I don't want to have to take 'em into town each time they need a new shoe, or when I need a wagon wheel fixed. We're going to need a buggy before long and it might be a good idea if Mose comes along and checks it out. I don't want to get cheated."

"He'd like that. He surely would, although he's mighty shy 'bout goin' into town. I doubt he'll ever go."

"You might as well tell everyone at your camp that there's no need to be nervous about going to town now. Sooner or later, everybody in town is going to know about all of you, if they don't know already. I suppose Isaac has already told you about the little incident we had in the store."

Rose smiled. "Yes, he did and the way he told it, you wuz like a general in charge of his army. He said the store keeper wuz awfully nice to him after that."

"Rose, I haven't met too many people around here but so far, all that I have met are fair and seem honest. Not everybody thinks the way I do but so far they haven't given me any trouble and I don't expect any.

"I surely hopes you's right, Miss... sorry, Aim-ee, but don't be surprised when you do meet them other kind, 'cause I guaran-tees they's out there everywhere."

"I've already met one of the worst, Rose. I surely have."

A rap on the door made Aimee jump but Rose waved her to sit back and went to the door. Albert stood grinning.

106

"Abraham's workin' on makin' the chicken pen bigger. He's done got the post holes dug and him and George's 'bout ready to drop 'em. It won't take no time to nail that wire up. He kin put them nestin' boxes up after the chickens git here and he'll make roosts for 'em. We gots about a dozen old apple crates at home that we collected, and they's still in pretty good shape."

"Good grief, I'd forgotten about the chickens. I told Mister Owens I'd be there at nine." She went to the bedside table and picked up her pocket watch. "It's just now eight. I'll have to leave in about half an hour. Can you get the wagon hitched for me, Albert?"

"Yas suh, I kin. Do you want me and Dewey to go pick 'em up?" he asked. "We doesn't mind."

"Thanks. I do think it's a good idea for you to drive me and for Dewey to go along. It probably would look better if I had you along to load them up. He's throwing in a rooster and he did mention it's a mean one. I wanted to warn you before we get there".

Albert nodded. "I'll go tell Dewey and we'll get the wagon hitched."

"I'll be ready when you are," Aimee said, and went back inside to finish getting ready.

Rose made Aimee's bed, gathered clothes to be washed, and had stew meat sizzling in the skillet. Aimee stopped and looked around. Rose dropped the fork she held, placed one hand on her hip, and pointed a finger at Aimee.

"Now, don't you say a single word, Miss Aimee. As house-keeper I gots to do something, I jest can't sit around here all day. I'm 'fixing a stew for tonight and when I was lookin' 'round I found what looked like the beginning of a gown. If you don't mind, when I get the stew on, I'll rest a spell and sew on that gown.

"I've never seen one like that, but I really likes it. Some of the workers used to have sleeveless dresses they wore in the cotton fields but my ma wanted me covered from chin to shin. My next one will be just like this 'un. Where'd you get the idea for it?"

"The idea was what I would like to wear instead of what I'm supposed to wear, and that's what I came up with. Do you think Albert will let you wear it?"

"Miss Aimee, I tries to dress pretty for Albert and I tries to dress proper but at night, when the lights are out, Albert don't mind what I'm wearing. I think he'll like it just fine."

At the sound of snorting horses and the creaking wagon, Aimee grabbed her hat, slipped into her coat, and pulled her gloves from the pocket.

"Miss Aimee, you need to get you a few ties. I knew something was missin' but it jest came to me what is. Ties. Most men wear ties when they go to town or do business. Git yerself some ties 'n vests."

"Thanks, Rose, I will. See you later."

Albert jumped down and started to help Aimee up, until he saw Rose frowning from the doorway. He grinned and pretended to check the harness before climbing back on the seat and grabbed up the reins.

They drove down the lane and just as they turned onto the road, Aimee heard someone yell a greeting. She turned her collar up, pulled her hat down, and slipped on her gloves.

"Morning, Mister Kaymey. Albert. What a glorious morning. Care if I ride along with you?"

"Can't stop you," Aimee said gruffly.

"You wouldn't be heading up to the Owens' place, would you? That's where I'm going. Just picked up the bill of sale and transfer deed, so all I need is his signature and I can start moving in."

Aimee stiffened. "Thought you had to build a place," she said, looking at him from under the low brim of her hat.

"That's what I thought but come to find out, there a nice big farmhouse further back on the property. Seems his father built it when Henry was a small child. After the old man's wife died, he just couldn't stand to live there anymore, so he built the house where Henry lives. Henry said he almost forgot about the house. He let it go with the property, furniture and all. So, I'm all set. I'll just clean it up, buy supplies, move in, and start fencing."

"U-h-h-m," Aimee mumbled.

"I didn't hear you say, are you heading there?"

"Yas suh," Albert answered, as Aimee stared into the woods. "We's gonna pick up some chickens from Mister Owens. Mister Kaymey bought about three dozen hens and a rooster."

"Chickens?" mused Lucas. "Maybe I need a few. Fresh eggs would surely be an easy meal."

~ Nine ~
Unexpected Bonus

They rode in silence for several miles. If Lucas noticed that Albert and Dewey were a little nervous, he hid his feelings well.

"Here we are Mister Kaymey, suh, is this it? The second trail off the road, right?"

Aimee nodded as Albert directed the horses up the path and through the trees.

Lucas jerked his head around. "Let me get ahead of you, Albert. I've been up there twice. I can lead you through this maze. It really gets confusing."

"Yas suh, thank you."

Lucas maneuvered his horse along the tree line and paused beside Aimee, peering down at her. She glanced up and acknowledged him with a nod, as he worked his way ahead of the team.

Albert followed behind and Aimee realized she might have never found the house if Lucas hadn't been along. It sat in the center of a large dirt clearing, and Aimee could see a small house to the left, at the end of a path veering off from Henry's house. A bent-over old man sat on the porch, smoking a pipe, rocking slowly and gazing blankly across the yard.

Henry Owens walked out on the porch amid several young children. "Emma, come get these kids," he hollered. Emma gathered her children and ushered them inside, nodding slightly to their guests. "Mister Kaymey, Mister Chase, go ahead and take a seat."

Aimee jumped down and reached the porch about the same time Lucas did. She paused and then climbed the steps ahead of him.

"Boy, take that wagon over by the barn. Little Henry Three is waitin' to help you load 'er up. You can bring them crates back next week or such. Ain't got much use fer 'em right now."

"You might, Mister Owens," Lucas said. "That is, if you

110

have enough chickens left so I can buy a dozen or so?"

Aimee sat down and leaned forward. "If you don't have enough, I'll just take two dozen and Mister Chase can have the others."

"That won't be necessary," Henry said with a laugh, waving his hand. "I got plenty. Uncle Hank, over on that porch there, got more layin' than he can eat, so we won't miss another dozen, I promise you."

"Little Henry?" his father yelled. "Git yor brother to hep you crate up another dozen fer Mister Chase, here."

"Yes sir, Pa," the boy replied.

"Mister Kaymey, that'll be 'bout one dollar and twenty five cents fer them chickens, since the rooster ain't gonna cost ya nuttin'. Glad to git rid of that 'un. He's a mean 'un, he is, but he does keep them hens smilin'. I got several more roosters, if you want one, too, Mister Chase."

Lucas nodded and watched Aimee try to count out the money in her gloved hands. Finally she rose, turned her back on the men at the table, pulled one glove off, counted the money, and laid it on the table."

"Ma," yelled Henry Owens. The tiny, dark-haired woman came out of the house smiling from ear to ear when she saw the money. She moved in a blur, scooped it up, and disappeared back into the house without a word.

Henry grinned as he leaned back on the legs of his chair. "Ma handles all the money. She can make a dime into a dollar. I ain't no good at it.

"Mister Chase, you got them there papers I'm supposed to put my mark on?"

As Lucas laid the papers out on the table, Aimee rose and started toward the wagon.

"Thank you, Mister Owens. I'll be seeing you around."

"You bet, Mister Kaymey, glad to be able to hep you out. Drop by anytime. I 'preciate yer business."

Aimee only made it a few yards toward the barn when the

wagon rolled out of the barn. Albert and Dewey had the crates safely stacked in the bed of the wagon, with Dewey holding onto the last one. The rooster kept pecking at him through the wooden slats of the crate causing him to jerk his hands back.

"He's a feisty one, he is," Albert said, looking back over his shoulder, while Aimee climbed aboard. "You's gonna have to watch out for that 'un when you get them eggs."

"I'm thinkin' of puttin' a window inside the barn, so Mister Kaymey can check for eggs without goin' into that pen any more than he has to," Dewey said. "I can fix it so it opens into the back of the nestin' boxes. It may take a week or so 'fore I kin git to it, but I think you needs it."

"Good idea," agreed Albert. "Them roosters have spurs on the back of their legs that can rip you open or poke you bad iffin you ain't careful."

"Spurs?" squealed Aimee, causing Dewey to stare at her. She grabbed her throat, and pretended to cough to clear it.

"What do you mean, spurs?" She repeated in a deeper voice.

"It's like a big, single claw on the back of their legs just above their feet. Some folk back home raises 'em to be extra mean and puts 'em in rings to fight one another. Then they bets on who's gonna win and who's gonna die. They's fights 'til one of 'em is dead. Never favored that practice. They's jest dumb chickens but death shouldn't be no entertainment."

"That's horrible and unusually cruel," Aimee agreed. "I hope no one around here does that."

"Ya never knows," Dewey said from the back. "When it comes to gamblin' ain't nothin' folks won't do."

"Hello, the wagon, hold up," shouted Lucas as he came galloping up from behind, his two crates of chickens bouncing on the rear of his horse, where they were tied.

He tipped his hat to Aimee and slowed his horse to keep pace with the wagon. "I was afraid Mister Owens might want to chat a while but he's a no nonsense kind of fella. Once the papers were signed and I handed him the money, or rather handed the money to his wife," he chuckled, "Henry just got up and disappeared into the house. I waited a while but when he didn't come back, I figured I'd been dismissed. I told his son to tell him thank you for me."

"You gots family near here, Mister Chase, suh?" Albert asked when Aimee didn't pick up the conversation.

Lucas smiled at Albert. "I was born in St. Louis, but when they discovered gold, I had to try my luck. I'm the youngest of four boys and since the three older ones get the bulk of the inheritance, I decided to take off on my own. I've been in California for the past couple of years. My sister lived in San Francisco with my aunt and was engaged to be married, so it wasn't like I'd be alone."

"Didja have any luck, Mister Chase?" Albert asked when Aimee still didn't respond.

"Not at first. Just enough to keep me from starving to death," he chuckled. "But about a year and a half after I started, my partner and I followed a creek up into the mountains, found a cave and, lo and behold, there she was. The..."

"Mother lode," Aimee burst out unexpectedly and almost clamped her hand over her mouth.

Lucas froze. His eyes widened and his mouth gaped.

"Uh... yes, mother lode," he managed to say. "My sister can never remember that phrase." He turned and stared ahead.

"Is that there your turn off, Mister Chase?" Albert asked as they approached a space along the road where brush had been removed and a red cloth tied to a tree as a marker.

"Yes, it is," Lucas answered, as he slowed his mount to let the wagon pass.

"See you 'round," Albert called out and wav-ed.

"Yes. You can bet you will," Lucas said, stopping to watch the wagon roll away.

~ * ~

Lucas stared after the wagon. He forced himself to breathe

slowly. Never in his life had he felt so confused. He hadn't been riding alongside his neighbor, Mack Kaymey, he knew it without a doubt. He had been riding beside Aimee McKay, the woman who haunted his every waking minute, and many of his dreams since he met her aboard the S.S. Sonora a lifetime ago.

Although her dress and demeanor had been cold and strict, there had been something so fragile about her that brought out the protective instinct in him. She held herself too straight and squared her shoulders too confidently. There was something mysterious beneath the layers of propriety. Her moss green eyes appeared haunted and he ached to see them sparkle. He longed to touch her shiny chestnut colored hair and that heart-shaped face with flawless porcelain skin.

He spent days searching for her in Charleston, running into one blank wall after another. He couldn't imagine how a person could have vanished without a trace. In the confusion, no one he spoke to even remembered seeing her. His search had been in vain, and now, here she was.

~ * ~

Aimee twisted slightly and shot a quick glance over her shoulder as the wagon passed, with Lucas sitting there watching. She felt her face flush hotly as their eyes met. Tiny laugh lines creased the corners of his blue eyes and he smiled that crooked, familiar smile. She quickly faced forward again.

Being around Lucas left Aimee feeling extremely warm and slightly queasy. "Albert can't you make the horses go any faster?" she asked faintly, and placed her hands over her cheeks to hide the redness.

"I could, but them chickens might lay scrambled eggs tomorrow if I bounce 'em all the way home," Albert replied.

"Oh, yes, the chickens," Aimee said absently.

No one spoke during the remainder of the trip, though Albert glanced often at Aimee. When they reached the front yard, he pulled up to the front door and Aimee climbed down. Albert continued around the driveway and stopped at the far side of the barn. Isaac ran proudly up to the wagon pointing back at the completed chicken pen. Abram and George were just putting the hammer and nails up when they saw him. Both grinned broadly and hurried to help unload the wagon.

~ * ~

Dewey set the crated rooster aside and began handing the boxes of laying hens to Abraham, George, and Albert. Isaac had gone inside the pen and pulled the boxes to the far side as the men set them inside the gate. After all the crates were unloaded and in the pen, Albert closed the gate and Isaac ran in the barn to get a bag of chicken feed.
George made a feeding trough by nailing two long boards together in a V-shape with a square board at each end for balance. Isaac slipped into the pen, shook feed from the bag along the bottom of the trough, and scattered some all around the crates for the chickens.

The sound and sight of the feed were all the chickens needed, as they rushed from the cages. George gathered up the empty crates and set them outside the gate. Albert waited until the other men were safely out of the pen, and then stood near the gate. He reached down, opened the crate, grabbed the back, shook the rooster out, and then darted out of the pen taking the cage with him.

When the rooster hit the ground, his eyes flashed as if he expected a fight. Finding no adversary, the bird calmed down and strutted among the hens. Abraham filled a bucket with water and pour-ed it through the fence into a watering trough George built. After the men stacked the crates inside the barn, and washed up, they found a comfortable, shady spot to have lunch.

~ * ~

Inside, Rose helped Aimee with her coat, then put the gloves in one pocket and hung it, along with her hat, on a peg. After leading Aimee to a chair, Rose immediately poured a hot cup of tea, pulled a sugar cake from the oven, and set the aromatic dessert on the windowsill to cool. Rose waited until she could stand the silence no longer.

"Didja have any trouble getting them chickens?" she asked, as she bustled around the kitchen.

"No," Aimee answered vacantly.

"Do you feels okay? You's acting kinda funny, Miss Aimee." Rose poured a cup of tea and sat across from Aimee.

"Rose, what is wrong with me? Why do I let Lucas Chase get to me every time I see him?"

"Was he at Mister Owens' place?" Rose asked, her eyes wide.

"Yes. No. We met him on the road and he rode with us to Henry's place, since he had papers for Owens to sign." She rubbed her face and ran her fingers through her hair. "He makes me so uncomfortable, Rose. I just get the feeling that he knows I'm a fake. What am I going to do?"

"Now, Miss Aimee, that's jest the scared girl in ya talkin', not the brave survivor I know and love. How come you can talk so strong and independent to me and then lets that man rattles ya so? Are you sure it ain't sumpin' else?"

Aimee sipped her tea, the warmth and sweetness pulling her together. "Rose, that's ridiculous. What do you mean by 'something else'? I'm just nervous he'll recognize me. I have no problems with the men in town, since they never knew Aimee McKay. But Lucas Chase? Now that's another story. He met me as Aimee, talked to me as Aimee, and even helped me up the steps during the storm. I sat across from him on the train to the last ship we boarded."

Rose reached over and squeezed Aimee's hand. "Are you sure that whut you's worried 'bout or could it be he stirs sumpin' deep inside ya? Sumpin' yous doesn't wants stirred?"

Aimee jerked her hand back. "I don't mean to be rude, Rose, but you don't really know enough about me to assume something like that. I can assure you that one of the main reasons I became Mack Kaymey was to disguise myself and put distance between Aimee McKay and men in general.

"The other reason is that I refuse to be put in the position of being used, abused, and discarded like a worn out pair of shoes. All men really want is to strip women of their identity, make them bow to their will, and create slaves out of them. I'm not a piece of property, Rose, and I am never going be treated like that again. I will never be hit, ridiculed, or abandoned." Her hands shook and tears gathered in her wide green eyes.

Rose calmly rose, and went to Aimee, wrap-ping her arms around her.

"Oh, Miss Aimee, I had no idea you's been hurt so bad. Men can be cruel that's true but all men ain't likes that, 'n you know it. My Albert is a kind and lovin' man and there's lots of kind and lovin' men in this world."

"It wasn't just the man, Rose. True, he was mean, cruel, and possessive but it was me, too. What I became because of him, and what I allowed him to do. The things I believed, and the dreams I had. The pain I caused my family, and I can't, no, I *won't* be that stupid again. I simply refuse. Do you understand?" Then the tears she tried so hard to control spilled down her cheeks.

Rose refilled Aimee's teacup, then went back to her chair.

"Tells me about him, Aimee," Rose said gently. "Tells me. Git it out. Don't let it fester like a canker sore 'n make you sick. You has to talk about it sometimes. Now is as good as any. You'll feel better when you does. What was his name?"

Aimee took a deep breath. Her head ached just above her right eye and her voice trembled as she began.

"His name is Marcus Alexander and my brother, Edward, brought him home for a visit. It was my birthday and I felt old at twenty, and a little lonely. Marcus treated me like a princess and I believed all the lies he told me. He discovered that my mother left me a sizable inheritance and all her jewels. He convinced me, against my father and brother's objections, that we should take the money and jewels and start a life in California.

"He assured me that he was an expert gambler and could

double the money in a few weeks. My father and brother warned me that Marcus was a scoundrel but I didn't listen. I wanted to believe that it was me he wanted. Marcus made me feel beautiful, special, and wanted. And I did so need to feel those things. Nevertheless, my family was right. Marcus lost all the money, sold Mother's jewels, beat me, and left me marked."

She pulled her hair back and fingered the scar. She told Rose every detail and with each word, her burden of secrets became lighter but reliving those days fired up her emotions.

"Why would God do this to me? Doesn't he have better things to deal with?" Aimee cried bitterly.

"Hush, now, Miss Aimee," Rose said. "We mustn't blame the good Lord for all the mountains we has to climb in our life's journey. He gives us the gift of free will and our choices makes consequences we has to deal with. Supposin' I gives Isaac a whole dollar and he goes off and buys hisself a knife and then ends up stabbin' somebody with it. Would you blame me for that man's death? After all, if he didn't have the dollar, he couldn't have bought the knife, and if he hadn't bought the knife, then he couldn't have stabbed that man."

Aimee shook her head.

"Of course you wouldn't blame me for givin' him the money, so don't blame the Lord for givin' you choices. We all makes mistakes. Some change our lives and we must live with the actions of them mistakes forever unless we turns them 'round and makes them lessons. That's what you gots to do."

Aimee's voice hitched with a sob. "I'm not sure I know how," she said shakily. She wiped her tear-filled eyes and stared at Rose.

"Of course you does. You escaped, didn't you? You wuz out halfway across the world on your own, wasn't you? You done fooled enough people and ended up here, didn't you? You has to git yourself together, makes a plan, stick out yer chin, and be the woman, or the man, you needs to be. Now, drink your tea, dry your eyes, and go out and see them new chickens."

Aimee finished her tea, rose and snugged down the baker's hat. "You're a real jewel, you know that?"

Rose smiled, went to Aimee and hugged her. "Go on, now."

Aimee paused at the door. "Did I tell you Marcus saw me on the boat at the dock, just as the ship was leaving, Rose? He must know by now that all the women survived. You don't think he'd come after me, do you?"

"From whut you told me 'bout him, I thinks it would be too much work for that man. I 'spect he's just moved on to someone else to bully and steal from. That kind don't never change."

"I hope so," Aimee said doubtfully, and walk-ed outside.

~ * ~

Albert, Isaac, and the others sat under a large, heavy-limbed shade tree, eating their lunch. Aimee smiled at the men, then walked to the pen and saw the hens busily pecking and scratching while the cocky, but colorful rooster marched around the yard like a squatty little monarch surveying his kingdom.

Aimee suddenly realized she was going to have more eggs than she needed. If each chicken laid one egg a day, she would have thirty-six eggs each morning. Thirty-six times seven was two hundred and forty-two eggs a week. Even if she only gathered half that much, it was still one hundred and twenty-one eggs a week. What had she been thinking? Even half that amount was too many.

She marched over to where the men were sitting and they all jumped up when she approached.

"Don't do that," she said scowling. "We're equals here."

"That's your thinkin', Mister Kaymey, but if'n anyone wuz a'lookin', they'd 'spect us to git up," Albert said, a worried frown on his face."

"You're right, Albert. Sorry. What I wanted to say is that I need you to crate up two dozen of those chickens and take them up to your place. I must have been mad to think I needed three dozen chickens. We can get you another rooster later on."

"Are you sure, Mister Kaymey? We's be glad to takes 'em but only if'n you're sure. How much is they?"

119

"Please, Albert, you would be doing me a favor. What would I do with over two hundred eggs a week, if they all lay, I mean? Please take them. I may not need the dozen I have left but I think they'll be fine."

"Dewey, go gits a strong branch to keep that rooster away from us, while Abraham and I catch them chickens. George, you go gits a couple of them crates. We'll have 'em crated up in no time. I's gonna let George put 'em on a horse and take 'em home. He'll need to put up some kind of pen for them. We have some old tin layin' around we kin use fer a temporary pen till we can do it right."

"Great, I feel better now. Please take plenty of chicken feed. I won't need it for just the dozen I have left."

Albert suddenly froze. He stared down at the ground as if listening intently. "Mister Mack, someone's a'comin'."

Aimee looked at him curiously.

"We's learned the signs of approachin' horses when we wuz—that is, when we wuz a'travelin'."

Nodding, Aimee went to the cabin.

"Gloves," Albert reminded her. "You needs to cover them tiny hands," he said softly, so the others couldn't hear.

"Rose," she said when she went inside, shutting the door behind her. "Albert says someone is coming."

"You sits down and let Albert sees to it. A boss don't run out and greet every visitor," Rose told her sternly. "She has the servants tend to that. You never told me much 'bout your home and how you wuz raised. Y'all had servants, didn't ya?"

Aimee took a deep breath and looked at Rose sadly. "It seems that was another life. But yes, we had servants, and yes, they greeted the visitors, cleaned the house, cooked the meals, washed the clothes, and did everything for us. This past year has erased so many memories. I'm so used to doing for myself that I forget. What would I do without you?"

Rose grinned. "You'd do jest fine. You might stumble a little but you'd do jest fine."

120

Aimee smiled and tiptoed over to the window to peek into the yard. A strange man stood beside an enormous workhorse, then he handed Albert the rope to three cows.

"Cows," Aimee exclaimed loudly. "Someone is bringing me cows. I only wanted one for now, but I get three. Oh, Rose, there's a bull on the other side. I don't even have any fences up yet. Hand me my coat, I've got to see what's going on."

She pulled her hat over her hair and rushed out to the men.

"Howdy," she said with a smile. "I'm Mack Kaymey. What's going on?"

"Howdy, Mister Kaymey. I'm Jonathan Price. Matthew, down at the store, said you wuz in the market for a few head of cattle, some cows, and a young bull. I told him I had some for sell and he told Mister Gaines, who took a look, and said they'd be fine. I've also got six horses coming behind me. It's okay, ain't it?"

Aimee gave a harsh laugh instead of the giggle bubbling in her throat. "Yes sir, that's just fine. Albert, how close is that second corral from being done?"

"Suh, we can finish it by this afternoon," he said with authority.

"Fine. Go ahead and put the cows and bull in the corral for now. We'll put the horses in the barn when they get here and put the cattle out in the second corral when you get it finished. What do I owe you, Mister Price?"

"Mister Gaines said he'd take care of it if you would jest sign this bill of sale and charge ticket."

"That's fine."

"Mister Kaymey, suh. Wuz you gonna ask about some plow horses? This here 'un that Mister Price is riding is a fine horse. We could sure use somethin' like that."

"Sorry," Jonathan Price said with a grin. "I've only got two draft horses. I bought 'em when I was in Savannah a while back. Needed 'em to pull stumps with. I might know a feller that has a good pair of plow horses. Ya want me to send 'em out here or check with Mister Gaines?"

"You needn't bother Mister Gaines. Have him bring them by here and Albert can take a look at them. He's my farm manager. He makes all the decisions concerning the farm. Tell Mister Gaines I do appreciate him taking the time to get me the cattle and horses. I know he's a busy man and I'm mighty obliged."

"Yes sir, I will. And I'll tell this feller I know to come by. His name is Wilson Carter. He's a good man. You don't need worry 'bout Wilson selling you no crippled old horse. He wouldn't do that."

"I believe you, Mister Price but I'll let Albert deal with him. That won't be a problem, will it?"

"No sir," he said quickly. "That won't be a problem. I thank you for your business. I'll be going now."

"Thank you, Mister Price. When you get ready to make another sale, come by and see me."

"I surely will, Mister Kaymey. I surely will. Nice to have met you, see you later." With a tug of his hat, Jonathan Price leaped up, struggling to straddle the monstrous draft horse. With a snort and a stomp, the giant horse turned and trotted away.

"I ain't never seen no horse that big, Pa," Isaac said.

"Can't say I did neither, son. That horse is a giant. We'll finish that corral and box up them chickens 'fore we leave. I'll send Abraham back a little early to get that pen ready fer us."

Aimee nodded and wearily walked back to the house.

~ Ten ~
A Surprise Visit

The next few days were end-of-summer days. The nights became chilly and the days warmed up only to cool off again when the sun dropped behind the hills. Albert and his crew worked alternate days since most of men from the camp came down to work on enlarging the corrals and securing the fences along the woods. Everyone wanted to make a little money but Albert made sure the payroll stayed the same by setting a schedule.

A few days after the cool weather hit Aimee noticed the men wearing two shirts, and shy away from working directly in the wind. She had to insist they only work five days a week since she knew they had chores to tend at their campsite.

A month had passed since she went to town and one, crisp Friday morning Aimee prepared to drive in. She finally convinced Rose to go with her and, by ten o'clock, they pulled up to the general store.

"Have you got your list, Mister Kaymey?" Rose asked with a smile.

"Yes, I do, and that's going to mean work for you ladies at home."

"What does that mean?" Rose asked, curiously.

"I'm going to buy some thick work shirts and coats but some of them may have to be altered. You need to help me there."

"Oh, how we's ever gonna pay you back?"

"Hush up, woman." Aimee grinned. "We're also going to buy some material for shawls and do you think we need any more blankets?"

"Mister Kaymey we has 'nuf blankets, but we could use some shawls."

"I know I bought blankets earlier, but I thought you might could make coats for the children out of blankets."

"Oh, that would keeps 'em good 'n warm," Rose said.

Aimee eased the horses up to the rail, tied the team, and went inside. Matthew Barker hurried up to the pair, smiling and friendly.

"Good morning, Mister Kaymey. What can we do for you to-day?"

"I need you to fill this list and Rose, my housekeeper, and I, will just walk through and pick up the items we need."

"Yes sir, whatever you need, Mister Kaymey, we'll take care of it."

Aimee and Rose walked along the rows of tables gathering up piles of blankets as Rose whispered to Aimee how many children needed coats. Rose glanced sideways at the bolts of material on the shelf, and when Aimee noticed, she began to point at several different patterns. When Rose nodded, Aimee pulled down the bolts, and when she had all that Rose wanted, she called to Mister Barker to take them to the counter.

"What the women don't use for dresses and curtains can be used for quilting and shirts for the men and boys," Aimee said, while she and Rose continued to stroll down the aisles.

Aimee ordered as many boxes of supplies for the camp as she had earlier and stocked up for herself. As Matthew and his son, Nathan, loaded the supplies from her list, Rose picked out several spools of thread and a dozen needles.

"Mrs. Barker? Please, double whatever sewing supplies she gets. She needs them, believe me. There's lots of sewing that needs done," Aimee told the store keeper's wife.

Once the supplies were loaded and Aimee paid the bill, she and Rose headed to the wagon for the trip home. Just as she was about to climb up she heard a dreaded voice.

"Mister Kaymey, hello, so nice to see you again. Ma'am," Lucas said and he tipped his hat to Rose, who looked shocked. "See you're loading up again. We're in for a big change in the weather, or so I hear. It's supposed to get mighty cold in the coming weeks. At least that's what the blacksmith says."

Lucas paused, looking hard at Aimee. "I was wondering if you'll have a drink with me in the saloon over there. We never did get a chance to look over the surveyor map. Your farm manager always said you weren't feeling well. Hope you're better now."

"I appreciate your offer, Mister Chase, but I'm in a bit of a hurry right now. Maybe another time, sir."

Lucas grinned. "I wanted to tell you I've put up a fence and I'm fairly sure I didn't encroach on your land."

"I'm sure you did a fine job, Mister Chase. I'm not worried about your fence being on my property."

"I'm sorry you don't have time for a drink. Another time perhaps?" Lucas chuckled, tipped his hat again, and walked across the street to the bar.

~ * ~

Back at Eagle Creek, work continued. The wind had turned sharp and Aimee could see the men working, hunched over against the cold. Dewey and George unloaded the supplies for the house, and Rose and Aimee distributed the coats to the men. While Rose put on a pot of coffee, Albert and Abram pulled the wagon into the barn to get the horses out of the cold, leaving them hitched for the trip to their camp.

As Rose and Aimee organized the kitchen, they chatted and didn't hear the tap on the door. The rapping became louder and Rose jerked the door open, expecting see Albert.

"How do, ma'am," Lucas Chase said, standing with hat in hand. "Since Mister Kaymey wouldn't have a drink with me, I thought the least he could do was offer me a cup of coffee on my way home."

"C-come in, Mister Chase," Aimee said, quickly slipping on a pair of soft, thin gloves she'd bought at the store earlier. Then she turned up her collar, and became Mack Kaymey.

"Rose, would you get Mister Chase a cup, please?" Aimee said roughly. "Sit down, Chase, sit down."

"Call me Lucas, won't you?" Lucas pulled off his gloves and removed his hat. Rose took the items and waited for his coat.

"Mack," Aimee said and pulled out a chair. "This is Rose Washington, my housekeeper."

Rose poked at the fireplace until a roaring fire drove out the chill Lucas let in when he arrived.

Aimee turned her head away and pulled her hair down to make sure the scar was covered. She took the cup of coffee Rose handed her, and watch-ed as Lucas smiled his thanks when Rose passed him a cup.

"I see you've bought yourself a few cows, a bull and some nice horses," he said. "Those are good looking horses. Did you buy them from that Price fellow? He's thinking about moving to St. Louis, he told me. Said he was planning on coming by here to see if you wanted to buy all his stock. That is, except those draft horses. Said he was going to use them to pull his wagon. Sorry, but I tried to buy them when he told me."

"We tried a month or so ago, he wouldn't sell them then, either," Aimee said and sipped her coffee.

"Your place is really looking good. Your men are doing a fine job."

"Yes, they are. I'm lucky to have 'em. Got a good deal on 'em," Aimee said gruffly. "You might want to check around and see if you can pick up a few."

"I don't want to get into a political or moral argument with you, but owning slaves is not something I'm comfortable with."

"That so?" Aimee answered after taking a bite of sugar cake Rose had set on the table between them. "You against slavery?"

"Since you asked so directly, yes. Yes, I am. I believe that the time will come when all men will be free, and slavery will be a crime, no offense."

"No offense taken, Lucas. Each to his own belief, I say. Here, have a piece of cake. Rose is a wonderful cook."

126

Rose coughed to hide her smile and handed them both a fork. Aimee had been breaking off bites with her gloves.

"Are you cold, Mister Kaymey? Why don't you sit here, nearer the fire?" Lucas rose and gestured toward the fireplace.

"It's not the cold, it's... " Aimee searched for the right word.

"... a skin problem. Master Kaymey has a skin condition," Rose finished. "Exposure to sun and cold makes his skin peel and crack. He has to protect 'em."

"I'm sorry, I didn't realize," Lucas said, keeping his eyes glued on Aimee.

The sound of chopping came from outside.

"Sounds like the men are finishing up the woodpile," Rose said. "We may be in for a long winter. Have you found some help for your place, Mister Chase?" Rose asked.

"Yes, I have, Rose. A couple of drifters offered to temporarily stay around and help out, and then decided to stay at least until spring. Mister Barker sent three or four men out the day Mister Gaines had the papers signed and everyone signed on. They seem to be good workers. We'll have to wait until spring to see how many move on. The gold fever is still as enticing as ever and I'm afraid some of these are passing through going on to California and Colorado. It's a long, hard row to hoe, but who am I to try to discourage them? Gold gave me my life."

"Mack, if Price does decide to move to St. Louis and comes by to see you, let him know that I'll take whatever you don't buy."

"I'll do that, Lucas, I surely will."

"Well, I've got to get on home. I'm afraid I don't have as much confidence in my hired hands as you do with your men. Sometimes I think they stop working the minute I leave." He chuckled.

"Thanks for stopping by," Aimee said, coming to her feet.

"Don't get up, Mack, I'll see myself out. Thanks for the coffee and cake, Miss Rose. Mack is right. You are a good cook and you make a great cup of coffee," Lucas told her.

"Thank you, sir. I 'preciate them kind words," Rose replied, giving him a small curtsey.

"Come by again," Aimee added, as she picked up her cup.

"You too, Mack. You're welcome at my place anytime. Anytime at all." Lucas reached out to shake Aimee's hand, but his stare caused Aimee to jerk her hand free.

Rose grabbed Lucas's coat, and held it for him. He slipped it on, then accepted his hat and gloves. He turned up his collar when he stepped outside, and Albert met him in the driveway with his horse ready to go. After Lucas left, Albert tapped on the door and Rose let him in.

"I's mighty sorry that feller got past me. We wuz a'hammerin' on the fence and George was choppin' wood. I jest didn't hear him rides up. I must be losin' my touch."

Rose smiled widely. "Warn't your fault. It had to happen sooner or later. Miss Aimee done herself proud. I thinks it went well. She didn't make a single slip."

"Still, heading off strangers is my job. It won't happen again," he said with determination.

"I'm almost glad it did," Aimee replied. "We can't hide forever. I'm not going to take any foolish chances, but we have to face the inevitable. I'm going to run into Lucas now and then. I just have to be ready. Don't worry about a thing. Thank you, Albert, it's nice to have someone who cares."

Albert grinned sheepishly and Rose laughed. "See what you done. You made him blush. Albert Washington, you gits on back to work." She laughed and pushed her husband out the door.

"I'm goin' to take the rest of this coffee to the men. I'm sure they could use a hot cup. You relax now, Miss Aimee. You looks kinda tuckered out."

Rose picked up several tin cups and grabbed the coffee pot. Aimee held the door for her and when she was gone, collapsed in the chair. Rose was right, stress was exhausting.

~ * ~

Lucas slowed his horse to a walk once he reached the road. He inhaled the crisp fresh air and watched as leaves fell, swirling and dancing over the ground.

"You know what, Bailey, old boy?" he asked the horse and leaned forward to scratch his ears. "It's a small world when the woman I've searched for all this time shows up right under my feet. What are the odds I'd be drawn to the same out-of-the-way little town? I feel dumb as a rock. I'm not sure what I'm supposed to do now or how to act around that woman."

Bailey's ears flicked back and forth at the sound of his master's voice. Not knowing whether it was a command or not, he kept plodding along, still alert.

Lucas gazed at the sights along the road as pictures of Aimee filled his mind.

"She has the most beautiful eyes and flawless skin. What could have happened to make her want to hide way out here?"

Bailey snuffled and twisted his head as if looking back at Lucas. Bringing his head down, he almost jerked the reins from Lucas's hand.

"Sorry, boy. I guess I was daydreaming. Won't happen again. Guess you don't have any advice, either." Lucas chuckled, tightened the reins and kicked Bailey into a full gallop.

~ Eleven ~
The Masquerade Revealed

A few weeks after Lucas's visit, Jonathan Price made a second trip to see Mack Kaymey and announced he was, indeed, moving north after he settled his affairs.

"My father has been ill and I'm going to take over the farm, with me being the oldest and all," he explained.

Jonathan laid all his papers on the table and Aimee carefully read each line.

"I've got forty solid, healthy young mares and five young stallions, as you kin see there on the paper. I have two hundred and fifty steers, cows and a couple of young, healthy bulls. That is a list of buyers when they get heavy enough. You kin makes a nice profit in time. You did say to check with you, so here I am," Price said.

"Mister Price, I'll take them all," Aimee said, after reading the inventory list.

"Great, this is just great," Price said and slap-ped his knee. "I need to get to my Pa's 'n I wuz afraid I'd have to break 'em up and sell just a few at a time. No tellin' how long that'd take."

"By the way," Aimee said slowly. "There's a Mister Lucas Chase who has the place next to mine. He bought some chickens from Henry Owens, and he's in the market for some cattle and horses. If you know of anybody, send 'em over to his place. I told him that if I didn't buy all your stock, I'd send you to him but that won't be necessary now."

"I met him earlier. I'll send Wilson Carter over to him. He's the feller I told you had the horses, and he'll give Mister Chase a fair deal.

"Don't look like your men have much experience with cattle. Since mine are gonna be needing new jobs, think you'll have any opening for cow hands?"

"I can use a few wranglers but I have plenty of farm hands. Mister Chase might hire them. Do you think your men will mind helping mine out a while?"

"Don't think you'll have any trouble at all. I've hired several Negroes and they're among the best I got.

"Say, Mister Kaymey, would you interested in the hay I've got in my barn? This time of year, you're gonna need to stock up on grain and hay to supplement them cows and horses during the cold months. I'll sell ya the hay and what grain I got at a good price, and I'll have it delivered to boot." He jotted down a price and showed her.

Aimee nodded and wrote Jonathan one of the checks she picked up from the bank. Price and Aimee went out into the yard to check with Albert.

"Albert, do you think you and the other men can drive the cattle from Price's ranch to our place? He has several men who will help you drive them. I may be hiring two or three hands to take care of the herd while you take care of the farm."

"That sounds fine, Mister Mack. I don't mind gittin' 'em here but farmin's whut I knows," Albert admitted. "It's best you hire some real cowboys for that. I hear they fix fences, too. That'd be a help."

"Good," Price said. "I'll ride with them and see you Monday. Sir, it's been my pleasure doing business with you. Good luck."

"Thank you, Mister Price, and good luck to you. Give my regards to your father."

~ * ~

Aimee went back inside, shook her hair free, and began to dance around the room. Suddenly, she stopped, thoughts turning to her dream house. She wanted to start the designs as soon as possible.

The first drawing resembled her childhood home. She scratched it off and started again. This house would be different and it would be special. She wanted this house to live on for hundreds of years. It would be Eagle Creek Manor. This would be a house that would not only hold her memories but also allow someone else a place to create memories of their own, and be the house of many dreams thanks to Abram and his gold. The Manor should be filled with laughter of children and smiles of loving parents. Aimee hunched over the table and began to put her dream down on paper.

First, she drew an outline of a three-story house with large bay windows and a big glass-double front door. A large porch was added around the entire house and a balcony that followed the porch around the front and both sides. On the third floor, she drew a balcony in the rear, overlooking the meadow and woods beyond. Sketching gardens in the back yard with two small fountains and several small statues scattered throughout was the perfect touch. The springhouse should look like a decorative summerhouse. In the front yard, she drew small pathways winding throughout flowerbeds that surrounded a large fountain.

After the initial sketch, Aimee added shutters, windows with many tiny panes, gingerbread trim on the porch, and then she drew in flowers, climbing vines, bushes, and trees. Sitting back and staring in amazement at what she'd done amazed her. It was just what she wanted, and she loved it. Now, she would have to design a floor plan for all three stories. She never thought she could draw and design a house, but she did. Now, she knew she didn't need an architect to design her house but she would need one to explain and direct carpenters to build what she created. She started on the first floor and before long, realized she'd spent the entire day working on the plans.

132

The next day was Saturday and Rose and the men were off work. Aimee looked forward to the peace and quiet. She loved Rose, Albert, Isaac and they were all becoming family. Still, she looked forward the weekends so she could wander around as herself.

Aimee woke to a quiet and peaceful Saturday morning. She took her time getting dressed, and eating breakfast. When she finished cleaning the kitchen, she went for a hike around her property. After giving the horses a couple of forks of hay, she gave them each a helping of grain. Aimee fed the chickens and gathered the eggs in a basket, then put them on the doorstep.

Today she felt free. The horses and cattle would be delivered next week, the crew was off so she didn't have to wear her gloves or hat, and let her hair blow in the breeze. There wasn't much to blow, she thought, as she ran her fingers through the wild curls. She wanted to race through the fields and sing as loud as she could. Just to be careful, though, she slipped her gloves in her back pocket and let her hat hang down her back.

She had done some exploring but there was a lot of land she had never seen. Finding a deer trail, Aimee began walking the slight incline that soon leveled out in the forest. Trudging along for well over half an hour, she came upon a gurgling stream. Stopping, she knelt down for a drink of cool water. The sun reflected off the churning ripples and as she watched, she caught a glimpse of something metal in the water, like nothing she had ever seen before.

Walking nearer the submerged object, she picked up a broken branch and began to poke around in the water. Suddenly, the water churned and Aimee found the stick jammed. She began to tug and yank, and slowly the stick gave way allowing her to pull the object out of the mud. Dragging it onto the bank shifted the leaves on the ground, allowing Aimee to see a chain.

Following the chain, she saw that it was tied to a nearby tree with the other end attached to the sharp-toothed contraption clamped onto the end of her stick. It was some type of trap.

Anger boiled through her body, and she jerked at the chain until it came loose from the tree. Heading back to the house, dragging the trap behind her, Aimee's rage increased with every angry step she took. She couldn't believe someone set animal traps on land that didn't belong to them.

Her eyes riveted on the trail in front of her, the weight of the beaver trap seemed to be getting heavier with each labored step. Moisture beaded on her forehead and her breathing became heavy.

Pausing to rest, two deafening shots rang out behind her, and she heard a deep, gravelly voice somewhere in the nearby bushes.

"And where do ya thank you're 'goin' with my traps, ya thievin' sidewinder?"

Aimee froze, her stomach tightening.

"How dare you pull a gun on me while standing on my land? Your traps were on my land, in my creek and the last time I read the law, that makes them my traps, not yours," Aimee said bravely, although her heart pounded wildly.

"The town does have a lock-up and the mayor has authority to hold you until the circuit judge comes to town. If you don't want to be arrested for discharging your firearm on private property and trespassing, you'd better turn around and head on out of here." She reached up, pulled her hat low on her head and slowly slipped on the gloves she always carried.

"Who do ya think yor 'quotin' the law to, mister? I don't see any sheriff or lawman or nuttin' 'round here to back up them puny threats and demands." The man snarled as he stepped onto the trail cradling an old shotgun, with a second one in a sling on his back. He dropped the one he held, and quickly pulled the one from his back around front and pulled back both hammers.

Aimee pulled herself up as tall and straight as she could and lowered her voice. "My name is Mack Kaymey and I own Eagle Creek. You have placed your traps without my permission and it is my right to remove them and ask you to leave my property. Now!"

The man's massive belly jiggled as he smirked, spat a brown, vile-smelling wad on the ground near her feet and squealed, "O-o-o-e-e-e, I'd better watch out. Yer about to skeer me to death with all them words. Cain't you see how bad I'm a'shakin'? Cain't you hear my teeth a'clickin' together? I surely do hope my tremblin' fingers don't hit this here trigger and accidentally blows your fancy talkin' head clean off."

Aimee's stomach churned as the man stepped closer to her and the stench of dead animals emanated from his unwashed body, filling her nostrils. She watched him lift the shotgun from his arm and aim it at her chest.

"Now, I gotta idee. Iff'n you care to keep on a'breathin' why don't you jest hand my trap over to me real slow like and I jest might leave you with a few cuts and bruises rather than a belly full o' rusty old buckshot."

As they stood face to face, another voice from the nearby trees cut through the silence.

"Although I'm impressed that an idea was able to make it way out of your thick-boned head and through that nasty, greasy, bug-infested growth of a miserable excuse for hair, I propose a better idea."

Lucas Chase slipped noiselessly from between the trees and jammed his rifle barrel into the center of the hairy man's back. "Like I said, I have a better idea. Why don't you just point that rusty blunderbuss toward the sky slowly, and I do mean slowly, release the hammers and hand that gun over to Mister Kaymey. Then, empty your pockets of shells on the ground in front of you and step to your right, holding both your filthy hands high over your head."

The man raised the gun, released the hammers, and handed the shotgun to Aimee. Then he dropped the shells from his pocket to the ground, and started to move.

"Your *other* right, genius, and put those hands back up," snapped Lucas.

Aimee quickly joined Lucas, dragging the heavy trap behind her.

"You 'messin' wit sumpin' whut ain't none o' yor business, stranger," growled the trapper.

"That sounds like the pot calling the kettle black to me, doesn't it to you, Mister Kaymey?" Lucas asked with a grin.

Aimee nodded and prayed her pounding heart would slow down.

"What's your name and what gives you the right to treat People like Mister Kaymey here in such a rude manner while standing on his property?"

The man glowered at Lucas. "I'm Bundy Owens 'n I stays behind my brother's place, well, my half-brother, anyhow." He waved his upraised hand behind him.

"Brother? Who's your brother, uh, half-brother?" Aimee asked in her low voice.

"Henry Owens, that's who's 'n I been trappin' around here since I wuz knee high to my pa 'n nobody never dared told me I wuzn't to. This here is Injun land and I wuzn't botherin' nuttin'."

"You were bothering me, Mister Owens," Aimee snapped, feeling braver, now that Lucas had disarmed him and she was calmer.

"Generally speaking, I have no problem with someone being on my property. They are welcome to walk, ride, or cross it going from place to place but you cannot hunt or trap here. These are things that need permission and you do not have it. What you used to do doesn't matter. What matters is now. I own Eagle Creek and I'll not have a stray cow or horse stepping into a trap, or any other animal for that matter, and I'll not have you shooting my livestock.

"Your attitude is deplorable. You have no respect for other people's property. Therefore, you, Bundy Owens, are to stay off my property and never set foot on it again. Do I make myself clear? The next trap I find or the remains of a butchered animal, I

136

will call the mayor and have you locked up. Do you understand?" Aimee paused and took a deep breath.

Bundy Owens' mouth pinched into a tight white line, his eyes gleamed with hatred and Aimee could see his fist clenched in anger.

"This ain't right. Them varmints I trap ain't no good for nuttin' 'cept for killin' 'em for the furs. I ain't no greenhorn. I ain't gonna shoot no cow or horse. You ain't got no right to insult me like that."

"Every creature is good for something," Aimee insisted.

"Skinning those poor defenseless animals for fur isn't any different than scalping humans."

"Well, I might have taken a scalp a time or two myself, to them what's needed it," sneered Owens.

Lucas reached over and took Bundy's gun from Aimee. He broke open the gun and slipped the shells out and stuck the gun out toward Owens and nodded for him to take it.

"Mister Kaymey has the right to restrict his property any way he wants to. Most ranchers don't allow hunting or trapping and you know that, don't you? You thought that you'd test the new owner, flex your muscles if caught, but it didn't work out for you, did it, Mister Owens?

"I think your brother told you Eagle Creek had a new owner and maybe his description of Mister Kaymey made you think that you could bully him around and have your own way. I think you're lucky that Mister Kaymey didn't bring his gun along. He would had a perfect right to blow your head clean off, Mister Owens. Wouldn't you have in his position?"

The defiant poacher didn't look very confident as he began to shift from one foot to another.

"Mister Owens, I don't want to get off on the wrong foot with my neighbors. Your brother and I have done business to-gether and he seems like a good man. Now that you understand how I feel about hunting and trapping, let's consider this matter over."

"Kin I git all my traps 'fore I leave? I have a lot of money tied up in 'em."

Aimee looked hopefully at Lucas for advice. Noticing the gesture, he nodded in agreement. "Mister Kaymey will give you the rest of the day to gather them up and get off his land. Tomorrow, I'm sure he'll have this area checked carefully for poaching and trespassing, and I suggest he find nothing out of the ordinary. Now, go on, get your things and get off this land."

Bundy nodded, reached down and snatched up the trap at Aimee's feet. She stepped back quickly and cringed when he leered at her. "This ain't no place for greenhorns and fancy-jawing sissies, and yore a greenhorn 'n a sissy iff'n I ever saw one. Lucky for you this feller come along when he did. What would ya have done iff'n he hadn't, huh?"

"Mister Owens, speaking of luck, yours is about to run out. Now, go on, before I change my mind and just take you to the mayor's office."

With a grunt, the would-be poacher turned and stomped into the woods.

Once he was out of sight, Aimee felt her knees start to give way and she reached out and grabbed a tree trunk for support.

"Hey, are you all right?" Lucas leaped forward and grabbed Aimee's arm.

"Y-yes, I guess I'm more tired than I thought," Aimee whispered. "Just give me a minute. I'll be f-fine."

She inhaled deeply and closed her eyes for a moment. The world around her spun, then her legs turned to jelly. A moment later she felt herself hit the ground and Lucas Chase cradled her head and shoulders in his lap.

He removed her hat, sprinkled a little water from his canteen over her face and gently patted her cheek.

~ Twelve ~
The Truth Will Set You Free

Aimee struggled to get up, with her heart racing and pounding every bit as hard as it had when Bundy Owens stood pointing his gun at her.

Tiny pinpoints of light marred her vision and she heard a voice, which sounded far, far away.

"Lie still a moment, Aimee. Relax. Take deeps breaths." He reached for her hat and began fanning her face.

Although the breeze soothed her, tremors shook her body. *Did she hear him right? Did he just call her Aimee?* Sound faded in and out and she knew if she didn't get up, she would pass out completely. Lucas was tall and muscular and she had learned long-ago struggling against someone stronger was use-less.

As he put the canteen to her lips, she sipped the cool liquid and some of the water ran along her face and into her hair. Lucas snatched his kerchief and dabbed at the water.

He jerked his gloves off and with his bare hand, lifted the damps curls up along her hairline, smoothing it back against her head.

"I knew it was you. Although for a while I must admit, I thought I was losing my mind. I have searched for you since the day I was rescued. Aimee, why are you dressed like this? What happened? Why did you disap- pear?"

Aimee worked her mouth but it felt dry as cotton and no words came out.

"Your sweet, innocent, hurt and frightened little face has haunted me day and night and here you are. What's going on?"

Aimee struggled to an upright position and buried her face in her hands. She felt tears burning her eyes and she began sobbing uncontrollably.

"Please, Aimee. Mrs. McKay, I didn't mean... I'm so sorry. What can I do?" He put his hands on her shoulders and gently squeezed her. "Please forgive me."

"No, d-don't apologize. You have n-nothing to apologize for. It's me. It's a-all m-me. I'm a phony and it was just a matter of time before someone found me out. I h-hoped and prayed it was behind me, but when I saw you here in Sycamore Grove, I k-knew my plan had been too good to be true. I was so afraid you'd recognize me and now you have."

As she twisted around and pushed to her feet, Lucas never let go. His strong arms supported her as she stood, and swayed against him a moment or two before regaining her balance.

"I'm sorry, I just don't understand," he said gently.

"I know," she whispered. "I'm not sure I can explain it so you will understand. I have lived in a web of lies for so long, they almost seem real to me. I started turning my back on the truth so long ago, I can hardly remember."

Lucas took her arm and led her down the trail. "Why don't we get back to your house and you'll have a chance to freshen up a bit. I'll put on a fresh pot of coffee and if, I repeat, just if, you want to talk about it, we can. If not, then at least you will be safe at home."

They walked down the path a bit and Lucas turned her arm loose long enough to walk a few feet into the trees to retrieve his

140

horse. He lifted Aimee up on the saddle and then leaped up behind her.

Aimee's skin burned with a strange tingle when Lucas'ss hand brushed hers as he reached over and took the reins. His breath on the back of her neck was disarming and unsettling, yet, at the same time, so warm and comforting.
She had been so filled with confusion and regret at her outburst earlier and almost lied again with some outrageous story to keep her identity a secret until she felt him so close, his chest pressing against her back. She would tell him the truth, the entire truth, and if he couldn't accept her for who and what she was, then they would go their separate ways, or one of them could move on.

When they rode into the yard, Aimee was stunned to see Albert, George Cooley, and Dewey Jackson, standing shoulder to shoulder, all carrying sticks except Albert who held his rifle in both hands. Albert slowly brought the gun up to his shoulder as Lucas urged his horse forward.

"Albert, it's okay. Mister Chase just rescued me from a poacher."

Albert lowered the gun but none of them relaxed.

Lucas slid from his mount, put his hands around Aimee's waist, and lifted her from the saddle.

"We heard shots and come a'runnin'. You sure you is okay? Who didja say done the shootin'?" Albert eyed Lucas suspiciously when he saw the way he helped Aimee from the horse. The other men looked confused.

Aimee went to Albert. "Everything is fine, Albert. A man named Bundy Owens fired the shots. They were just warning shots. I found one of his beaver traps in the creek and was bringing it back to the house. He didn't like that idea and tried to scare me into giving it to him.

"Mister Chase was nearby and disarmed Mister Owens, took the shells from his gun, and threatened to take him to the Sheriff if he didn't leave. I'm afraid the heat and excitement overwhelmed me. Mister Chase revived me and brought me home. You don't know how much I treasure your concern. Thank you so much.

"Now, please, go back to your families and enjoy your time off. I'll be just fine."

"You sure now, Mister Kaymey? We don't mind sticking around if you needs us," Albert said, staring hard at Lucas.

"That's kind of you, Albert, but, the poacher is gone now, and all I want is a cup of coffee and some rest. Mister Chase is going to join me for the coffee. Go on home, Albert. Thanks again."

Reluctantly, Albert nodded to George and Dewey and they slowly started toward the camp, looking back over their shoulders occasionally.

Aimee watched until they were out of sight before she turned to go inside, and motioned for Lucas to follow.

Aimee pulled off her gloves, went to the washstand and splashed water over her face. Lucas stoked the fire and prepared a pot of coffee.

"How did you survive? I watched from the Ellen when the ship went down. I thought everyone... ," she paused, as tears filled her eyes. "I thought everyone on board perished."

"Several of us were lucky." Lucas stared out the window. "There were chairs, crates, life buoys, and other floating objects that many of us were able to cling to. Some couldn't hang on long enough. Dozens of good men slid into that unforgiving water.
"I'm not sure how many were taken aboard rescue ships. I ended up in the hospital where I stayed a couple of days. Once I was on my feet, I contacted my family and tried to locate you. It was if you vanished into thin air. Eventually, I decided to take a different road and start a new chapter in my life but you were always on my mind."

Heat rushed to Aimee's face. "Lucky for me that you were here when I was confronted by that brute in the woods, I'm afraid Albert and the others might have done something dangerous had I returned home beaten up."

"I have to admit I'm a little puzzled over the way you and your slaves interact. Aren''t they generally quartered near the main house? Aren't you afraid they'll run off, living so far away?" Lucas asked as he searched the cabinet for the cups.

Aimee dried her hands and face, walked to the cooler, took out cream and the sugar bowl, and added some to the cups on the table.

"We have a very unusual relationship," she answered.

"Almost too unusual to believe. Are they part of those lies you mentioned earlier?"

Aimee heaved a loud sigh. "Well, in a way, they are."

She sat down heavily in the nearest chair, unbuttoned the neck of her shirt, and ran a hand over her throat.

"They know, don't they?" Lucas asked, leaning forward and placing his arms on the table.

"Well, Albert does. He's the tall one who was holding the gun. He's married to Rose, who figured it out and we had to tell Albert. Their son, Isaac doesn't know and neither do the rest. We thought the fewer who knew the fewer chances of slip ups."

When the coffee was ready, Aimee rose, grabbed a towel and poured the steaming liquid into their cups. She put the pot back, and stirred her cup slowly while gathering her thoughts.

"You don't have to talk if you don't want to. Trying to make a new life alone is hard enough. That is the case, isn't it?"

Aimee nodded, a lump rising in her throat.

Lucas reached over and patted her arm. "My aunt lost her husband several years ago and couldn't make it alone. She moved in with my grandparents and still grieves over her loss. I think you're very brave and courageous to do all this on your own."

Aimee leaped from her chair, knocking it over and rushed to the fireplace, leaning her head against the mantle.

"Oh, Mrs. McKay, I've done it again, haven't I? Please, forgive me. It wasn't my intention to remind you of your loss."

"No, it isn't that, Mister Chase," Aimee said. "I've just realized that I led your sister to assume a fact that is most incorrect. I am not a widow. I couldn't be because I've never been... I've never been... "

"Mrs. McKay," Lucas interrupted. "Please call me Lucas. I think circumstances have warranted a first named basis, don't you think?"

"Yes, you're absolutely right, Lucas, but my name is not Mrs. John McKay. It's Aimee, Miss Aimee McKay. Not Widow McKay, not Mrs. McKay, just Miss. Miss Aimee Amelia McKay. Foolish, stupid, disobedient, unmarried, disgraced, and brainless Miss Aimee McKay."

Lucas raised his eyebrows as he calmly sipped his coffee. "Aren't you being a little hard on yourself, Miss Aimee Amelia McKay? I don't think you're old enough to have that many titles of disrespect."

"You said earlier you didn't understand and that's obviously true. I went against my father's wishes, took my mother's inheritance, and ran off with a man who promised me the world, and that takes care of foolish and disobedient. He didn't marry me, and then stole my money and my mother's jewels. He treated me like a common... a common... " Once again, she covered her face as the unwanted tears began to flow.

Rubbing her swollen eyes, she sniffed and took the handkerchief, he offered, and continued. "That's unmarried and disgraced, as well as stupid. Then he proceeded to lock me up, punch and slap me each time he lost at the gambling table, blaming me for his bad luck, and I say that's brainless. Finally, one night, I escaped, bought a ticket on a doomed voyage and here I am Miss Aimee McKay who changed her name, accepted a tired old man's gift of his life's gold and tried to lie to the world about who and what she is. That's also brainless." Aimee exhaled a long breath and practically collapsed back into her chair.

"Please, don't be embarrassed into staying. I hold no ill will against your opinion of me." Aimee rose, rewashed her puffy face and ran her damp fingers through her unruly curls.

Hearing a slight rattle, she turned, expecting to see Lucas, hat in hand, heading for the door. Instead, what she saw was a man pouring two fresh cups of coffee and holding out a towel for her.

"What are you doing?"

"Getting more coffee and warming yours up. Is that okay?"

"I--I--I just thought... " Aimee paused and rubbed her forehead.

"Me thinks my lady thinks too much," Lucas said, bowing and sweeping his hand dramatically. "Why don't you sit down, Miss Aimee, and let me take a turn talking?"

Aimee sat and picked up her cup with trembling hands.

"My father is the head of a large banking firm and is one of the most successful investment brokers in the nation. My two brothers happily followed his example and they, too, are successful. I was, what did you call it, 'the disobedient one'?

"Against my father's wishes, I took off, with my mother's blessing, to California. My father was furious and refused to speak to me before I left. I wrote Mother, and apparently, Father will never forgive me for going against his plans for my future.

"On the way to California, I brought a horse that came down with colic, another which turned up lame, and in a card game, I lost most of the money my mother slipped me before I left. I know the other player cheated but I had no proof. I've had my share of love 'em and leave 'em ladies, so it looks like I have the stupid, careless, disobedient, foolish, and every bit as shameful background as you do.

"The difference, Aimee, is that men don't get labeled as women do. Men are called explorers, ladies' men, and independent entrepreneurs when they take advantage of a situation for their own gain. 'Boys will be boys,' is the most common excuse for male mistakes. The gander can get away with most anything

145

while the poor goose is chained, labeled, and treated like a sec-ond-class citizen. No, I take that back. Second class citizens are treated better than some women."

Aimee continued to sip the hot coffee while staring in dis-belief as Lucas champ- ioned her cause.

"Aimee, don't you see that you haven't done anything every man on earth hasn't done, or if truth be known, many women? Everyone makes mistakes. Some get away with them, some are labeled, shamed, and ostracized. And then, there are those, like you, who punish themselves every day."

"I humiliated my family. I disgraced myself. I accepted a gift I had no right to accept, and I lied. How can I *not* punish my-self?"

"Your family will always love you. They will be saddened by your plight, that's true but they'll love you. You were seduced, lied to, robbed, and abused. That's not your disgrace. That be-longs to the low-down, dirty scoundrel who took advantage of a sensitive, naïve, young woman who believed in love. You can't blame yourself for that.

"You took gold that would surely be lying on the bottom of the ocean if you hadn't. The man who gave it to you must have seen in you the dear, sweet, lovely, brave girl that I do. You lied because you were afraid. No one can blame you for that. We've all known fear. We've all lied. You're human, that's all. Aimee, you're the victim here, not the villain."

"You don't you don't find me repulsive?"

Lucas fought to keep from laughing aloud, but he couldn't suppress a smile. "Aimee McKay. Miss Aimee McKay, I find you the least repulsive person in the entire world. You have no idea how glad I am that you are sitting here in front of me, single, safe, and so beautiful. I can't believe I didn't see through that pitiful dis-guise before. I am the one that should be ashamed. I'm the one who should feel foolish.

"Nevertheless, and regardless of that, I feel happy I've found you at last. You are everything I thought you would be, if

146

not more. You're good, kind, thoughtful, generous, and brave. All the mistakes in your past can't change that."

Tears of relief streamed down Aimee's face and then she smiled.

"Now, tell me about your slaves."

Aimee blew her nose, dried her tears and smiled at the mention of Rose and the others.

"Lucas, these are wonderful people who have a great deal to contribute to this world. Due to no fault of their own, they have found themselves in need of a friend. Someone who can give them a second chance at a good life."

"Aimee, does that statement sound familiar?"

"I don't know what you mean?"

"Due to no fault of their own they find themselves in need of a friend? You have stepped forward to be that friend. Why can't you give yourself the same chance? Let me be your friend."

"I... " Aimee's face brightened at Lucas'ss words.

"We all need help at one time or another. I have. Remember when I told you that I lost almost all the money my mother gave me in a poker game?

"That could have been the end of my quest to reach California but there was a man in the saloon that night who took me home with him. I couldn't even pay my hotel bill.

"When I awoke the next morning, he cooked breakfast, told me that he had gone back to the saloon after I fell asleep, and won nearly half my money back for me. Aimee, why would he do that? He wanted to be a friend. He got nothing out of it, except to do a good deed. I got his name and a few months after finding gold, I sent him an anonymous check, personally delivered, so he could be on the receiving end of a good deed for a change. That's what you're doing.

"Can't you see that? Your friend, Mister Ginsberg did a good deed by giving you that gold and now you're passing on that good deed to others. It's easy to see how hard this is on you, Aimee. You look exhausted."

"I am tired," she said, closing her eyes and taking a deep breath. "Pretending every minute keeps me so tense. Promise me, Lucas you will never tell anyone. The world is too small and my family and... the person I left in California must never know where I am or even that I am still alive. I couldn't bare it any other way. I would rather my father and brother mourns for the daughter and sister they lost, than know I'm alive and have to live with the shame I brought on them."

"But, Aimee... "

"No, Lucas," she said loudly, reaching for him. "I couldn't live with them knowing the outcome of my folly. And I may be mistaken about anyone looking for me but the thought frightens me so."

"You have my word," Lucas said. "I will not betray your trust. I will honor my pledge as long as it's the right thing to do."

"Thank you. You can't imagine how terrified I've been since I first saw you in my yard that day asking for directions."

"Afraid of me? What kind of man do you think I am?"

"It wasn't you. It was the fear of being recognized, revealed, and unmasked. I was just getting comfortable in my guise and I was afraid of being shown up for the phony I am."

"Oh, my dear girl, what horrors you have lived with. No more. With your friends working side by side with you, and now that I have found you, your life will be different. I promise you."

A sudden frantic knocking on the door ended their conversation abruptly. The banging grew louder and more urgent.

~ Thirteen ~
A Meeting of the Minds

Aimee jumped up, wiped her face, and searched for her gloves.

"It's all right. Wash your face and take your time. I'll get the door. Relax, Aimee."

As he raised the latch, the door flew open, and a small dark figure with flashing eyes, lips pressed tightly together and hands clenched into fists, ran inside.

"Where's Mister Kaymey? Whut you done to 'im? Whut's goin' on? Who tried to shoot 'im?"

"Miss Rose, how nice to see you, won't you come in?" Lucas said with a grin.

Rose rushed over to Aimee, her puffy eyes revealing she had been crying and Rose spun around to face Lucas.

"You gots a lotta nerve 'comin' here pertendin' to be a friendly neighbor when ya ain't. All you wants to do is stick yer nose where it don't belong. What gives y'all the right? Whut kind of person is you?" Rose paused just long enough to inhale a deep breath before continuing, "You, my fine feathered friend, has done walked into a den full o' lions jest like Daniel in the Good Book, but iff'n you think for one minute that things are goin' to turn out for you like ... "

"Rose, please... " Aimee said.

"Mister Kaymey don't you bother your little head... uh... yourself... one little bit... "

"He knows, Rose, and it's all right. He hasn't come to expose me to the world."

Lucas stepped toward Rose and Aimee. "Please, believe me, I mean none of you any harm."

"Whut ya gonna do with whut you done learned, Mister Chase?"

"Rose, please, can we sit down? Won't you invite Albert in? I'm sure you have him and several others outside, don't you?" Lucas asked. His eyes twinkled and his lips twitched with a smile.

Rose lowered her gaze. "Yes, I reckon I did think I might need some strong backs. I'll git Albert to come in. I'm sure he feels awful guilty for leavin' Miss Aimee in the first place, 'specially after the tongue lashin' I give 'em when he got home."

"Poor Albert, I tell him one thing and you tell him another. I'm sure the poor man is dizzy with confusion. I'll bring him in and reassure the others," Aimee said as she started toward the door.

"You best let me. We's the suspicious type anywho and he might thinks you's being forced to call him in. He knows nobody could force me into nuttin' I done set my mind not to do," she said and chuckled.

Rose opened the door wide and stepped outside. "It's fine," she called. "Mister Kaymey wuz telling you true, Albert. He's jest fine. Albert, you kin come in, Isaac, you go on and play,

150

and the rest of you go on home. I'm obliged to ya. Albert, come on in."

Albert turned to the other men and said something, shaking his head and grinning. They returned his grin and nodded as they started home. Lowering the hammer of his rifle, Albert leaned it against the kitchen wall once he entered the house.

"Woman, don't ya think ya should tell me what the blazes is a'goin' on," grumbled Albert. "First, Mister Kaymey tells me everthin' is okay, then you flay me with that tongue o' yers and now ya tells me that everthin' is okay."

As he sat down at the table, Rose walked over and rubbed his shoulders. "Sorry Al, but I's jest worried. You know as well as I do that things ain't always the way they's looks. I jest had to see for myself and if Miss Aimee thinks we can trust Mister Lucas, then we have to thinks it too, unless he goes 'n proves us wrong," she finished with a furtive glance at Lucas.

Aimee looked at Lucas to see his reaction to Rose's comment. He smiled slowly and nodded.

"Miss Rose, Mister Washington, I realize you don't know me and have no reason to trust me considering the circumstances. I'll have to admit that I spent my early years in a privileged world, that my problems since I left are a mere speck of dust compared to the desert of trials and tribulations your family and friends have had to endure. Neither have I been through the pain and disappointments that Miss Aimee has, still, I do understand adverse situations. All I ask is for a chance to help Miss McKay and you. I'll not interfere with your lives, nor will I utter one harmful word."

"We's 'preciates that, Mister Chase," said Albert. "All we ever wanted in life was a chance. We knows the need for chances. We've spent our lives a'dreamin' and a'prayin' for a chance to stay together, raise our young'uns, provide a warm home, and share life with good friends. We doesn't want to hurt nobody, take nothin' from nobody, or be beholdin' to nobody. We just wants to be left alone by those that want to separate us, that's all. Do you reckon that's too much to ask fer?"

"No, Albert, that's not too much to ask for. That's what everyone in the world truly wants, whether they realize it or not. We shall have all that and more. It's people like you, Rose, and all your friends who made life easy for thousands of people like me. You may not be aware of it but there is a thunder of voices in the north that predicts the storms of war. There are those jealous of the profits of sugar cane, cotton, and the money the south makes. People that resent the business of slavery are raising their voices to protest the inhumane practice and are insisting that slavery be abolished. I'm afraid war is inevitable."

Rose, Albert, and Aimee looked shocked.

"It ain't gonna matter what them people say, Mister Lucas. Rich folks is always gonna want the poor to do their work. Raising their voices didn't stop my people from being clubbed, shackled, and crammed on ships to die or be whipped into slaves."

"You're wrong, Albert. You all have no idea what's happening. Those men caught your people by surprise, captured them without warning, and managed to destroy entire families before they had any idea what was going on. Those people do not represent the majority of voices and the majority will succeed.

"The thunder is preceding the storm that will demand slavery be declared illegal, and not just in the minds of men but in their hearts as well."

"My children will be free," Rose said breathlessly.

"Now, Rose, it ain't gonna happen that fast," argued Albert.

"Still," she sighed. "Our children and their children have a chance to dream."

"That's what I meant about chances," said Lucas.

"That and hope," added Aimee.

"Oh, yes, let's not forget about hope," agreed Rose. I hopes this baby has all his or her dreams come true."

"Oh, Rose, with all that has happened today, I haven't given a thought to your condition," Aimee said.

"Well, I guess congratulations are in order," exclaimed Lucas as he stuck out his hand to Albert.

Albert shook Lucas'ss hand vigorously.

"What does Isaac think about a new brother or sister? I haven't heard him mention the baby," Aimee said.

"To be honest, we ain't told him yet. We jest been so busy and wanted to wait until the right time." She ran her hand gently over her slightly protruding stomach. "I guess we needs to tell him fairly soon."

"You look like you have plenty of time," Aimee noted.

"Not really," Rose said. "This 'un should be making an entrance next month or so."

"Good Lord," Lucas roared. "And here you are running around. You need to get plenty of bed rest and someone to come in and take care of you."

Aimee smiled at his outburst and Rose patted his hand.

"Mister Lucas, our living ain't quite whut you's used to. I'm sure in y'all's world, the ladies is pampered, petted, and treated sumpin' special at a time like this. You gotta know though, in the other world, folks like us, and I'm a'talkin' 'bout folks of all colors, who must do their own work, are used to a different kind of life.

"The thought of this here baby and us bringin' a new life into our family is a time for joy and gettin' ready. We jest ain't got time to rest or sit back. We gotta cook lots of vittles up for our men folk for when we can't cook, so they's kin still eat. We gotta sew new clothes for the little one and wash up all our kin's clothes so they ain't gonna go dirty. We gotta do our chores as we pulls our own weight. Now, I admits that I does get a lot of help." She glanced at Albert, her eyes soft and moist.

"When I needs water, firewood, and totin' the wash in and out, Albert is right there to tote it. Albert helps with the dishes after meals and sees that Isaac is cared for. He fusses over me to rest after dinner and he rubs my aching feet at the end of each day. It's all I needs. A woman's gotta be strong and fit when it comes to birthin' a baby and steady work makes you fit."

Lucas shook his head. "All I can say is I'm glad the good Lord saw fit to give that chore to the women. I'm afraid that if it were up to men, the world's population would be greatly lacking."

"I, uh, think that's 'nuff talk 'bout babies. I'm 'fraid Albert ain't used to such private talk," Rose said looking at her husband.

"Albert, forgive me. I'm not used to talking much in mixed company. If I've offended anyone, I apologize, truly," Lucas said.

To fill in the silence, Aimee changed the subject. "Did Mister Price drop by and give you the name of that horse rancher?"

"Yes, he did but I've already made some other arrangements. My brothers had some sales lined up for me. They'll be driving a herd down in the spring. I'm just not equipped to handle them right now. My barn needs a lot of work and we're still finding fence posts that need replacing. I didn't realize there was a fence started until recently. The wire is still good, but several posts are rotten. It's going to take me until at least spring to get the place ready.

"The house is in pretty good shape, just a few minor repairs. It was a great surprise to find a large house like that buried deep in the forest. I'm set up quite well."

"I'm sure you are. Men aren't as particular as women when it comes to a house. In a way I'm glad I only have this. I've started drawing the house I plan to build here. I don't think I would be satisfied trying to make someone else's house mine. I want the walls, windows, and rooms in certain spots, and I want to design gardens around the house so I can sit in any room and stare at a lovely, restful area from anywhere in the house. I want... "

Lucas chuckled. "I think we get the idea. You want every board, nail, and swipe of paint to be something you choose, not something that someone else selected. Got it."

Aimee lowered her head as her cheeks flushed. "I've never had anything of my very own. This will be it. I intend to live the rest of my life here come wind or high water. I'm going to build to bring happiness to many, many families after I'm gone."

"You needs to be thinkin' 'bout bringin' that happiness to a family of your own," Rose said. She placed her hands on her hips and raised one eyebrow.

"That's out of the question. In order to keep possession of this farm, I must remain Mack Kaymey, I can't even think about that sort of thing. Until the law in the South changes and women can be landowners without inheriting, what can I do?"

Rose frowned. Her eyes grew moist and her mouth worked as if she was about to say something but the room remained silent.

Lucas coughed. "I really must go. I'm glad I was able to help you with Mister Owens and all of you can be assured that your secrets are safe with me. We have a new life ahead for all of us and now that we understand one another, I think that life is going to be a good one." He rose and shook Albert's hand. "You know where I live if you ever need me."

"Miss Aimee, please don't go roaming alone for a while until we know for sure that Mister Owens and his friends understand their boundaries. I'm sure Albert or one of the hands won't mind accompanying you around for a while. See that she listens, won't you, Miss Rose? I have a feeling you have more influence over her than any of us.

"And Miss Rose, please take it easy until that little one comes, if not for your- self, for my nerves and Albert's. By the look on his face, you haven't convinced him that you're as tough as you act." Lucas reached and patted Rose's shoulder.

"I will, Mister Lucas. You men jest don't know how we treasure the lives we's carry. We'd never do nothin' to put them in harm. Still, y'all keeps talkin' and worryin'. We really likes all the attention you give us," Rose said with a smile.

155

"Lucas," Aimee said softly. "I don't know how to repay you for saving me from that monster in the woods. I won't go out alone, I promise. And I'm glad you know. Like I keep telling Rose, Isaac, and Albert, you can never have too many friends."
She stuck out her hand and Lucas looked at it a few moments before taking it in his. Holding her small hand in both of his, he looked deep into her eyes. "If you hadn't worn that hat so low and kept your head down, I would have recognized those eyes that very first day. I've seen them in my dreams over and over." He seemed to realize what he had said and grinned boyishly.

"You take care, Miss Aimee, and by that I mean keep your eyes open and be careful. I will see you very soon." He turned and left the room, shutting the door firmly behind him.

Albert and Rose exchanged glances.

"Well, Miss Aimee, things are a little different, now. First Mister Gaines, then us, now Mister Lucas. Pretty soon everybody's gonna know about all our secrets. You realize the more people who know, the bigger chance of all of us being exposed," Rose told her.

"Rose, is you sayin' that you don't trust Mister Chase?" Albert asked.

"I ain't sayin' nothin' 'bout nobody. I jest said whut I meant. More mouths there is to jaw, more words to spoil the milk. Some- times, harm come when ain't no harm meant."

"This is all my fault. Why did I think I was smart enough to carry this off? What gave me the right to put other people's lives in jeopardy? Who did I think I was to do something so stupid? That just goes to prove that nothing has changed in my life. I did stupid things in the past and I'm still doing stupid things."

"Oh lordy, Miss Aimee, I ain't placing no blame on you. I'd never do that. You ain't done nothin' but good things for us. You got the best heart of anyone in this here whole world. I was just sayin' that... "

"She didn't mean you was to blame, Miss Aimee," Albert said.

"But it's true, isn't it? If it wasn't for me, you wouldn't be worried about anyone around here knowing anything about you. What have I done?"

"Miss Aimee, our time was flat runnin' out," Albert said. "It was jest a matter o' when 'n how. We wuz sick, starvin' an' warn't sure if we could survive one more hard freeze. Our blankets wuz thin and there's warn't enough of 'em.

"Possum was gettin' scarce and squirrels had moved onto Mister Owens' property. Most 'o the time our traps came up empty and I don't mind tellin' you I wuz scared that the end was nigh. We'd already talked 'bout movin' on, only we didn't know where. You saved us, Miss. You saved us all. That's whut you done."

"Miss, the old folks and the young'uns knows what real food tastes like for the first time in so long some of the babies can't even 'member. You don't got no idea what it was like the day Albert brought in a big hog. We used to jump at ever little snap or footstep. Now we sleep sound. We eat good. Now we laugh and enjoy our days. For a second I forgot about that 'till Albert started talkin'.

"It don't matter now who knows what. Things'll work out. I feels it. I knows it. Now you must pulls yourself together and get good thoughts on your mind," Rose said firmly. "What's done is done. We got to keep on. You hear me, Miss?"

Aimee hitched a breath as Rose talked. When she finished, Aimee inhaled deeply and smiled. "You're both right. They say the road to hell is paved with good intentions but if we continue to make those intentions work, then we'll be okay. There is still a lot of today and all of tomorrow to spend tending to your place. Rose, I don't want you coming in Monday. I'm going into town and I won't be back until late.

"Lucas did have the right idea about you getting rest. You may not rest at your place but that's up to you. I don't want you coming back here until after the baby is born. There is not much to do around here for a while anyway. My plans for the new house are going to take up a lot of my time and the men will be dealing with the livestock. They can bring their lunches and you know I can cook for myself. Is that clear?"

Rose smiled. "Yes'um, that's clear. We be goin' now. I gots Albert 'n Isaac planting me some winter root vegetables and they's still got some diggin' to do. I'll drop in for a visit sometime next week. Come on Albert, holler for Isaac and let's go on home.

~ Fourteen ~
Home and Holidays

"Mister Mack, Rose wants I should tell you that she'd truly be happy if you'd join us next Thursday for a celebration dinner fer the end of fall harvest, and the new baby that's a comin'. She woulda come herself only it's getting a little harder for her to climb up on that wagon now. Granny Alma's been a'harpin' fer her to gets in bed but you knows Rose. She's like a mama bear readying her den fer the new cub. It would please her so if you could come by and share our turkey and some of her mama's sweet tater pie." Albert grinned shyly.

"Oh, Albert, please tell everyone how sorry I am. I forgot about it being so near her time. I got so wrapped up in this place and getting it ready for winter that I... "

"Mister Mack, we knows that when you's a farmer or rancher, work ain't gonna wait fer babies or weather. We knows that. We done all the huntin' and brought home everythin' the women needed. Nearly all of us got a turkey or deer, and we's let the women folk worry 'bout the meal. Please come and share our good fortune. We got lots to celebrate fer this year, and praise to the Lord that he sent you to make this fall harvest party special. It jest ain't right fer you not to be there."

Aimee turned toward the window when she felt tears sting her eyes. "Albert, I would be honored to eat at your table and celebrate your new baby.

"Oh, mercy, if fall is coming to an end already, then that means Christmas isn't far off. What kind of person am I to get so involved with my own private business that I forgot all about such important holidays? I need to pull my head out of the sand and see what's going on around me."

"Mister Mack, we'uns knows when you's a farmer or rancher, work ain't gonna take a holiday. We knows that. We done all the huntin' and brought home everythin' the women needed. Nearly all of us got a turkey or deer, and we's let the women folk worry 'bout the meal.

"Please come and share our good fortune. We got lots to be thankful fer this year, and praise to the Lord that he sent you to make this holiday special. It jest ain't right fer you not to be there."

Aimee turned toward the window when she felt tears sting her eyes. "Albert, I would be honored to eat at your table. Oh, mercy, that reminds me, Christmas isn't far off now. What kind of person am I to get so involved with my own private business that I forgot all about such an important holiday? I need to pull my head out of the sand and see what's going on around me."

"You gots a lot to think about 'round here. Do you knows what all you done in jest a few months?"

"Has it only been months? It's seems like a couple of years but no matter, you're right. Time waits for no one. Still, I'll tell you one thing, as soon as the harvest celebration is over, we need to turn our attention to Christmas."

Albert smiled and nodded, "Yassum, the women folk done started on that. They's hiding lots of stuff from the chill'uns and I knows for a fact Rose sneaks 'round after she 'spects I's done gone to sleep to sew on somethin' she don't wants me to see."

"That's all fine and good but Albert, I need to make this a special Christmas. I may have overlooked the harvest celebration but I want to have you all here at Christmas. Do you think Rose will object?"

Albert looked around and grinned. "My Rose ain't gonna say a word but I reckon you might wants to wait 'till you gets a bigger place. With all of us, Rose, Isaac, her mom, my brother, and the new 'un, I truly don't think there's 'nuf room."

Aimee followed Albert's gaze and burst out laughing. "Oh my, I guess we might have to take the bed out and move a few things around but nevertheless, we're going to make it a wonderful holiday. The more I think about it, the more excited I get. Now, I have to tell you that this will be the first Christmas I've celebrated since I left home.

"Growing up, I went to the finest stores in Boston and charged all the gifts for my father and brother. My father and brother bought gifts for everyone else. Under Papa's supervision, the staff decorated the entire house, planned and prepared the dinners. And last year... well, last year I was starving and alone on Christmas Day. I've got a lot to learn about being in charge of a celebration of this size but I will learn and it will be great."

"I's sure it will, but we's be havin' the harvest celebration on Thursday. Just thinkin' 'bout a'chawin' down on that turkey

160

and them sweet taters makes my mouth water. We'll be looking for you 'bout noon. See you then." Albert grinned as he put on his hat and took the reins of the horse, and swung into the saddle.

"I'll be there. Should I bring anything?"

"Jest be good 'n hungry," he called over his shoulder and headed home.

Aimee walked around the house and wandered in and out of the barn. She brushed Dusty and hugged his neck. He and Puck had both put on weight since settling at Eagle Creek, and both had grown a thick winter coat. Slipping each a carrot, they munched happily, and Aimee smiled, pulling her coat tighter around her, the sharp wind bit coldly as she headed to the house.

Inside, she immediately added another log and poked at the fire until it began to blaze. She slipped out of her hat and coat, and pulled off her gloves. Pouring herself a cup of strong, black coffee that had been sitting on the back of the stove all day, she pulled out the sketches of her future home and flipped through the pages until she came to the one she had created for the sitting room.

In all her planning, she had never considered holidays but now she wanted to make sure the kitchen was designed for prepa- ration of large meal, and the dining room could accommodate a dozen or more guests, and the parlor had enough room for a mas- sive Christmas tree and still be large enough for many people to enjoy the festivities. Her excitement grew as she drew and imag- ined the house filled with colorful decorations and the aroma of delicious food coming from the kitchen.

At the second swallow of her coffee, Aimee's mouth puck- ered up at the bitter taste of the cold, over-cooked liquid. She put the teakettle on, slipped out of her work clothes and dressed more comfortably. Then, as she worked on the drawing of the sit- ting room, her thoughts drifted back to her childhood.

She fought hard not to copy the parlor from her childhood home. She remembered her mother directing servants to place the boughs of cedar and holly down the staircase and over the mantelpiece above the fireplace. They fastened large red bows along the greenery and cook always designed a large towering centerpiece of apples on the sofa table, surrounded by shiny, green leafed holly speckled with bright red berries.

Aimee recalled another yearly tradition where her papa made such a production of selecting the Christmas tree. Around the twentieth of December the entire family bundled up and climbed into the sleigh for a trip to the tree lot where Papa and her brother, Edward marched up and down the paths between the trees, while Aimee and her mother trailed along behind. Occasionally, Papa paused and murmured something to Edward, who in- evitably nodded, turn to Mama and say, "What do you think of this one?"

Mama always smiled but Papa, turning his head from side to side, and moved on inspecting other trees. Aimee swore that each year, Papa looked at every single tree on the lot before choosing the one he thought perfect enough. She often wondered why he just didn't go alone and surprise them, as he was the one who made the final decision anyway. Back then, she and Edward thought they all chose the tree but that was the whole idea. Papa was a genius at making people think his idea was also theirs. Aimee paused her drawing and bowed her head. She only wished that his genius had worked the day he tried to dissuade her from becoming involved with Marcus. What would her mother have said about the man who all but destroyed her daughter's life?

Mama had been a bit of a mystery. Aimee couldn't remember ever seeing Mama disagree or argue with Papa. However, Mama always seemed to get her way. She was a beautiful woman, generous, kind, and affectionate, and she adored Clark, Aimee's papa, and Aimee knew she spent more time with her children than any other mother. The family always had meals together. That was an unbreakable rule, unless one was sick in bed. Mama read to Aimee and Edward each evening, teaching them letters when they were young and words as they grew older.

As Aimee returned to her sketch and began drawing a tree into the picture, she could see Christmas' past in her mind. Papa and Mama were always up and in their robes by the time she and Edward awoke on Christmas morning. Edward never went downstairs without Aimee. She smiled to herself as she recalled him leaning over her, gently shaking her and whispering loudly in her ear, "Aimee, wake up. It's Christmas morning. Aimee, do you hear me? Please, sleepyhead, get up. I hinted for an archery set all summer. I want to see if I got one. Aimee, don't you want to see what you got? Ai-m-ee, get u-u-up!"

Those were beautiful days, with wonderful people in a grand house. She wanted those days repeated. Maybe those future days wouldn't be for her, and maybe she would never know those wonderful people who would have those days but she could build a house so that life could be beautiful for someone.

She mentally brushed the cobwebs of memories from her mind and concentrated on the drawings.

After making the parlor much bigger, sketching in the huge tree and piles of gifts and toys, she turned to the drawing of the dining room. She enlarged the room, drew in a large table and after adding several additional chairs and a long serving buffet; she began work on the kitchen. Adding eight feet across the back wall, she gave it two cook stoves side by side, several work tables, and she penciled in an enclosed porch off the side where baked goods could cool and be stored until serving time. She drew a covered porch off the back door of the kitchen and a lovely garden to enhance the view.

Taking a sip from her second cup of tea Aimee frowned at the drink she allowed to become ice cold. Straightening up, she felt the twinge of stiff muscles in her lower back, and glanced at the clock. She had worked for four hours, and the fire had burned down. Aimee stretched and slipped her drawings back into the folder and slid them onto the shelf.

After washing her face, brushing her hair and undressing, she pulled on her nightgown, locked the front door and crawled into bed.

~ * ~

The next morning before Albert and the others arrived, Aimee rose, picked out what Rose called her, "Sunday-go-to-meetin' clothes," and prepared to ride into town. Before she fell asleep the night before, she decided to take the plans for her house to Ernest for his opinion. She didn't have a clue as to how to proceed with the building of the house but Ernest had connections and perhaps he could suggest someone.

Leaving the work in Albert's capable hands, Aimee left for town and arrived as the restaurant opened its doors. As she was about to enter, someone reached in front of her, twisted the knob and shoved the door open for her. She jumped and whirled around to see Lucas Chase grinning from ear to ear, his blue eyes sparking as he nodded and touched his hat.

"Mister Kaymey," he said loudly, "good to see you. How's the work coming at your place?

"Good, Lucas, very good," she answered in a deep voice. "What brings you to town so early?"

"I could ask you the same thing. Would you join me for breakfast and we can discuss our ranching problems?"

"Delighted to, Lucas, just delighted," Aimee bantered back, enjoying the game.

They chose a table and as soon as they sat down, the waiter appeared with two cups of steaming coffee and menus. They ordered steak, eggs, grits, and biscuits and after the waiter left, Lucas leaned in closer.

"Have you had any more trouble from trespassers?"

"No. I haven't seen or heard anything unusual lately. George and Abraham check the woods and creek regularly note any signs of poachers, if they spot any." she said softly.

"Good. I hope you don't mind but I did make a call on Henry Owens and mentioned the fact that some of the neighbors

164

are complaining about traps found on their property. I didn't mention your name or accuse his brother but from the look on Henry's face, I could tell he wasn't pleased to hear the news.

"He told me he hadn't had any problems but if he heard anything, he would report it immediately. I have the feeling that Owens takes care of his own problems and I wouldn't be surprised if Bundy didn't get a firm warning from his brother.

"Henry may be a bit strange but everyone around here thinks highly of him. His father was wild and wooly, or so the rumors go but his mother was a well-liked local. Although Henry's brother still lives in the house next door, I suspect he's senile. Henry seems to be a kind man that takes care of his own and I think he'll want to keep a clean and honest reputation. You can't blame Henry for what his brother, that is, step-brother, does."

"Of course not. Mister Owens was very pleasant to do business with, although, you're right. He is a bit strange."

The waiter brought their breakfast and the conversation turned to lighter chitchat about the horses, weather, and as they neared the end of the meal, Lucas said, "You never did say what brings you into town so early."

"I have some business with Ernest at the bank and I wanted to look over some of the items at the general store for possible Christmas gifts to give to my..." Aimee paused and glanced around to make sure they couldn't be overheard. "To my friends."

"The general store is a fine place," Lucas grinned, "but I don't think you're going to find as wide a selection as you would in Charleston. I'm taking a trip there in a week or so. Would you like to travel with me and see if there is anything might like to pick up in the city?"

Aimee thought for a moment and then nodded. "Yes, I would. At least there I could buy a few things and everyone in town wouldn't know about it five minutes after I left."

Lucas threw back his head and laughed. "I see you've finally got the feel of living in a small town. You're right. Nothing goes on around here that isn't local gossip within a few hours. I'll

let you know exactly when I'm leaving so you can make plans ac-
cordingly."

"Thank you." As she reached in her jacket pocket for her
money clip, Lucas held out his hand.

"I believe I asked you to join me for breakfast, Mack.
Please. I'll take care of the bill."

Aimee lowered her gaze. "Thank you, Lucas. I appreciate
that. I really must get to the bank before Ernest gets busy.

"I enjoyed breakfast and the offer to go to Charleston with
you. I'll talk to you later."

As they rose and parted company, Lucas walked to the
waiter to take care of the bill and Aimee headed out the door and
down the wooden sidewalk toward the bank. Inside, the teller escorted Aimee to the back office.

"Mister Mackey," Ernest cried loudly. "How good it is to
see you." He closed his office door and added, "What can I do for
you today?" With the door securely closed, he took Aimee's hand
and kissed it. "Good morning, my dear. How are you doing?"

"Ernest, I have drawn up some ideas I have for a house I
want to build. I hoped if perhaps you know someone that might
look at them and be able to draw up the blue prints. I'd like to
start building next spring."

"You know, I do have some connections in Charleston and
Savannah. Let me look at your plans for a while and maybe I can
find someone who will work on it for you. You need to give me a
couple of weeks anyway."

"There's really no hurry as long as we find someone who
can start next spring. Thank you, Ernest. I'll let you get on with
your banking. I'll be waiting for hear from you."

~ * ~

Aimee returned home happier than she had a right to be,
or so she thought. Ernest was evaluating her plans; she was going
into Charleston for the first time since the sinking of the S.S. Central America; and she was going to spend a wonderful day with
people she had come to love. Still, in the back of her mind, fear

lurked. She couldn't truly enjoy her good fortune for worrying that any moment her tower of good luck might come tumbling down.

The next couple of days passed quickly as the cold moved in and the freezing rain descended.

On Thursday morning, Aimee rose, dressed in her best men's suit, shirt, tie, and hat, then saddled up Dusty for the trip to the Washington camp. Aimee had ordered supplies a couple of week prior and the men had winterized all the cabins and small barns in the camp for the coming cold.

Aimee arrived in camp to see Albert waiting for her, just as Rose came out to greet her.

"Rose, shouldn't you be resting?" Aimee asked worriedly.

"Now, I ain't in the mood fer you to start in on me, too," Rose chided. "That's all I hear these days. I thinks I knows my own body better than anybody else does. I feels fine. Mama ain't let me do nothin' if I wasn't sittin' down. So, believe me, I been on my bottom more than I been on my feet. I feels this need to clean, sew, and get ready. Mama says it's like a bird readying the nest. Here, let me take your coat and hat."

The aromatic smells of roasting turkey mingled with the sweet, tangy scent of pies and cakes filling the cabin, and Aimee's mouth began watering the minute she stepped inside the door.

The serving table against the wall was loaded with bowls and tin containers heaped with vegetables, relishes, fresh churned butter, and steaming loaves of bread. Another shelf displayed pies, cakes, and jars filled with cookies.

Albert stood formally by the table holding out a chair for her to sit in. Rose's mother's chair was at one end and Isaac rushed in to hold the chair for his grandmother.

"Albert, you sit next to Benjamin and Isaac, soon as Mama sits, Isaac will say the blessing and we'll eat."

Isaac did his mother proud with the blessing and the meal was delicious. Aimee couldn't help but think what a wonderful cook Rose was.

Late that evening, Aimee started back and already her thoughts were on the Christmas holiday that was soon to follow. She wanted Christmas to be just as special as the day she'd just had, and although Albert was right about her little cabin being too small, she knew if she removed the bed, she could make room for everyone. Thinking of her first Christmas in her own home brought a smile to Aimee's lips.

~ Fifteen ~
The Wanted Poster

The next week and a half passed quickly. The horses found the pond and were content in their new home, and the recently delivered cattle grazed comfortably in the back pasture behind the horse meadow.

Albert took the wagon, together with Price's wagon, and transferred the hay Aimee bought to her own barn. It took several trips but they finally got it home.

The weather changed abruptly and the sky became a cold, steel gray. The repairs to the property were completed and most of the men came to work only a couple of days a week to check the livestock and run the fence line to check for breaks. They were looking forward to springtime when the planting would begin and once again, they would be doing something familiar.

Rose had told Isaac about the baby the a few weeks earlier and he was thrilled when the baby girl named Annie, was born. Now he could be a big brother, protect his sister from all harm, and teach her all about the woods and animals.

During the day, Aimee made notes on how she would decorate her house and in the late evenings, Lucas occasionally dropped by. He usually stayed until just before sundown, looking at her drawings, drinking coffee, and discussing plans for his farm, and listening to what Aimee planned for hers.

One Sunday afternoon, Aimee heard a horse galloping up into the yard. Thinking it was Lucas, she hurried to the door and jerked it open. Instead of Lucas, she saw Ernest Gaines dismounting from his horse.

"Ernest, how nice to see you. How's your family?"

"They're doing just fine, Mister Kaymey," he said with a grin.

"I think I have news that you're really going to like," he huffed as he caught his breath and swept off his hat. How 'bout cup of coffee?"

"Sure, come on in. What's this about some news?" Aimee smiled.

"Well, I looked over the drawings you showed me and was very impressed. I sent them to a friend of mine from Charleston who has just opened his own architect and design studio. His

brother has a building material company and they often work together, and have built some of Charleston's finest homes."

"Do you think he would?" Aimee's eyes glistened with excitement.

"Aimee, you don't mind me calling you that when we're
alone, do you?" Ernest quickly asked.

"No, of course not, Ernest. You're one of my dearest
friends."

"Thank you, my dear. Your secret is safe with me. As I was
saying, not only will he do it, he is excited about. With the South
grumbling about the North's complaints about slaves, most the
money is going into politicians pockets and the building of new
houses has slowed down considerably. Of course, I didn't mention
your finances and with the economy so uncertain, he'll be more
than fair about the price of working up a blueprint for the carpenters to follow. 'I'm sure his brother will be also. He did have several questions he wanted to go over with you." He sipped his coffee that Aimee had poured him and watched her reaction.

"How soon do you think I can meet this gentleman?" Aimee
asked. "Don't you think he'll be suspicious of the type of house I
designed considering that there is no apparent woman around?"

"Heavens no, Aimee. Andrew, that's his name, Andrew Harmon, is a professional and he is working on the plans for your
house out of immense interest, that's all. You must admit, those
drawings you made are incredibly beautiful and elaborate. Andrew was deeply impressed with your artistic ability. Even the individual rooms you sketched out were extraordinary. He asked me
if you had any schooling in architecture.

"Let me see if I can recall his exact words... 'the choice of
stained glass windows and their locations are awe inspiring.' Andrew is a genius in my mind and I feel his remarks were most flat-
tering toward your work and believe me, they were genuine.

"I know for a fact that when we had our house built, I was
given a selection of plans which, ask my wife if you don't believe
me, she had more say in it than I did but no one knew that except

170

me. We men like to give the impression that we make all the decisions. Andrew probably thinks the house is being built for a future Mrs. Kaymey."

"Excellent. Please set up an appointment with Mister Harmon for me and we'll get started as soon as possible."

"I'm sure he's anxiously awaiting your reply."

"Aimee?" Ernest said slowly, staring into his cup. "I've been toying with an idea that I think might alleviate some of your concern of your true identity being discovered."

Aimee leaned forward. "What is your idea? I'm very interested."

"I've been thinking that perhaps your sister might come down for a visit now and then and help you with the house." He glanced at Aimee and saw the stunned look of total confusion spread across her face. He continued, "You know, like picking out wallpaper, drapes, carpet, and the kitchen arrangement. Architects and designers are always grateful for a woman's touch when it comes to that part of the building."

Aimee shook her head slowly and spoke softly. "Ernest, I'm not sure what's going on but one of us has a terrible problem. Either you have lost your mind or I am going crazy. What in blazes are you talking about?"

Ernest grinned and leaned back. "Aimee, I'm talking about the woman that can walk out that bedroom any time she wants to if she stayed here with her brother now and then."

Aimee's eyes widened at the implication. "You mean…," she paused, and then rose and went to the window, looking out across the yard.

After a few moments, she whirled around. "Ernest, you are absolutely brilliant. I did not think, due to my past experience, that I would mind not being a woman but I was wrong. Things… well, things have changed and I didn't have a clue how I would handle those feelings. I must admit I miss the feel of silk and satin, buying new hats, selecting new shoes, you know, the vain, silly things that women pleasure in, and you have just given me the perfect solution.

"A sister. Yes, Mack should have a sister. Someone who can assist him in all those decorative little nuances that give a home character and personality, without thinking him odd, or the center of distasteful conversation.

"Oh, Ernest, what a dear friend you are. I will cherish your kind thoughts for my lifestyle forever. I need to think on this and decide how my sister will come into my life. Go ahead and arrange a meeting with Mister Harmon and hopefully, by that time I will have come up with an idea."

"There is one more thing, at least to me, that is more exciting than your house," he paused and grinned. "We have been extremely fortunate in our investments with your money. Naturally, with the government being in controversy over this slavery thing, stocks and bonds are shaky. Still, the investments we made are doing quite well... quite well, indeed. In fact, your account is growing steadily and in no time, your investments may double. I think you need to get some of your money in a personal fireproof safety box and put it in the vault. This unrest in the North is making me nervous. Better be safe than sorry."

"Oh, my," whispered Aimee. "This is more than I could hope for. Poor Abram would be so pleased. His family's investment made all this possible. Thank you, Ernest, for taking such good care of his legacy. I will put some money aside in one of those boxes. You have my authority to do just that."

Ernest smiled and his cheeks flushed with pleasure.

After about a half hour of chatting, Ernest rose, and with a promise to let her know as soon as the appointment with the architect was set up, he left.

~ * ~

Aimee poured herself another cup of coffee and sat down at the table. The idea of being a woman again, even if it was just playing Mack Kaymey's sister, was intriguing. Just thinking of feeling feminine once more caused her to shiver. She rubbed her cheek against her shoulder feeling the rough, heavy surface of the work shirt she wore.

It wasn't fair, she thought, that men didn't enjoy the smooth, cool surface of fine fabrics in their clothes as women did. She knew that the wealthy men did purchase high quality fabric for their shirts and suits but there should be some way that most men could buy clothes that would give them the best comfort possible. It was certainly something to think about.

As she sat nibbling on a piece of Rose's honey cake, her eyes kept flitting over to the bed. Suddenly she jumped up, brushed her hands off, rushed over and knelt on the floor bedside her bed. She pulled out the carpetbag and unbuckled the fastener. Opening it, she pulled out the only pieces of feminine clothing she owned and slung them on the bed. They had been rolled up and stuffed in the bag the day she cut her hair and dressed as Mack Kaymey.

Smoothing out the wrinkles, she placed the blouse above the skirt and laid the jacket beside it. She walked over to the wood stove, shoved a couple of extra sticks of wood in the fire, and closed the lid. She placed the heavy iron on the top, and got out the piece of wood been used to press her clothes. She turned two of the chairs back to back, pulled them apart about three feet and laid the plank across the back of the chairs, then placed a folded sheet on top. She refilled her coffee cup and waited for the iron to heat up.

Carefully and tenderly, Aimee smoothed out all the wrinkles in her clothes with the hot iron. She repeatedly reheated the iron and ran it over a piece of paper she placed on the fabric to keep it from scorching. When she finished, she undressed, pulled on her stockings and shoes and began layering on her underclothes. Thrusting her arms into the sleeves of her blouse, she paused, relishing the feel of the cool shimmering cloth against her skin. After pushing the tiny pearl buttons through the carefully stitched buttonholes, she shoved her upper body into the voluptuous folds of her skirt and let it fall to her hips. Aimee hooked the little metal hooks into the loops of the waistband and fastened the wide cloth belt around her middle.

Standing still for a moment, Aimee savored the movement of the skirt around her legs. She walked to the small dressing table and sat down to look at her reflection in the mirror. Picking up her brush, she began pulling it through her tangled curls. It wasn't long enough to gather up in the back and was too short to cover her neck. She felt tears sting her eyes and dropped the brush.

"I'll never pull this off," she said with a small, harsh laugh as the irony hit her.

She had been terrified that she could never pass as a man and now, she was terrified that if she became a woman again, everyone would know what she had done.

Sitting at the dresser, she suddenly had a feeling that she was not alone. Aimee whirled around and saw Lucas standing quietly just inside the door.

"I knocked, but I guess you... you didn't hear me," he said softly noticing her watery eyes.

Aimee jumped up and found herself at a loss for words.

"I wondered how long it would be before you were tempted to remind yourself what it felt like to be a woman. Aimee, you look beautiful. That dress makes your eyes sparkle. Weren't you wearing that dress the first day of the voyage?" Lucas asked, smiling.

"I can't believe you remembered. Yes, and I was wearing this just before we arrived in Charleston. It's hard to believe it survived all that. My father bought this for me for my birthday, the one I had just before I left home."

"How does it feel to be Miss Aimee McKay from top to bottom?"

"Not from the top," she complained. "I don't have enough hair to pass as a woman."

"Aimee, you must have led a very sheltered young life. Certain shops carry dozens of hairpieces that hair stylists design for women. Ladies can wear different styles for an assortment of events. All you have to do is find one that you are comfortable with and that you feel is appropriate for your style," he said as he twirled his hand over his head.

"And you know this because...," Aimee replied, cocking her head to the side, eyeing him curiously.

"Because my mother had a shelf lined with little wooden heads with a dozen of these hair pieces attached to them. Her hairdresser kept them styled in the latest fashion for her use at a moment's notice.

"She had one that was a bunch of curls with pearls and rhinestones poked in them. She wore that one to the opera and theater; another was a twisted thing-a-ma-jig that she wore at the nape of her neck when she attended her ladies meetings and city socials. She also had two little braided what-cha-ma-call-its that had long curls hanging down that she pinned to both sides of her hair just in front of her ears when she went to balls and formal dances.

"There were several others, but I can't remember what they were. She always had little hairy little poofs and pomps sitting around. I'll bet you can find something great. Not here, of course but in Charleston, I'm sure."

Aimee smiled at the mention of the thing-a-ma-jig and giggled at the what-cha-ma-call-its, then laughed out loud when he popped off about the hairy little poofs and pomps. The tears were gone and her face radiant when Lucas finished.

"That's a wonderful idea. I really wasn't that sheltered. My mother wore a few hairpieces but I never used them, although I can see now that they certainly do come in useful. I think Rose and I need to take a trip to Charleston."

"What brought up the idea in the first place?" Lucas asked.

"Actually, it was Ernest's idea. He suggested that Mack have a sister. I guess I never really thought about Mack having a family. The more I thought about it, the better I liked it."

"I take it you've decided that Mack's sister is coming to visit, then?" Lucan grinned hopefully.

"Yes, your little hairpiece suggestion did it. I hadn't thought about using them. Thank you."

"At your service, milady," Lucas responded, giving Aimee a deep bow. "Now, when do you think you'll be starting on the house?"

"Ernest is setting up a meeting with the architect, a Mister Harmon so we can discuss the blueprints. His brother is the owner of a building supply company, so I feel this combination is a pretty good one. I don't imagine we'll start until the spring. It would break my heart to start and then have to stop halfway through because of bad weather."

"Speaking of weather, would you like to get out for a ride today? It looks like it might get too cold and rainy soon and we won't have another chance for a while."

"Sure, let me change clothes and I'll meet you at the stables," Aimee said. She was still smiling at the idea of being a woman as she stepped behind the bedroom curtain and slipped off her jacket.

"I'll saddle up your horse," Lucas called over his shoulder as he walked out the door.

Aimee changed into her work clothes, and pulled on her boots and gloves. As she walked out the door, she pulled her hat low over the scar, and saw Lucas talking to a stranger, laughing now and then.

He pointed as the stranger shaded his eyes and looked across the fields behind the house. The man with Lucas was about six feet tall with wide shoulders, like Lucas but his dark hair was cut short under his wide brim hat. He wore chaps over brown trousers and a matching vest over a blue chambray shirt.

Something about him caused fear to run through Aimee's body.

She adjusted the scarf around her neck, pulled up her collar, and walked toward the two men.

176

"Mack, come over here and meet James Evans, the new marshal. Marshal Evans, this is Mack Kaymey, owner of Eagle Creek."

Aimee stuck out her gloved hand and firmly shook James Evan's hand. She pretended to cough heavily and spluttered in a fake weak voice, "Caught a bit of a cold the past few days. Please excuse me," she said in a low gravelly voice.

"Don't worry about it," Marshal Evans said. "This time of year is hard on everybody. I've had a sore throat for a week now."

"I didn't realize that a town the size of Sycamore Grove was able to afford a sheriff much less a marshal," Lucas chuckled.

James Evans smiled ruefully and took his hat off, running his fingers through his hair.

"Actually, a marshal is appointed and hired by the federal offices of the individual states. A sheriff is elected and in charge of a local area, like a town or community and they have county boundaries. We have no boundaries. As a United States marshal, there are no lines I can't cross between Canada and Mexico."

"What brings you to this little, out of the way town, Marshal?"

"This does," Evans answered, pulling a poster from the inside pocket of his leather vest. He pulled the rolled-up poster from beneath his vest and found it mashed flat from pressed against his chest under the vest that sported his silver-circled star.

Lucas unrolled the paper and Aimee heard an unexpected gasp.

"You know her, Mister Chase?"

"No, oh, no, I was just surprised that it was a woman. I was expecting a bearded, mustached, evil-looking rogue, that's all. I was taken off guard."

Luca studied the poster for what seemed like a very long time before slowly handing Aimee the paper.
"What has this person done, Marshal?"

177

Aimee looked at Lucas as he talked to the marshal and when she looked down at the paper, she felt the world shudder beneath her feet and a sharp pain lodged itself just above her right eye. There on the paper, was a beautifully sketched picture of her, just as she was dressed the day she boarded the S.S. Sonora. The likeness was uncanny. Below the picture were the words:

'Wanted: Aimee McKay
$500.00 Reward for any information leading to her whereabouts.'

"It seems she robbed her companion of several thousand dollars' worth of gold in California, and then disappeared without a trace. Those poor miners are real suckers when it comes to a pretty woman. Between money-hungry saloon dancers and gold diggers, those poor chumps are easy pickings. Most just crawl away and lick their wounded pride but this here feller won't stand for being cheated. He's flooding the law offices with these flyers and with that size of a reward that McKay woman is in a world of trouble."

"Why would they think she was here in South Carolina? We're a long way from California," Aimee croaked.

"The feller she robbed, Marcus Alexander, saw her board a ship whose passengers were bound for New York. They ran into a storm and all the women and children were rescued and taken to Charleston."

"Have you talked to any of the passengers?" Lucas asked.

"That's why I'm here," Evans said with a grin. "I understand you were aboard the S.S. Central America and were one of the survivors. Do you remember Aimee McKay?"

Lucas scratched his head. "Marshal, there were over five hundred people on board, plus the crew. My sister, her husband, myself and a few of our friends pretty much stayed to ourselves. Do you know which class she was in?"

James Evans pulled out a small notebook and flipped through a few pages. "I believe she was in steerage class. The passenger list puts her in one of the bottom rooms."

"There," Lucas snorted, as he threw his arm up in the air dramatically, "That's your answer. We were in first class and I can assure you that steerage didn't mingle with first class. It just isn't allowed." He raised his eyebrow and sneered.

As frightened as Aimee was, she almost burst out laughing at Lucas's performance.

"I see," murmured the Marshal as he replaced he notebook back into his shirt pocket. He looked hard at Aimee as he spoke to Lucas. "So, I'm correct in saying that you don't remember seeing Aimee McKay aboard the S.S. Central America?"

"Please, not if she was in steerage," Lucas repeated haughtily. "I do understand that all the women and children were rescued. Did you check the hotels and rescue units there in Charleston? Perhaps some of the steerage passengers remember her."

"That's the strange thing," Evans said, running his eyes from Aimee's hat down to the heels of her boots before looking at Lucas, "the crew aboard the Ellen took names of all the passengers they rescued and her name wasn't on any of the lists. She didn't check into to any of the hotels and to be honest, I can't find one single person who can remember for certain if they met her."

Lucas swallowed hard before he asked his next question. "Maybe she drowned. Have you talked to my sister? She was on board, too. She's the type that notices everything and everybody worth mentioning."

"I haven't talked to her in person since she had already left for New York, however, she was contacted and said that she had no knowledge of the woman."

Aimee let out a long sigh of relief at that remark. Lucas's sister, Adeline Easton, surely did remember her. She had gone out of her way to be kind and considerate to Aimee. Aimee knew Adeline was suspicious of Aimee's story and was simply protecting her.

There was no doubt in her mind that Adeline had outright lied about knowing her, and it was obvious that Lucas and his sister were two of a kind. They were both protecting her as best they could, even though his sister hadn't known her that well. Aimee smiled to herself. Just when she had convinced herself that most people were cruel and uncaring, here in the past few months, she discovered she was wrong. The marshal being here wasn't good news, and could cause more problems. This was a man who looked like he didn't lose often.

"Looks like you're out of luck here, Marshal. Sorry I can't help," Lucas said.

"How about you, Mister Kaymey? I haven't heard a word out of you," said James Evans.

"It's just strange," Aimee answered in a low gruff voice. "This reward poster doesn't read like most I've seen. It doesn't mention the woman's crime or that the reward is for her arrest. It just mentions information leading to the location of the woman. If she had stolen all this money and that man involved the law in this, why doesn't he want her arrested?"

"The way I understand it," Evans drawled as he scratched his chin, "he doesn't want the woman in jail. He just wants to recover his money. I think maybe he's still in love with her and doesn't want to see her hurt or humiliated."

"Ah." Aimee spit the exclamation out before she could stop herself. "As if these posters wouldn't humiliate her enough, doesn't it seem a little suspicious to you, Marshal?"

"Unfortunately, we aren't hired to give our opinions, sir. Mister Alexander has employed a private detective to scour Charleston for any clues that will lead to her location. We receive these posters and it is our duty to investigate them. Once again, I'll ask you," he repeated as he tilted his head and tried to look Aimee in the eye unsuccessfully, "Is there anything you want to tell me? Have you seen this woman?"

"Marshal, if that woman has all that money that Alexander claims, what would she be doing in Sycamore Grove? She's probably in some big city looking for the next sucker. You're following the wrong tracks and barking up the wrong tree. She isn't listed on the rescue list. No one recalls seeing her on board the ship that took in the women and children. I think this feller has sent you on a ghost hunt."

Lucas added, "If you recall, the Sonora took us as far as Panama City in South America where we transferred to the S.S. Central America. That was the ship that was lost in the hurricane. If you ask me, that McKay woman disembarked in Panama City and is probably still down in South America. That's where I would be. I'd focus my hunt down there if I were you."

"That thought has crossed my mind, too," Evans said thoughtfully. "Still, I was in the area and thought I'd check everything out. I appreciate your time. Much obliged for your advice. Y'all have a good day now," he said as he mounted his horse, with a tip of his hat. As he started down the path, he turned one last time and stared at Aimee several seconds before turning back around and riding away.

"Ai... Mack," Lucas called. "Wait."

Without turning, she said, "I'm tired, Lucas. I need to think. Please. I'll see you tomorrow."

~ Sixteen ~
A Lady for the Season

As Aimee entered her little house, she could hear Lucas riding away. She slipped off her gloves, removed her hat and untied the bandana around her neck. She shook her head when she realized she had a silly grin still lingering on her face.

Aimee chuckled as she went to the stove and poured herself a cup of strong coffee and practically giggled as she sat down. She was amazed.

The once weepy, frightened, nervous, scared little girl who inhabited her body had disappeared, had been replaced with anger when she saw the poster. In place of the scared girl was now a strong, independent, self-assured young woman who simply wouldn't stand by and let anyone intimidate her. Not a marshal, not the fear of discovery, and certainly not by any poster that a detestable, insufferable, loathsome, savage brute like Marcus Alexander made public.

He once ripped her heart from her very soul, destroyed her relationship with her family, gambled away every physical memory of her sweet mother, and now he had laid claim to her future. Not in this lifetime. Not now. Not ever. Marcus Alexander would never see one penny of the gold that Abram had so generously shared with her.

She had seen men who devoted their lives to acquire a future for themselves and their families, and were then forced to throw it away for the sake of survival. Aimee would make sure the gold in her possession was only be used for life and happiness, and that certainly did not include Marcus Alexander.

Lucas must have sensed that Aimee had come to the end of the lying, hiding, and pretending that she did not exist. Had he not jumped in at the end of Marshal Evans inquiry, she might have said the wrong thing, exposed herself for who she really was. But, he had changed the subject and now the marshal was gone - at least for now.

Somehow, deep inside, Aimee didn't believe the marshal had accepted their stories, and she wouldn't be surprised to see him again. This time, however, she would be ready for him. But for now, she had other things on her mind. Marcus Alexander would not rule her life.

She finished her coffee and took out her pen and paper. She couldn't wait to have a big Christmas dinner this year, even if they had to move the bed out into the yard and she had to sleep there for a couple of days. It was time to start her lists. One for the decorations she would need and the food she should buy for dinner. The second was for gifts for her friends and she wanted to think of wonderful, personal things that they would treasure.

~ * ~

The next morning a dusting of snow covered the farm. Isaac arrived with his father and George, who quickly broke the thin ice on the water troughs, fed the livestock, and milked the cows. Isaac fed the chickens and gathered the eggs. When they were through, Aimee called them in for hot chocolate and cinnamon toast.

"Sky looks mighty heavy," grumbled George. "I ain't favoring snow, that's fer sure." He took a large bite of the sweet toast and washed it down with a gulp of cocoa.

"I'm not that familiar with the weather here near the coast. What are the winters like around here?" asked Aimee as she buttered more bread.

"Last winter," piped Isaac, "it didn't snow at all but we had an ice storm that froze us in for three weeks. I'll take this here snow any time over that."

"We've been 'round here near on four years," added Albert, "and winter here jest ain't that predictable. Sometimes it's mighty cold and other times jest chilly. Ya never know fer sure what it's gonna be."

George nodded at Albert's description. "That's true, ya don't," he mumbled, his mouth full of toast.

"What was it like at your house when you was my age?" Isaac asked, his eyes sparkling. "What did y'all do?"

Aimee smiled and tried to keep her voice low and force herself to remember that Isaac was still thinking of her at his age as a little boy.

Ordinarily, she would have told him that she and her mother made snow ice cream, angels in the snow, and gathered holly in the woods to decorate the house. However, she had to try and remember how her brother, Edward spent his time during the winter.

"Sometimes, Nicholas, my father's assistant, would take me ice fishing. We would cut a hole in the lake, drag a couple of pieces of logs near the hole and drop our lines in the water. I was amazed when the fish bit, but they did," she said with a smile.

"What kinda fish does you catch in a frozen lake?" asked Isaac. His eyes had widened at the mention of ice fishing.

"As I remember, there were yellow perch, sunfish, and a few northern pike. Some of the bigger and deeper lakes had lots of pike and sometimes we caught a fish called a walleye."

"I heard of perch and sunfish. We got some of them down here but I ain't never heard of pikes and walleyes. Are they good to eat?"

"Now that was a long time ago. I really don't remember if cook ever prepared them or if we gave them away," Aimee said, and honestly couldn't remember ever eating the fish Edward caught.

"That don't sound right," Isaac said. "Why would you freeze your bottom a sittin' on a log fishing just to give 'em away?"

"Isaac," Albert snapped at his son. "You ain't got no call to speak to Mister Mack like that."

"He's right, Albert. It does sound silly when you tell it. I guess we just did it to have something to do during the cold weather."

"I didn't mean nothin', suh," Isaac said.

"I know you didn't," she said. "Besides fishing, we used to go for sleigh rides, horseback riding, skating, sledding, and hayrides. Sometimes we'd build a bonfire and sing songs or just sit around drinking hot cocoa. We had lots of fun."

"Didn't you have to chop wood, feed stock, hunt, and gather roots?" Isaac asked. The disbelieving look on his face alarmed his father.

"Isaac, whut am I gonna do with you, boy?" Albert said, sounding perplexed.

"It's alright, Albert. It's a perfectly normal question for him to ask. Sorry, Isaac but no, we didn't have to do any of that. I realize we were quite spoiled now that I look back."

"You said we. Who is we?"

"I have a sister," Aimee quickly answered before Albert could snap at Isaac again. He was just asking the questions that his curiosity prompted him to.

"This place where all the lakes is froze up, is it far from here?" continued Isaac as one question prompted another.

Albert rolled his eyes at Aimee and shook his head, looking relieved when she smiled patiently.

"Yes, Isaac, it's a long way from here and someday I'll tell you more but right now, let's talk about here and now. It's almost Christmastime."

Isaac grinned and nodded. "It's kinda like the fall harvest, the way Ma cooks."

"But what about the presents and the toys that Saint Nicolas leaves?" Aimee asked.

Isaac's eyes widened and he looked at Albert, his face registering shock.

"Pa, whut's she talkin' 'bout?" his voice almost a whisper.

Aimee realized she had made an error. She looked at Albert and saw he was struggling to find the right words.

"I'm sure that you're moving here probably caused Saint Nicholas to be unable to find you," Aimee said quickly.

"Pa, who is she talking 'bout?" Isaac asked again.

"I'm 'fraid Saint Nicholas ain't ever knowed where we lived," Albert said.

"Well, I-I'm sure he knew that the owners of Deerborn Estates wouldn't allow you to keep his gifts," Aimee sputtered. She had opened a can of worms and now she had to make things right.

"Who is this Saint Nicholas? Why would he leave gifts?" Isaac insisted.

"Isaac, you have a wonderful surprise ahead of you." Aimee said softly, scooting her chair near him. "Your see, Saint Nicholas comes to the homes of good boys and girls during the dark of the night on Christmas Eve and leaves gifts as rewards for being obedient and helpful to their parents.

"He hasn't been able to come to your house because he was afraid someone would see him and find where you were hiding but now that you are safely living here, I know he'll feel comfortable visiting you on Christmas Eve, and leaving all you children presents."

Isaac had a wondrous look of amazement on his face but now a smile spread. "Pa is this true? Can that Saint Nicolas feller find our house and leave presents?"

Albert's grin matched Isaac's inch for inch. He nodded and looked gratefully at Aimee. "Yep, that's pretty much true, son. I don't think Mister Mack would tell a fib that big, do you?"

Still grinning, Isaac turn to Aimee. "I's didn't mean no disrespect, Mister Mack. I wuz jest trying to believe all I heerd."

"I understand, Isaac. I just wanted you to be prepared for the holiday of a lifetime."

"You sure that Saint Nick feller is a'comin'?" Isaac asked anxiously.

"I'm sure," Aimee said reassuringly.

"Even if it snows?"

"Isaac, that's enough," barked Albert. "Enough is enough. Mister Mack said he wuz a'comin' and if Mister Mack say he is, then he is."

"Especially if it snows," Aimee said, smiling. "He loves cold weather. I hear he lives at the top of the world where it snows all year 'round."

186

"Wow," was the final exclamation from Isaac, as he glanced quickly at his father.

Aimee turned to Albert. "I think if you and I sit down and work out a work schedule for the men, we can eliminate them all from having to come out in this weather every day. I know they have lots to do around their own place in the winter.

"The horses and cattle will need fresh hay a couple of times a week and the fences will need to be checked every once in a while. I'll need someone to ride the fence and look for wolves and coyotes regularly and also check the woods for traps. If we work out a schedule, the men should only have to continue to work a couple of days a week and rotate so they can take care of their chores at the camp and get the work done around here at the same time."

"That's mighty good of you, Mister Mack. I knows that they'll 'preciate that. We'll makes do just fine on a couple days work. I don't reckon most have spent any of what's they's made so far." Albert said.

"Albert, you all won't be getting shorted in your pay. You'll be getting full salary. When spring comes, planting starts, and all of you will be working longer days, and harder hours so on an average it works out evenly in the end. You tell the men that for me. The pay for each week will stay the same."

Albert looked at Aimee with wide eyes. "Mister Mack, that ain't right," he said. "We don't 'spect to get paid a day's wages for doing nothin'."

"Wait 'till spring, you'll remember those words."

Albert nodded and grinned. "Come on, Isaac, we best be headin' home or your ma will have my head."

"Tell Rose I said hello," Aimee called, as the pair went outside.

~ * ~

The next morning Aimee was surprised to see Lucas and Ernest riding side-by-side, talking and laughing. She met them in the yard and Ernest pulled out a letter and waved it toward Aimee, grinning and nodding.

"Just got a letter from Andrew, and he loved the drawing you made of your house. I've never seen him so excited. He can't wait to talk to you and get started on your house. With work being slow and people holding tight to their purse strings, prices for supplies are at an all-time low."

Aimee couldn't contain herself. She laughed and began clapping as she two-stepped around the yard. Both men looked at one another and then back at Aimee.

"It's alright, gentlemen. I'm just fine."

Lucas grinned and Ernest chuckled. "For a minute," Ernest said, "I thought you'd lost all your marbles."

"I just get tired of pretending all the time. It's nice to have some friends I can be myself around."

"Well then, have you decided about that idea I mentioned?" Ernest asked.

"Not only has she but I'm taking her to Charleston tomorrow to buy some clothes and a few of those thingys that ladies wear to poo-poo up their hair styles. I think she's planning on doing some Christmas shopping, too," Lucas said.

"Tomorrow? I'm ready today," Aimee said with a laugh.

"I guess we could go today, if you really want to."

"No time like the present," Ernest chuckled. "Besides, you might want to go before she changes her mind. If she's anything like my wife, she might decide to forget the whole thing by tomorrow."

Lucas thought for a few seconds. "Actually, today would be fine. I just need to tell my foreman, get the wagon, and throw a change of clothes in a bag and..."

"Change of clothes?" Aimee blurted out. "What's this about a change of clothes?"

"Aimee, a trip to Charleston will take one or two nights. Don't you remember the trip you took to get here? Think, my girl, this is not like running into Sycamore Grove," Ernest said gently.

Lucas swung into the saddle and smiled. "I'll be back in less than an hour. Can you be ready by then?"

"I've already told the Washington's that I was going tomorrow. They've finished for today and gone home. Ernest, could you wire about five hundred dollars to the bank there in Charleston for me?"

"I won't have to. I'm heading in to do some paperwork right now. If you two will stop by and tap on the back door on your way through town, I'll have the cash ready for you."

"Ernest, you're a wonderful friend. We'll be there. Run along now. I've got to get ready."

Ernest grinned at her bubbling joy and mounted his horse.

Soon Lucas was back, dressed for the trip, driving the wagon. Aimee left a note in the barn for Albert showing a picture of her and Lucas in a wagon going down the road, and then they were on their way.

The trip was smooth and easy, and there had been no more snow, leaving the temperature crisp and chilly but pleasant.

After stopping and collecting Aimee's money, the pair continued on to Dawson City where they spent the night.

Renting a small room each at the hotel located above the saloon, they met for supper downstairs. There was an excited air as patrons spoke happily about the new gin mill coming to town, and Aimee noticed the little town didn't look unkempt as it had a few months ago when she first saw it.

The next day at breakfast, Lucas seemed to have caught Aimee's enthusiastic attitude. He, too, made a shopping list for gift to send his family. And when they arrived in Charleston, Aimee felt giddy.

"Where to first, Mister Mack Kaymey?" Lucas asked.

"Do you know where your mother bought her hair pieces?"

"Why, Mister Kaymey, I believe I do. If not the exact location, I think I can get you close. All those shops are all in the same area. You might be able to find some new clothes for you... uh...

your sister. We can shop all week. We do have a change of clothes with us. We're not under any time schedule, are we?"

"Not really but we can't stay all week. It wouldn't be right. I need get back and besides, it just isn't proper for us to be spending time alone... Uh, together, that is, without a chaper-one."

"Mister Kaymey, who is going to care one way or another about two ranchers taking a trip into Charleston on a buying trip? You forget yourself, sir."

"Lucas," Aimee scolded, "there are several people who know the truth and what would they think?"

"Times are changing, Aimee. Besides, the people who know the truth know you, and they know this trip has a legitimate pur-pose. You spend too much time worrying about what people think."

"Let's find that store. We have a lot of shopping to do. True, we may not be able to finish it today but we are not, I re-peat, are not, staying any longer than necessary," Aimee stated, one hand on her hip.

"Whatever you say, my good sir." Lucas laughed.

"There," Aimee cried. "There's the wig shop." She jumped down from the wagon and suddenly stopped.

"Lucas, what do I do now?" she gasped. "I can't go in dressed like this and buy hair pieces."

"Sure you can. Look, we'll stop over there at the café first and have some coffee. You can make a list of what you want, take it in and pretend you are getting them for... uh... your mother, or sister, or heck, woman, use your imagination. Tell 'em they can't travel or something. I'm sure the shop owner doesn't give a hoot one way or another as long as a sale is made."

"That sounds reasonable."

Aimee sipped her coffee and described the pieces she wanted while Lucas wrote them out. "I'd write them, but I'd have to take off my gloves."

"I know, and they'd give you away."

190

"You want to come in with me?" Aimee asked, hopefully.

Lucas guffawed. "Not on your life. Never been in one of those places and I don't intend to start today. Here, take this list and get your do-dads. There's a shop down the street I want you to see."

Aimee looked at him curiously, nodded, and walked across the street.

When Aimee entered the store, she knew Lucas had been right when he said she had led a very sheltered life. She had always admired her mother's hair, and now she knew how her mother managed such beautiful styles. While gazing at the shelves of wooden heads adorned with masses of curls, braids, hairy little poofs and pomps, a tall elegantly dressed woman glided across the floor, all smiles and glowing with the prospect of a sale.

"Good morning, sir. How may I help you?" she asked warmly.

"My sister is unable to travel and she has given me this list to fill," Aimee said in her practiced gruff voice.

"Of course, sir. May I see the list?" The sales clerk examined the list carefully and looked at Aimee. "If you would look at this sample sheet, could you point out the color and texture of your sister's hair?"

Aimee stared at the sheet containing tiny ribbon-tied curls of various colors and textures of hair. The more she looked, the more confused she became.

"Actually, her hair is very similar to mine," she finally said.

"Do you mind?" the woman asked as she reached toward the hair sticking out the back of Aimee's hat.

Aimee stepped back and cocked her head at the sales clerk. "I beg you pardon?" she growled.

"No offense, sir," the woman explained. "If I could touch your hair, I could find styles on your list that would match your sister's hair almost perfectly."

"Of course," Aimee said quickly. "You must forgive me. This is new to me."

"I understand. Could you remove your hat, please?"

Aimee took off her hat and the woman fingered her hair briefly and then took off across the room to remove several heads from the shelves and placed them on a nearby table.

"I'll give you a selection of five or six to choose from. I'm sure you know your sister's preference better than I do but I am familiar with the latest styles. All of these," she said, "are of the finest quality and are seen at the most prestigious events."

Aimee walked past the table and wished she could take her gloves off and touch the shiny curls. "I'll take them all," she finally said.

"All?" the woman asked incredulously.

"Yes, I can't make a decision like this. I'll take them all."

"Do you want the head supports also?" The saleslady asked eagerly.

"Yes, just box them up. I'll pay you now and pick them up later."

"Thank you, sir, and Merry Christmas."

"Same to you." Aimee eyed the total, counted out the bills and walked out into the crisp air.

For a while, she had been so engrossed in the wig store she had forgotten the main reason for trip to Charleston. It was only when the saleswoman had wished her Merry Christmas did the excitement of the trip lighten her step.

She jammed a hand into her jacket pocket and took out the list of Christmas presents she had carefully made.

~ Seventeen ~

192

'Tis the Season

Lucas handed his list to the salesman at the Turner Emporium. Aimee clutched hers tightly in her gloved fist. The sign out front stated they carried the finest assortment of high quality merchandise and Aimee couldn't help but agree. However, she also realized that she certainly wasn't an expert at judging quality merchandise. She had to reflect again that, other than her time with Marcus, the fabric for her clothing had been selected by her mother, handmade by a seamstress, and most of the items needed were either delivered or purchased by someone else.

Although Aimee could have handed her list to the anxious and eager store manager, she preferred to select her items personally.

She chose two dresses, a fancy hat, gloves, and a handbag for Rose, a dress and perfumed soap for the other women at the camp. She had Lucas select a special rifle for Albert with a cleaning kit, and three good hunting rifles for the men at the camp to share. Choosing four toys each for the children at the camp, Aimee still couldn't decide what to buy to Isaac that would be special and personal. For Albert, she bought a new pipe and plenty of tobacco. The other men would receive knives to field dress game.

She bought a family Bible for Ernest and his family, and an assortment of books, tablets, pens and ink.

"Sir," she said softly to the attendant who was dutifully following her from place to place. "What do you suggest for a self-made man who can buy himself anything he wants?"

The young man frowned, thought for a moment and then smiled, "Perhaps a first edition book by his favorite author?"

"I don't know his favorite author," she replied.

"Oh," the young man looked down at the floor a moment. "And the price range?" he inquired nervously.

Aimee smiled. "He's just a friend. I do not want to make a statement, just a personal thank you for the kindness he's shown me."

"Ah," the young man nodded. "Perhaps a nice riding crop with a silver handle, inlaid with mother of pearl."

"May I see one, please?"

"Could you have his initials engraved in the silver on the handle?" she asked, as she examined the beautiful crop.

"Certainly. We'll have to send it out, but it can be ready within the hour."

"Please do and have it gift wrapped before I pick it up. Speaking of gift wrap, I'd like all the others gift wrapped and I have to list of names to put on them here," Aimee requested, as she handed the young man her list.

"This may take a while," the man said. "In fact, with as many gifts as you have, I could ask the ladies to work late tonight."

"No," Aimee said quickly. "I don't want anyone put out because of me. I can pick them up tomorrow afternoon, if that's enough time."

"They will be ready shortly after noon. Will that be acceptable?"

Aimee nodded and walked to the cashier where she paid for her purchases. She stepped outside, still wondering what gift to give a boy like Isaac and bring him hours of joy.

It was then that fate stepped in to change the lives of Aimee McKay and Isaac Washington.

"Mister Kaymey, what are you doing in Charleston?" A booming voice from behind Aimee stopped her in her tracks.

She spun around to see Marshal James Evans striding toward her.

Snugging up her gloves, Aimee turned up her collar, and yanked the wide brim of her hat down. "Marshall Evans. Still looking for that female terror?" Her voice dripping with sarcasm.

"Call me Jim. No, actually, there's been a turn of events in the case against the McKay woman. It's out of my hands now. I just came into town to finish up some reports, and ran into an old friend who came into town to sell a few of his hunting dogs."

Aimee wanted to ask about the turn of events he mentioned, but the mention of the dog diverted her attention. "Hunting dogs?" Aimee asked, a smile playing along the corners of her mouth. "What kind of dogs?"

"They're a new breed he just brought over from Europe, called English Setters. He's been breeding them for the past few years and swears they're the best hunting dogs he's ever seen."

"Where is he? I might be interested in getting a couple of those dogs," Aimee spoke deeply, and pulled her coat up around the bottom of her face, pretending to be cold.

"He has a wagon down near the dock. Oh, there's your friend, Lucas. Maybe he'd like to see the dogs, too?" Jim said waving at Lucas.

After a brief explanation to Lucas, they took off toward the dock. Jim found the wagon and Aimee was delighted to see several handsome leashed dogs, as their owner raved about their attributes to a small audience.

"Let me tell you, ladies and gentlemen, you are looking at a one of a kind animal. They are loyal to the point of obsession, superb watchdogs that will guard you and yours with their lives. And, my friend, I'm telling you right now that if you're looking for a hunting dog that will make your hunting trip as easy as a trip to the market, then these are the dogs for you." He paused only to suck in a deep breath and was off again.

"These here dogs can smell any bird in the vicinity. They'll swim the deepest water to retrieve a downed duck. They'll sniff out a bird and hold a frozen point until you shoot. They can tree a raccoon or squirrel, and track down a deer or elk, and I'm here tell, they've even treed a bear or two.

"I guarantee you that you won't be disappointed if you take home one of these beautiful, well trained, animals, they'll end up as a member of your family. You might even train them to cook the duck they drop in your hand."

"How much are they?" Aimee asked when he finally paused.

"Glad you asked," the man said loudly. "Sir, they'd be a bargain at half the price. These here fine animals been brought over the vast ocean from England and carry the finest hunting bloodlines known to man. I have been with these incredible hunting machines from birth and made sure these champion setters have had the best of care and was only fed the finest..."

"How much are they?" Aimee repeated. She was bored with his rhetoric and wanted to get down to business.

"Hey, Jackson, how ya doin'?" said James Evans loudly, as he stepped into the circle formed by the crowd and clapped his friend on the back.

"Jim, you old hound dog, I heard you were in these parts. Is this here feller a friend of yours?" he asked nodding toward Aimee.

"You could say that," replied the marshal. He looked o at Aimee with a sly grin on his face. "He's interested in your dogs."

"Mack, this here is Jackson Wheeler. Jackson has dealt in hunting dogs for several years now. He's good at his job and is as honest a man as I know. I can vouch for that."

"Well, now, friend, if you're a buddy of Jim's and it's a dog you want, you've come to the right place. I can make you a special price you can't say no to. Let me tell you... "

Aimee stepped forward and passed over the adult dogs to look over two small crates, peering in at young puppies about six to eight weeks old.

"Are these all from the same litter?" she asked.

"No sir, those on your left are from Queenie, tied there at the end. Those on your right are from Duchess, that handsome bitch lying under the wagon."

Lucas wandered around looking at the dogs, and stepped up behind Aimee, then leaned down close. In one crate, seven small puppies wiggled from nose to tail, squirming and yipping. In the second crate, most of the puppies were wrestling with each other, growling, chewing at an assortment of ears, legs, and tails that appeared and disappear as the squirming mass changed positions constantly.

"What are you doing, Mister McKay?" Lucas chuckled. "What do you need a dog for?"

"I was thinking perhaps I could solve two problems at once. One, Isaac would love these dogs and two, if they are as good a watch dog as he says, we might be able to flush out Bundy Owens and get rid of him once and for all."

"That's all well and good but do you realize how young they are and we don't know a single thing about training dogs?"

"That may be true but there is another way."

"Sir," she called to the man James had called, Jackson.

"Have you found the critter what stole your heart, mister," Jackson grinned.

"I have a few questions," she said in her growling, Mack voice.

"Shoot," said Wheeler. "I have most of the answers, as long as they pertain to the dogs."

"How difficult are they to train? Is it possible to find someone in the area to come to my house and train one? How much are they? Can you guarantee their success, and how would I go about establishing a breed line of my own?" Aimee listed her concerns to the astounded Jackson Wheeler.

"Well, sir, I don't think I've ever had anyone asked such great questions before. I like the way you think, sir, and I'm proud to say I've got all the answers for you. Would you like to sit down over here and we'll discuss it in detail?"

He motioned for Aimee to follow him and they walked around the back of the wagon where two chairs and a small table had been set up. After they sat down, Jackson Wheeler withdrew a packet of papers from the inside pocket of his coat.

"These are the certified papers for the line of dogs you see here, from their grandparents bred in England. I have a sire and a bitch from three separate lines and these dogs are the ones I breed. I usually keep the strongest male and female from each litter and start a new line from those.

"I'm only in these parts for a short while and usually don't encourage competition but since I'm based in Pennsylvania, I don't think you'll hurt my business."

"Mister Wheeler, you've misunderstood me." Aimee grinned. "I don't intend to breed and sell. I simply want to buy a couple of puppies and, perhaps, a male and female and perhaps produce a litter that might survive our area for future generations."

"Nothing would please me more, Mister Kaymey, than to know that some of Queenie and Duchess's offspring have made it across the country and are continuing the line."

"Mister Wheeler, before we discuss the other answers, I insist you tell me what you're asking for them. I don't mind buying something of value but I do not throw my money away."

Wheeler straightened up and leaned over. "I may sound like a ticket salesman at a circus side show but I assure you that when my name goes as guarantee against my dogs, you can take it to the bank that those dogs are worth the money. I have a reputation to protect and I stand behind my dogs for every penny I ask."

"The price, Mister Wheeler?"

"The pups sell for twenty-five dollars a male, thirty-five for a female, seventy-five for an adult male and one hundred for an adult female. The females I sell have already produced one litter. I insist on assuring the buyer, and myself, the bitch is capable of birthing a healthy litter before I sell them.

"The males also have sired a litter therefore, I can guarantee their ability. I can afford to sell them cheaper since I have already gotten paid for their offspring. As far as training, the adults are thoroughly trained and I'd suggest you take an adult and a young one and let the adult train the puppy. They learn a lot faster following in the footsteps of one of their own."

Satisfied, Aimee stood. "Then I guess I'd better pick out my dogs, don't you think?"

Wheeler looked at Lucas and James in astonishment. "Yes, sir, I guess you'd better."

Aimee walked around the end of the wagon and began to examine the beautiful dogs. "I take it Queenie and Duchess are not for sale," Aimee remarked.

"Sorry, but they are the Alpha dogs of my tribe." Jackson smiled. "I couldn't let them go for any price."

"I don't blame you." She knelt beside a sleek and gentle-eyed female who sat quietly and watched Aimee intently. "What is her name?"

"That's Gypsy. She's from the line of Lady Tasha. You have a good eye, sir. She's one of my finest. She'll do ya proud, I guarantee".

Aimee looked down the line. A young male who had been watching Aimee closely, mimicked the female she had chosen. He sat very still, his eyes never leaving her but his tail banged loudly on the packed ground behind him.

"This one?" Aimee ran a gloved hand over the dog's head. The dog stayed in a sitting position but began to tremble with excitement, and his tail was almost a blur as it swished back and forth.

"That's Duke, he's Queenie's son from her first litter last spring. He's a fine animal. Loyal, loving, and very energetic. I hope you've got plenty of room for a large run."

Aimee smiled. "I've got plenty of room. He'll have acres and acres to exercise in the likes of which he's never had before. I'll take Gypsy and Duke. I'd like to pick a couple of puppies."

Jackson's eyes grew even larger. "Puppies? Yes sir. Right over here." He rushed over to the two crates. "Each crate of puppies is from a separate litter of an entirely different lineage. Any two will make a handsome set of parents but I'm afraid you'll have to name them yourselves. We usually leave the puppy naming to their owner."

Aimee's interest had fired up the crowd to start looking at the dogs with a closer eye, and once she chose Duke, they began to move in and examine the animals first hand. Jackson's young fourteen-year-old son guided the crowd from dog to dog mimicking his father's barker-style speech.

Aimee leaned over the crates and watched the puppies play. Most ignored her with the exception of one who not only reached up for her but also began to yip for her attention. She reached down, scooped up the dog and cradled it in her arms, sneaking a peek to determine its gender.

The puppy began to nuzzle Aimee's neck and lick her chin.

"What a sweet little girl, you are," Aimee whispered. "You want to go home with me? I have a friend that would give you such a wonderful life."

She turned quickly and handed the squirming dog to Lucas who, startled, grabbed it and jerked his head back when the dog started licking his chin.

Aimee walked over to the other crate and watched the second group of puppies. Unlike the first bunch, all these lively pups were yipped, seeming to yell, "Pick me, pick me."

Smiling, she began to pet each one. They fought for her attention and one in particular struggled up the side of the crate to escape the madness. Aimee grabbed him as he reached the top.

"If you want to get at me that badly, come on little feller." She checked to make sure he was indeed a feller, and once she was satisfied, she turned to Lucas.

"That's it. I'm ready to go home now. We need to find crates big enough for the dogs, pick up the gifts and hairpieces, and then I want to get on the road."

She went Jackson Wheeler and after a short conversation, handed him the correct amount of money, waited for a receipt, and then joined Lucas as he and Jackson's son labeled the dogs she had chosen and placed them each in their own crate.

"Mister Wheeler, we have some merchandise to load up, and we'll be back after lunch to pick up the dogs," Lucas said. He turned to Aimee and leaned in close.

"Now, did you find out what they eat and how often you feed them and did you ask what they..."

"Mister Wheeler gave me a sheet of paper with all the information I need for the dogs," Aimee said. "Don't you have any faith in my abilities?" She grinned at the sheepish look on his face.

"Sorry, I don't know anything about them but they are beautiful creatures."

"Yes, they are and I think Isaac will be thrilled. Let's finish up and get out of here."

"Don't you want to shop some more? How often do you get a chance to spend time in the big city?" Lucas asked with a grin.

"No more shopping. I guess I am just a small town gir... guy at heart but I do need a favor. When we go back to pick up our packages at the Emporium, I need you to purchase plenty of ammunition for the men at the camp. You may need to show them how to care for it and some may need some instructions on how to use it. I promised them I'd buy the guns and ammo but I didn't think it would make Sycamore Grove happy to know that several slaves in the area had firearms. Though it's really none of their business."

"I will, if you buy yourself a good rifle. You're out there all alone and with the unrest about slavery from the North, you need to protect yourself," Lucas said sternly.

"Yes, you're right. However, I will need some practice. When I was a girl, Papa taught me how to shoot a rifle and I was pretty good if I do say so myself. It got to be a competition between my brother and me, but it's been a long time. I have a pistol, but I'm not very comfortable using it. Can you help me with that?"

"No problem, my dear friend. If you learn to handle a rifle then I will feel better, and you do need practice with a pistol."

Within three hours, they purchased three rifles and ammunition, loaded the presents and hairpieces, bought the dog food,
and Aimee picked up several other items and stuffed them in the
wagon. Lucas stored his gifts under the seat and after picking up a
loaf of bread, a chunk of cheese, and several slices of ham, they
left the bustling city of Charleston.

Lucas noticed a change in Aimee as soon as the city was behind them. She was silent most of the ride to their first campsite,
only answering when absolutely necessary. She seemed lost in
thought and Lucas didn't know what to say to make things more
comfortable.

They ate a light supper before going to bed, and Lucas
slept lightly listening to Aimee tossing and turning most of the
night. It seemed like he had just fallen asleep when he was jolted
awake by a horse whinnying. He jerked awake and breathed a sigh
of relief when he saw Aimee hand feeding her favorite riding
steed.

Coffee perked and ham sizzled in the pan. Slices of fresh
bread lay on plates and eggs were ready.

"When did you buy all this?" Lucas asked.

"I told the merchant to bag them up while you were helping to load the wagon. I knew after a sparse supper, you'd be hungry this morning. I wanted to get an early start, so I can be in my
own bed tonight."

"That means we won't be getting to Sycamore Grove until
nearly midnight."

"That's fine with me as long as I wake up at Eagle Creek."

"I heard that's what it was called. I thought maybe you'd
change the name to something personal."

"I thought about it, and actually Eagle Creek fits it about
as well as any name I could think of. After all, it is home to the
eagles that fly, and now it's home to the many golden eagles I
have hidden around the place."

"Aimee McKay, you can't be serious. I understood you put
your gold in the bank. If any rumor get started that there's gold

buried there, the scum of the earth will start creeping around and all of you will be in mortal danger. There are people who'll cut a person's throat for fifty cents. They'll slaughter everyone on this land for what they only *think* might be there."

"You are the only person who knows, Lucas. The only one. I don't know why I told you. It's just that sometimes you need to trust and believe that... you know, to have a friend. I can't tell Rose or Albert. It wouldn't be fair to burden them. They would make it their personal goal to have someone guard me every minute. That in itself would be like posting it on the front page of the Sycamore Press."

"I'm glad you told me. Maybe together we can decide how to handle it."

"I've already decided what to do with it. Later on, we'll talk about my idea. I do need your advice on who to get to help me."

"It's a deal."

~ Eighteen ~
Birth of a House

On Christmas morning, with the turkey baking in the oven and the side dishes bubbling on the stovetop, Aimee looked around her little house, pleased with what she saw. The bed had been removed to the barn the day before and Aimee slept on a pallet the previous night. George and Dewey had finished four stools and a bench several days earlier and sanded them smooth. Aimee baked a plum cake from a recipe sent from Ernest's wife. Martha had volunteered to bake it thinking Aimee was a man but Aimee insisted she wanted to attempt it herself. It smelled good and Aimee just prayed it tasted as good as good as it smelled. She had also baked a peach pie from some home canned peaches bought at the general store. Myrna, the cook from her childhood, had taught Aimee many cooking secrets.

Albert, Rose, Isaac, his uncle, Anton, grandmother, Allie, and new baby sister arrived shortly before noon, bearing a basket filled with packages.

Aimee mixed up a pot of rum, cinnamon, brown sugar, with slices of oranges floating on the top. She also fixed a pan of hot chocolate. The aroma filled the small house with a delicious smell and the meal was greeted with ooh's and ah's. When they were all seated, Aimee and her guests held hands and gave thanks for their bounty and for the glory of the birth of the Baby Jesus.

Chatter began as soon as the first bowl was passed and murmured compliments filled the room as each of Aimee's friends filled their plates over again. A smile of triumph lit her face. Soon, chairs were pushed from the table and empty plates filled the dishpan. The fire blazed, the rum toddies were sipped, and Isaac blew gently on his hot chocolate while admiring the tiny tree Aimee had gaily decorated.

"You know something, Isaac?" Aimee asked softly. "A strange thing happened last night."

"What?" Isaac asked, his eyes growing large at the mysterious sound of her voice.

"I had gone to bed when there was a weird ringing sound outside. The horses were whinnying, the cows were restless, and the chickens started clucking loudly but when I went outside to check, all was quiet. I checked the barn, behind the house, and even walked to the drive but I didn't see a thing."

"What does you think it wuz?" The boy asked, frozen in place.

"I wasn't sure but when I came back in the house, it seemed to me that there were a lot more presents under the tree than there were before I left. I can't help think perhaps it was Saint Nicolas."

"Wha... " Isaac jerked his head toward the tree and peered around.

"I think it's time to see what's under there. Do you think you can make out everybody's name? You have been practicing your letters, haven't you?"

A grin spread across the child's face as he hurriedly sipped his chocolate. "Yas suh, I has... have. I think I kin makes 'em out."

The gifts of the dresses found their way to Rose and Allie. Aimee also surprised each woman with lovely hair combs. She gave Anton the pipe, tobacco, and a hunting knife. There was a heavy coat and hat for Isaac and Albert was speechless when he unwrapped his pipe, rifle, and several boxes of ammunition. Aimee received several hand-stitched handkerchief and aprons, which Isaac said that no man should ever have to wear, and a beautiful quilt Rose and her mother made together.

Finally, there was only one small box left. It was tied to a limb of the tree. Aimee rose, untied the ribbon, and turned to Isaac.

"This must have been left by Saint Nicolas. It has your name on it."

He carefully opened the ribbon and unfolded the paper.

"Read it out loud, son," said Albert.

"It says, l-lo-ok in the cr-ate jest ins-si-de the b-a-rn. Take g-oo-d c-are of what you f-find. Mer-ry Chr-is-t-mas." He turned toward his father. "Can I go look, can I? Huh, Pa?" He twisted back and forth between Aimee and Albert.

"Go." Aimee laughed.

A knock on the door announced Lucas's arrival. He too, bought gifts for Albert's family. Ribbons and brushes for the la-dies, a field dressing knife for Albert, a warm scarf and a sharpen-ing stone for Anton, and a slingshot for Isaac.

"I thought you were coming for dinner?" Aimee asked.

"I was but one of my mares decided to drop her foal on Christmas day, can you believe it? She seemed a little nervous and I just couldn't leave her alone."

Aimee smiled. "I would have done the same. Let me fix you a plate. There's plenty left over. In fact, I'll be eating on this for two or three days."

"That will be great. I'm starving."

He took the plate Aimee mounded with food and looked at her curiously.

"Have you told them the news, yet, Mack?" Lucas asked grinning.

"What news?" Rose asked, her eyebrows rising slightly.

Aimee looked at Lucas questioningly.

"You know, Mack," Lucan said slyly, "the news about your sister coming to visit."

Rose almost choked on her toddy. Albert looked stunned, while Allie clapped her hands.

"That's jest whut you needs, Mister Mack, a woman to takes care of things. Men thinks they's takes care of us women but they'd jest be lost without us. Ain't that right, Albert?" Allie said as she reached over and slapped Albert's knee.

"Yassum, Mother Allie, you sure is right on that one but I don't believes I ever heard you mention a sister, Mister Mack." He spoke slowly turning his head toward his wife.

"Well, uh, as I told Isaac, I've been away from home a long

time. I just haven't settled any one place long enough to recon-
nect with them.

She turned to Lucas, giving him a stern stare. "I didn't realize you were so interested in my personal life, Lucas."

Lucas'ss smile wavered and then disappeared. "I'm sorry if
I spilled the beans. With her arrival so imminent, I thought you
might want Rose and the others to know about her visit."

"This is so exciting, don't you think so, Rose? Mister Mack,
when is she arriving? Where is she to stay? You ain't got no room
here. Where's you goin' to puts her?" Allie rose and began to look
around the tiny cabin.

"Mama, apparently Mister Mack done made his plans concerning his sister, ain't that right, Mister Mack? I guess he don't
need no help." Rose looked scathingly at Aimee.

Aimee realized she should have told Rose her plans to appear as her sister. Aimee could see by Rose's demeanor her
friend's feelings were deeply hurt.

"Her visit was a spur of the moment decision. Rose, I would
have told you all about my sister's visit, except with the arrival of
your new baby, the holiday shopping, and all the preparation of
winter, it just skipped my mind."

"And when wuz you gonna to tell me?" Rose scowled.

"Really soon, I assure you," Aimee insisted.

"Rose Washington, I never seed you be so rude to somebody a'fore. Why should Mister Mack tell you about his sister? It
ain't like he's your family, young lady," Allie snapped angrily.

"No, Miss Allie, Rose is absolutely right. She is in charge of
my house now, and she has every right to know what is going on. I
should have told her sooner but Rose, you must understand, I was
going to tell you. I swear."

Thankfully, Isaac came inside with an armful of pups. "Mister Mack, are... are these... m-mine?" he asked in disbelief.
"They w-wuz in the crates and the card did s-say my gift wuz in
the crates, didn't it?" Aimee rose and took one of the struggling
pups from Isaac's tight grip.

"Yes, son, they are both yours. I found them and a couple of grown dogs. They're behind the barn. There was a note telling me that the grown dogs were mine and the pups were yours. They're hunting dogs and the note said the older ones will help train the pups."

"Wh-what's their names?"

"That's up to you. The big dogs had a tag that said Gypsy and Duke but you're going to have to name yours. I guess Saint Nicholas wants all puppies to be named by their owners."

"Pa, didja see? Didja see whut that Saint Nicolas done gone and got me?" Isaac's eyes shined with joy and Albert's eyes filled with tears of joy for his son's happiness.

"Yes, son, I sees. Them is fine huntin' dogs. I can tell that this time next year, our smoke house will be full."

"You bet it will, Pa. I'll work with them every day, I promise."

Putting the pups down, Isaac sat on the floor and watched them. "This one I's a'gonna call Merlin. You know, like that magic feller in the story you read me, Mister Mack? And this one, I reckon her name is Lady. Lady and Merlin. You like them names, Pa?"

"Those... "Aimee corrected, "those names, not them names."

"Those names," Isaac repeated sheepishly. "Do you like those names, Pa?"

"I surely do like them... uh, those names jest fine, son," Albert said. "Where'd you gets them... uh, those names?"

Isaac grinned and glanced at Aimee. "They're from a book Mister Mack read one day 'bout a wizard, that's a magic man, and a king and his queen."

"Kin I go see them other dogs, Mister Mack? Did you say they wuz in the barn?"

"Sure you can. Take the puppies with you. I'm sure they'll all enjoy being together. I'm counting on you to take Gypsy and Duke out on a daily run. You will, won't you, Isaac?"

"I surely will, Mister Mack... ever single day, I promise."

"Oh, Lordy, I almost forgot," Lucas said, as he jumped up and went out the door with Isaac.

A few seconds later, he returned with a letter in his hand that he held out to Aimee.

"I ran into town yesterday and Ernest had that letter for you, so I told him I was coming out today and would be happy to deliver it for him."

Aimee grabbed the letter, pried the wax seal loose, and lifted the top flap of the envelope.

Her eyes quickly scanned across each line and as she read, a smile appeared and spread across her face.

She looked up, her eyes shining. "It's from the architects. They've accepted my drawing and have agreed to build my house," she gasped.

"That's wonderful," Rose said, rushing to Aimee's side.

"That's not all." Aimee smiled. "I wasn't sure how to tell you but I've also made arrangements to have all the buildings at the camp remodeled and upgraded."

Rose squealed. Allie looked confused. "What are you saying?" Allie's voice dropped to a whisper.

"When I sent my sketch in, I included a rough sketch of the campsite and the buildings. I told them I wanted all the houses upgraded and modernized. Actually, we are going to discard the lean-tos and replace them with cabins.
"It's all included in his bid here and there's a note from Ernest that says the bid is way below normal. Construction is a bit slow now, so I've picked a grand time to get started."

"When are you getting started?" Rose asked, her voice sounding shocked from the news.

"I didn't think they would start until spring but from what they say in the letter here," Aimee paused and took a deep breath, "they want to start immediately."

"What about the cold and wet?" Albert asked. "Won't that slow them up?"

"I don't think they have a lot of building going on right now and they're rather anxious to work," Aimee explained. "I must say I'm thrilled that they want to start now. Actually, once I made up my mind to build, I was ready yesterday."

"With the weather so cold and nasty, how are we going to live while they're a'workin' on our house?" Allie asked.

Albert gave a harsh laugh. "Mama Al, does you remember how we wuz livin' when we first found this place? All us us wuz crowded under a coupla of pieces of old rusty tin."

"Yes, Mama," scolded Rose. "Whut we have now ain't nothing compared to that first winter. Whut we'll do is each of us will takes in a family under our roof until their house gits finished and then they'll do the same for us."

Allie looked sheepish. "I didn't mean to sound ungrateful and complaining. This is a wonderful thing you're a'doin' Mister Mack. We'll work it all out. Don't you worry."

Aimee smiled gently. "After what you all have been through, I don't worry about you at all. I just want to make your life easier. Any change is stressful, I realize that, believe me. There are always sacrifices to make now and then. I'll make sure they work as quickly and as efficiently as possible so you can get back to your normal life."

"We've all been blessed this Christmas," Rose said softly. "Albert, let's help Mister Mack clean up and get back home. We'll take care of the dishes, while you and Anton git Mister Mack's bed back inside and put it back together. The baby's getting' fussy and I'm a little tired. I'm sure Mister Mack and Mister Lucas have things to talk about with the news of the builders and all."

"No need to help clean up. I've got everything organized and it won't take any time at all. Lucas will be happy to help, won't you Lucas? You all load up the wagon and get yourselves home for a nice rest.

"Rose, there is a box in the barn with dresses for the other ladies at the camp and Albert, there is a crate by the box of dresses. That crate is for the men. It's the rifles I promised. There is also a sack of ammunition that goes with it."

Albert stood very still and Aimee could see his eyes begin to glisten. "Mister Mack, I... uh..."

"Albert, since I haven't had much hunting experience maybe you all can bring me a chunk of venison or ham now and then to put in my smokehouse? I really would appreciate it," Aimee said, saving Albert from stumbling for words of thanks.

"We'll have that there smokehouse overflowing in no time," Albert said gruffly. "You jest watch and see." He grabbed up some of the boxes Rose had ready and started for the wagon. "We is gonna put that there bed up, though," he insisted, and left before Aimee could protest.

"We're to know what a normal life is," Rose smiled. "There was a time when I wasn't sure that would ever happen. You know, we even talked about moving out west for a spell. Of course, that was long 'fore you came. Thank you."

"Thank the Lord, Rose. If I hadn't bought that ticket for that fateful voyage, if a hurricane hadn't hit, if I had met that wonderful gentleman, Abram Ginsberg, if the ship hadn't sank, if I hadn't been saved... " Aimee's voice trailed off.

Rose threw her arms around Aimee and hugged her tight. "I'm so glad you were."

"Rose," her mother yelped, "what would Albert say? Mind your place, girl."

"Sorry," Rose said and grinned, stepping back, winking at Aimee. "I just got so carried away with the holiday season. Merry Christmas, Mister Mack. I'll be over soon to get your house in order. Mama, if you'll get the baby ready to travel I'll help Albert and Isaac load up the wagons.

"I'll be over to clean this house in a couple of days, Mister Mack. I think I needs to have a talk with Mama and share some facts with her iffen you doesn't mind."

"That's fine, Rose, just fine. I think it's about time Miss Al-lie knows, too. It just might come in handy someday." Aimee returned the grin and wink.

After putting the leftovers away and washing dishes, Aimee and Lucas poured themselves a fresh cup of coffee. Lucas sat down at the table and Aimee went to a shelf and retrieved the gift she bought in Charleston.

"Here," she said softly, as she thrust the brown wrapped package toward Lucas. "Merry Christmas. This is just a little appreciation for your friendship and your support."

"Why, Mister McKay," Lucas said, smiling. "That is a very thoughtful gesture." He took the parcel and slowly untied the string and unfolded the paper.

His eyes widened at the sight of the silver handled riding crop with the intricate engraving of his initials.

"Aimee," he whispered as he examined it in detail. "This is absolutely beautiful. I've never had a gift I've admired more than this."

Aimee's face flushed at his words. "I'm glad you like it. I wanted something to show you how much you, well, how much I enjoy having you as a trusted friend and neighbor."

Lucas rose and went to his coat hanging on the hook by the door. He reached into pocket and pull out a small, gaily wrapped box.

"I, too, know how to say things with gifts," he said. "Hope this says what I'm thinking." He took Aimee's hand and placed the small box in her palm.

Aimee pulled loose the end of the shiny red bow, releasing the ribbon and watched the paper fall away from the velvet box.

"Lucas, I...," she stammered, unsure how to react.

"For heaven's sake, Aimee, open it before you say anything."

Aimee opened the soft lid and gasped at the delicate onyx and ivory cameo necklace hanging from a thin gold chain.

"Lucas, I love it. It's the loveliest thing I've ever seen. You shouldn't have. I've done nothing but create problems for you."

"Nothing I can't handle, my dear Aimee. I feel honored that you feel you can rely on me. You can, you know, rely on me, that is. I'm here for you. I'll always be here for you," he said with a catch in his voice.

"Thank you, Lucas. I'll treasure this for the rest of my life."

A knock on the door broke the tension. Lucas opened the door and stood back as Anton and Albert toted in Aimee's bed. Another trip produced the mattress and Aimee busied herself making up the bed. With laughter and handshakes, Albert and Anton left to join the women and make the short trip back to the camp.

Aimee and Lucas sat back down at the table, with another cup of coffee.

"Merry Christmas, Aimee. It's been an unforgettable day, but I must get home and check on the new colt. The riding crop is magnificent."

"Merry Christmas, yourself. You didn't do so badly with the necklace, either. I'll walk you out."

Aimee shivered as Lucas swung up into the saddle.

"I can't believe that Harmon fellow is starting construction in this weather," Lucas said, looking around.

"Times are hard nowadays and men need work. I'm sure they are all anxious to get started. I'll fix up the barn with some cots and plenty of blankets. Albert can hook up an old wood stove in there and some of the men can stay there if they need to and at least get in from the cold and have some hot coffee and a bowl of stew to stay warm."

~ * ~

Soon the holidays faded, they prepared room in the barn for the workers, and after several communications back and forth, the crew began to arrive. Andrew Harmon arrived a few days earlier and stayed with Ernest and his family. Aimee found him to be

213

intelligent, charming, and anxious to build the home of her dreams.

There was only one thing that put a kink in Aimee's plans. Andrew wanted to completely raze her little cabin, and give her a large, roomy basement over which he wanted to construct her house.

Aimee hated to demolish the cabin. It had been the site of her first new beginning, her first Christmas gathering, and had housed the bed where she first dreamed of her new life. She knew in her heart that it had to go but when Andrew swept his arm across the site, explaining what he wanted to do, Aimee cringed at the thought of destroying her cabin.

The men drank coffee while waiting for Andrew and his brother to arrive with tools and more workers. Aimee dressed warmly and walked into the woods, deep in thought.

With her head down and her gloved hands thrust deep in her coat pockets, she wandered along the path. Pausing by the little waterfall, she sat on a log and watched the colorful leaves swirl in the icy water.

"Aimee?" said a voice from the woods.

Alarmed, she jumped up and peered through the trees to see Lucas making his way through the damp underbrush.

"What are you doing out here? Are you moping? I thought you'd be ecstatic about the new house?"

"I was... I am..." She shook her head and smiled. "Andrew, that is, Mister Harmon, wants to demolished the cabin and start from scratch. He thinks I need a cellar right where the cabin is and I... well, I just hate to see it go. It was, after all, my very first house."

"But Aimee..."

"I know. He's right of course. Down deep I knew this would happen but I just..." tears welled and she grinned ruefully.

"But Aimee..."

214

"I know. I'm acting like such a baby. I don't know what came over me. Of course, the cabin will have to go. I don't know what I was thinking."

"Hush a minute." He joined Aimee on the log and slipped his arm around her, pulling her close. "You're not acting like a baby. You're acting like a woman who's about to lose something very dear to her. But, please, don't cry. I can't take it when you cry. I think I may have a solution."

Aimee looked at Lucas in wonder. Her eyes wide with hope.

"Why don't you have them dismantle the cabin and move it somewhere special? You know, a place where you can go to reflect later on in life when you need a quiet place to meditate. It can be your own little secret hide-a-way."

"Oh, Lucas, that's a brilliant idea. I love you."

Stunned at her words, she jerked back and jumped to her feet, dropping her eyes to the ground.

When she was able to make herself look at Lucas, who hadn't moved, she smiled.

Lucas gazed at her as no man ever had. His hand rested on the log where it had fallen when she jumped up and he extended his other hand toward her, palm up.

"I love you, too. You know that, don't you? Don't you, Aimee?"

"I... I... " Her expression resembled a frightened deer. "I know how you make me feel when I'm around you but I won't dare..."

"Please dare, Aimee. I beg of you, please dare. I've never been able to get you out of my mind since I first saw you on the ship."

"But I tried to dress as plain and unattractive as I could, how could you have..."

"It was those beautiful, deep, sorrowful eyes. That shy smile or maybe it was that little turned up nose, or it could have been..." Lucas stood and drew her to him, cupping her chin in his hand and turning her face upward.

"Your clothes, hairdo, and nervous shyness just couldn't hide that special something about you. My every waking moment was of you. I just couldn't forget you. I started searching for you the moment I reached land. Even Mack Kaymey reminded me of you." He laughed. "Imagine that."

"I want to take care of you, Aimee. I want to give you the stars and the moon..."

A look of horror suddenly spread over Aimee's face. Her arms stiffened. She pushed away from Lucas, stumbled, and threw her hands out in a protective gesture. Her mouth worked soundlessly as she turned and fled through the forest, leaving Lucas stunned.

When he was able to speak, he called out. "Aimee, what did I say? Aimee, come back." However, she was gone.

~ * ~

Lucas headed back home, trying to figure out what happened. He had been so engrossed in the moment, so swept up in the happiness of Aimee's words, that he couldn't recall his exact words. It must have been something he said, although he couldn't recall anything other than professing his love for her.

A thought suddenly struck him. What if she had realized that her feelings for him were just gratitude, not genuine affection or love? He needed to think and he couldn't ignore what happened. Taking long strides, Lucas went home to figure out what he would do next.

~ Nineteen ~
Discovery

The shock of hearing those words from Lucas sent Aimee into a shock. Marcus Alexander had said those very same words to her a lifetime ago. Those words had seduced her into a nightmare that she almost didn't survive. Did all men use the same line? How could she have been so blind? They were all alike. They used beautiful words to turn a girl's head and warm her heart and then...

Blinded by tears she almost collided with Andrew Harmon, who was sighting through a strange contraption at a man across the yard who held a pole.

"Whoa there, Mister Kaymey. Are you alright?" he asked, as he grabbed her arms to keep her balance.

"Ah, yes, I ran into a swarm of gnats that flew into my eyes. I just need to wash them out. Excuse me." Aimee lied and rushed into the house.

Rose stood at the stove stirring a large pot of chicken stew, and started when Aimee flew through the door, securing it firmly behind her.

"Lordy girl, what's the matter? Are you hurt?"

"No, Rose, I'm fine. I just had a valuable lesson, that's all."

She splashed water over her face and patted her flaming cheeks with a towel. Pulling her hat down over her eyes, she turned and headed back out.

"Mister Harmon?" She called to the architect. "I've made a decision. I'm going to move into town and I want you to have the cabin dismantled and moved to the edge of the woods at the far end of the back pasture. I'll have my men store the furniture and other items in the loft of the barn until you have it rebuilt. I don't want it destroyed, it has a great deal of sentimental value to me."

"Please, Mister Kaymey, call me Andrew, we're going to be seeing quite a lot of each other over the next few months. I'll have my crew help your men store your things. We'll have the cabin moved and restored in a week's time."

"Good, Andrew, and call me Mack," Aimee said gruffly. "I'm going to pack my things for town. I'll be leaving in the morning."

After Rose heard Aimee's decision, she called to Albert, and with George and Dewey's help, they boxed all the food items in the cabin and Rose helped Aimee pack up the things to take into town with her.

That night Aimee tossed, turned, cried, and finally drifted off into a restless sleep. The faces of Marcus and Lucas floated hazily before her, each pleading with her, promising her the stars and moon that circled around her head.

She rose early and although she still felt tired and exhausted, she dressed and made ready to leave for town before the first carpenter awoke. By the time Albert arrived, the men loaded the wagon and began transferring the few pieces of furniture to the barn. Aimee waited anxiously to leave and apparently, the carpenters were ready to dismantle the cabin.

~ * ~

Lucas worked around his place for several days before he worked up the courage to ride over to Aimee's place. He wanted to make sure she recovered from whatever he said to upset her. He wasn't surprised that the cabin was gone, and was pleased she had taken his advice about moving it. There were still a few piles here and there waiting for the men to load and carry them to the

218

backfield but overall, the spot where the building once stood was bare.

George and Dewey, along with a couple of other workers raked away the debris in order to start digging for the basement. Lucas did not see Rose anywhere and the only response he could get from the workers was that she moved into town.

Having planned to ask Aimee to stay at his place until the men rebuilt the cabin, he cursed his bad timing. He had worker's quarters behind his house and planned to stay there while until Aimee's new home was ready. He hoped that whatever caused her to flee from him that day had faded, and she would be receptive to his company. Even though she hadn't bothered to tell him she was moving into the hotel in town, he still hoped she would see him.

Rose, he thought. Rose would know. He knew how close the two women were, and surely Aimee would have confided in Rose. He simply couldn't stand not knowing what he had done or what came over Aimee. He wasn't going to lose her now - he couldn't, especially after all she had gone through.

Even though she told him about her life with Marcus Alexander, along with the cruelty and pain she suffered, he knew there was no way to express a hurt that deep, or the pain and disillusionment that went with that type of betrayal.

That Alexander creep had almost destroyed her and yet, she somehow survived, although damaged and weakened in her belief in love and trust of men. He had broken her spirit and now she was on the mend. Alexander had probably told her all the things Lucas had, and then he remembered his own words. "I want to give you the stars and the moon." No, surely she hadn't heard those words from Alexander? He shook his head angrily.

What made him think his words were original? He had never been in love before. He didn't need to find Rose now. He knew. However, even that revelation didn't solve the problem. How was he ever going to convince Aimee that he meant those words sincerely? Especially when there was a chance she had heard those same words before and they resulted in nothing but lies, deceit, physical abuse, mental pain, and betrayal? Could he ever make amends? Right now, he wasn't sure. The look on her face had been pure terror.

Lucas headed toward the road and when he reached the gates of Eagle Creek, he paused. Wrestling with his conscience for a few seconds, he turned the horse toward town at a full gallop.

Reaching the edge of town, Lucas slowed his mount to a walk. Trying to look relaxed and unconcerned, he rode up to the hotel, dismounted and wrapped the reins around the rail. He took a deep breath and tried to think of what he was going to say to Aimee. There would be no privacy and she would still be Mack Kaymey, so this wasn't going to be easy.

He brushed himself off, adjusted his hat, and straightened his coat. Holding his head high and forcing a bright smile, he pushed the hotel door opened and headed for the desk. While his opening words were churning in his head, a sharp voice broke his reverie.

"What are you doing here?"

He turned awkwardly and found himself looking into the flashing green eyes of the woman he came to see. Dressed in a heavy wool suit, a muffler wrapped around her neck and chin, and her hat pulled low, Aimee stood warily, her hand on one hip.

Suddenly his mind went blank. Those shamrock green eyes glaring at him numbed his mind. He reached for her and stiffened when she stepped back.

"Excuse me, I am meeting someone for breakfast," she stated. Her voice cold and flat, as she brushed past him and headed for the dining room.

"Aim... Mack, I need to discuss something with you," he pleaded. "It's very important."

Aimee stopped short and turned. "You'll have to make an appointment, Mister Chase. I'm building a new house, as you well know, and I don't having any time to spare. I'm a very busy man. If it's financial, or concerns our real estate boundaries, you can see my banker; if it's about the farm, you need to talk to Albert. If it's personal, you'll just have to wait until I have a free moment and. And I don't know when that will be. You must excuse me now, I'm running late." She spun and stomped into the dining room where she joined a tall, thin stranger who appeared to be waiting for her.

Lucas stood stunned as he watched Aimee shake hands with her breakfast companion and place an order with the hovering waiter.

It was no secret, as small towns often know more than they should about their citizens, that Mack Kaymey had money. No one knew the true extent of his wealth, but as the supplies for his house arrived and were loaded and carried up to Eagle Creek; tongues had started wagging and wouldn't stop. Obviously, the townsfolk saw no expense spared for the new house and were all speculating on just how rich Kaymey was.

As tempted as Lucas was to stay around and see if Aimee might need some protection or support, he knew Mack Kaymey was perfectly safe in a public dining room of the popular hotel. Still, his longing to be someone she leaned on, depended on, and needed haunted him as he left the hotel.

He heard the screen door of the hotel bang loudly behind him, and turned to see Aimee stomping angrily down the wooden sidewalk, muttering to herself. Before he could react, the man she met inside came out and trotted off after Aimee, trying to shove a handful of papers into a folder.

"Mister Kaymey, please, be reasonable," he shouted after Aimee. "This is a buy of a lifetime and it's in your best interest. Times are changing now and the South must stay true to its traditions. This is the time to act. You must believe me."

Aimee quickened her pace and the man ran hard to catch up with her.

Lucas leaped onto the sidewalk and raced along the wooden planks. The man quickened his step behind Aimee, caught up with her, reached out and grabbed her sleeve at the elbow. At the speed she was traveling, being stopped so suddenly caused her to lose her balance. She wavered, swayed, and toppled backward.

Lucas watched as Aimee fell, and saw shock on the man's face as he tried to prevent her fall. Aimee stumbled back, her arms wind milling as she tried to regain her balance. Her boot heel slipped off the edge of the sidewalk plank, and she flew backward into the railing. The horses tried to pull away, rearing and kicking in fear.

The man stood frozen as Lucas passed him, shoving him out of the way. Quickly slipping one arm under Aimee's shoulder and the other under her legs, Lucas scooped her up.

"The doctor?" Lucas yelled. "Where's the doctor?"

Several people had crowded around curiously and one woman pointed across the street.

Lucas took off running, searching the storefronts for some type of sign designating the office. When he reached the other side, he saw a small wooden board at the corner near the alley with the medical insignia on it and an arrow slanting upward. He raced around the corner, spotted the steps, and hurried up two at a time, kicking open the door when he reached the landing.

A tiny, gray haired woman quickly stood, when she saw Lucas standing in the doorway.

The doctor?" he panted. "Is the doctor in?"

She nodded stupidly and jerked her head toward the back. Lucas passed her and opened his hand under Aimee's legs, twisted the knob, and burst into the room. A small boy sat on the table as the doctor put the last piece of tape across a square bandage on his knee.

"She fell... I mean... he fell and struck his head on the rail. I think..." Lucas felt his throat close up. He swallowed and dropped his head as tears filled his eyes.

"Run on, Tommy, your knee will be fine. Just watch where you're going next time." The doctor muttered as he lifted the boy to the floor and shoved him out the door.

222

"Here, lay your friend here. Let's have a look at him."

The doctor began to check Aimee's eyes and laid his head on her chest to listen to her heartbeat. A puzzled look crossed his face and he glanced at Lucas. He began to slip off her coat, remove her tie, and loosed the collar of her shirt. He slid his hand down the front of the shirt and jerked it back, stiffening and glaring at Lucas.

"Is this some kind of joke?" he snarled.

Before Lucas could answer the door flew opened and Ernest Gaines came bursting in. He saw the expression on the doctor's face and turned to Lucas. "Son, would you step out just one moment, please. I need to talk to Norman for a minute while he's examining Mister Kaymey."

"You don't understand, sir, Mack is..." Lucas began.

"I know, son, remember, I know. We can trust Norman here but I think he needs a few words of explanation that will ease his mind."

Lucas nodded, his eyes never leaving Aimee's unconscious figure.

As soon as Lucas left, Ernest leaned over. "I guess you know by now that Mack Kaymey is a woman. She is a dear friend of mine, and this is a very delicate situation. I'll explain everything later. We must keep this information between us, Norman. This is very important and I know I can rely on you. We go back a long way, dear friend, and you must know that I'd never deceive you without a darn good reason."

Norman Tucker parted Aimee's hair and tenderly probed the back of her head. When he removed his hand, there was a smear of blood across his fingers. She moaned slightly and stirred.

Dr. Tucker pulled out a drawer, opened a bottle, and waved it back and forth under her nose. She gasped, jerked, and slowly opened her eyes.

Norman pressed down on her shoulders as she struggled to sit up. He glanced at Ernest, grinned, and looked back at his patient.

223

"Mister Kaymey, I'm Dr. Norman Tucker. You've got a concussion. That was a bad fall you took. You're a lucky man that your friend brought you here so quickly. Had you come to and tried to go on about your business, you might have suffered from blackouts and been hurt even more severely. As it is, you must get to bed immediately and I don't want you up for at least three days."

Aimee looked around slowly. "W-what h-happened?"

The door opened and Lucas stuck his head in. "Is she... he alright? Why doesn't someone say something?"

"Lucas?" she whispered weakly. "What happened?"

Norman and Ernest both turned to him curiously. "Yes, son, what did happen? Mrs. Vasquez came in the bank fretting something that someone assaulted Mack Kaymey and then I heard horses trampled him? Is that what happened?"

"Is he alright?" Lucas repeated anxiously.

"A slight concussion, some bruising, and a large lump," stated Dr. Tucker. "Nothing life threatening, but she, uh, he is going to have to have bed rest for the next few days."

"What about the attack and the horses?" Ernest asked again.

"No, he wasn't attacked or trampled by the horses," Lucas said impatiently. "Some yahoo grabbed Mack by the arm to talk to him. Mack lost his balance, stumbled off the boardwalk and fell, hitting his head on the rail. The fall frightened the horses but she... he wasn't struck. I don't think."

Ernest nodded and turned to Aimee, giving Lucas a quick glare. "Son, you need to watch your pronouns. Who grabbed you?"

"I don't know. I-I can't remember," she said, as she screwed up her face and winced.

"Mister Kaymey, what do you remember?" The doctor asked, inspecting her eyes once more.

"I-I remember getting undressed for bed. I heard the noise from the street. I'm having a hard time sleeping in the hotel. I walked down to breakfast and... then... then... I'm not sure. I woke up here." Tears gathered as she rubbed her forehead.

"That's not surprising," explained Norman. "A head injury of this type occasionally causes temporary loss of memory. They call it amnesia. I expect she'll, pardon me, he'll regain every moment he's lost in a day or two. The blow caused bruising in the brain. The brain and the body sometimes shut down in order to heal. I think that's what happened here. I wouldn't be too worried as long as you see that Mister Kaymey gets plenty of rest and allows the healing to continue."

"Can we move him back to the hotel?" asked Ernest.

"No!" shouted Lucas. "Sorry," he apologized, lowering his voice. "I think Mack should be moved to Hill Crest, my house. I'll contact his housekeeper to come and look after him. He needs someone with him until he's well. I don't think he'll able to take care of himself right now."

Before Aimee could protest, the doctor ran his fingers through his thick silver hair and nodded. "That's an excellent suggestion. We must move him by wagon. He's in no condition to travel on horseback. He'll need a few stitches and I'll put some antiseptic cream on the wound, bind his head, and he'll be ready to travel by the time you return with the wagon."

"But... " Aimee objected.

"No buts, young man, it's been decided. You will recover in the home of your friend here, as long as you are cared for and have day and night assistance from your housekeeper," the doctor paused and looked at Lucas with a raised eyebrow.

"Certainly his housekeeper will be there night and day. I would never allow Mister Kaymey to be left alone."
"That's not possible. Rose has a new baby and..." Aimee protested hoarsely.

"She can bring the baby with her, or her mother can help out. Whatever is decided will work out," Lucas said firmly. "It's final. You're coming home with me."

With a sigh, Aimee closed her eyes again as the pounding in her head increased.

"I'll give you a sedative for now and some medicine to take with you. I'll explain the dosage when you return. Run on now and get that wagon, son, and let me get to work."

"Thank you, Norman," Ernest said gratefully, pumping his friend's hand vigorously.

Norman grinned as he prepared his table. "You know I wouldn't do this for anyone else but you. I expect a lengthy explanation over an expensive dinner tonight, old friend. You've given this old shaman a delightful diversion.

"Bandaging skinned knees, lancing boils, and delivering babies is what takes up most of my time. Now I have this delicious piece of information that would cause every tongue in town to waggle until they fell off. This is powerful stuff," he said with a chuckle. "You know that, don't you?"

Ernest grinned and nodded. "Tonight at six in the dining room of the hotel."

"Six." Norman nodded and turned to his patient.

Lucas hurriedly rented a wagon at the livery stable and by the time the horses were hitched and he returned to the doctor's office, Aimee had been stitched, bandaged, medicated, and given a heavy sedative for the trip.

Gently lifting her, Lucas took extra care not to jostle her. The doctor and his nurse followed with blankets and a heavy quilt to prepare a cushioned bed for her to travel on. The doctor gave Lucas a small basket filled with clean bandages and two bottles of medicine. He carefully explained the dosage and after Lucas assured the doctor he understood, climbed into the wagon and slowly started for Hillcrest.

Ernest had sent a rider out to Eagle Springs to tell Albert and Rose to meet them at the Chase spread. Lucas resisted any offers to have someone ride out with him. With Aimee under sedation, he feared she might say something to expose her true identity.

226

As careful as he might drive, it seemed to Lucas the wheels of the wagon found every rock and hole in the road. Aimee seemed to rest comfortably but winced at each bump, and by the time the horses turned up the drive, Lucas was exhausted from the tension and worry.

Rose waited for them on the front porch, concern creasing her face. She rushed down to meeting the wagon.

"Oh, Mister Lucas. Is she hurt bad? Albert said she done been injured but he didn't know no details. What happened?"

"She tripped and fell, hitting her head on a hitching post. The doctor said she has a concussion and needs several days of bed rest. She has some stitches, the bandages will need changing, and she has to take some medicine. Will staying here be a problem, Rose? I have plenty of room for your mother and the baby if you need to bring them." Lucas tenderly lifted Aimee from the wagon and started toward the house.

"Actually, I brought them both with me. Mama wasn't planning on staying but I know she won't mind if we need her." Rose fretted as she followed Lucas up the winding staircase. Allie came out of the kitchen and followed Rose.

Before Lucas laid Aimee on the bed, Rose began pulling off her boots and socks. He lay her carefully on the turned-down bed and stood, his brow furrowed in worry. Rose turned to him and patted his cheek.

"Why don't you go down to the kitchen and start us some coffee? Mama will help me get Miss Aimee undressed. I brought a couple of my nightgowns for her to use. In fact," she smiled, "Miss Aimee made them for me. Mama used her pattern to make several for all the women at the camp. They're very popular."

"You scoot on down, Mister Lucas," Allie prompted. "That Chinaman you got a cookin' for ya don't seem to care for women in his kitchen. That's awful peculiar to me. Where didja find him?" She sniffed her disapproval of a man in the kitchen.

Lucas couldn't help but smile. "Actually, Chan found me. A group of Chinese workers were in Charleston working the docks.

Chan cooked for them, and when he heard I was rounding up a farm crew, he applied for the cook job. I hired him on the spot. I wasn't sure what he cooked but I knew it had to be better than what I was fixin'."

"Men," Allie fumed. "Hepless, that's all, jest plain hepless. What kind of name is Chan?"

"Mama?" Rose pleaded. "Please, don't start. Help me get Miss Aimee changed."

"We need some hot water and bathing cloths," Allie snorted. "Think you kin manage that?"

"Yes ma'am" Lucas said. "Right away, ma'am." He hurried to the kitchen. Unsure why Allie was in such a state, he feared Rose might have told her Aimee was upset with him. Whatever it was, he was grateful they were there to care for Aimee.

~ Twenty ~
Conspiracy Club

Aimee's mind struggled against the fog of medication. She stretched, and grimaced in pain as she turned her head to look toward the light pouring in through the window.

An involuntary moan escaped from between her clenched teeth and pinched lips.

The door flew open and Rose rushed to her side.

"Don't you move now. Don't you move at all."

Aimee's eyes widened at Rose's worried face. Her gaze wondered around the room and she stiffened at the unfamiliar setting.

"W-where am I? Rose, where a-am I-I?"

"You're at Mister Chase's house, Miss Aimee." She hovered anxiously at Aimee's side. "Don't you 'member nothin'?"

"I-I was at the hotel…"

"That's right", Rose interrupted, "… now think hard."

"I went downstairs and saw Lucas… "

"That's more than you remembered yesterday at the doctor's office," Lucas said, sticking his head in the door.

"Yesterday? Doctor's office?" Aimee looked bewildered.

He stepped in the room. "Yesterday," he repeated. "You've been out since yesterday when Doc Tucker gave you a sleeping draught. He wanted you to get plenty of rest and be completely relaxed for the drive out here."

"Yesterday? I-I don't remember yesterday."

"Now, don't you worry your little head about yesterday," Rose told her. "We gonna take good care of you. Mama is here with me and you're to stay right in this here bed until the doc says you kin get up. He'll be out this afternoon to check on you."

Lucas leaned against the post and kept a steady gaze on Aimee. "You're looking better already. You're still a little pale but you were white as a ghost yesterday and last night."

"Last night?"

Rose swiveled her head around and glared at Lucas. "Mister Lucas, you best go on downstairs and do whutever it is you do around here. Mama will be bringing up Miss Aimee's breakfast any minute and we need to freshen her up and she needs some privacy. Understand?"

"Sure, privacy. Yeah, I gotta go down and... and do whatever it is I do." His grin faded, as he straightened up under Rose's stare and left the room.

Rose washed and gently dried Aimee, and helped her into a clean gown. Aimee's head felt like a spinning top, although not as bad as when she first woke. Gingerly, she touched the bandaged area at the back of her head and pain had shot around her head and slid behind her eyes. She closed them tightly and when she opened them, Rose stood patiently beside the bed holding a spoon filled with amber liquid.

"Open wide," she said softly. "You need to take two spoons of this before you eats and 'nother dose jest before lunch. This other stuff is some kinda elixir that's gonna make you stronger. The doctor's gonna bring some more when he comes later."

Aimee opened her mouth and grimaced as the bitter liquid slid down. The second spoonful was just as nasty.

Allie appeared through the doorway and placed a tray filled with coffee, scrambled eggs, and dry toast across Aimee's lap.

Aimee grabbed the coffee and sipped hurriedly to wash the taste of the medicine from her mouth.

"It's horrible," she complained.

"Then it must be good for you," Rose's mother said confidently. "I ain't never got well from medicine that tasted good. In fact, I don't think I never tasted no medicine at all that tasted good."

"Surely in this day and time, doctors can make it taste better than this."

"You'd think so," agreed Rose.

"If it ain't bad, it ain't good," Allie said determinedly.

"Eat," commanded Rose. "You're supposed to take your medicine with meals. It might upset your stomach if you doesn't eats something."

Aimee bit off a piece of toast and shoveled a forkful of eggs in her mouth.

"M-m-m-m, this is delicious. Rose, these are the best eggs I've ever had."

Allie smiled broadly as Rose explained, "Mama cooked those. She taught me everything I knows 'bout cooking but they's still a few things I can't make as good as she can. Eggs, turkey stuffing, and cherry pie is a few of them."

"Allie, I didn't think I was hungry until I tasted this."

"Well, you must be getting better. Really bad sick folks usually don' eat much. Eatin' is good fer you, Miss Aimee, really good."

"Allie, how did you feel when Rose told you about my masquerade? Were you upset?" Aimee asked.

"Upset? Mercy, no. You has to remember that us folks are used to trying to fool people. The more I thought about it, the more I knows jest how brave you were. We stayed to ourselves but you, you jest faced the world. You wasn't 'fraid to test everyone. The world needs more women likes you."

Aimee smiled at Allie's kind words. She could see how sincere the words were, and Allie's eyes sparkled as she spoke.

"Thank you, Allie. That means so much to me."

"Now, no more talkin'. We gotta lets Miss Aimee eat. We be back in a little while fer the tray. Jest set it 'long side you when yer through and try to rest."

"Yes, ma'am," said Aimee obediently. Allie was right. It didn't take much to tire her out. As soon as she was finished, she set the tray on the bed alongside of her and drifted off to sleep.

Aimee woke around noon by a gentle shake from Rose, who gave her some more bitter tasting tonic, and a bowl of chicken soup. Rose washed her face and arms, gently brushed her hair, and Aimee was pleased to find that the early dizziness had dissipated some.

She pushed herself up in the bed and leaned back against the pillows Rose plumped up behind her. Rose walked to the window and twisted the metal crank, allowing a slight breeze in. She turned to Aimee. "Riders a'comin'. I think one man is a doctor, he's carryin' a black bag. Then there's the banker man, and there's a stranger with them."

A noise in the hall grabbed Aimee's attention, as Albert hurried through the doorway with Allie on his heels.

"That fella is back, Miss Aimee," panted Albert. "I comes over jest as fast as I could. Rode through them woods and 'cross the creek. It's that marshal feller, you know, the one that came by when Mister Lucas wuz there. He done come back."

"Take it easy, Albert," fussed Rose. "Miss, that is, Mister Kaymey is too sick to see anybody. I'll makes that plain when I goes down to let the doctor in. Mister Gaines will go along, I'm sure. You goes on downstairs and out the back door. We don't need him to sees you and think we's got sumpt'n to hide."

Albert nodded, turned, and disap- peared down the hall.

Rose rushed to the bed and motioned for Aimee to slip down flat. She removed the pillows from against the headboard and placed them beside Aimee, then pulled the covers up to her chin and grabbed a towel lying on the nearby table. Soaking the towel in water, she rung it out, folded it into a wide strip, and laid it over Aimee's brow.

She pulled down the shade and closed the curtains, plunging the room into semi-darkness. Rose stood back and examined the results, then walked to the door and looked around from that angle.

Nodding to herself, she whispered, "Now, don't you move, Miss Aimee. Don't you twitch a muscle. I'm gonna go downstairs and when I comes back up, you listen to what I'm saying and follow my lead. Just nod if you understand."

A slight nod from the bed gave Rose the signal to meet the guests.

As Rose reached the landing, she saw Lucas greeting the doctor, the banker, and a stranger, who stood with hat in hand.

"Doctor Tucker, this is Rose Washington, Mister Kaymey's housekeeper. She's taking care of Mister Kaymey. His house is under construction and I felt it was better if he recovered here," Lucas explained, looking at his guests but specifically the stranger, who kept glancing up at Rose.

"Rose, you know Mister Gaines. This is Doctor Norman Tucker, and Marshal James Evans."

"How do, gentlemen. Doctor, if you'll follow me, I'll takes you up to Mister Kaymey's room."

"Is he any better today, Rose?" Doc Tucker asked loudly, giving Rose a strange stare.

Hoping she was reading his signals correctly, she lowered her head and shook it worriedly. "Not really. He seems to drift in and out. I has to spoon feed his food and his medicine."

"Has he said anything yet? Anything you can make out?" He asked, still looking at her in the same odd way.

"Naw, sir. He mumbles some now and a bit but I can'ts understands a word he says. I'm real worried."

"Rightly so, my dear, rightly so."

They disappeared out of sight and Lucas turned to James Evans. "What brings you back here? Last time we saw you in Charleston you were off duty."

"Sycamore Grove was added to my circuit. When I arrived yesterday I heard some worrisome news. A woman told me that a citizen was attacked and the doctor is worried about his recovery. I did some checking and when I found out it was Mister Kaymey, I checked around, talked to the doctor and Mister Gaines. Doc says he was coming out today so I rode along with them. I'm sure Mister Kaymey will want to press charges. It's just that I need to talk to him and find out just exactly what happened."

"I tried to tell the marshal that some of our townsfolk have a tendency to color the facts but he insisted on coming out and

seeing for himself," said Ernest, a look of apology on his face."

"Ernest is right, James. I was near enough to see everything that happened. It was an accident. The man grabbed Mack's sleeve to slow him down, Mack jerked around, lost his balance, and fell against a hitching post. It's as simple as that."

James reached in his pocket and brought out the same scrubby, stained, little notebook he had the last time he was out at Eagle Creek. "Let me see, a Mrs. Judith Denton said that a man accosted Mister Kaymey and threw him against the hitching post and a Mister Chase, I guess that's you, Lucas, shoved him away and carried Mister Kaymey across the street to the doctor."

"No, no. I don't think I shoved anyone. Still, I might have pushed him out of the way but he certainly didn't attack Mister Kaymey."

"Good," James murmured as he jotted down Lucas'ss story. "Now, after I take Mister Kaymey's version, I can make my report and put this to rest."

"I'm afraid that won't happen today," the doctor said as he came down the steps. "Mister Kaymey is in serious condition and I won't allow any visitors and certainly no interrogations as long as he is this unstable."

234

"Sorry to hear that. I'm due in Savannah in a few days to meet with the gentleman I mentioned on my first trip here, a Mister Marcus Alexander, and I was hoping I could take care of this while I was here."

Lucas blanched at the mention of Marcus Alexander.

Ernest noticed his discomfort and called up to Rose who was following the doctor down the stairs.

"How about a cup of coffee, Miss Rose?" I'm sure the marshal and doctor could use a cup. I know I could."

"My mama's in the kitchen," Rose said, returning his smile. "She's here hepin' with the baby, while I care for Mister Mack. She always keeps a pot warm."

"Yes, that's a great idea," agreed Lucas. "Please, come this way."

When the men entered the kitchen, Allie had three cups of steaming coffee waiting for them. Rose followed behind the men and began to place a slice of butter cake on small plates. Chan stood back, frowning at this woman who bullied her way into his kitchen and practically taken over.

"This looks wonderful," Ernest exclaimed, as he picked up his fork.

"Smells even better" James bent over the table and inhaled deeply. "You have no idea how long it's been since I've had homemade cake. Traveling as I do, it's usually hardtack and beans on the trail. I generally sleep in the jails when I make my rounds."

"You're welcome to drop by here whenever you're in the area, James. In fact, I insist you stay here when you're in Sycamore Grove."

"I should resist the temptation," admitted James, "and refuse your kind offer. However, I must be getting old. I appreciate the invite and it'll be nice to sleep in a real bed. Thanks. I'll take you up on that offer."

"W-wonderful, that's wonderful. It will be an honor, James. I look forward to it. W-would you care to stay tonight?" Lucas held his breath.

"Oh, no, thank you kindly. With Mister Kaymey ill and all, I'd only be in the way. I'm staying at the jail tonight. I have to pick up some wanted posters in the morning and then I'll be on my way to Savannah."

Lucas took a slow sip of coffee, trying to decide how to bring up Marcus, when Ernest jumped in and relieved him of that problem.

"Wasn't that Alexander fellow the same one that distributed those posters a while back? You know, the one offering a reward for information on some woman?"

"The same," mumbled the marshal scooping a large piece of cake into his mouth.

"I thought he was from... wasn't it California?" asked Ernest.

"Yes, originally but after not being satisfied with the results he was getting from across the country, he decided to follow some of the reports personally. He hired a private detective who claims to have found a witness or two. He started in Charleston and has worked along the coast westward toward Savannah."

"He's found proof that she's in Savannah?" Lucas asked.

"No, he's found a merchant who told the detective that a woman came in around the time the survivors arrived and bought some used clothes. He didn't seem to think it was the woman in the poster, and the detective agreed that it wasn't important. Not to this Alexander fellow, though. He seems to feel the buyer was the woman he's looking for."

"Persistent bloke, isn't he?" growled Ernest. "Why does he need you, if he's found the man?"

"To be honest," said James with a frown, "the sheriff from Mountain Springs in California contacted me after discovering Alexander was headin' toward my jurisdiction. He's concerned that this guy might be really dangerous. He did some checking and found out Alexander was one of the men that was suspected of murder back near San Francisco. There wasn't any proof and now he's left town. The sheriff asked me to keep an eye on him."

236

"Sounds reasonable but why you? Why can't the sheriff handle it?"

James snorted angrily. "He told the sheriff he'd been working with me and was following leads that I provided. The only thing I ever told Alexander was every lead I followed led me to a dead end. I'm going down there to straighten this out and give that guy a piece of my mind. I also need to tell him that he could be charged with... impersonating an officer of the law. I can't have every Tom, Dick, and Harry pretending to be working with my office. Someone might get killed in the name of the law, which he doesn't represent. That yeehaw needs to go back to California and accept his losses."

"You think you can convince him to do that?" Lucas asked.

James shook his head ruefully, "I doubt it. I think this joker is thinking with blinders on. He has one thought, and that's getting his money back, if indeed, it's his money, and nothing else. I'm afraid nothing I can say is going to deter him from his search."

"You said, *if* it's his money?" asked Ernest. "What do you mean by that?"

James wiped his mouth on the napkin Rose had placed by his plate. He sat up and leaned over on the table like a conspirator. "What I'm about to tell you mustn't leave this room, gentlemen." He looked around and seeing that Rose had left, he lowered his voice.

"Something about that guy didn't sit right with me," he confessed. "I sent a few wires to friends of mine on the coast and received some very interesting information about Mister Marcus Alexander. It seems he's a con artist and gambler, and isn't very good at either. Nobody, and I mean nobody, ever recalls him winning more than enough for a beer. There jest ain't no way he would have a large amount of gold in his possession. Heck, that loser couldn't hold on to a nickel. My contacts reported that he lived in a shack in shantytown, owed every gambling house in the area, and has a reputation of sweeping rich women off their feet and fleecing them before he dumps them.

"There was a rumor that he arrived with a beautiful young woman who seemed to disappear shortly after they settled down around Mountain Springs near the gold fields. In fact, there have been several women that have disappeared in that area and a few turned up with their throats cut. I'm afraid that's what happened to the first one.

"He's been a suspect in robberies, muggings, and one of my friends even suspects him in the murder of those women I mentioned. He was questioned but never arrested. Jest didn't have hard evidence. The sheriff has a hidden card up he's sleeve and he wants to keep Alexander from disappearing completely. He's clever, this Alexander but if he thinks he's moving his action into my territory, he's got another think coming."

With that, James appeared to looked a little guilty at revealing so much about his business. He rose and smiled at the wide-eyed audience around him.

"I really gotta go. I've got to get back and see to business in town. I hope Mister Kaymey makes a complete recovery. I'll be back next time around and hopefully I can finished this investigation then and put it to rest.

"Thanks for your hospitality and I will be back in a month or so."

"Remember, I insist you stay here," reminded Lucas. He wanted to make sure he was first to get any information about Marcus Alexander.

"Absolutely, Lucas. I appreciate that. Good day gentlemen," James said, as he went toward to door. By the time he reached the front door, Lucas was on his heels and Rose stood stoically holding his hat.

"Safe trip," said Lucas, as they shook his hand. "See you next time."

James nodded and turned to Rose, "Great coffee, ma'am and even better cake. Never had none better."

She gave a little bow and sighed in relief after she closed the door behind him.

238

She and Lucas looked at one another and smiled. Lucas started back to the kitchen while Rose rushed upstairs to tell Aimee what she heard.

When Lucas entered the kitchen, he found Ernest and Norman in a hushed conversation.

"Let's see what Lucas thinks," said Ernest.

Allie topped off everyone's cup with fresh coffee and once again disappeared.

"I've told Norman everything I know about Aimee McKay and Mack Kaymey. It never occurred to me in the beginning that illness or accident might reveal our secret. I don't know if Aimee talked to you about this, Lucas but I suggested to her some time ago that she might be able to regain her femininity by creating a sister."

"Yes, she did. We went to Charleston before Christmas and she picked up some hairpieces and I think she bought some dresses, although I didn't see them."

"Good. I thought this would be a good time to bring the sister into the picture but Norman fears that Alexander fellow might turn up and recognize her. He is the one she's afraid of, right? We noticed the expression on your face when the marshal mentioned him."

"Yes, he's the one," Lucas admitted. "She hasn't told me everything but from the pain in her eyes and her fear of trust, I gather he's a real evil piece of work."

Norman cleared his throat, stood, and quickly went to the back door and stared out the upper pane across the field.

"Norman, are you all right?"

The doctor turned and faced his old friend.

"I am so grateful that you have confided in me. I can assure you that you have not placed your trust in the wrong man. We all have our secrets and I'm no different.

"My father was a kind and loving man. I adored him and when we lost him to a fever in my younger years, I vowed that I would become a doctor and make sure I did all I could to keep good men on this earth. I was taught to trust and look for the good in everyone but like Aimee, we can all be fooled.

"Before I came here, I was married to a wonderful woman, Dora, and had a lovely little girl we named Patricia. My beautiful daughter met a young man, William Vargas, who was visiting our church. He and Patricia were drawn to one another and he spent a great deal of time at our place. He told us his family had passed away and he was interested in settling in our little town. I sympathized with his loss and to make a long story short, in time, I allowed my daughter to marry him.

"I don't know why I didn't see through his lies. Maybe I didn't want to because my daughter was so enamored with him. Regardless of the reasons and excuses I tell myself, my daughter endured horrors I can't even imagine, or maybe I don't want to. The bruises were always explained away, until my wife finally cornered her one day and she admitted that Martin beat her often. She had been too ashamed to tell anyone, and blamed herself for not being a good enough wife, that he was under stress, or that she had put extra pressure on him.

"There was always one excuse after another. He was a closet drinker, so no one knew except Patricia. He was a mean drunk. She thought she could fix him because she loved him so. Love wasn't enough. One evening a neighbor went to their house to see if some cattle that wandered onto his property belonged to Pat and her husband.

"He found my precious Patricia dead, beaten to death and left on the ground. Martin was passed out in the barn, still clutching the hammer he used on her in one hand, and an empty bottle of whiskey in the other. He was sentenced to prison but we lost our daughter, our only little girl...," his voice broke and his breath hitched with a strangled sob.

"Norman, I am so sorry. I... what happened to your wife? I didn't even know you were married," Ernest said softly.

"She grieved herself to death. She stopped eating, fell into a deep depression, and started taking long walks and one day she didn't come home. We found her dead, sitting against a tree trunk on a hilltop overlooking the cemetery. She wanted to join her child and I... I guess she did. I found a doctor to replace me there and I moved here seven years ago.

"This Alexander fellow has got to be stopped. If he is the man who killed those women in California, he won't stop. Demons like him can't stop. Someone has to stop him. Just tell me what you want me to do. I couldn't help Patricia but maybe I can help Aimee McKay."

"I'm sorry, Norman," Ernest said, laying his hand on his friend's shoulder. "I didn't know."

"Nobody did, Ernest. I was ashamed and kept it to myself. Why was I ashamed? Why was she ashamed? It wasn't my fault or hers. Why didn't I make a scene and warn young women and parents about that kind of evil preying on innocent women? Abused women should tell the world about men like William and Alexander, instead they are raised to keep the family together, hold their heads high and muddle on, ignoring the faults and failures of husbands. That's dead wrong.

"I hope we can stop Alexander, then maybe Miss McKay will be able to live her life without fear."

"You're right about that and you're right about stopping Alexander. We can't let another woman become his victim. He can't get to Aimee," Lucas said through clenched teeth.

"I don't think this is a good time for Kaymey to have a sister show up. If Alexander comes here, he's sure to recognize her." Worry apparent on Ernest's face, as he spoke.

"You're right," agreed Norman. "She'll have to wait until we get rid of Alexander."

"How are we going to do that?" Ernest asked.

"We'll have to come up with a plan. Let's meet here tomorrow night and see if we can come up with something. I think we're clever enough to outsmart that maniac, don't you?"

Ernest and Lucas nodded thoughtfully, as Norman stood and shook their hands.

"Tomorrow evening, about eight?" Lucas asked with a confirming nod.

~ Twenty-One ~
The Bad Penny

Aimee sat up in bed and listened in disbelief as Rose recounted the conversation she overheard downstairs.

"I never imagined in my wildest dreams he would become so obsessed with me. I thought I was just a throw-away, a piece of used up garbage to him. What is he thinking?"

Despite Rose's objection, Aimee struggled to stand. Shaking away her dear friend's hand, she began to dress.

"No, you don't, young lady," Lucas said firmly. "Rose, don't let her bully you. You're getting back in that bed. The doctor said it would be a few more days and you'd be as good as new. More stubborn maybe but good as new."

Aimee smiled weakly. "Maybe you two are right but you don't understand."

"Yes, we do. We all do and you're not in this alone."

"What does he want?" Aimee moaned. "He can't know for sure that I'm here or that I've got money. Why can't he just let the past go and move on."

"Honey chil'," Rose explained gently, "there are some men whose ego is bigger than their brain. Some men jest can't admit

242

they ain't in charge no more, that they's been outsmarted. It eats at them until their thoughts are sour and rotten. It's like a disease that takes 'em over, 'specially the mean 'uns. They has to have the last word or in his case, the last punishment. It's true, ain't it, he was good at punishments?"

Tears welled in Aimee's eyes, and her hands balled into tight fists. "Yes, it's true but those days are over. It won't happen again. I won't let it."

"Aimee, we won't let it happen again. You have friends now, and you're not alone. Please remember that," Lucas said firmly, and Rose nodded in agreement.

"Have you remembered anything about the man who grabbed you? Is he connected with Alexander? What did he want?"

"Now, Mister Lucas," barked Rose sharply, "what did I tell you about...?"

"It's all right, Rose. I remembered this morning. It's been coming back in bits and pieces but I can recall events farther back than just yesterday," Aimee said and smiled wanly.

"Who was that yokel?" Lucas asked.

"Nobody we have to worry about," she sighed. "He's just some snake-in-the-grass who was in Charlestown when the supplies for the new house were loaded. He got the idea that the person building the house might be in the market for slaves and when he found me, he tried to talk me into investing in a cargo of slaves to be delivered in Savannah in a couple of weeks.

"He wouldn't take no for an answer and when I left in the middle of his well-rehearsed speech, he was upset. I could tell he was determined but I didn't realize he followed me out until I heard him calling to me. Then I felt him tug on my arm, and I lost my balance trying to free myself from his grasp. Truly, however, I don't remember much after that."

"No wonder," exclaimed Rose. "That fall done got you a cracked skull. You coulda got yerself killed. Maybe that marshal was right, and you should press charges. It makes me sick to think of them people in Savannah just waiting to find out their fate."

Lucas looked at Rose. "We're not the only people who think that way, Rose. It's not a popular subject in the South but slavery won't be around forever. Trust me. Man was not meant to be a slave."

Rose smiled sadly, as she plumped Aimee's pillow. "Man has always been a slave one way or another, Mister Lucas. Some is slaves to money, some to their jobs, or some other thang, while others is a slave to fear. It ain't an easy battle to win that's fer sure."

"Miss Rose, you are a jewel. You never fail to amaze me with your wisdom," Aimee said.

"Mama says my tongue may be the death of me."

"Not while I'm around, it won't," Lucas said, as he reached out to touch her arm.

"Rose, I'm doing so much better now. I know Albert and Isaac need you home. Won't you please go home and get on with your family?"

"In the morning," Rose said. "I'm goin' home in the morning. Mama is gonna stay another day to make sure you is on your feet. She ain't gonna take no fer an answer, so don't waste your time arguin'. I think she really enjoys being needed," Rose said.

"Good," Aimee sighed. "Now, I won't feel so guilty about getting hurt."

"Pshaw," Rose sniffed. "Likes you could help it. Now, get some rest."

"I will, Miss Words-of-Wisdom."

Rose ducked her head. "I really does has a hard time keepin' my mouth shut. Lucas, go do..."

"I know," he grinned, "...whatever it is I do." He winked at them both and left the room humming.

For the next few evenings, Lucas, Ernest, and Norm, met after supper in the quiet, warm, aromatic kitchen at Hill Crest.

~ * ~

Since Aimee could move around the house, Allie went back home. The headaches faded, the wound on her head was healing,

244

and the dizziness was nearly forgotten. She felt antsy, bored, and wanted desperately to check on the construction of her house. The doctor assured her that in a few more days, she would be able to go, although Aimee wondered if he was dragging his heels for some other reason.

Lucas, Ernest, and Norman played cards in the evenings and discussed the growth of Sycamore Grove. With new construction, expanding businesses, and the new gin expansion in the next town, Sycamore Grove needed a strong council to oversee the development of the town. The idea sounded reasonable to Aimee but she doubted the need to meet every evening.

After Allie and Rose had gone back home, Lucas included Chan in Aimee's secret, and the little Chinaman took over the duties of a nurse with a vengeance. He popped into Aimee's room every half hour with hot tea, scones, fresh water, and hovered over her as if she were royalty. He was so joyful to have the house back in his care that he practically danced down the halls when he walked.

He gave Aimee privacy for her toiletry needs and dressing, otherwise he brushed her hair, laundered her clothes, and waited on her hand and foot. It was only when she demanded to Lucas that Chan allow her to walk in the garden alone, did he limit his hovering, and even then, she could see him peeking out the window, watching her every move. Despite his smothering actions, Aimee was growing fond of Chan.

A little over a week after her accident, Aimee felt more like her old self. Chan reluctantly agreed to stop playing nurse and Aimee prepared to check on the construction of her new house the following day. She pretended to get ready for bed and instead, decided to bind herself up when the door opened and Chan walked in carrying a pile of freshly ironed clothes. Seeing Aimee in her half-dressed state, he dropped the clothes, grabbed a small medallion that hung around his neck and began to beg her forgiveness as he babbled incoherently in his native tongue.

Aimee grabbed a blanket to cover herself as soon as she saw Chan and quickly turned her back.

Chan, bowing and murmuring, backed out of the room and careened into Lucas as he came to see what the commotion was all about.

One glance into the bedroom told Lucas of the intrusion. Aimee peeked over her shoulder, her cheeks flaming when she saw Lucas's grin. He followed the muttering Chan down the stairs assuring him at every step that his patient was forgiving and wouldn't hold his unexpected interruption against him.

Aimee stripped off the bindings, and slipped on her gown and robe. She climbed into bed, then heard a light tap on her door.

"Come in," she called. Chan entered carrying a tray of hot chocolate and cinnamon toast. He averted his eyes as he approached the bed and stared at the tray while settling it over her lap. "Chan, please look at me," Aimee pleaded.

He held up his hand to silence her and spoke softly.

"Chan did not give mistress proper respect. His shame is very great. Please allow Chan to redeem himself in her eyes."

"Chan," Aimee said gently. "You have become a dear friend. That was not a show of disrespect, it was an accident because I didn't lock the door. It was not your fault and I do not feel disrespected. Please forgive yourself and let us continue as before."

"Thank you, thank you. Chan will fix this, yes, yes, yes. Chan will fix this."

Before Aimee could answer, he rushed from the room.

Aimee plopped down in the bed and gently rubbed her forehead. Her new life was proving more difficult each day. She wasn't handling being a man very well and apparently being a woman was bringing on a new set of problems. Her aim to become tough and independent was crumbling and she felt as vulnerable as ever.

She heard a buggy drive up and looked out the window to see the doctor jump out as one of Lucas' men held the horse.

Although she didn't know the doctor very well, and couldn't see him after a long day of delivering babies and tending to the sick, he seemed pleasant enough. And she worried what his wife thought of him spending so many hours with Lucas.

There was definitely more to this card playing than Lucas revealed. Waiting for nearly half an hour before blowing out the bedside lamp, Aimee shoved her feet into her house slippers. She tiptoed to the door and opened it as quietly as she could, then listened intently before peering down the hall.

She knew Chan would be busy preparing coffee and snacks for the guests, so tonight she decided to find out what was going on. Aimee had a bad feeling they were about to get themselves into trouble. They didn't realize what a vicious, underhanded, evil, human being Marcus was or that he would do everything in his power to destroy her.

Tiptoeing down the hallway, Aimee paused at the landing. The foyer remained quiet and dark except for a couple of wall sconces burning low. She tested each step for squeaks and creaks as she slowly descended.

When she heard the faint murmur of voices from the kitchen, Aimee scuttled across the hallway and slipped into the dining room, engulfed in darkness. Freezing in place, she closed her eyes and tried to recreate the room in her mind. Concen- tration was the key. She stretched her hand out and touched the wall. Suddenly, in her mind there was the buffet a foot to her right, with two large candlesticks on top and a large crystal bowl filled with pears between them. There were two doors at the end of the room that Lucas told her were installed so the kitchen help would not run into each other during meals. One was for the serving from the kitchen and the other was for taking dishes to the kitchen.

Reaching out, she touched the buffet and crept along until she reached the door. She placed her ear against the wooden panel of the kitchen door and held her breath.

"We've met three times, created three scenarios, and discarded three plans. My wife is becoming suspicious at my leaving each night after being such a homebody for so long. I don't know about you two but I'm beginning to doubt our ability to come up with a workable scheme to stop this Alexander fellow," Earnest said.

"Come now, fellows, we are three fairly intelligent men of the world here. We have met monsters all across the land and I have no doubt we can trip this rascal up if we put our heads together long enough," Lucas said.

"That may be true," Ernest agreed, "but at what cost? Don't misunderstand me, I'm not making excuses, and I don't mean to be unfeeling but I have a family. My wife feels neglected, my baby girl won't recognize me soon, and the servants have started whispering behind my back."

"Maybe, I could help," Aimee said softly, as she stepped through the door.

"I thought I told you..." Lucas snapped. He jumped up and pulled out a chair. "I'm sorry, Aimee. It's just that you mustn't be involved in this. Your exposure is just too dangerous."

"There is no way I can stand idly by and let you three kind, generous, and brave men put your lives, the future of your families, and your reputations on the line for my problems."

"Aimee," Lucas said, sounding exasperated.

"You might as well resign yourself, Lucas. I am the reason Marcus is here. He may be a crude, cruel, heartless, swindler, and from what Rose overheard, a possible murderer but he is here because of me.

"Sycamore Grove isn't his typical mark. He canvasses places where new money is, along with innocent, foolish men and women who aren't experienced in recognizing common predators.

He looks for big money and that's rarely found in small towns like this."

"We're going to stop him, my dear," Norman said. He patted her hand to reassure her. "You've had enough of him for a lifetime. It's time for you to step aside and let us take over."

Aimee smiled. "Like I said, that isn't going to happen, Doctor Tucker. Whatever happens, I am going to be a part of it."

Norman opened his mouth, but Aimee held up her hand.

"You must understand. I have to do this. I can't put that part of my life behind me while I know Marcus is still looking for his next victim. If he's going to be stopped, then I'll be a part of it. There will be no closure otherwise. You can't get rid of me. I promise you that."

"Chan?" Lucas called and the servant quickly entered, hurrying to his side. His eyes settled on Aimee and she squirmed uncomfortably under his scrutiny.

"Would you fix Miss Aimee a cup of cocoa? She's decided to join us tonight."

With a look Aimee couldn't quite interpret, Chan nodded silently and went to the stove. How he could work in the kitchen and make little or no noise amazed Aimee, but Chan was Chan, unreadable and remarkable.

"Now, in the little time we have left, does anyone have any suggestions we can discuss?" Norman asked.

"Boomerang," said Chang as he set Aimee's cup on the table.

"I beg your pardon?" Ernest asked, looking at Chan.

"Boomerang, sir," repeated Chan, his eyes averting the group as he refilled their coffee cups.

"I've heard that word," said Norman, a puzzled look crossing his face. "But I'm not sure where."

"Boomerangs come from Australia," explained Chan. "They are deadly weapons made of carved wood that is curved. The shape of the wood allows the piece to travel long, precise distances and return to its owner. If you are unfamiliar with a boomerang and unaware of its trajectory, you will be caught off guard and seriously injured."

"How extraordinary." Norman said, looking at Chan with a wide smile. Chan returned his smile shyly and nodded as Norman slowly rocked back and then forward.

"Boomerang." Norman grinned. "Yes, that's it. Boomerang."

"Have you completely lost your mind?" Ernest frowned, pulling out his watch to check the hour.

"Gentlemen, Chan has just solved our problem." Norman rose and stuck his hand out to Chan. Chan looked at the group, smiled, and with an embarrassed nod, shook Norman's hand as he bowed.

"What?" Lucas asked, confused.

Norman sat down and leaned over. "We can't possibly out think Alexander. I wouldn't be surprised if the fellow is slightly mad. We did call him a maniac, if you recall. You can't predict how madmen think but we do have a clue to his mental goal. Taking other people's money, winning the game, no matter how, and making vulnerable people succumb to his treachery. These things make that man tick.

"The only way we have of defeating him is beating him at his own game. Boomerang. We must let him formulate his plan, throw it into action, and make sure he isn't prepared when it turns on him."

~ Twenty-Two ~
Ante Up or Fold

The meeting lasted another half hour before Ernest excused himself and left for home. The three remaining schemers sat around until nearly midnight bouncing ideas off one another, considering, eliminating, and rejecting half a dozen more. Norman's yawning finally alerted them all that it was time to call it a night.

Lucas and Aimee walked to the porch to bid the doctor good-night and watched him head down the drive. Aimee shifted her gaze to the starry skies above.

"Why is it that the night sky seems so much clearer and magnified during the winter months?" she wondered aloud.

"I've noticed that, too," Lucas said. "The summer sky is beautiful but the winter sky seems larger and brighter. It feels like we're closer to heaven."

Aimee nodded and shivered slightly as she gathered the collar of her robe close. Lucas moved behind her and slipped his arms around her.

"We'd better go in. Don't want you catching cold."

"Just another minute."

She ran her hand through her short curly hair.

"I need a haircut," she remarked, pulling a curl out straight.

"I hate to see you cut your hair."

"I have to. We need to see this through to the end. If I make public my true identity, I'm afraid the people would feel deceived and I don't want to embarrassed or insult anyone. Besides, with Marcus in the neighborhood, I can't take any chances. I'll get Rose to cut it tomorrow when I ride over to check on the construction."

"I wish you wouldn't go out right now. I know how curious you are to see the place but now isn't the right time. I haven't told you this because I didn't want to get your curiosity up but that Andrew Harmon fellow is doing a fantastic job at your place."

"You've been there and didn't tell me. That's just mean."

"The doc said to wait but I was going to tell you tomorrow. I didn't know you were planning to go over until you told me tonight and I didn't want to go into detail with Doc and Ernest still here."

Aimee smiled. "It looks good?"

"It looks great. I've already talked to Andrew about doing some remodeling for me after he's finished with your house. I may even ask you for some ideas if you've got time, after we've gotten rid of Alexander, I mean."

"Lucas?" Aimee placed her hands on his chest. "Do you think we really have a good chance of making him go away forever?"

"Better than good," he assured her as he leaned down and kiss her forehead.

For just a second, he felt her body lean into his but before he could react, she stiffened, pushed herself away and turned her back on him.

"Go to bed," Lucas ordered gruffly. "... and I want you to sleep in tomorrow."

"I will. I'm just going to sneak through the woods to Eagle Creek. I have to take a peak. I'll be careful that no one sees me. I promise."

She moved toward the door paused, then glanced back quickly and all but ran inside and up to her room.

~ * ~

Lucas slammed his open hand against the post and leaned his cheek on the chilled wood. He needed advice, suggestions, help in his quest to convince Aimee of his sincerity. There was no doubt in his mind this was not infatuation. The other women in his life had all been innocent flirtations. He had practiced his craft at wooing, winning, and moving on until looking for the special person he would spend the rest of his life. And Aimee was the one.

This was not easy; in fact, it was the hardest thing he had ever had to do. Spending cold nights curled up in flimsy tents wasn't hard. Digging, sifting, and panning in icy waters wasn't hard. Standing guard on a rocky mountainside, protecting his claim while his partner raced into town to have their samples assayed, was nothing to trying to convince the woman he loved with all his heart and soul that he was the man she was meant to be with.

He stood on the porch a few minutes more looking at the same twinkling stars knowing Aimee had stared at them, too. He bowed his head, said a quick but sincere prayer and went inside.

The next morning as Lucas walked Aimee to the door, a loud voice came from outside and Lucas hurriedly opened the door. Aimee slid in beside him just in time to see Ernest practically leaping from his horse.

"He's here." The banker panted and bent over, placing his hands on his knees, gasping for breath. "He's here."

"Whoa, Ernest. Get your breath and start from the beginning. Who's here and what's the rush?" Lucas asked.

"That man we were talking about. That Alexander feller. He's in Sycamore Grove. He's got a lot of nerve. Can you believe it? As soon as I heard he was in town, I headed straight out here to tell you. We've got to get busy, Lucas. We've got to get this beast."

"Calm down, Ernest. The marshal's in town. Alexander won't try anything that will blow his cover. He thinks everyone here is a dumb hillbilly. We'll figure something out. Don't worry about that. Thanks for letting us know, we appreciate that."

He put his arm around Aimee's trembling shoulders. He pulled her close until she steadied herself.

"Aimee, you're white as a ghost. You need to get back into bed. I've got to get the boys out to check fences out at the Owens' boundary. Ernest, you get back to town and see what you can find out. Where's he staying? How long does he plan to be here? What brought him to Sycamore Grove? Things like that."

Ernest nodded and hurriedly mounted his horse.

"Ernest," Lucas called. "You'd better stop by the doctor's office and fill Norm in. We can't afford any slip-ups of any kind. He won't know Alexander from the next stranger. He needs to know he's here and what he looks like."

Again, Ernest nodded, reined his horse around and started for town at a full gallop.

"You all right?" Lucas asked softly.

"Yes, I need to get to Rose and get my hair cut. I've got to stay away from him. Marcus will recognize me in a second. Surely he won't go to Eagle Creek, will he?"

"James knows Mack Kaymey is recuperating here. He won't take Alexander out to any property when the owner isn't there. If you insist on going to Eagle Creek, Tom will take you by way of the woods. I'll tell the men to lookout for you. They all know Mack Kaymey isn't well. Tom'll take good care of you. Don't take too long and stay on the path."

Aimee nodded and headed to the barn for her horse.

As Aimee and Tom zigzagged over deer trails toward her house, a strange feeling came over her. When she crossed the creek and heard t hammering and sawing of the workers at Eagle Creek, she knew what she had to do. Surprised to find Rose and Allie standing within the framework of the house, she watched Rose point and nod, while Andrew scribbled frantically on a small pad.

Aimee rode up and dismounted.

"Aim...azing that you're out of bed so soon, Mister Mack. Do you think that's wise?" Rose glared at Aimee after recovering nicely from her mistake.

"Thank you, Rose, I'm feeling some better, now. How's everything coming along?"

"I was jest telling Mister Harmon of some of the little details you wanted in the kitchen area. He agreed completely they'd

would be welcome additions to his plans."

"Thank you, Rose, I trust you completely. I wonder if I could speak to you privately for a moment, please?" Aimee asked, her eyes sparkling.

"Yes sir, Mister Mackey. Right away, sir." Rose grinned and nodded to her mother and Andrew Harmon as she joined Aimee.

"Rose, I need your help. You may not agree with my plan of action but before you react, think hard and put yourself in my place. Let's take a walk."

After a few moments, Rose said, "Aimee, ain't there nothing I can do to change your mind?"

"Look deep, Rose. How can I keep ignoring the inevitable? Marcus isn't normal. If he's crossed, he must destroy the source. I can't allow Ernest, Norman, and Lucas to become a part of his world."

"D-do you want to c-commit suicide?" Rose hiccupped, as tears threatened again.

"Of course not," Aimee insisted. "But I do want my life back. I need your help, Rose. I won't force you but I don't have anyone I trust as I trust you. I can end this but I can't do it alone." She looked at her friend beseechingly. "If Marcus goes away, then Mack can go away and Aimee can return to a normal life. I'm tired, Rose. I don't want to pretend anymore that I'm someone I'm not. Help me, Rose. Please, help me."

"Stop that," Rose snapped. "Of course I'll helps you. Just tell me what you wants me to do."

"I have to think. Ernest, Doc, and Lucas have been meeting every night this week to come up with some plan to get rid of Marcus. I think they're planning to trick him into some sort of scheme that will backfire in his face.

"They don't know how clever that man can be. It won't be easy conning a con artist. He'll be on to every trick they come up with. He's used them all. I have to get my plan together before they do."

"Have you thought of asking the marshal for help?" Rose asked.

Aimee nodded slowly. "Actually, I have. I think I can pull this off. Marcus may be smart and no doubt he's madder than a rabid fox but his greed overrides both those traits. I've been thinking and, you're right, I need to talk to James Evans. Just remember, this is between you and me. Don't let Lucas find out about what I'm going to do."

"At least, you're gonna talk to someone with authority," Rose said with relief.

"Only if I feel I can trust him," Aimee said.

~ * ~

Rose watched Aimee mount, wheel her horse around and head for the road toward town. She said a quick prayer and turned back and walked toward the house, her face contorted in worry.

Albert looked at her and she knew he was concerned. It broke her heart that she could not tell him Aimee's plans but she had promised. She hoped he would forgive her when it was all said and done. Aimee was their freedom and if she failed, they all failed. Still, she would stand by her friend no matter what.

"Everthin' all right?" he asked as she drew near.

"Sure," she answered and gave him a forced smile. "Mister Mack was just checking on the house. He's feelin' right good now and, despite my objections, is takin' a little ride into town."

Albert nodded as she spoke, but Rose suspected he knew her well enough to see the concern in her eyes. He may not know exactly what was wrong but Rose knew he'd keep it inside until she was ready to tell him. She bit her lip and hoped when the time come, she'd give him good news.

~ * ~

Aimee felt a slight headache trying to develop over her right eye but she knew it was worry, rather than the result of her fall. It was a nagging little ache that she recognized from several episodes in her past. She had suffered from the pain when her father tried to talk her out of seeing Marcus, it was there when Marcus began screaming at her when they first ran out of money, and it was there the day she slipped out of the shack to sell the last of her mother's jewelry to buy the ticket for her escape.

She chuckled wryly. After all this time, Marcus was still able to cause her pain. But this time, she was ready for him. This time she would meet him head on, face to face, and she wondered if anyone had ever stood toe to toe with Marcus and lived to tell about it. She would soon find out. Life was precious and she wasn't about to spend what time she had left worrying about him. He wasn't worth it. Nothing was.

257

~ Twenty-Three ~
Long Arm of the Law

Aimee found James Evans in the town hall, sitting at a long table leafing through a stack of papers. He shifted his gaze when he heard the door open before looking back at the papers. He jerked his head up again when he realized Mack Kaymey had walked in.

"Mister Kaymey, glad to see you up and about. Last time I talked to Mister Chase, you were in bad shape."

"Yes, it wasn't one of my proudest moments. Falling off a sidewalk is not the most adventurous way to sustain an injury."

"Injuries come in all sizes and from all sorts of accidents. Sometimes our poor choices in life result in serious injuries. We don't all get hurt from exciting adventures," Evans said wisely. "Sometimes we can get hurt in the most unsuspecting ways."

"You know, don't you?" Aimee's eyes narrowed.

"I suspected the first time I met you," James said softly "But I didn't want to jump to conclusions before I knew all the facts."

"What gave me away?"

"Miss McKay, it is Miss Aimee McKay, isn't it?" When Aimee nodded, he continued. "Miss McKay, I've been on my own since I was around twelve. I was taken in by a kindly old sheriff when I was fourteen and for the next ten years, I walked his every step, took in his every word, and Lordy, did he ever teach me plenty.

"I learned to read people, listened to what they had to say and hear what they didn't. I learned to see what they tried not to show, and when I took over his job after he passed, I was good at judging people. Mind you, I stumble every now and then but I never take anything at face value. I never assume my feelings are right on until I weigh every aspect of my doubts. I investigate, study, and when all the facts are in, I am the jury.

"Sometimes, I'm sorry to be right. Sometimes, people get sucked into breaking the law out of stupidity, retaliation, desperation, anger, jealousy, and, believe it or not, love. And, sometimes people are just mean, evil, and lots of 'em were born that way. They hit the ground running around trying to hurt, steal, and spend their lives working hard at not working. They want what everybody else has but they want it handed to them on a silver platter. They want to take it from those who already have it. Those are the people who create my job."

"If you thought it was me Marcus was looking for, why haven't you reported your suspicions to him?"

"One reason is that everyone back in California figured you were just one of Alexander's victims, and are fairly well convinced that you're dead. As I told you, if I have any concerns about someone, I do a full investigation. I couldn't find any proof that Marcus Alexander was, at any time, in possession of the amount of gold he claims was stolen from him. He swears he won it from a miner during a poker game. Quite the opposite, in fact.

"Alexander, despite his personal opinion of himself, is a loser. His only talent is his gift of deception and I will have to say he is very good at that. He's always on the move to keep his creditors at bay. Neither the sheriff there nor I could find hide nor hair of the miner who lost all his gold to Alexander. The man just does not exist. I don't know where you got your money or how he found out you had it but that's his next game... relieving you of your fortune."

"Have you got a minute, Marshal Evans?" Aimee sighed as she sat down heavily in the chair across from him.

"Only if you call me Jim." He smiled and leaned forward, giving Aimee his full attention.

For the next half hour, Aimee painfully related how she met Marcus, and how he convinced her that her father didn't understand how much he loved her. She told him about his drinking, gambling, and abuse. She recounted the events of the trip when she escaped, meeting Lucas, and the disastrous hurricane. She explained how she met Abram Ginsberg and his gift, and her decision to become someone else. James Evans listened intently and occasionally clucked sympathetically during her account.

"I thought when I found Sycamore Grove, I was safe. I knew Marcus stayed where there was gambling, land scams, and money to be found. I never dreamed he would become so obsessed with me, he would go to these lengths."

Jim looked at her curiously. "Why have you told me all this today? Is it because you heard that Alexander is in town and you thought he might recognize you?"

Aimee bit her lip and shook her head. "I think I could avoid him indefinitely. If you're as astute as you say, you must know that others know my true identity. I don't believe they'll betray me, neither do I think you will. I'm here because I want this charade ended in a calm and calculated manner. I don't want Ernest, Norman or Lucas injured in any plan they may be devising..."

The marshal chuckled. "Those three are planning something? How many others know of your disguise?"

"Rose Washington, you met her the night you went to see Lucas. Also her mother, and her husband, Albert, who work for me."

"I see. Anybody else?"

Aimee shook her head. "No one else. I do not intend anyone else to ever find out because I don't want them to feel duped or tricked. I'll take care of the masquerade in a way no one will feel slighted."

"And your plan for Alexander is what, exactly?"

"I want to face him and disprove the lies he's spreading. I want to reveal, once and for all, what a brute and cheat he is, and I... I... I want him out of my life now and in the future."

"Did you come here to ask me to shoot him?" Jim asked.

"No," Aimee gasped, covering her mouth. "I wouldn't do that. That would be murder. Do you really think I'm that kind of person?"

Jim grinned. "Not really, just wanted to see if I had you figure out. I do."

"I want you to know the real facts so when I confront him, you know the truth and not just what he wants you to think is the truth."

"When is this confrontation going to take place?" Jim asked, his faced now stern with his eyes boring into hers.

"I'm going to send him a message and ask him to come out to my place Saturday night. I thought it would be best to do this in private."

"I thought your place was torn down and the new house still under construction."

"The new house is under construction but the original cabin has been moved to the back of the property. We can meet in the cabin. I'll offer him some money and a ticket to anywhere he wants to go. I'll set him up in a new place with a new life."

"You realize, don't you, that once he finds you and you offer him money, he will blackmail you for the rest of your life."

"That did cross my mind but I don't know what else to do. I can't live knowing that so many people are willing to put themselves in danger because of me. I need to end this face to face."

"You said Saturday. You know that's tomorrow night, don't you?" Evans asked.

Aimee nodded.

"Are you going to tell Lucas or the others?"

"No, I don't want them there. They'll only get hurt. Norman lost his wife and daughter to a cad like Marcus, and Ernest is such a dear man he wouldn't stand for me to pay off a man like Marcus."

"What about Lucas?" Jim asked, cocking his head to one side.

"I-I don't think Lucas has ever been in the kind of world Marcus comes from. You can tell someone about the horrors of war but unless you've been there, you just don't know. Lucas doesn't know how dirty Marcus can play."

"In other words, you're afraid Lucas couldn't beat Marcus."

"I didn't say that." Aimee's voice rose and her brow shot up in defiance.

"Of course, he could, that is, in a fair fight but Marcus doesn't fight fair. Beside his pointed tail and forked tongue, Marcus stabs people in the back the first chance he gets."

"But you think he'll listen to you?"

"No but he might listen to the clink of gold," Aimee said sharply.

"What time tomorrow night?"

"Why?" Aimee stood and put her hand on her hip. "What do you plan to do?"

"Plan? Why Miss Aimee, whatever do you mean?" The marshal rose, took her arm, and walked her to the door.

"Time?" he repeated.

"Six, I'll meet him at six in the evening."

"Good luck." James said and touched his fingers to his forehead.

As Aimee walked along the wooden sidewalk, she heard a familiar voice call her name.

"Mister Mack. Mister Mack, over here."

When she shook the thoughts of Marcus from her mind and looked up, she saw Isaac holding the leash of his young dog. He waved at her from across the street. As he stepped down into the dusty street and began to trot toward her, the dog jerked forward and yanked the leash from Isaac's grip. The boy stumbled and lunged for the dog.

Automatically Aimee glanced up and to her horror, saw a horseman galloping full speed toward the hotel, which was right past Isaac.

"Stop," she screamed. "Isaac, look out."

Hearing her shout, James Evans rushed outside just in time to see Aimee jump into the path of the horse to rescue Isaac.

The rider pulled back on the reins when he saw the boy, the dog, and the man scrambling in the middle of the road. The horse reared and the man grabbed the saddle horn to keep from being thrown. Wrenching the horse to the left, he brought him under control, leaped to the ground, and strode angrily toward them.

Aimee snagged the dog's collar as she passed and with dog in tow, pulled Isaac to the hitching post out of the way. She bent over in panic when she saw Isaac's feet leave the ground.

"You stupid little piece of trash," a loud growl cut through the ringing in her ears.

Looking up, Aimee saw Isaac dangling two feet off the ground by the front of his shirt. The man's head jutted toward Isaac, putting them nose to nose. Her heart tightened when she saw Marcus' familiar face, wild with fury.

"What are you doing out of your cage? Don't you know your kind isn't allowed to mingle with white folks, boy?"

"Put him down, Mister Alexander. This isn't how we do things here in Sycamore Grove." James Evans took a firm grip on Marcus's arm and tightened his fingers as he spoke.

"You didn't see what happened, marshal," snarled Marcus. "This little cuss almost killed me. If I hadn't been able to control my horse..."

"...and if Mister Kaymey hadn't intervened, you might have run right over the boy."

"What would be the loss?" Alexander smirked. "One less of them to have to deal with."

"I don't want to have to tell you again to put the boy down." Evans voice became dangerously low.

Marcus lowered his arm and pushed Isaac away. Aimee grabbed him, and pushed him safely behind her.

"So that's how it is here," sneered Marcus.

"That's how it is," James said calmly.

Aimee cleared her throat and lowered her voice. "This boy belongs to me and I don't like anyone manhandling my property."

"Well, maybe you'd do a better job if you kept your slaves in the fields where they belong and out of the way of decent people."

"Decent people?" Aimee squeaked.

"That's enough," Evans said quickly, seeing the surprised look on Alexander's face. "Mister Kaymey, perhaps you and your boy best be getting on home. This is Mister Marcus Alexander. Mister Alexander, this is Mack Kaymey, one of our most affluent citizens. Mister Alexander, didn't you have somewhere you needed to be?"

Marcus twisted his arm from Jim's grip. "Don't you worry. It won't take but a few days to clear up my business. Believe me, I don't want to stay in this town any longer than I have to."

"Well," drawled Evans, "I'm glad to hear that. The Saturday Night Poker Club has heard the rumor that a professional poker player arrived in town and I must admit that made them a little nervous. They're just some good, ol' local boys who like to get together once a week and brag about their bank accounts. I was worried that you might want to join them but business is business. I'm sure you won't have time for cards, after all you being a professional and them just playing a friendly little game. It just wouldn't be fair."

"Is there some law preventing me from playing a friendly game with them?" Marcus's ears perked up.

"This is a very small town and these people play for social enjoyment, not for their livelihood."

Aimee pulled her collar up and her hat down before nearing her nemesis. "The marshal has a point," she said hoarsely. "Why not ride out to my place Saturday night for a good home cooked meal and some good brandy. My housekeeper prepares a first class dinner and sets a handsome table."

Marcus laughed and kept his eyes on James. "I'll pass on the home-style cooking, Mister Kaymey. That really isn't my style. I'd rather a card table than a dining table. After completing my business, I just might drop in and see if that bunch is as friendly as you seem to think they are. I'm sure they won't object to additional money in the pot."

"Thought you were in hurry to complete your business?" James asked.

"Poker is my business," Marcus snapped. "This investigation I'm conducting is an off-spring of that. I was robbed, remember?"

"That's right," interjected Aimee. "I saw your poster. This woman is supposed to have stolen a great deal of gold from you. She must have been very clever to have outsmarted you."

Marcus shot a warning glare at her. "What's it to you?"

"Excuse me," retorted Aimee. "If that's the attitude you have when you ask your questions, I'll be surprised you get any cooperation."

Marcus' eyes widen for just a second and he seemed to transform before their eyes.

"Please," he responded, "forgive me." He looked down at Isaac who still hid behind Aimee. "I'm sorry, boy," he said gently. "I was so worried about your safety that I lost control. It would have devastated me if a hair on your head had been harmed. Mister Kaymey, your kind invitation was very thoughtful and I truly appreciate it. This..." he paused dramatically and lowered his head. He wiped at his dry eyes and looked up, a tragic expression on his face. "This situation has upset me more than anyone knows.

"You see, I truly care for the woman on the poster. I had planned to make it my life's work to treat her like a queen - to give her the moon and the stars."

Aimee cringed. Hearing those words again and knowing Lucas had repeated them to her caused the irritating pain to return over her eye.

Marcus continued without missing a beat. "I worked day and night to afford her the best of everything. Nothing was too good for my sweetheart. Her betrayal of my love is a painful truth that I must live with day after day. I mustn't let it affect my relationship with those I meet. I humbly apologize. Please forgive me."

The speech made Aimee nauseous. She could feel the bile rising in her throat. The urge to reach over and scratch out his eyes was almost overwhelming. Instead, she pulled her hat lower and nodded.

"No harm done," she murmured gruffly. "Come on, Isaac, we need to get home."

"Nice to have met you," Marcus said politely. "Sorry to have frightened you, boy. Best you learn to look before you leap."

Before Isaac could respond, Aimee pulled him forward and they headed down the street.

"What are you doing in town alone?" Aimee asked, roughly.

"I came in with Dewey and George to see 'bout the main gate," he answered excitedly, missing Aimee's irritation. "They toted it in to have the new hinges attached by the blacksmith. His anvil is way bigger than the one they have at camp. I went down to the general store to gets some rock candy. Want some?" he held out a small piece of brown paper that held the amber sweets.

Aimee smiled and took a small piece of candy, casually looking back where they had been. Marcus had remounted and was heading for the hotel, while James watched the stagecoach pulling up to the delivery station. She watched him stride hurriedly over to the stage and greet two men who were climbing stiffly from the coach. He shook hands with both, talking briefly to one and then he did something Aimee thought was strange. One of the passengers picked up the luggage the driver handed him and James insisted on taking the suitcase of the other passenger. He escorted both away from the hotel, and across the street where they entered a small house just passed the row of shops and businesses.

Aimee started toward them when Isaac tugged on her sleeve.

"Mister Mack, ain't we goin' home?"

"Yeah, sure," she said. "Come on. My horse is at the town hall. I'll get you back to the house. You run tell Dewey you're going with me."

When they arrived at Eagle Creek, Aimee cringed when she saw Lucas walking back and forth in front of Rose. She realized she had been gone far longer than she should have been.

His face lit up when he saw her and then darkened immediately when he realized she was safe.

"I thought I told you..." he began.

"Don't," Aimee snapped. "I'm sorry I worried you but I'm grown now and don't need anybody's permission to go where I please."

"But..." he answered.

"Please," she pleaded.

"Where's George and Dewey, Isaac?" asked Rose, looking down the road. "Why didn't you come back with them?"

Aimee whirled to hush Isaac but his back was to her and with waving hands, he proceeded to recall the events in town.

"I seed Mister Mack in town and wuz crossing the street to meet 'im. A man on a horse was a comin' real fast and Mister Mack snatched me out of the way. The marshal man came over and the man on the horse got real mad and started a'yellin' and Mister Mack and the marshal talked to him and he got really nice and said he was sorry."

"This man," asked Rose slowly, "wuz he someone we knows?"

"I thinks the marshal-man called him Alyzana, didn't he, Mister Mack?"

Rose stared at Aimee in horror. Lucas was stunned.

"Yes, Isaac, it was Mister Alexander." She returned Rose's stare and glanced at Lucas.

"He's a lookin' fer someone," Isaac went on. "But he sez he might stay and play cards with the poker club in town. Isn't that what he said, Mister Mack?"

Lucas waited for Aimee to answer.

"Yes, I think that's what he said. It's not a matter for us to be concerned about." She shot Rose a warning glance. "He's just passing through. He'll be gone soon and we can just go on with our lives."

"That he will," hissed Lucas as he leaped into his saddle, jerked his horse around, and took off toward town.

"Men," moaned Aimee as she ran to mount her horse. She had to catch up with Lucas before he ruined everything.

He was halfway to town before Aimee overtook him and practically forced his horse off the road.

"Get out of my way, Aimee," panted Lucas. "This can be ended once and for all."

"I thought you and the others were making a plan. Don't do anything foolish. If I can't stop you, at least go talk to the marshal. He was there and from what he said to Marcus, I think he has something up his sleeve. You really need to talk to him."

Lucas' face turned from angry to puzzled. "What did he say?"

"It was really what he didn't say that was interesting. He almost dared Marcus not to join the Saturday Night Poker Club."

"The what?" Lucas asked.

"The Satur..." Aimee started to repeat.

"I heard what you said. It's just that I've never heard of any such club. I've talked to most of the men in town and as far as I know the only clubs are the Cattleman's Association and the Town Council. I wonder what Jim was talking about?"

Aimee smiled. "Maybe that something up his sleeve has to do with a bogus card game."

"You're right. I do need to talk to Jim. Don't worry. I'll stay far away from Marcus Alexander, at least for the present," he winked. He started to ride off but before he left, he reached out and grabbed Aimee's hand.

"Aimee, please, for me, go home. I can't worry about you and Alexander at the same time. I swear I'll tell you everything I find out when I get back. I'm not trying to run your life, just protect you. It won't help if I'm worrying about you while I'm trying to talk to Jim. Won't you please let me handle this?"

As she nodded, he squeezed her hand. "Aimee, this is neither the place I would have chosen... nor the time. I'm not good with words. I found that out earlier. I've practiced a dozen speeches and thought of where I'd take you to hear them, but to be honest, I'm terrified that I won't know the right time or the right place, so here goes.

"Aimee McKay, I love you. No fancy words to frighten you and no pretty phrases you wouldn't believe. I know you've heard them before but you must hear this. These words come from my heart not just my mouth. I love you. Now, please, go home and think about it. Think about whether you believe me or not or even if you want to believe them. If you do, I'll spend the rest of my life proving it to you. If you don't, I'll never bother you again. This I swear."

He swung around and spurred his horse into a full gallop, while Aimee sat frozen in the saddle and watched him disappear around the corner. She sat there until the dust settled back on the road. Slowly she pulled the reins around and started back to his house at a gentle walk.

Dismounting at the front steps, she sat heavily on the porch. She heard the words Lucas said but more than that, she also heard the sincerity in the timbre of his voice. The shield around her heart had begun to soften when he spoke and now she began to experience a longing she denied herself for so long. The urge to race into town, find Lucas, and throw herself into his arms seemed to overwhelm her. Suddenly, the need to see him, touch him, and hear his voice filled her with hope. Lucas was the man she could grow old with and share life's dreams with.

She walked into the house and went to the guestroom.

~ * ~

Chan quietly followed her upstairs and saw the dreamy expression on her face. After she curled up in bed, he pulled the door closed and made a decision he hoped was the right one. He pulled on his coat, went outside and hitched up the buggy. He climbed in and drove toward Eagle Springs.

~ * ~

When Lucas returned home, it was late and the only lamp shone through the dining room window.

Chan opened the door and took his coat. Lucas waited for Chan to hang it up and motioned for him to follow. With a glance

270

upstairs and a nod from Chan, they walked into the study and Lucas closed the door tightly and turned the key in the lock. He went to the cabinet and poured them both a drink. After downing the burning liquid, Lucas grinned and began to fill his house manager and good friend in on his part in an elaborate scheme James Evans concocted and Chan had something he wanted to add.

~ **Twenty-Four** ~
The Plan Begins

The morning dawned as usual but for Aimee, she expected more. Looking out the bedroom window, she searched the skies for storm clouds that would match her mood. Aimee felt different. Today felt different even though it looked the same.

A tap sounded on the door and Rose entered, carrying a large bundle. Chan stood quietly behind her.

Aimee raised her brow and tilted her head to the side. She eyed the bundle and frowned when Rose sat down and stared at her.

"What?" She asked, curiosity reflecting on her face.

"We is... are... sorry to hear 'bouts your setback, Mister Kaymey," Rose said slowly.

Aimee's eyes widened at the statement. "What?" she repeated.

"Oh yes, very, very sorry," said Chan moving into the room. "Your trip into town was too much for you. Your accident, your head injury, and your rescue of the little boy was responsible for the relapse of your past ill health and caused you to collapse upon your return. That in turn, resulted in us sending to town for the doctor."

"W-what?"

"Oh, yes. Yesterday, Mister Lucas done sent a telegram to that sister of yours to come right away. The doctor is mighty concerned 'bout your health. He's sore afraid that fall done caused some permanent injury. He 'spects you have a blood clot in your brain from the fall and he wants your sister here mighty quick."

Aimee shook her head and started to speak.

"Please, don't say what again." Rose grinned. "Doctor's orders."

While Aimee sat trying to figure out what they were talking about, Rose began to shove pillows under the blankets and bunch the covers around them. When she finished, there was only the outline of a figure, seemingly snuggled down under the quilts.

"Now, you has to git yourself into this here trunk we done brung up."

"Now, can I say 'what'?" Aimee asked, jumping to her feet, hands on her hips.

"Mister Lee here came to me yesterday with an idea. We done drove into town and found Mister Lucas with the doctor, Mister Gaines, and Marshal Evans. They's had an idea, and when they stirred Chan's idea together with theirs, they told us we should get you outta town and bring in Mister Kaymey's sister."

"And that means I have to be shipped out in a trunk?" Aimee said shaking her head.

"You gots a better idea of not being seen… by anybody?"

"No, not really, but…"

"No more what's and no buts," said Chan sternly. "You dress now. You please get in trunk and we do the rest."

Aimee dressed quickly and climbed into the trunk. Rose carefully folded some clothes and placed them all around her, shielding her from the trunk wall. Chan had meticulously removed brads along the upper portion of the trunk base and across the lid to allow air to enter. A knock on the door was the signal. Aimee snuggled down and Chan lowered the lid and fastened the lock.

Rose opened the door and whispered, "Y'all come in and be's quiet about it. Mister Kaymey done had a relapse but this trunk must gets on the stage this evening 'cause he done put some fancy crystal inside. Don't bump anything and for goodness sake, don't drops it, you hears me?"

Tom nodded solemnly. He and another man entered, picked up the trunk and with a quick glance at the bed, and carried it out, handling it as if he saw Rose fill it with dynamite.

Rose slipped on her coat, touched Chan's arm warmly, gave him an appreciative smile and together followed the men out to the wagon. She climbed onto the seat beside Tom, after making sure they had handled their cargo with kid gloves, she waved at Chan as they headed for town.

Rose argued for a good fifteen minutes before convincing the ticket master that she wanted four seats on the six-seated stage. One for her, one for Tom and the other two for the trunk that she wanted beside her inside the coach. Eventually, the clerk gave in after she explained that the space was for paid tickets and as long as she paid, he could not legally refuse her. The men gently placed the trunk on the seat, Rose mounted the steps, clamored in and snuggled herself across from her precious cargo. Tom sat next to Rose. He wasn't sure what was going on, but Mister Lucas paid well and if he told Rose to tell him to ride with Rose to Dawson City with a trunk, then that's just what he would do, no questions asked.

Within five minutes they were on their way down the road and in a couple of hours, they reached Dawson City. About two miles from town, Rose rapped on the roof of the carriage and the driver pulled to the side of the road. She told the driver they were being met there, and he helped Tom unload the trunk. When the stage was out of sight, Rose opened the lid.

"Are you alright?" she asked, reaching for Aimee's arm.

"I couldn't have done this in the summer," Aimee gasped. "There was enough air to survive but it was so stuffy I thought a couple of times I couldn't stand it any longer."

"I'm so sorry, Miss Aimee but Chan said you'd be jest fine. Lots of people in his country done escaped from soldiers this a'way."

"I'm just fine. Chan was right. It's a perfect way to get around without anyone knowing. It's just that once you're inside you feel so helpless and I don't like being locked up or at least feeling helpless. It's over now. You two failed to tell me the rest of the plan. What's next?"

"What's next is that we waits right here for Chan. He's gonna be 'bout half an hour behind us. While Mister Kaymey is being cared for by my mama, his sister is on her way to take over his care herself.

"Mister Ernest is done spreading the news of her arrival

whiles we sits here. The doctor done been confiding to the loosest lips in town 'bout how worried he was 'bout Mister Kaymey's serious relapse. Mister Lucas done been to Eagle Creek to talk to Mister Harmon and tell him that he is to continue on the house, that it don't matter 'bout Mister Kaymey's condition, and here we are."

"Oh, my, you all have been busy. This was all Chan's idea?"

"The escape plan wuz his idea. The rest wuz hatched between the other gentlemen, Mister Lucas, Mister Gaines, the marshal, and the doctor. You got a bunch of good friends, Miss."

Tears filled Aimee's eyes. "I never thought this would happen the day I came to Sycamore Grove. I never felt so lonely in my life. Now, like you say, I've got more friends than I ever had but you're the best, Rose. You're the very best. None of this would have ever happened without you."

Rose reached out and took Aimee's hand. "I had my momma, my man, my friends, and my youn'uns. You had no one and you's frettin' over your father and brother's reputation pushed you deeper into them shadows of loneliness.

"The thought of you hidin' every time a body came by reminds me of how I lived for so long but at least I warn't alone. I jest couldn't bear the thought of you livin' in fear the rest of your life. You terrified me when you told me of your plan to face that Alexander man and the more I heard 'bout him, the more 'fraid I became. But I knows that you done taken fear from my life and I wanted to help snatch the fear from yours. Everyone is right. We must gets rid of him, once and for all."

"What do we do now?"

Rose shifted to the side, looked past Aimee and began waving wildly. When Aimee followed her gaze, she saw an enclosed carriage coming quickly down the road with Chan in the driver's seat.

Chan pulled the horses off the road and climbed down. He opened the door and motioned for Aimee to quickly enter the coach. He and Rose lifted the trunk onto the back and fastened it securely. After helping Rose inside, he climbed back into the driver's seat, coaxed the horses to swing around and headed back down the road.

"I thought we were going to Dawson City?" Aimee asked when she realized they had turned around.

"Oh, no. Chan has a place where you can change. The story is that you arrived in Dawson City and we picked you up there."

"Wouldn't it be better to wait until he ...? Marcus, left town. He...he might recognize me," Aimee said nervously. "I don't want to put Lucas or the other men in danger."

"No, you needs to get back. Your face'll be covered with a heavy veil. Mister Lucas'll make sure that you's seen 'round town as Mr. Mack's sister. The doctor is spreading the sad news about Mister Mack's terrible turn for the worse and the marshal will make sure that Mister Alexander is as busy as a three-legged dog in a smokehouse when you arrive."

Chan took a road to the left that bounced and jostled the coach around until it finally pulled to a halt. Rose jumped out with her carpetbag and gestured for Aimee to follow. A small shack sat hidden in the trees a few yards from the coach.

"Me, Albert, and Isaac found this here place back awhile. It ain't much but you kin change in there. I think most folks done completely fergot it's even here."

They went inside and with Rose's help, Aimee quickly changed and Rose attached a thick, curled hairpiece that hung down the back of her head, and a tiny but smart little hat with the full, dark veil covered Aimee's face. The last item was a small box that Aimee recognized and with a lump in her throat stood still as Rose hung the cameo necklace Lucas had given her for Christmas around her neck.

"This here is fer luck," Rose said with a smile.

Aimee touched it tenderly as Rose fastened it around her neck.

As they walked out, Chan smiled broadly.

"Wouldn't know she our little missy or that she our Mister Kaymey, you wouldn't. This lady look very well dressed with fancy hairdo. She look like she from very fancy family."

Aimee returned his grin as she and Rose climbed into the coach and Rose stowed Aimee's other clothes in her bag.

A while later, as they drove into town Aimee pulled the veil over her face. Rose adjusted it around the sides and then stepped out. Lucas came hurrying up to greet them and leaned near Aimee.

"You look beautiful," he whispered. "Not that you're not a nice looking man but believe me, this is what you were born to look like."

His eyes paused at the necklace around her neck and looked back into Aimee's eyes.

"It's a lovely necklace but your beauty makes it pale in comparison."

Aimee blushed and smiled behind the veil. Lucas took her hand and tucked it under his. As locals ogled them, he led her into the hotel where they walked into the restaurant and sat at a table in a dark corner. Suddenly, the sidewalk outside became crowded by slow-walking rubber-neckers, who tried to pretend they were just casually passing by. Lucas order iced lemonade and before the waiter could leave, Norman joined them.

Lucas rose and introduced Norman to his companion and the citizens noted the doctor kiss her hand. He sat down, pulling his chair near hers and talked softly and earnestly, while the on-lookers shook their heads as she scrambled for a handkerchief, which she slipped under her veil and apparently dabbed at her eyes.

The waiter returned but Lucas shook his head and handed him several coins. Then his companion rose, took the doctor's arm and they hurried outside, where she was helped into the waiting carriage. Lucas and the doctor joined her and Chan pulled away from the hotel at a steady trot, pushing them into a gallop as soon as they were at the edge of town.

Heads nodded and tongues wagged before the dust settled from the carriage. Within five minutes, the citizens of Sycamore Grove had practically buried Mack Kaymey with their gossip and speculations. That is just what Lucas had hoped for.

Chan delivered his passengers to Lucas's house and waited patiently for the doctor to finish his part in the charade so he could take the doc back to town. It was important for not only the town to witness the charade but for the men who worked at Hill-crest to see the performance.

Upstairs, Aimee threw back the heavy veil and gasped, "This is one item of ladies clothes that I hope I don't have to wear often. I feel claustrophobic in that thing."

"I can't say that I blame you," agreed Norman. "I'm un-comfortable camping out in a tent. I sure don't want any kind of net over my face."

"You may have to wear it once or twice more," said Lucas with a frown. "I don't want Marcus recognizing you too soon at the card game and, of course, you'll have to wear it at the fu-neral."

"Card game, funeral?" Aimee shuddered. "What are you talking about?"

"We're holding the Saturday Night Poker Club at the hotel restaurant. It will be closed by then but there will probably be several last minute customers. I want you to be there. Norman, Ernest, James, and a friend of James' has a little surprise for your friend, Marcus Alexander. I think you'll really enjoy it."

"...and the funeral?" Aimee prodded.

"Oh," Lucas said, his face feigning exaggerated sorrow. "I'm afraid Mack isn't going to make it. Isn't that right, Doc?"

"Aimee, now, you know we talked about this. Ernest said you understood that the only way you could live a normal life was to have Mack... well...have Mack out of the way. I'm sorry to break it to you like this."

"Are you'uns outta ya minds," cried Rose. "You folks is act-ing like Mack Kaymey is a real person and you is about to murder

278

him. Get a grip on yourselves. Aimee, I's told Mother and Isaac the truth 'bout everythin' an' we're in charge of the funeral. Mother says it's about time and Isaac thinks you're the bravest thing since King Arthur, that knight fellow you done told him all about.

"Now, let's get down to business."

"Rose is absolutely right," Norman agreed. "Lucas, you get on back to town and help James get everything set up. Aimee, you need to get something to eat and it wouldn't hurt to take a dose of elixir. You look pale and shaky. Rose, you take care of her and make sure Chan gets her to town and go in through the front door of the hotel before eight o'clock tonight. We want everyone to see Mack's sister once more. I'll follow Lucas in and go directly to the funeral parlor and get things going on that end.

"We don't have time to waste. Things are coming to a head and we all need to be ready and in our places when the boomerang is thrown. Are there any questions?"

Lucas grabbed his hat and as he passed Aimee, he slipped his arm around her waist and drew her close. To her surprise, in front of everyone, he leaned down and kissed her firmly.

"I know you are ready to resume a normal life but I guarantee, I am more ready than you are. I love you, Aimee Amelia McKay, and there is nothing in this world that will ever change that. I promise that after tonight, our lives will never be the same again. We'll be saying goodbye to the past. Are you ready?"

Aimee stared at him and she could feel her heart pounding in her chest. She couldn't fool herself anymore. She loved Lucas, but the words stuck in her throat. All she could do was squeeze his arm and nod.

That was all Lucas needed. He gazed into her tear filled eyes and quickly kissed the tip of her nose, before turning and rushing out the door.

Aimee took a deep breath and when she turned, she saw Chan quickly look out the window. Norman stared at his boots and Rose beamed with delight.

"Well, now that we done got that straight, we needs to get going," Rose said with a chuckle.

Chan hurried out and Rose closed the door firmly behind him.

"What shall I wear?" Aimee asked as she struggled out of the dress she wore.

"I has it all picked out. All you needs to do is wash some of the traveling dust off and get into this blouse and skirt I'm gonna lay out. You still has to wear that veil for a little while."

Aimee giggled as she washed her arms and neck.

"What's so funny?" Rose asked as she smoothed out the skirt.

"If I'm Mack Kaymey's sister and I have to use his name. You'll have to call me Aimee Kaymey. Isn't that funny?"

"Aimee Kaymey," Rose repeated. "Aimee Kaymey. What sort of parent would name their child Aimee Kaymey?"

"No one, silly. That just the way it worked out with my real name and my alter ego's pretend name."

Rose giggled. "I see now, Aimee Kaymey." She giggled some more and cocked her head toward Aimee. "You needs to remember that and not to name your son, Stace Chase."

Aimee blushed. "I don't know what you're talking about, Rose. That kind of talk is ridiculous."

"Is it, now? Is it really?" Rose continued to stare at her. "You knows Mister Lucas is bad in love with you. He be doing everything in his power to give you the life you want and need. Tell me, Miss Aimee, that you ain't leading that poor feller along by an invisible ring in his nose without knowing. Please, tell me true." Rose pinched her lips together and furrowed her brow.

"Rose, I wouldn't do that. I couldn't."

"Then what's you got in store for that man?"

"I..." she gasped as Rose tightened the laces in the back of her corset. "I..." Rose pulled again and tied the laces. She reached for the skirt. Aimee reached out and grabbed Rose as she went to slip the skirt over her head.

"Rose, I know you care for me and Lucas."

Rose sat on the bed and shook her head." I ain't got no right questioning you. This ain't none of my business, but Aimee, things done spiraled out of control and I'm scared. Mister Lucas is putting himself in a dangerous spot tonight and it's all for love-his love for you. I done seen it in his eyes. He ain't fer sure how you feels, still he's said them words serious like, and them words that came out of his mouth today weren't in fun. His heart was hangin' on those words out in plain sight for all the world to see. He said it in front of the good Lord and all of us. And the way he said it, he don't ever mean to take 'em back. Maybe if you ain't in love with him fer sure, maybe... maybe you could learn to be."

Aimee sat down beside Rose on the bed. "I don't have to learn to, Rose. I do love him. It started growing the first time I saw him on the S.S. Sonora. I didn't know it then but the seed of affection was planted. That was before we were aboard the ship that sank. His eyes were so kind and gentle and I saw them in my dreams. When he showed up here, my heart nearly broke. Here was a man that I thought I could never have, living right next door. I tried not to love him. I never wanted him involved in the mess I'd made of my past."

"But he done got himself involved," Rose insisted.

"I know and although I'm sorry, I feel that I have a chance to be happy with him, and a chance to be me."

"Oh, Aimee, it's gonna work out. I feels it. You knows I got the gift. You gots too many good people on your side."

Before Aimee could answer, Chan rapped loudly on the door.

"You ready, missy? Sun going down and we go."

Rose jumped up and called to Chan, "Gets the buggy ready and gives us a few more minutes. It won't be long. We's nearly finished."

Aimee buttoned the blouse and Rose finished slipping the full dark skirt over her head. While Rose fastened the skirt, Aimee readjusted her hairpiece and drove a large bejeweled pin through the small hat, anch- oring to her hair.

Before Chan could rush them again, they jerked opened the bedroom door and hurried down the stairs. Aimee slung a velvet cape she bought in Charleston over her shoulders and Rose grabbed her woolen shawl.

Once in the buggy, Chan snapped the horses into a quick trot and they headed for town.

~ Twenty-Five ~
The Final Hand

They arrived at the hotel just as the sun began to disappear below the horizon. Ernest waited inside the front door of the hotel, and kissed Aimee's veiled cheek. Then, as everyone around watched, he whisked her upstairs to a room that had been reserved just for her. Rose hurried along behind and as soon as Earnest closed the door, Marcus Alexander exited a door just down the hall and proceeded to follow Norman downstairs.

In the dining room a large table had been placed in the back corner of the room with seven or eight chairs around it. There were still a few tables vacant against the far wall but as rumor spread about the strange poker game and an even stranger club that no one had ever heard of before, people who had never eaten out before, suddenly decided to eat at the hotel restaurant.

By the time dusk faded into the dark of night, every table except the poker table was filled and the 'closed' signed had been placed on the door. As was the custom, patrons in the restaurant were allowed to order and eat if they arrived before the sign went up. The cook worked overtime, as he and his helper worked furiously to fill each order.

Ernest and Norman selected a few close and trusted friends to participate in the poker game, and although they didn't know all the details, they willingly agreed to set a trap for a man the marshal was anxious to apprehend.

As Lucas, Norman, and Ernest selected the chairs they would use, a waiter set up a long table nearby with several bottles of liquor, a few plates of snacks, and placed ashtrays around the table. The chosen poker players wandered over to the table and soon there were only three chairs left unoccupied.

James entered, chatting earnestly with a man Lucas did not recognize. Ernest gave a quick nod to him, when James neared the table.

"Hello, boys," James said loudly. "This is my old friend, John Smith. He's passing through and I thought he might join us if you have no objections.

"No, not at all. Here, let me get you a chair. Waiter, bring Mister Smith a drink. What's your poison, Mister Smith?" asked Norman.

"Thank you, just call me John and I'll have coffee for now."

A minute later the loud voice of Marcus Alexander roared into the dining room. "What do you mean you've never heard of the Saturday Night Poker Club?"

Lucas jumped up and hurried into the lobby. "Here, Mister Alexander, we're in here. I'm afraid most of the men don't advertise the club due to repercussions from their wives. A little discretion, if you please."

"Men around here ain't got any backbone if they live their lives in fear of the wrath of a worthless, pitiful female," he guffawed. "You won't catch me quaking in my boots afraid some woman might disapprove of the way I choose to live.

"Women belong to their husbands and if they cause a problem that problem should be dealt with like you would deal with a stubborn mule, leave 'em out in the cold and let 'em go without food for a day or two. If that doesn't work, then a whack or two should put them in their place, if you ask me."

Ernest reached over and gently rested his hand on Norman's trembling arm to quiet him.

"Have a seat here, next to me," Lucas steered Marcus to the table. "Ernest, will you name the game and begin the deal?"

"Five card stud, nothing wild. Straight poker, gentlemen. Will you ante up, please? Five dollar ante, if you will."

"Five dollars," spat Marcus. "Gentlemen, if you call this poker, I'm afraid your little game is a might too tame for me. I'm used to seeing hundreds, if not thousands of dollars on my playing table."

As he started to push back his chair, the stranger James brought slapped a small sack on the table. He opened it slowly, enjoying the anticipation on Marcus's face as he revealed a dozen or so similar sized golden nuggets.

"Each of these is worth approximately one hundred dollars. Is that rich enough for you, mister?" he asked slyly.

"And who am I addressing, good sir?" Marcus' voice suddenly sweetened and his sarcasm flipped to charming.

"Why, my name is John, sir. John Smith. These nuggets come fresh from the western coast. Have you ever been there, Mister Uh, sorry,I didn't get your name?"

"Alexander, Marcus Alexander. Yes, I've passed through that area, although, I'm originally from the east, Boston and Philadelphia. My family has roots there, you know. My father made his fortune there. Some of the same fortune that woman I'm looking for stole from me."

"I see. Well, I spent some time in Boston and am familiar with most of the businesses in the city. What does your family do there, Mister Alexander?"

Marcus looked uncomfortable. "Ah, well, they're in investments, sir, and you probably never ran into my family. My father is an entrepreneur who chooses to keep his identity private. You understand, I'm sure."

"I'm sure," John Windham said curtly.

As they talked, Ernest shuffled the cards, Norman cut them, and Ernest proceeded to deal. With a nod from Ernest, all his friends nervously slid their hundred-dollar ante to the center of the table and peeked at the cards in their hands.

Within the next couple of hours the men won a few hands and a lost few hands. Everyone was about even until Marcus and John Windham began to raise, bet, and raise again. Close to three thousand dollars lay on the table, and Marcus stared hungrily at the pot. Every other player folded, and the game came down to Marcus, John, and Lucas.

Suddenly, as Marcus studied his hand, Lucas glanced down,

scooted back his chair, and threw his hand face down on the table. "Gentlemen, I'm sorry but it seems we have a problem. This hand is over and we'll return everyone's ante."

"The blazes we will," Marcus shouted, jumping up and facing Lucas.

"I'm sorry, Mister Alexander but there's a card on the floor by your feet. We cannot continue this hand without all the cards in play."

"Wha- ?" Marcus gasped as he stepped back and peered in the direction Lucas pointed. "Hey, what kind of people are you?"

"That's what I want to know about you," growled John.

"What are you accusing me of?" Marcus demanded, as he scooted his chair back. "That card ain't mine."

A new group had entered the dining room during the last half hour and sat at a table against the wall. One patron rose and approached the table.

"Here," said a soft feminine voice. "I see it. Let me get that for you."

A tall blond woman, wearing an emerald colored dress and a tiny white hat with a short veil covering most of her upper face, approached them. She bent over, her colorful bracelets jangling in the process. Straighten- ing up, she handed Lucas the card.

"Thank you, ma'am. I don't believe I've had the pleasure," Lucas said, as the other men rose.

"No, you probably haven't," the woman replied and lifted the veil.

"My name is Veronica Hays and I'm from San Francisco. My father runs the Golden Slipper Gentlemen's Club there." She paused dramatically as Marcus slowly turned toward her.

His eyes widened in shock and a slight tremor passed through his body.

"You?" he said.

"Yes, it's me," she sneered. "You thought I was dead, didn't you. That's the only reason I survived that night, wasn't it? After you beat me senseless and tried to strangle me, you really

286

thought I was dead." She threw back her head and laughed.

"They said, that is, I heard...," he stammered. "The newspaper said you were dead. What's going on here?" He snarled as he turned to find James and John pointing guns at him.

John Windham stepped forward, reached behind Marcus, and removed a small handgun he had hidden in his belt snuggled in the small of his back.

"I said I was from the west. Actually, my name isn't Smith, it's Windham. John Windham, the sheriff of San Francisco. The newspaper was very co-operative when I told them I wanted her death reported. She was the only witness we had that could identify her attacker and possibly stop the man responsible for a series of attacks and murders that occurred on the waterfront. A friend of Veronica's gave us an excellent description of the man she saw Veronica with, and I've been searching for you since you left town."

"You're crazy, the lot of you. I've never seen this woman before."

"But you just said you read about her death in the paper," another female voice said.

He jerked around to see Aimee standing beside Rose.

"There, there's the thief that stole my gold. I knew I'd find you, you two-timing witch. She's a wanted woman. Why don't you arrest her?"

James moved near Aimee and took her arm. "I'm afraid you're mistaken. May I present Miss Amelia Kaymey, gentlemen. This is Mack Kaymey's sister. Mister Kaymey has taken a turn for the worse after his fall and Miss Amelia has come to nurse him." The men around the table mumbled their well wishes and looked stricken at the news.

Marcus looked stunned. "Veronica tell them. You know Aimee McKay. You saw her with me. Tell them who she is."

Veronica Hays lifted her eyebrows and snapped open her fan. "Whatever do you mean, Marcus? There were rumors, of course, that every time you pawned a piece of jewelry, every

287

time you bet a jewel or coin, that they belonged to some woman you kept locked up in shantytown.

"I've even heard some of your low-life friends laughing about the woman locked away in your shack, too injured from your beatings to move. They bragged about how you'd taken every penny, even her poor dead mother's legacy, but see her? Marcus, you made sure no one around town ever saw her. You couldn't take the chance she'd tell, or try to run away and have you put in jail. From what I hear, she's probably dead, killed by your hand.

"No, Marcus, I can't identify this woman as Aimee McKay." She smiled seductively and fanned herself.

"This is a frame-up. You can't prove I killed anyone. Do you have a witness? No. Is there any evidence I was with them? No. If there was, you wouldn't be playing cards with me, you would arrest me and put me in jail."

"Actually, I'm arresting you now for the attempted murder of Veronica Hays and the burglary of her apartment. I do have a witness for that. There is a shop owner waiting to testify that you are the man who sold him jewelry that Miss Veronica has identified as belonging to her. Her father reported it missing shortly after we found her unconscious. We also have a witness, her personal maid, who says she saw you leaving the same apartment just before she was found."

"That's absurd. Veronica, this is a horrible mistake. You know how I feel about you. Remember our moonlight walks and the nights we sat on the beach talking. I can't live without you. I want to give you the sun..."

"The moon and the stars," Aimee and Veronica chimed in. They both burst out laughing and so did everyone else.

"Ka-boom," Norman shouted as he ducked the imaginary, invisible boomerang.

"You're crazy," screeched Marcus. "What was that for?"

"Why, that's the sound a boomerang makes when it levels the unwary," Lucas snarled, and then burst out laughing. Norman and Ernest's guffaws joined Aimee and Veronica, who were still laughing.

Marcus growled, cursed, and struggled as James tied his hands behind him while John Windham held him in an iron grip. He hissed at the two women and tried to spit on them.

"I wouldn't be surprised if we get more evidence on him once I get him back to California," Sheriff Windham said. Once it's known he's in custody and folks don't have to worry about getting their throats cut, I 'spect more witnesses will come forth. I won't give up until I hang him for those murders."

"Fat chance, you miserable, tin-starred coward," Marcus spat.

As James and John dragged Marcus off toward the jail-house, Lucas, Ernest, and Norman divided the poker money among the volunteers and thanked them sincerely. Most left to go home but Aimee invited Veronica to have a cup of tea, although Veronica opted for whiskey.

Norman and Ernest cleared the dining room and stayed behind to make sure only Rose, Aimee, Veronica, and Lucas remained. James and John returned shortly and James poured all the men a tall, stiff drink.

"It's very brave for you to come all the way from California to confront that horrible man. I commend you for that and I am so glad you've recovered from his attack. Thank you for coming here and stopping a monster like that, Miss Hays."

"You're very welcomes, Miss McKay. I assure you, it is my pleasure," Veronica Hays said in a soft whisper. "However, I can't take all the credit. If not for you and your determination to survive, he still might be roaming free to ruin another woman's life."

"What...what did you call me? My name is..." Aimee's lips grew numb.

"Please, I know who you are. He told me you were his sister. I did see you once with Marcus when you first arrived and once again later. Your eye was swollen shut then and you had a bandage..." She paused, reached over and gently moved Aimee's hair back, "right about there," she finished as she tenderly touch Aimee's hated scar.

"He told me you drank a lot and fell." She took a deep breath and continued. "I believed it because I wanted to. He was so sweet at first and I thought he needed me and loved me. I'm sure you know what I'm saying." She downed her drink in one swallow. "What a fool I was. Why are we so stupid when it comes to men? We either pick the wrong one or we let the right one get away."

She laughed harshly and held up her glass for a refill.

"Why did you, um, why did you..."

"Lie?" Veronica laughed. "Let's just say I was taught by the best, weren't you? You haven't been truthful since you've been here, have you? We both have become the victims of his cruelty and we lied in order to survive. People lie mostly out of fear. Occasionally," she smiled, "people lie for a good reason."

"I didn't mean to seem rude," Aimee said softly as she touched Veronica's arm. "I, have turned into someone I don't even recognize."

"I know," she smiled sadly, "that I'm not a well-bred lady like you, Miss McKay. But I wasn't born in the gutter either. My pa runs a Gentlemen's Club, that's a fancy name for a high-class saloon, and he brought me up to be honest, hardworking, and truthful. I'm not so naive however, that I don't know about men like Marcus but I never thought I'd be fooled by a man like him.

"That friend of yours, Lucas Chase, is sweet on you, isn't he?'

"I... Well... I..."

"You don't have to say anything, it's obvious, James told me he expected a wedding soon. You're not as good a liar as you thought you were.

"Everyone but you can see you two were meant for one another. You know, Ma used to say that everything happens for a reason. Maybe you and I had to experience the dark side of this world before we could recognize the good when we see it. You hang on to that Lucas feller, Miss McKay. I've got my eye on James Evans. He treats me like I'm someone special."

"You are someone special, Veronica Hays. You saved my life and are putting away a monster. Maybe, in a way, you're saving James's life, too. None of us is supposed to live alone, without love." Aimee leaned over and hugged Veronica, who blushed.

"Well, ladies, I'm glad to see you two are getting to know one another." James grinned as he walked to their table.

"Is he..." Aimee looked worriedly at James.

"Mister Marcus Alexander is trussed up like a Christmas turkey and locked safely away. Several citizens are keeping watch on him until John can get him back to California. Norman has even volunteered to let James swear him in as a deputy and accompany him to San Francisco. He is as determined to see Alexander get his just reward as anyone involved."

He turned to Veronica. "Norman is our resident doctor and his daughter was abused during her marriage and eventually beaten to death by her drunken husband. This will help him get closure for his daughter's murder since he wasn't able to save her himself."

Veronica dabbed her eyes. "Bless his heart," she sniffed. "I know exactly what he's going through. My father has suffered so much over this. He blames himself that he was not there when Marcus attacked me. Each time I came to in the hospital, Pa was sitting beside me and most of the time he was crying. I'd never seen Pa cry before and that just added to my determination to see that someone stopped Marcus. It's bad enough to snuff out a person's life but the damage done to those left behind is something they live with all their lives."

Lucas stood behind Aimee, his hand draped gently over her shoulders.

"This has been a long hard day but I must say more than rewarding. Miss Hays, you must be exhausted after the trip and having to go through all this. We have your room ready for you if you would like to rest."

Veronica slipped her fan inside her muff and tucked her small purse in with it. "You're right. After all this and my glasses of celebration, I'm ready to call it a day."

Both women rose and Veronica hugged Aimee tightly. "I'll be leaving on the morning stage. I'm so glad to have met you and know that you're doing so well." She paused and glanced at Lucas. "I think you've got your brave knight to protect you from now on."

James leaned forward. "I don't think you'll have to worry either, Miss Hays," he said with a shy grin.

"Good-bye, Miss Hays, and I'm glad this is all behind us both. Have a happy life," Aimee said.

"Thank you, I will. Goodbye. Goodbye to you all." She turned and let James lead her from the dining room.

"Are you ready, Amelia?" Lucas asked.

"I'll never get used to that name," she said as she shook her head." I was given that name after an aunt and I always thought she behaved horridly to my mother. I just shiver when I hear it. I can't bear to hear you call me Amelia."
"Sure you can. We'll shorten it to Aimee after a bit. After all, Amelia is your middle name isn't it?"

"Yes, but how did you know?"

"I'm afraid I'm to blame for that, my dearest," came a deep voice filled with emotion.

Aimee turned, her hands flying to her mouth. A tall, well-dressed, white haired gentleman stood inside the dining room door, leaning heavily on a cane. A younger man stood beside him steadying him by his other arm. Both smiled at her and Aimee burst into tears as she flew into their arms.

"Papa, oh, Papa... I'm so ashamed. I'm sorry, so sorry," Aimee sobbed and buried her head on her father's shoulder. Her brother wrapped his arms around her and hugged his sister and father in a tight embrace.

"Edward," she cried. "I've missed you both so. Can you ever forgive me?"

"Shh," comforted her father. "None of us are without having made foolish decisions. Anyone who claims to be perfect has one great flaw, they're liars."

"Come sir, won't you sit here?" Lucas asked and pointed out a large cushioned chair inside the door.

"How... how did you know? Who...?" She stammered as she followed her father to the chair, holding on to him as if she were afraid he'd vanish.

"Now, that blame is mine," Lucas admitted. "No girl needs to go through life without the father and brother she loves."

"How could you think that we cared more about gossip than we did you? Your Mama taught you better than that, Baby Sister. As Papa always said, 'The only reason people gossip is to keep the spotlight off of themselves,' isn't that right, Papa?" Her brother stated, smiling happily.

"Never met a busybody that didn't have a secret or two they were trying to hide." The old man grinned. "I hear you've come into some money and you're building a beautiful house."

"How? Oh, you again?" She looked at Lucas.

"Guilty as charged," he answered.

"Papa, there are some things I need to tell you... or do I?" Again, she turned toward Lucas.

"Well, there didn't seem to be any place to stop," he said, sheepishly.

"Aimee, my darling, I would have never thought it possible for you to have survived the way you have. It was an incredible journey for you to make all alone. A loving, caring person like you would just naturally attract those people who end up wanting to protect you and aid you. Still, your world became so empty and lonely."

"I wasn't too alone, Papa, and I wasn't lonely long. First, I found Abram, then, Rose, Albert, and Isaac, along with their friends. Next, there was Lucas, and Norman who stepped forward to keep me from stumbling and making any more foolish mistakes.

"I have friends who have protected me and surrounded me. I haven't been alone here, that's for sure."

"Yes, here, you have friends, but before that...," tears flooded his eyes and his voice shook.

"That was yesterday, Papa. We can't change yesterday. We don't have to keep looking back. We're here today and that's all that matters.

"I still don't understand? How did you find my father? I never told you...," Aimee looked beseechingly at Lucas.

"Marcus Alexander isn't the only one who hired a private detective. It didn't take him long to locate your father. He wired law offices from Boston all across the country inquiring about you and Marcus. Few made it this far south, however. Unfortunately, Marcus was afraid of that and shied away from towns with sheriffs and marshals in the Midwest but it was his inquiries that led the detective to your family."

"I wanted to spare you, Papa. Can you ever forgive me?"

"I want to ask for your forgiveness. I know my actions in the past must have influenced your decision not to return home when you had the chance. There is nothing you have done to forgive. Am I forgiven, daughter?"

"Always, Papa, always. I love you and Edward so much. I thought my heart would burst when I saw you two."

Aimee felt a slight touch at her elbow. Rose whispered in her ear. "Miss Aimee, I needs to get on home. You are in good hands now and I needs to hold my baby. I forgets how powerful the pull of love can be. I know it's strong and it's pulling me home."

"Oh, Rose, how thoughtless of me. Papa, this is Rose Washington. She and her husband, Albert, their son, Isaac, and all their friends work for me. I couldn't have made it without them."

"Mrs. Washington, allow me to offer my thanks and appreciation for looking after my little girl. I will make it my life's mission to repay you and your family for what you've done for us."

"You ain't owin' us nothin', Mister McKay. Your daughter done gave us our freedom and nothing can top that."

Joseph McKay nodded solemnly and bowed to her.

Ernest stepped forward. "Rose, I'll be happy to get you home. Come with me, my dear."

Lucas slid his arm around Aimee. "I suggest we all get home. I'll have your bags sent to my house. We can all ride home together. Chan, my right hand man, will drive us."

Later that night, after a cold supper of ham, sliced melon, tomatoes, hot biscuits, dripping with fresh churned butter, gallons of steaming coffee, and hours of reminiscing, hugs and tears, Aimee lay in bed, exhausted, but wide awake.

Tears burned her eyes but they were tears of relief, joy, and the comfort of having her family back in her life. She rose, slipped her house shoes on and wrapped a blanket around her. She shuffled to the window and sat on the cushioned window seat, peering outside.

A movement caught her eye and she squinted down into the yard. Lucas stood on the graveled walk gazing into the velvet night. She waved but realized his back was to her and he couldn't see her. Without hesitation, she silently left the room, and went downstairs and out the front door.

Hearing the door close, Lucas turned around. His face lit with a loving smile.

"Aimee," he whispered. "Are you all right? You should be asleep. It's been a stressful day."

She peered into his face and reached out to stroke his cheek. "I can't sleep. I thought it was the excitement of seeing my family and the strain of facing Marcus but I was wrong. I can't sleep because of you."

His blue eyes twinkled and his smile lit up the darkness. "I knew down deep you truly cared but I was afraid you'd harden your heart against any involvement."

"I do care and I was afraid... I'm still a little afraid but I'm more frightened at the thought of losing you."

His smiled faded. "What would make you think there was a chance you'd ever lose me? Didn't I tell you I love you? You have witnesses, remember? Aimee, I came looking for you."

"Yes, I know but you really didn't know me then. Now that you've rescued the princess and see her for what she really is, do you have any second thoughts?"

Lucas pulled Aimee into his arms, one hand slid into her short curly hair, as he leaned down.

"I left California with the idea of sailing across the Atlantic and touring Europe. I finally made my mark in life, thanks to the gold fields but I had no goals ahead.

"I'm here because of you. The first time I saw you, I forgot to breathe. After meeting you, there were no other sound in life but your voice. There was no touch so dear as when I held your arm as you struggled to reach the deck in that storm, and no goal but to find you when I finally reached Charleston. Second thoughts, you ask? My only thought would be, how long could I live without you? The only answer is why would I want to?"

He lowered his head and kissed her tenderly. Throwing her arms around his neck, she pressed against him.

After the embrace, Lucas held her face in both hands.

"You sweeten the air I breathe and brighten the world I see. I can't imagine living without you."

He kissed her lightly and released her face, only to grab her hands as he dropped down on one knee.

"Tell me you'll marry me. Tell me you'll be the first thing I see each morning when I wake and that you'll kiss me goodnight each evening before I sleep. On my final day on earth, I want your beautiful face to be the last thing I see and when I close my eyes, I want to feel your hand in mine. Marry me, Aimee McKay. Complete my life, my sweet, sweet girl. I love you so."

Tears sparkled in his eyes and all Aimee could do was sob and nod.

After Lucas asked Joseph for Aimee's hand in marriage, there was a private celebration. Joseph and Edward McKay stayed another two weeks. They met Albert and the rest of the people from the camp and watched Aimee's new house take shape. Shortly before they left, the news of Mack Kaymey's death circulated around town and speculations that the McKay's were dear friends who would escort his body back to his hometown. Amelia would remain behind to supervise the building of his house and rumor was that she had inherited his entire estate. There were whispers that Lucas Chase was smitten with Mack Kaymey's sister.

Doc Norman also whispered that he would not be surprised if there were wedding bells in the future for the handsome couple.

Lucas and Aimee stood in front of Eagle Creek Manor, as the workers put the finishing touches on the magnificent house.

"Lucas do you know a good sculptor?" Aimee asked, leaning against his chest.

"I'm sure Mister Harmon knows several. Do you want something carved in stone or wood?"

Aimee smiled. "Neither, I'm thinking more of bronze. In fact, I'm thinking of several more for the back garden. Something to remember how we met. I picture a large pond with a fountain and statues of mermaids, mythical sea creatures, you know, that sort of thing. We could put benches around the edge. It would be perfect to enjoy the early mornings or late evening."

"That sounds great. I'll ask Andrew about it. You've got sketches, I suppose."

"Yes," she said with a wide grin. "I've got sketches. You know me pretty well."

"Not as well as I plan to," he answered, pulling her closer. "Not nearly as well as I plan to."

~ The End ~

~ About The Author ~

Bobbie Shafer is the author of more than three hundred short stories and articles but *Love's Golden Dream* is her first full-length novel. The second book in the Secrets of Eagle Creek series, **Legacy of Eagle Creek**, will follow in spring 2012, and a third book in the series is coming at a later time.

As a member of the East Texas Writer's Guild, and a free-lance author, Bobbie enjoys writing young adult, contemporary, and historical stories.

She is the proud mother of four children, with three grand-children, and lives with her husband, Gordon, outside Troup, Texas, where, as an animal lover, she has rescued many cats, dogs, and other critters.

Visit Bobbie here:
http://www.bobbieshafer.com/
https://www.facebook.com/profile.php?id=100002683627022
https://twitter.com/#!/BobbieShafer